What Would You Sacrifice?

She was being pulled downward with the grace of a broken ragdoll, and her brother was dwindling in the distance. However, she felt a spark of hope as she was reminded of the two other things she had here.

K'tar shrank his size down to that of a normal wolf, before landing on Kukkug's back and starting to rip at one of his wings. Qiàn simply dove straight down, using the power of her own wings to catch up to the falling angel. Unfortunately, the raven's wings weren't strong enough to support them both.

"You have to fix my wings!" Gabriella shouted.

"How?"

"The hard way!"

Qiàn did her best to straighten the angel's right wing. She ignored the pained noises from Gabriella that followed every "snap." Once finished, the single mighty wing was enough to finish halting their descent. Qiàn then quickly helped straighten her overall body to make it easier for Gabriella to restore her spine.

The angel's left wing was bent and twisted far worse than the right one had been. It was actually pressing down on her left shoulder, preventing proper use of that arm. No matter how hard Qiàn tried, the wing refused to budge.

"Yǎniū, I can't fix the left one!" she yelled.

Gabriella pulled out a sword with her right hand and nodded to the wall. With Qiàn's help, she got close enough to bury the blade into the stone. She then braced herself, facing the wall.

"You need to reach inside my right wing," she told the raven, who was hovering behind her.

"What?"

"Just do it!"

Qiàn reached her hand forward and gasped as it seemed to disappear inside the blood-soaked wing.

"I give you my sword, of my own free will," Gabriella mumbled.

"What did-" Qiàn stopped talking as she felt the pommel of a sword appear in her hand. She tightened her grip and drew Gabriella's flaming sword.

"Qiàn, I need you to cut it off," she said sternly.

"What are you talking about?"

"What do you think?" she muttered, bracing herself more carefully.

Qiàn's eyes went to the twisted remnants of her left wing. "No," was all she said.

"Do it now, hurry," Gabriella insist.

"I can't!" Qiàn started to cry.

"It's in the way! Do it!" the angel shouted.

"Yǎniū, you said your wings were-"

"*Soul, I command you!*"

Wolves and Ravens

Book 3
Broken Angel

Richard Spegal

Other books by Richard Spegal :

Eternal Nights Series

Prequel:
Book 1 – Redemption
Book 2 – Origins

Series:
Arrival – (forthcoming)

Wolves and Ravens Trilogy

Book 1 – The First Law
Book 2 – Choice
Book 3 – Broken Angel

Dedication

To my wife as always, and all the
little ravens running throughout
the house. When they aren't trying
to destroy things or hurt each other
they really are quite adorable.

Prologue

Market District, Capital, Raven's Realm, AS 1077

"And just how is the newest member of the family doing?" The former Raven Queen beamed as her daughter approached with the tiny bundle.

"Better than I am, to be completely honest, mother." Queen Shūfāng held the infant out to give her mother a better view, but she was not yet willing to let go.

"Well," the old raven flicked the tiny nose. "I have to admit she just may be the cutest raven ever born."

"Except for me, of course," the Queen arched a brow.

"I have said what I have said," she mumbled confidently, continuing to coo at the infant. "You are still certain of Xuě?"

"Yes, stop trying to name my daughter," Shūfāng laughed.

"It doesn't even snow here, and you hate the cold." She gently blew the infant's wispy hair as she spoke. "Just seems an odd choice is all."

"It's a perfect choice. I find snow to be quite beautiful, and now I can see it without the silly discomfort of being cold."

"You are a strange person, dear."

"What a lovely thing to say to your daughter," she smirked. "Anyway, Alger will be along in a moment. Where's father?"

"He's still at the barracks with your uncle. No doubt threatening the soldiers with all sorts of horrors if everything isn't completely perfect," she chuckled.

"Do we really have to bother with all that silliness? I hate parades. We should skip right to the festival."

"You've been queen long enough to know better, dear. This is a significant day. Let the soldiers show off for you, and then look the other way later when they start drinking." She quickly snatched the bundle away while Shūfāng was distracted by the surrounding commotion.

It was the seventy-fifth anniversary of the great victory against the Soul Eater Thraxsis, and hordes of people had spent the last week decorating. The parade would march throughout the city and end here, where a platform and dais had been constructed opposite their most sacred shrine. The entire district was lined with tables, laden with all manner of food and drink, as the city prepared for its largest annual celebration.

Even holding the delightful infant, the former Queen couldn't look at the shrine without tears forming in her eyes.

It was a depiction of an angel in mortal form leading her parents to safety. The same angel who would later, in not quite mortal form, save them all. Unlike her daughter, she had met the angel personally, many times in fact. Although that was a long time ago.

Měilíng was approaching her seventy-fifth year, making her the oldest raven in recorded history. There were many others close to her, but she had still been the first. The first raven to live longer than the second day of her seventieth year. She had been the final proof that her parents had fixed the world.

With the angel's help, of course.

Unfortunately, it hadn't saved them. It was hard to not cry even now, over fifty years later, as she remembered how young her mother Qiàn had been when she died. She hadn't even lived to be fifty. Just because Měilíng understood didn't make it fair.

Like all ravens now, Měilíng knew the truth. She understood that her mother had done too much. She had *been* too much. Her mother's generation lacked the proper balance in their bodies, and the same light she had repeatedly used to save her people had destroyed her.

And it had taken her father the same day.

Her parents had warned her it would happen that way and swore her to secrecy. She knew it was what they wanted, but that didn't help much at the time. It had been difficult for the realm to accept, but given what their lives had accomplished, it was decided they were simply needed elsewhere. The angel never came back after that day.

"You probably shouldn't be holding a baby if you plan to simply stare at nothing, mother," Shūfāng spoke up, holding her arms out expectantly.

"Of course, dear," she said, turning and gently returning the bundle.

"Oh, I'm sorry," Shūfāng whispered as she saw the tears in her mother's eyes.

"I wish you could've met them."

"Considering how many stories you've told, I feel like I have." She gave her mother a smile of encouragement. "Well, look who finally decided to join us," she squinted her monolid eyes as her wayward husband made his appearance.

"There were a few matters to attend to."

"Yes, there were," she indicated the small bundle. "Some rather disgusting matters, in fact, which you never seem to be present for."

"Odd how that keeps happening." He tapped the sensitive nose that always warned him when to be somewhere else as his yellow eyes laughed. He leaned down to kiss his wife and steal the now freshly cleaned baby.

"A pleasure, Your Majesty," he offered to the former Queen as he kissed his daughter's tiny forehead.

"All-Father's sake, Alger," she rolled her eyes. "I'm not the Queen anymore. You *should* be calling me mother."

"Why? You're her mother, not mine," he tried to look honestly confused. "I still can never tell when your husband is trying to be funny or not."

"Just ignore him. It works for me," Shūfāng mumbled as she surveyed the final preparations.

Alger responded by reaching a large hand over and pinching her backside.

"What's the matter with you!" She squealed, jumping in surprise. "In front of my mother?" she scolded loudly.

"Not to mention your subjects," Měilíng pointed out with a laugh.

"Just trying to teach you-"

The sudden explosion cut off what Alger had been saying, and pieces of the shine flew in all directions. Black ichor that seemed half liquid and half smoke fountained into the air, stretching to the furthest reaches of the sky. Shapes seemed to coalesce and detach from the ichor and began tearing through the surrounding people.

This was not the first time the people of this world had faced dark creatures, but these creatures were different. These were not the faceless, red-eyed shadows that Thraxsis's creations had been. These were actual demons, faces split with fang-filled grins as they were finally allowed to play.

Screams began coming from everywhere before the three of them even recovered from the shock of the initial explosion. Of course, this was no longer a broken world filled with confused races believing a lie. Even as the screams began, the ravens in the area started launching into the air on their feathery wings of golden fire.

Their slanted eyes, blazing with the same golden color, were determined as they sent arrows and daggers made of pure fiery light into the attacking horde. The stronger ravens even used staves to send uninterrupted streams of light into the enemy. Unfortunately, almost none had their wolves.

The wolves were gathering for the coming parade, and the few who remained in the area had been the demons' first targets. With the wolves dealt with, they began swarming the ravens. Several demons were burned into nothing, but it took multiple ravens to finish even these Lesser Demons.

Three much larger Greater Demons appeared amid the carnage, even as dozens of Lesser Demons attacked individual ravens. The alarm was sounded, but the remaining wolves were unlikely to make it here in time.

"Měilíng!" Alger shouted as he started to hand the infant over.

"No, Wolf, you need to go. Now!" Shūfāng yelled before her mother could respond. Both ravens already knew how this would end.

"You can't fight them without me!" He yelled over the growing volume of the screams.

"This battle is already lost. She has no wolf," she glanced at the infant, whose face was starting to contort in displeasure. No doubt angry at whatever was daring to interrupt her slumber. "Just her father.

"You must get out of the city. The rest of the wolves will be here soon, and we can evacuate with them." She could see the argument building in her husband's eyes. "Just go. I promise I'll be right behind you."

Alger could easily see the truth in her eyes and wondered again how it was so easy for the ravens to lie.

"You better be," he growled, playing into the lie, before turning and charging for the gates.

"You should go as well, dear," Měilíng commented as her eyes danced across the carnage.

"In battle, there is only one place for the Raven Queen. You taught me that, as your mother taught you." She argued, preparing to change.

"This is not a battle. This is something different. My place is here, but yours is with your family."

"You know I can't do that." "I know."

"We're wasting time," she said as she started to crouch.

"Wait," Měilíng held up a hand. "Something is wrong with this." She forced herself to look across the district filled with corpses and ravens still trying to fight. More and more demons seemed to pour from the non-stop fountain of ichor, yet none were approaching the two of them.

"Agreed," Shūfāng's eyes narrowed, "but if we act now, we can take advantage of it."

"Or, we can wait and ensure we attack the true enemy," she countered wisely. Despite her words, watching her people being slaughtered wasn't easy.

"Demons are our true enemy; we need to attack together."

"I suggest we ask this gentleman and see if he agrees with you," Měilíng said far more calmly than she felt.

Shūfāng turned her head and saw her mother looking at a dark-haired man who had suddenly appeared on the platform next to them. The man was dressed in a new tuxedo, complete with a formal coat, cummerbund, and boutonniere. Neither raven recognized the strange uniform, and the man seemed not even to notice them.

He looked around slowly, with a bemused expression, seeming to examine every surrounding detail with equal interest.

"Fascinating," came his barely audible mumble. "It's all so different." He turned slowly, finally noticing the two ravens. "Oh, hello."

The ravens braced themselves for an attack that didn't come. Instead, the man seemed to look over their attire carefully before looking down to examine his own body. Slowly, his strange clothing morphed into a dress identical to what Shūfāng was wearing.

Despite the surrounding horror, the ravens couldn't help but exchange an odd glance at the site.

"What?" He seemed to notice something wrong and appeared to examine their bodies again. "Oh, I see…female," he mumbled. Turning, he studied the multiple corpses throughout the district before his dress slowly morphed into clothes matching one of the dead men.

"A pity. I must have accidentally chosen my attire from a different world," he grumbled. "It's not my fault, it all looks the same," he complained before slowly descending the platform.

Měilíng held up a hand as she saw Shūfāng ready to attack. She knew they couldn't win whatever this was, and talking meant delay. Any delay could be enough for the wolves to arrive. It was their only chance to save at least some of the people in the city.

The man seemed to ignore them again, as well as everything else happening. He bent down to run his fingers through the dirt.

"Strange," he marveled as the dirt and small stones slipped through his fingers. "What is this?" He walked to one of the nearby tables and selected an item. "Wait, I saw things like this before. You put these in your bodies, correct?"

It wasn't entirely clear whether the man was directing his questions to them specifically or thinking aloud. Shūfāng was nearly trembling with the desire to fight, and Měilíng was also beginning to have difficulty holding back. The man sniffed the item carefully before slowly eating it.

"Nothing," he grimaced. "This body doesn't understand it." He looked to the side and up. Holding out a hand, one of the remaining ravens was pulled down and sucked into his grip.

They gasped in shock as the man put his hands on either side of the raven's head. She screamed in agony, but there was no outward sign of what was happening. They had no way of knowing he was forcefully pulling the knowledge he needed of this world from her mind.

The nearly brain-dead raven was tossed to stumble around until being ripped apart by the surrounding demons.

"Oh, that's much better," he exclaimed, sampling the food again. "This is amazing. Have you tried this?" He looked at the pair of angry ravens observing him.

Apparently, he had been talking to them after all.

"Who are you?" Shūfāng demanded through clenched teeth.

"Wouldn't you like to know?" he grinned. "You can call me Kukkug if you wish."

"If you do not leave-"

"A moment," Kukkug cut her off before returning to the carnage. He was only now realizing the totality of the slaughter. "I said only *half!*" He shouted into the mass of demons.

"Maybe I'm being unreasonable," he mumbled, looking back at them. "They've been waiting so long for this opportunity. Maybe I should just let them get it out of their systems." He rubbed his chin and looked thoughtful.

"As long as we balance it out later, does it really matter if none remain here? What do you think?" He looked back up at them. "Still," he faced the horde, "I will not be disobeyed."

Kukkug raised his arm, and the demons before him rose in a single mass.

The ravens were forced to cover their ears at the sounds of the impossible shrieks as they were shredded apart. He closed his fist, and the pieces imploded and vanished.

They looked at each other in confusion as the man instantly destroyed half of his attacking force. What was going on?

"I warned you!" He shouted at one of the much larger demons. "Get this under control, or you're next!"

The Greater Demon made a few strange noises before lumbering off.

"Conversation," he stated, facing them once more. "If I'm being honest, that's the one thing I truly miss. Proper conversation and intelligent debate," he specified. "As adorable as they all are," we waved toward the remnants of the horde, "they aren't up to the task.

"She and I used to have such wonderful conversations. Even our debates were enjoyable, despite how angry she used to get," he said wistfully. "I'd give almost anything to have that again," he cocked his head. "Agree to provide me with conversation, and I'll spare one of you."

Whatever nonsense this Kukkug creature was talking about, he was clearly waiting for them to respond. Knowing there was no longer any point in delaying, the two ravens finally allowed themselves to change entirely. Even compared to the brilliance of the other ravens, they were on an altogether different level.

Large golden wings instantly sprouted from both, matched only by the fiery light in their eyes. Both suddenly had their staffs at the ready as Shūfāng crouched to strike. Měilíng held her staff high, preparing to launch and take the monster from above.

"I suppose that's a no. Oh well," he shrugged. "I think your wings are magnificent," he nodded appreciatively. "Unfortunately, I do not yet possess the conceptual understanding to judge your bodies, but those wings," he trailed off with a smile. "Marvelous.

"Would you like to see mine?" Without waiting for a response, Kukkug unfurled his wings with a grin.

Mortal eyes couldn't handle what happened next, and even the ravens didn't fully comprehend it. It was as if wings of pure darkness extended into infinity, instantly encompassing their entire world.

All life everywhere was suddenly on the brink of death before the dark wings retracted to a more comfortable size. Although the sky seemed to have been permanently blackened.

"That was close," Kukkug smirked. "I'll have to remember to be more careful."

"We know what you are," Měilíng sneered. The sudden darkness seemed to do nothing more than accentuate both ravens' mighty wings. "There will be no more conversation."

Shūfāng quickly crossed her staff with her mother's, and they sent everything they had into Kukkug's body. They would distract him with the combined blast before separating and attacking from two sides. As the brilliant light from the attack faded, the ravens prepared to move but were briefly frozen in shock.

Kukkug was just smiling. Their combined light would have burned through a line of demons, but hadn't even affected his clothing.

"Sorry, ladies," his wings quickly scissored down over his shoulders, removing their heads, "but you have no idea what I am." He kept his wings crossed to shield his body from the brief spray of gore.

As the pair of headless bodies fell, Kukkug retracted his wings. He moved to look for and collect the pair of heads, even as he tried to flick a stray drop of blood that had found its way to his shoulder.

"Gross," he grimaced. "I didn't realize how disgusting you things are on this side." He continued mumbling to himself until he found what he was looking for.

Kukkug lifted the heads by their long hair, careful to keep his arms extended to avoid the dripping mess from the necks. Looking back and forth, it took a moment to make a proper decision. Finally, the older raven's head found itself being tossed unceremoniously over his shoulder.

Slowly, he brought the Raven Queen's severed head to his lips, kissing her slowly and passionately.

"Nothing," he pulled the head back, grimacing as he noticed the additional drops of blood on his clothes now. "Definitely not worth that. Wait," his eyes narrowed in thought. "I was supposed to do that when this was still attached.

"I see," he looked down into the still living eyes filled with hatred and disgust. "Don't look at me like that. Understanding takes time. What?

Surprised to still be in there? Well, say something about it then."

Shūfāng's lips moved silently, as burning eyes did the talking for her.

"It would seem the pieces you need to make sound are attached to that," Kukkug indicated her decapitated body. "A pity. Don't worry, even my power can't hold you in there much longer. Trust me when I say you should be grateful for every extra second you have."

He turned the head to whisper into her ear. "You're not going where you think you're going," he said in a sing-song voice. He started chuckling, but it turned into a disappointed sigh as he once again observed what his demons were doing.

"If you want something done right," he started grumbling. "Come along, dear. Time to punish the children," he laughed. He placed a hand in his pocket, while twirling Shūfāng's head by the hair like a child's toy with the other.

Whistling a pleasant tune, the Dark One strolled into the middle of the slaughter to remind his demons *again* of who was in charge.

Chapter 1

Castle Ruins, Former Capital, Raven's Realm, AS 1100

"Xuě, we shouldn't be here," Larg pointed out for the hundredth time.

"Give it a rest, Wolf." She rolled her eyes as they crept quietly through the deserted castle. "It took us almost six days to get here without horses, and I've been ignoring your warnings the entire time. How is it logical that I would listen now that we've arrived?"

"I don't care," he growled at his raven. "I'm going to keep warning you until that insane brain of yours listens."

"No matter how many demons are likely to come investigate the noise you're making," she whispered back.

"I'll take that risk any day, rather than be the one to tell Alger something happened to you. Your father's a lot scarier than any demon when he's mad, and he's got to be insane with worry by now. He'll probably kill me even if I get you back safe." He reached out to grab her arm, forcing her to turn around.

"Raven, you made me lie," his eyes burned with an angry yellow fire.

Xuě was about to answer immediately, but hesitated. He hadn't used this argument yet, but it had only been a matter of time. Truth be told, she wasn't looking forward to facing her father either.

"You didn't lie. I did," she pat his arm affectionately.

"I told him we were just going to hunt, and you still needed extra training. You knew he would disagree and trusted that I would argue the Raven Queen needed the training." He glared at her, and the raven found it difficult to match his gaze.

In fact, on this world of perpetual darkness, the ravens found it challenging to focus on much of anything. The term "day" had very little meaning anymore, although there was still a slight difference. Still, Xuě knew the difference between the sun and moon primarily based on size and positioning in the sky, and not the brightness they conveyed.

In the years since the world's extermination, the raven's night vision had adjusted to a degree due to necessity. Unfortunately, it wasn't enough for it to be safe for them to go very far on their own. Not that there were enough of them left for it to make much of a difference. There wasn't much of anything left.

Even with all the survivors' stories from various locations, no one could put together a proper timeline of exactly what happened. There was complete agreement on the day it began, but after that? If one believed the stories, it was simply over.

But that couldn't be true.

Xuě was willing to accept that it may have happened quickly, but she couldn't imagine it happening in just a few days. The Race of Man simply being dead and gone? Without any fighting?

According to the stories, the wolves and ravens had fought hard from the very beginning. However, despite being fully transformed, they accomplished precisely nothing. The survivors eventually gathered in the ruins of Henwick, and for some reason, had been left alone ever since.

Xuě had been just a baby when it all started, but she had heard the stories enough times to have memorized them by the time she was ten. Those weren't the only stories though. In vain attempts to give her hope, her father used to regale her with other exciting stories.

Stories of a time before this, full of exciting adventures and even more exciting people. It was hard to believe such stories now, but not much time had truly passed since then. Certainly not enough time for such important stories to have been forgotten or twisted.

So, as Xuě grew older, she began quietly asking questions of others who had been adults before this started. Wolves and ravens alike, and she saw as their eyes would glaze over wistfully when answering. She knew the stories were true, and so she began asking even more questions.

Xuě had already started making connections, but two years ago, she heard one final story that solidified her plans.

Her father was an amazing wolf, a fantastic *man*, but the decades had taken their toll. The survivors immediately began looking to him for guidance, and he took on the old title of Great Protector. Even as their numbers dwindled, he did everything he could to protect them all. All without his raven.

In her more honest moments, Xuě could admit, at least to herself, that she had not made his job very easy. He tried so hard, but a wolf couldn't raise a raven child on their own. Plenty of other ravens wanted to assist him, but Xuě had been horrible to them all.

She had secretly blamed her father for her mother's death for a very long time. All the remarkable stories of the time before had only made her more certain of this. Those stories taught that wolves were supposed to protect their ravens. It didn't matter to her that he had protected so many others.

What weight did the lives of others carry when compared to the raven who mattered most? The knowledge that he had to do it to save his daughter didn't mean much to her either, at least not to her child's brain.

Any other raven who sought to teach her was cast aside.

She was old enough now to understand how wrong she had been. To the extent she was able, she made amends to others. Her father had smiled and forgiven her easily. He always did. The others at least pretended to tolerate her now.

They didn't have much choice, considering she was the Raven Queen.

Unfortunately, the damage had long since been done. A raven's brain was a very delicate and complicated thing, and she had prevented any effort in ensuring hers developed properly. Logic could be far worse than senselessness if not appropriately guided.

The Queen could not admit to weakness, but she knew how worthless she was compared to those who came before. The final strange story her father told her had given her what she needed. The last piece not only finalized the connections, but it also told her what to do about it.

He had been rather pleasantly drunk and wanted to surprise her with a special story. Unlike the other stories, it was known only to the queens.

Passed down from Queen Qiàn herself, Alger only knew from his wife. Now, he could continue the tradition by telling the new Queen himself.

The story was straightforward, yet it could change everything.

Xuě remembered laughing to herself the next day when she had made the final connection. Of course, Queen Qiàn would have something to do with the answer. Why should being dead for nearly eighty years stop her?

Queen Qiàn.

Thinking of her brought mixed emotions to Xuě. The stories involving her and her husband from long ago had been as amazing as they were terrifying. She wasn't the only prominent figure in their history, but considering how recently she lived and what her reign had proven, she was at the top of the list.

What raven wouldn't want to grow up to be like her? Being her great- granddaughter had only intensified the desire. Unfortunately, it ended up doing nothing but increasing her hatred for herself once she had grown old enough to truly understand.

To understand that the entire time she had been idolizing perhaps the greatest raven ever to live on this world, Xuě had been living her life contrary to everything that raven had stood for. Oh, Xuě had recognized the arrogance someone like Qiàn must have had.

There were plenty of examples of Qiàn practically forcing others to follow insane plans and ideas through sheer force of will and a lot of shouting.

It had been all the justification her young mind had needed to keep others away. To keep anyone older and wiser than her from telling her that they knew better. It wasn't until Xuě was much older that she realized Qiàn had the perfect upbringing intended for the Raven Queen.

Qiàn had earned the right, through constant training and terrible testing, to be arrogant and to fly above all others. A right Xuě had merely assumed because of her birth. Not to mention that even in her most arrogant moments, Qiàn never truly operated in a vacuum.

At least, that is what the stories said anyway.

Xuě realized years ago that she didn't deserve the blood in her veins, but her great-grandmother had somehow still given her what she needed. It also wasn't too late for her to demonstrate at least one of Queen Qiàn's lessons.

If the answer's impossible, do it anyway.

She had been wanting to make this journey for some time, but it was out of the question. No one knew why, but the demons never attacked the survivors in Henwick. Any who strayed too far, however, never returned. So the elders said anyway.

One of the many connections she had made was that the demons rarely attacked anyone anywhere. Not that there was anywhere left with living people. In fact, it was extremely rare for the demons even to be seen anymore.

It had been a risk she was willing to take. Not that anyone would allow the Raven Queen to take it. So, Xuě had been forced to do the one thing she was best at. She manipulated the person who cared about her more than anyone else.

"As if being the Raven Queen is anything but useless words now," she finally responded.

"Raven, it's everything to us, as it always has been. Maybe even more now that there's so little else," he shook his head. "Even if I can't get you to agree with that, it doesn't change the fact that you drekking used me.

Again!"

"You didn't have to follow me when I ran off," she pointed out.

"Of course I did, which of course you already knew," he growled.

"If you were so much against this journey, why have you wasted all this time with words?" She allowed her eyes to twitch more than usual. "At any point, you could have simply picked me up and carried me back. I would have been unable to stop you," she pointed out logically.

"You *always* do this," he growled louder as he spun and put an angry fist through one of the wooden walls.

"Do what?"

"Act so drekking dismissive and arrogant! I swear, sometimes you don't give a pile of horse dung about anyone else." Larg recognized he was growing too angry and worked to control his breathing.

"Oh, grow up, Wolf." There were so many other things Xuě wanted to say instead. Telling Larg he was wholly right and how sorry she was, for example, but she simply didn't know how.

"You know I'm older than you," he smirked. Larg had been found as a pup by survivors in the beginning. It was difficult to be certain how old he really was, but he was at least a year or two older than Xuě.

"Maybe in number, but not maturity," she shot back, and immediately regretted it. Her first comment could have been simply dismissed, but what she just added turned it into a targeted insult.

What was wrong with her?

Since their people had become properly balanced, the wolves had begun maturing more quickly than in Qiàn's time. It still wasn't quite as fast as the ravens. Not enough time had passed to be certain whether this was a difference in their abilities or their genders.

"I'm mature enough to know that was a nasty thing to say," he said through grinding teeth. "Now I'm wondering if you've even thought of the worst-case scenario for all this?"

"I'm sorry for what I said, but as to that point, I contemplate my death every day we live on this hellhole," she admitted.

"I wonder what that says about a queen who considers the worst-case scenario to be simply her own death. I'm talking about your father."

"I know he's going to be worried, but he always forgives me," she shrugged.

"Odds are, he's already dead."

Xuě inhaled sharply. "How dare you say that to me," she hissed. Of course, she had considered the possibility. She knew the stories of how wolves were said to react on occasion after losing their ravens.

"It's a miracle he's been so amazing after that first day. Caring for you was a big part of that. Not that you ever seemed to appreciate it," he sneered. "Alger is one of the only things holding us together.

"If we lose him, we lose everything we have left. Xuě, if we lose you, we lose him. The joke I made earlier about being afraid to face him after this was mainly to distract myself from that possibility."

"He's stronger than that, and would never give up without seeing a body," she insisted, mostly trying to convince herself.

"There's seldom a body when the demons take someone, and from his perspective, we've been lost or missing for at least five days. Being lost isn't likely considering I'm with you."

Xuě could feel herself sliding down the wall she was leaning on, as her hands went to her head. Despite her usual control, she could feel her breathing become erratic.

"Why are you trying to convince me my father's dead?" Her hands moved to cover her eyes. "What is the point of this entire conversation? We're already here. Our decisions don't matter anymore." She lost control of her eyes as they danced back and forth, staring at the dark floor through slightly spread fingers.

"There's no logic to this conversation!" she started to cry softly.

"You're right, this is neither the time nor place," he said, kneeling down and placing a hand on her shoulder. "Look, Xuě, I'd be lying if I didn't say I think you deserve at least some of what you're feeling.

"Truth be told, however, I think I just needed to get some things off my chest. I'm really sorry that I took it too far." He gave her a quick embrace and kissed the top of her head.

Xuě's eyes froze in renewed anger with herself. Why couldn't she do that? Larg had just honestly demonstrated such a wide range of emotions. It didn't matter that he hurt her feelings, since he immediately made her feel better.

Why was her brain always stuck on one side? She quickly reminded herself that the answer wasn't relevant now and bottled everything back up where it belonged.

"I'm sorry too, but we are already here." She pointed to the room down the hallway. "It is senseless to turn back now. It's about six days either way, what's another few minutes?"

"Alright," he sighed, "but how long do you want to search for something that doesn't exist?"

"It exists, and until we find it." She tried to meet his gaze but failed again. "Just that room. If it's not there, then it's not real."

"I still say it was a pretty story your father told you to make you feel better. We don't have pretty memories to disappear into like the elders do, so you know they use stories to help us."

"Trust me."

Larg nodded as he helped her up and they made their way to what used to be the Raven Queen's bedchamber. It was eerie how little damage the castle and most buildings had suffered, although it wasn't surprising. The demons had little need to destroy.

All they did was kill.

The lack of residents had caused a level of disrepair everywhere in the world, even in Henwick, but it wasn't the same as widespread destruction. In some ways, it was worse. It gave a mysterious impression of emptiness, but the kind of impression that made you nervous to check around every corner to make sure.

Larg watched as Xuě quickly began tapping walls and testing floorboards, and tried not to roll his eyes. She really did believe this foolishness. Well, he agreed to help, and he really wanted to avoid another argument.

There was a small end table with drawers next to the bed, so he walked over and began searching. Barring the dust and evidence of insects, most of the contents of the room were no different from the day this started. He wondered if Xuě was too distracted by her strange quest to notice she was standing in her mother's bedroom.

No one had been left alive to loot anything, and he realized the amazing opportunity this had accidentally become. The clothing items weren't worth taking, but everything else went into his pockets and pack. He wouldn't distract her now, but once they got back, Xuě and Alger might appreciate the mementos.

A small wooden box in the bottom drawer drew his attention. All the jewelry had been in the top drawer, and this box wasn't nearly as ornate. He opened it carefully.

"Found it," he called out.

"What?" Xuě hurried over. "How could you possibly have found that so quickly?" She couldn't take her eyes off the box's contents.

"You were searching as if looking for a secret treasure. If I am expected to trust the story you told, this sounded more like a treasured memento. So, I looked there first," he pointed to the table and its mostly empty drawers.

"Oh," he noticed her confusion at the lack of contents. "I helped myself," he hefted the pack. "I thought maybe you might like some of your mother's things," he shrugged.

"My-" she cut herself off and started looking around the room. She had been so busy thinking of past generations, the most recent one never occurred to her. Xuě could feel her eyes misting.

"Thank you," she muttered hoarsely and leaned up to kiss Larg's cheek. "We should go," she quickly pocketed the box's contents.

"Okay, but are you sure that's what you think it is?"

"If it's not, it's the most disgusting memento I've ever heard of." They shared a much-needed laugh as they moved to leave the castle.

*****

"We need to head to the shrine," Xuě spoke up as they made their way through the castle grounds. Stealth wasn't very useful against demons, and so they stuck to the road leading to the main gate.

"I thought you said we were done, and there is no shrine anymore," Larg groaned.

"We are, but there's no point if we don't use it. Where the shrine used to be should be fine."

"Just do it now," he shrugged.

"Believe me, I want to. The thing is, I have no idea if anything is going to happen. We need to remove as many variables as possible before testing it. If it doesn't work there, then logically it won't work anywhere.

"We either try now, or make this entire trip again some other time," she smirked at his sudden expression.

"Fine," he relented.

They continued on, making pleasant small talk, until Larg suddenly stopped moving. He sniffed the air a few times, and she could see one of his pointed ears starting to twitch.

"What is it?"

"Drop your pack, now!" He dropped his as he shouted the command and turned around.

Xuě recognized the invitation and jumped on his back an instant before the wolf took off at full speed.

"Larg, what's going on?" She tried shouting into his ear as she kept her powerful legs wrapped around his waist.

"No one hears them unless they want you to." He knew there were at least four, possibly more, running parallel to them.

The demons wouldn't attack yet. Chasing their prey first was more fun.

"I can see two on the right, I think." Xuě was doing her best to squint through the darkness. Even her eyes couldn't miss the pair of gleeful, horrific faces.

"Are they close enough to shoot?" He knew her arrows wouldn't do much, but it was his only idea.

"With what?"

"What do you think? I doubt you can throw daggers that far." He was shouting loudly to keep from having to turn his head in her direction.

"You told me to drop my pack!" she shouted back.

"But not your weapons, you idiot," he growled angrily.

"They were in the pack! You should've given me better instructions." She tried to sound defensive, but the first notes of fear were already creeping into her voice.

"Do you remember if we latched the gate on the way in?"

"I don't think we did, why?" She asked an instant before the wolf brought his arms up and crashed through the metal gate, which was thankfully unlatched.

Even left open, the vibrations from the impact shook Larg's body enough that she almost lost her grip. He didn't even slow down.

"*Drek!* Are you okay?"

"I'm fine. I think there are six of them." "I heard a snap," she yelled in his ear. "That was the gate."

"Metal doesn't sound like that." She tried lifting herself to see the condition of his arms.

"Be quiet and stop moving around." He forced himself to run even faster.

"Get us to the shrine!"

"Are you insane! I can outrun them, but if I stop, we're dead." "Demons don't need rest, Wolf. You can't run all the way to Henwick." "I can drekking try!"

"You'll just die tired."

"You're really trying to be funny now?"

"It's not a joke. You're a wolf, aren't you? Would you rather die fighting or die exhausted? Those are the choices we have." She clamped down on the growing fear. If this didn't work…

Larg howled in rage. "Sometimes I really hate ravens." He managed to slowly change direction without breaking his legs by taking a wide arc to the old market district.

Honestly, he didn't even know where he was going, and he wondered how Xuě did. There was no longer any choice in the matter, however, so he continued following the directions being shouted in his ear. He was outpacing the demons, but he suspected they weren't really trying.

At least not yet.

The old market district and destroyed shrine were obvious, as they were the only areas in the city that showed actual signs of battle. The old stalls and buildings had been blasted apart by the ravens, who had been unable to hold back with their power. The demons had added to the destruction by ripping apart anything that stood between them and their prey.

Larg skid to a halt by the base of the destroyed shrine. Barely any of the pieces were large enough to show a resemblance to anything coherent.

Xuě jumped off and stumbled slightly, a bit disoriented from the flight.

Shadows even darker than the surrounding area seemed to gather around them, and there were sounds he had learned were the demonic equivalent of laughter. Red eyes opened and closed, appearing to change positions randomly. These creatures had more than just eyes, however, and Larg's vision could easily see the fanged grins.

He bared his own pointed teeth, even as he drew his greatsword. The massive blade was a two-handed weapon, even for a wolf, and he could feel at least two minor fractures in his left arm as he held it. The pain was growing, but he had no loss of mobility.

He started replacing his pain with pure rage. He knew he was strong enough to cleave a Lesser Demon in two with his well-kept blade. One Lesser Demon. Maybe. Now was not the time to worry that there were at least ten.

"Your arm!" Xuě shrieked when she saw the discoloration.

"Stay behind me!" He could see them finally coalesce as one charged him from the right. He had heard of the demons using this strategy.

The battle was contained and effectively already over. Instead of just attacking together and finishing them off, the demons would continue playing. It wouldn't change the end, but it could buy them some time.

Larg moved to dodge the incoming attack. "It's a trick! Above you!"

At his raven's warning, he forced himself to ignore the very real- looking claws coming for him. Instead, he twisted his body and swung the large sword in a powerful arc through the empty air above his head. He was rewarded by the feel of considerable resistance and a pained shriek that caused his ears to bleed.

The demon fell in two pieces before quickly dissolving.

A wolf's eyesight was far superior in the dark, but only a raven could genuinely *see* the demons. Everyone knew they were there *somewhere*, but a combination of speed and dark illusion made them impossible to predict.

Unless you had a raven's slightly slanted and ever-moving eyes.

Following Xuě's direction, Larg killed two more of the attacking demons. Not that "kill" truly applied to them.

"This isn't why we're here!" he tried to shout through his heaving breaths. "Do what you came to do!"

"You can't fight them without me!" Xuě didn't want to admit that she didn't know what to do. "On your right, up forty-five degrees, and behind you, dead center!" She ran forward and flipped onto the shoulders of the demon approaching Larg's back.

The wolf dove immediately to the left as he spun and tried to slice the stomach of the demon behind him. Xuě was doing her best to stab daggers into the same demon's eyes. It quickly reached around, easily plucking her from its back, and tossed her aside.

She picked herself up after crashing into what was left of the shrine's base. It was little more than a twisted plaque and the remains of what probably used to be feet. The demons were trying to ignore her.

Apparently, it wasn't the raven's turn to play yet.

Xuě knew they needed to be here and what she wanted to do, but she didn't know how. Her brain had gotten her this far, so she assumed the rest would become clear. It didn't matter that she had been right so far; they were both about to die because she couldn't figure out the next step.

"This fight is over the instant they decide it is," he growled from several paces in front of her. "Do something, *now!*"

She watched Larg start to move back and forth quickly. He was dodging randomly, even as he swept his sword in significant and unpredictable arcs. It was the only way he could fight without her sight to help him. She could see how bad his left arm looked, and there were already fresh slashes across his chest.

A demon collided with him, forcing Larg to bury his sword into its chest. With the weapon stuck, the demon grinned and began flicking its forked tongue to open lashes across the wolf's face. Larg was too close to kick it away, and so he tried to quickly wrap his powerful arms around it, but wasn't fast enough.

He howled as he felt the claws tear into his back.

Having no other options, he leaned in and buried his pointed teeth into the demon's throat. Who knew what the effect would be from ingesting whatever these things were made of? There was no time to worry about that, as he kept tearing the throat out and continuing to growl.

Xuě pulled the white cloth from her pocket as she felt her eyes starting to water. Despite its supposed age, the cloth and blood stains looked fresh. Having no other ideas, she closed her eyes and began to beg.

The demons must have decided it was finally time to move on, and Larg could tell he was being surrounded. He tried to dislodge himself to charge, but was interrupted by a lightning bolt impacting the ground before him.

Strangely, despite the proximity, the lightning itself didn't hurt him.

The strike did manage to send him hurtling backward to collide painfully with his raven. The pair tried to quickly untangle themselves to see what could have happened. When their eyes cleared from the blinding flash, it was hard to understand what they were seeing.

A fantastic figure had appeared and was moving through the district faster than any creature could possibly move. The stories said the ravens used to have feathery wings of golden fire, but this figure's wings were so brilliantly white it hurt Larg's eyes to look at them. The wings were also fully extended and seemed to stretch further than they should.

As the figure moved effortlessly through the demons, he could see it was a woman clad in shining, blood-red armor.

Something about her presence had dissipated the shadows, and the demons themselves were now clearly visible. There were more than Larg had thought, but it didn't seem to matter. He heard Xuě's matching gasp as the woman sliced them to ribbons with a pair of gleaming swords.

As she continued zipping through the area, the pure blonde hair and brilliant blue eyes were unmistakable. This figure could be no one else. Larg realized that until this very moment he had never truly believed any of the stories from the past.

She sheathed her swords behind her back, as a final trio of demons charged towards him. There was nothing else they could do, and they were desperate for at least a single kill.

Larg struggled to raise his sword, but there was little feeling in his left arm or back, and every breath sent fire through his chest.

The angel was suddenly between him and the demons, who now tried to turn and flee. She twirled in place, allowing her wings to slice them apart. Larg was close enough now that he could even hear her breathing.

Why did hearing an angel breathing seem the oddest thing about this situation?

"Well, that was fun." Gabriella smiled at the empty district before closing her wings and stretching her shoulders.

"You're, you're real," Xuě whispered as she moved up behind the angel.

Larg was equally amazed but was having enough difficulty standing to try doing anything else yet.

"Of course I'm real," she spoke, turning around to face the raven.

Xuě waited until the angel was halfway turned before striking her in the face as hard as she could. Gabriella fell back slightly from the blow, and Larg couldn't believe what he had seen.

"What is the meaning of this?" Her hand quickly went to her reddening cheek. "Why have you struck me?"

Larg stumbled forward and grabbed his raven's arm as it looked like she was about to strike the angel again.

"What are you children doing out this late?" She seemed to be ignoring or not understanding the pure rage in Xuě's eyes.

"It's early afternoon."

"Stop speaking nonsense," she said, her blue eyes glaring at them. "Go home and find your parents. You're welcome, by the way," she waved her hand to indicate the finished battle, before preparing to leave.

"Home?" Xuě shouted. "Don't you even know where you are?"

Gabriella cocked her head in annoyance. What difference did it make where she was? This could be any of the countless worlds with wolves and ravens fighting demons. Her assistance had already been rendered. It was time to rejoin her armies.

"Perhaps you should look closer, *Yǎniū*," the raven spat the name as if a curse.

Gabriella froze at the name. That name could only come from one world, and this wasn't it. She looked at the awe and confusion in the young wolf's eyes and seemed to finally notice the borderline hatred in the eyes of the raven.

"Měilíng, what game are you trying to play?" she scoffed at Qiàn's offspring. Měilíng had always been a wonderful raven but tended to be much less disciplined than her brother. Gabriella always thought K'tar was too easy on her.

"Who?"

"Raven, wasn't that your grandmother's name?" Larg was getting confused, but he was certain he remembered that much correctly.

"You can't summon me every time you want to play games, Měilíng. You have to learn to solve your own problems."

Larg was barely able to move his left arm fast enough to finish restraining Xuě before she could lunge at the angel. Even though he hadn't believed it was possible, he thought he knew what her original intentions were. He was no longer certain.

"This *was* our home. Can't you see it yet, fool?" Xuě was straining against her wolf's hold. "Měilíng is long dead, just like everyone else!"

Gabriella didn't appreciate being screamed at by a mortal, even if it was Qiàn's daughter. Some of what the crazed raven was saying, however, was starting to finally sink in. It was always so confusing to see properly with these eyes when she came to a mortal world.

She blinked a few times and started examining the area

more carefully.

Everything seemed very familiar, but at the same time, very wrong. Looking up, she could see this world's sun, but was it supposed to be this dark? It was hard to tell, considering how dark everything seemed compared to her home.

The raven was still screaming at her, but Gabriella ignored it. There was something vital about where they were all standing. When she finally recognized the pieces of the shrine, it all snapped together in her mind.

"What has happened here?" the angel demanded.

"The demons came," Xuě spat the response as the angel finally appeared to be paying attention.

"I know," Gabriella once again waved to indicate the prior battle. "Not *those* demons."

"I don't understand what you're talking about. What has happened here?

What demons?" Gabriella was rapidly losing patience with the situation. "*All the demons!*" Xuě screamed, nearly breaking Larg's hold on her.

"They did what you said. Everyone followed the instructions you gave, *and for what?*" Veins were beginning to bulge across Xuě's face as she continued straining in vain against the wolf's hold.

"They never stood a chance. This entire world is dead. *Because of you!*" She began pulling hard enough that Larg was concerned her arms would break.

He quickly leaned forward and snaked his arms around her chest instead.

Xuě was starting to flail so violently; it was difficult to hold her body still without breaking her ribs.

"I don't," Gabriella was having trouble accepting the information. "Why wasn't I summoned?"

"*You were!*" Xuě elbowed Larg's injured chest, causing the

wolf to let go and crumble in pain.

She lunged at the angel in a pure rage with a dagger in each hand.

Gabriella brought one of her wings forward and pointed the tip at the raven's forehead, and she was suddenly held in place.

"For twenty years, they called out to you. *We* called out to you. You never came. *You abandoned us!*" Every muscle in Xuě's body seemed to tense and contort as she fought against the angel's impenetrable hold.

"Raven, stop, please," Larg tried to shout through his coughing and heaving. "You said the plan was to bring her here to help us."

"I lied. All of this is her fault," she sneered.

Gabriella had to resist the sudden urge to step back. No one had ever looked her in the eye with such pure disgust and hatred before.

"I summoned you here to see the horrors you caused. To feel the suffering of the people who trusted you. I summoned you here because before the last of us finally die, I want you to get what you deserve." With her last statement, Xuě's mind had finally felt all the rage it could handle.

Sadness quickly took the place of everything else, and the raven crumbled in place, dropped her weapons, and started to cry.

Gabriella stepped around the crying raven. Something was definitely wrong here, but it would take time for her to understand it. Until then, there was a dying wolf that this raven seemed intent on ignoring.

She bent over Larg and smiled, as the wolf looked at her in awe. She placed a gentle hand on his chest and removed the injuries the demons had inflicted. It was much harder than it should have been. That was very odd.

"I'm afraid you're on your own with the arm, and I cannot return your lost blood, but I can take away the pain. I have also removed the poison that was beginning to spread within your body. You will feel weak for a time, but no further harm will come to you." She bent down and kissed his forehead.

"A fair trade, Miss Angel, thank you." He tried to bow from his half- crouched posture.

"You may call me Gabriella. I sense you destroyed several demons before I arrived," she let the statement hang.

"Well, only four, I think," he shrugged.

"That's still very impressive for one such as you." She bowed slightly as the wolf began to blush.

"Thank you, and I'm really sorry about," he finished by waving toward the crying raven.

"Don't be. She may be right." Gabriella helped the wolf up, and the pair moved to the raven. "What's your name, Raven?"

"Drek you!" Xuě shouted through her sobs.

"Whatever," Gabriella muttered as she grabbed the back of the raven's tunic and launched into the air.

She made sure she had a secure hold on the two shocked mortals as she ascended as quickly as she could. Something was very wrong with this world. She needed to see how far it had spread. She was over halfway to exiting the world before the increased struggles drew her attention. Looking down, she saw the strained faces and bits of ice forming in their hair.

Oh yeah.

She had forgotten mortals couldn't go where she was going. At least not without help this world didn't have. She quickly wrapped her wings around them for protection and let herself fall back down.

The trio tumbled downward through the atmosphere as Gabriella tried to see everything she could. Once the air and temperature had become survivable again, she extended her wings. There wasn't time to fly around the entire world this way, but she had to see as much as possible.

Sparing a glance at her cargo, Gabriella chuckled. As a raven, Xuě couldn't help but enjoy the feeling of soaring through the air. Larg just looked as if he was going to be sick.

"There must be somewhere safe." Her voice carried to them easily, despite the rush of air all around. "Where is your home?"

"I don't know where we are!" Xuě shouted back.

"Just hold a picture of it in your mind." Gabriella waited a moment before pivoting and diving downward.

Chapter 2

Henwick

Gabriella slowed her descent and curled her wings to land as softly as possible.

There was a scattering of wolves and ravens pointing and shouting at her sudden appearance, but she ignored them for now. The poor wolf she had been carrying could barely stand without her assistance, and his yellow eyes were wide with shocked terror. By contrast, the raven's eyes were those of a gleeful child.

"That was-"

"Horrible," Larg finished, cutting Xuě off, before keeling over and retching.

Xuě moved quickly to assist her wolf. The excitement of flying had temporarily interrupted her emotions, and she finally seemed to take notice of his remaining injuries.

Gabriella looked around carefully, still ignoring the gathering crowd. There was no mistaking that this was Henwick, but it wasn't the bustling city she remembered. She didn't see any direct evidence of battle or war. Certain areas seemed well-kept while others were in various and obvious states of disrepair.

The contrast was clear, giving the impression of a city far too large for the number of people inhabiting it. This was wrong. And why did she feel so strange?

Slaughtering the demons earlier had been no more difficult than blinking the eyes of this body, but healing the wolf had been a challenge. That didn't make sense. She also felt a bit tired after her flight, and that's not how her body worked.

Gabriella's physical body might be real, unlike the other angels, but it wasn't a normal mortal body. More accurately, her body was little more than a puppet for her pure essence. It was necessary for proper interaction on mortal worlds and fun to use, but she didn't need it.

Her consciousness and all the essential things she brought with her were stored in her wings.

"*Xuě!*"

Her thoughts were interrupted by the loud shout, and Gabriella saw a large wolf running toward them. Most of the crowd was quickly moving out of his way, but the wolf wasn't hesitating to shove aside anyone too slow.

"What foolishness have you been up to this time? Half the city's been searching for you for days!" He easily pulled the raven away from Larg. "Don't think being queen will stop me from giving you the lumps you deserve, you ungrateful little whelp!" His harsh words were belied by the fierce embrace he gave the daughter he feared lost.

"And you," he snarled at the injured wolf. "This is how you protect my daughter?" The older wolf growled and wasn't trying to hide his teeth.

"Father, you don't-" Xuě tried to answer.

"Be silent, child," Alger cut her off. "Answer me, pup!"

"Sir," Larg had recovered from his reaction to the flight but was still having difficulty speaking. He used his uninjured arm to point.

Alger turned, still furious, and finally noticed the angel standing in their midst. The joy of hearing his daughter was safe, mixed with the fury of her actions, had blinded him to the reason so many were gathering.

"Is this your doing?" he accused.

"It depends on what you mean by 'this,'" she smirked, but the wolf didn't seem overly amused or impressed with her. "He is in need of a healer," she pointed to Larg.

"Healer?" The wolf's anger flipped to sudden confusion at the angel's statement. "There are obviously no healers anymore." He waved for a pair of onlookers to tend to the injured wolf, and Xuě took the opportunity to escape after them.

"I don't understand." Gabriella's statement about a healer had been automatic, considering Larg's injury was obvious. She hadn't expected Alger's response.

"The Race of Man has been gone for decades," he shrugged. "Everyone knows that," he narrowed his eyes. "You're Yǎniū, aren't you?"

"I am."

"Why are you here?" Alger had mostly calmed down from his earlier emotions, but still didn't seem overjoyed at her presence.

"Honestly, I'm not sure yet. Can you please tell me what has happened on this world?" Gabriella was becoming increasingly frustrated with her lack of understanding.

Alger opened his mouth, but never got the chance to respond.

"*Demons!*" The shout came from somewhere in the distance and was quickly repeated throughout the area.

"Here?" Alger mumbled.

Gabriella didn't sense anything. Nothing specific anyway. Any time she closed her eyes to search, the entire world felt the same. As if she were standing atop a single vast demon, rather than a world filled with them.

There was no denying the demons must be somewhere close, based on the immediate actions of those around her. Before she could question the wolf further, however, he charged for the city gate. The angel was suddenly left to stand forgotten and alone in her confusion.

*****

She could see them now.

A massive formation of Lesser Demons was gathering on a hill a short distance from the gate. The city wall being in the way didn't affect Gabriella's sight, and she briefly focused on the enormous four-armed Greater Demon leading the horde.

This was wrong.

Before, she had destroyed the demons quickly and without hesitation. It had been nothing more than an automatic reaction to the enemy, but the more she thought about it, the less sense it made. Nothing the young raven had screamed at her earlier helped either.

These were actual demons. How could they be here in such numbers? On this world? In fact, she had seen the destroyed shrine with her own eyes. How? With this world's protection, none of this was possible.

It was as simple as that. Nothing she was seeing could be happening.

She looked around as the older wolf was shouting orders to the gathered crowd. Ravens began running up to man the wall and towers with their bows, as the wolves started to form into small units. She could see more wolves and ravens running toward them from other areas of the city.

She laid a hand on Alger's shoulder to get his attention. "You can't fight demons this way. Why haven't you changed forms yet?"

"We can't anymore," he looked over his shoulder to answer her. "Now, if you don't mind, I'm very busy." He quickly stepped out of her reach to continue directing the defense.

Not this again. She groaned the thought to herself.

In the end, it didn't really matter. At least not at the moment.

Questions could be answered later. Right now, there were demons to deal with, and that was at least something she knew how to do.

Gabriella closed her eyes and concentrated. The surrounding wolves and ravens stopped briefly in their movements as their weapons began glowing with a golden hue.

"It's the best I can do," she shouted to Alger. "Keep your wolves back to protect the gates," she ordered.

"Thank you for this, ma'am," he glanced at his glowing blade, "but with respect, we know how to fight."

"Sorry, but with equal respect, sir," she said, grinning as she drew her swords, "you'll all just get in my way." She shot into the sky before he could argue further.

If nothing else, Gabriella was glad to have a target for her growing anger.

Reaching the apex of her ascent, she twirled and dove for the center of the large horde. Having no need to slow her descent this time, she cratered the ground on impact even as she flared out her wings. The shockwave, combined with the powerful gust of wind, easily knocked the demons back from where she had landed.

Holding her swords close to her chest, she began to sprint. Once she built up enough speed, Gabriella leaped and began spinning her body parallel with the ground. As she spun, her wing tips continued pushing off the ground to keep her in the air and maintain her speed.

The mass of demons wasn't able to get close enough to counterattack without being sliced apart by the mighty wings.

As she broke through the edge of the formation, she planted a foot while allowing her other leg to sweep in an arc along the ground. It took a few rotations to finish dispelling her momentum, and she closed her wings in front of her body as she faced the horde. She winced in pain as the inevitable counterattack sent dozens of dark spines into her feathery shield.

That shouldn't have happened.

Her wings were the most sensitive part of her body, but only in terms of importance. They were akin to a mortal's head, or at least that was the closest comparison a mortal would understand. Unlike a mortal's head, however, they were not actually sensitive, or even vulnerable in any way.

Her wings contained everything she could bring to this level of creation, and they served as both powerful weapons and impenetrable shields. The dark spines hadn't hurt very much, but they *should* have bounced off harmlessly. She supposed it was yet another thing for her to worry about later.

Flaring her wings back out behind her, she ran for the center of the horde. Dark claws came at her from all directions, but were no match for her swords. Even better were the golden arrows finally starting to pepper the enemy. The delay in the ravens' attack was probably her fault.

Gabriella had forgotten to mention that the arrows couldn't hurt her, and the ravens had likely been hesitant for fear of hitting her by mistake. No matter.

It was long ago on this very world that Gabriella had learned the skills of a dual wielder. Skills she had easily mastered.

K'tar and Qiàn had shown her how to fight with the rest of her body as well, and observing the ravens moving on the training yard had given her plenty of additional examples. Even had she been merely a mortal, she doubted any of those she left behind in the city would be a match for her.

Of course, her experience as a mortal was long in the past.

She took the lessons she had learned and began making changes after returning home. Asking mortals to deal with actual demonic influence, even fighting demons themselves, was wrong. Even wolves and ravens who had been designed for that purpose should not be used in the mortal realm.

She believed now that it was her job, even if her celestial siblings continued ignoring her efforts.

Since the other angels wouldn't fight, she had formed vast armies of souls who were willing. She had also put a stop to wolves and ravens being placed in mortal bodies. Instead, she retained them in her armies back home, which allowed them to fight on the proper planes of existence.

The entire time, she continued teaching her body to fight, fueled by her true essence and power. Fighting non-physically was more straightforward and potent, but it was by far more dangerous for both sides. Destroying creation by accident was not a goal shared by anyone.

So, Gabriella and her armies would do things the hard way.

Adding the power of her wings to what she had already learned, she had turned herself into a being almost beyond comprehension by anyone witnessing her. Whatever mortals may or may not believe celestials were supposed to be, anyone seeing her in these moments couldn't deny their eyes.

Gabriella was a whirlwind of death.

She snarled, issuing very unangelic curses at the foul creatures that were daring to oppose her. A few of the demons broke from the rest and charged for the city. Given how many there still were, she was forced to let them go, but it was likely the wolves could handle the small number heading for them.

The more she fought, the more obvious another question became.

Gabriella was the Right Hand of the All-Father, and any demon would recognize her for what she was immediately. These were not the mindless creations of Thraxsis, but actual demons possessing independent thought. Challenging her was suicide for them.

When she first arrived, she had caught those demons by surprise. Even so, the last few had tried desperately to flee. So why weren't these?

Was it possible the Greater Demon had a stronger hold on its weaker brethren than normal? But even if that were true, why wasn't the Greater Demon trying to flee while the smaller ones slowed her down?

The unknown variables in this fight were becoming unacceptable, and she fought to get in range of her true target.

Any creatures lucky enough to dodge her swords were ripped apart by her wings. Once she destroyed the four-armed beast controlling the horde, the rest would likely scatter. Then she could figure out what was going on here.

Leaping into the air once again, Gabriella sheathed her regular swords.

The large monster waiting to meet her attack with its four dark blades deserved something special, and so she pulled a flaming sword directly out of her right wing. As she angled back down, she smiled at the unmistakable fear in the Greater Demon's eyes.

While the Sword of the All-Father was technically a myth, this sword had still been given to her by Him. Used at the time as a conduit to rejoin her consciousness with her true power, it was by far the most potent weapon at her disposal. The demon tried moving to the side, and she sneered at its efforts.

It didn't matter where this strike connected, so she didn't bother adjusting her angle of attack. The demon tried to deflect the blade, but the flaming sword easily sliced through both its left arms. Unfortunately, that's all it did.

Impossible!

The demon seemed to share Gabriella's thought, and for a brief instant, both combatants were equally stunned in shock. Worse was how unbalanced she was now. The demon should have been instantly destroyed, and so she had intended to continue straight through it.

She might not be bound by the laws of motion and physics, but her body was, and the demon's weight and mass were considerably greater than her own. Not being able to continue forward, she quickly used her wings to help her lean back so she could jump away. Whatever had gone wrong, it just meant she needed to take an extra swing at its head.

Unfortunately, the large demon recovered from its shock too quickly. As Gabriella leaned back, it plunged its two remaining swords downward through her chest.

Shock blocked the agony, but only for an instant, as she stumbled backward. Her eyes went cross, focusing on the large pommels sticking out of her chest. The blades had entered above her breasts, and she could *feel* them sticking out of her lower back. She was only still standing because this body's movements weren't controlled by its now severed spine.

Of course, her sense of pain was every bit as real as a mortal's, and it was all she could do to not cry out. Especially when the wounds didn't heal instantly. This wasn't the first time she had been injured in this form.

What was happening to her?

Time seemed to slow down as she finally fell backward, overwhelmed with pain. It was fortunate her body didn't really need to breathe since she was too busy choking on and spitting up blood to do so. She could see the grinning demon moving in to finish her off, and knew the smaller ones were likely closing in as well. She couldn't even move her arms enough to try to remove the blades.

This couldn't be happening, her mind kept insisting. *Where am I?*

As her vision began to darken, she could hear loud howling from everywhere. There was also a sense of many individuals suddenly charging through the area, swinging golden blades. Although all Gabriella was truly aware of was that she could no longer feel her wings.

Suddenly, the blades in her chest vanished, and her body was instantly restored.

She sat up quickly, clutching at her chest reflexively. The pain was gone entirely, but its memory would take longer to fade. She looked around and saw plenty of wolves, but no demons. It was clear this battle had been won.

So, she could still restore her body, but not until after winning the battle? That didn't make any sense.

"Angel!"

Gabriella turned to see a pair of wolves carrying Alger toward her and rushed to meet them. His chest was badly shredded, but he was still breathing.

"He killed the big one by himself, but," one of the wolves tried to explain while waving to the injury.

"Please back away," she requested as she took the large wolf in her arms and sat down. Gabriella wrapped her wings around him to ensure no one else could see or hear.

"I think you saved my life, thank you," she whispered, noticing he was still conscious.

"I believe I told you that we know how to fight," Alger tried to chuckle through his pained gasps.

"That you did." She rested a hand on his injuries, but nothing happened. Careful to conceal her surprise at not being able to heal him, she continued smiling.

"I am so sorry, but I can't save you. All I can do is take away your pain." She leaned down and kissed his forehead.

"I understand," he sighed in relief. "At least I got the bastard first."

"Yes, you did, and you don't need to be afraid. I have vast armies, and there will always be great battles to fight for those such as you," she kept whispering gently. "Will you fight for me when you wake up?"

"It would be my honor," he grunted.

"I used to be the Angel of Voice," she leaned closer to his ear. "May I sing you to sleep?" She couldn't help but start to cry. It was her job to save *them*, not the other way around.

"Only if you stop crying," Alger tried to insist.

"It is our honor to cry for you." She started to sing softly, as the wolf closed his eyes and smiled.

No sane mortal creature wanted to die, but what better death could there be for a wolf?

Alger had spent decades protecting his people, and his final act had been to kill a Greater Demon almost single-handedly. Not only had his actions saved an angel, but he was dying in that very angel's arms. Even better, for a wolf anyway, was the promise of even greater battles to come.

Gabriella tried to console herself with that knowledge as she continued to sing. She swore to herself his sacrifice would not be in vain. She would figure all this out and protect these people on his behalf.

It wouldn't be much longer before the soul passed through the barrier.

His eyes suddenly flew open, even as his facial features twisted in pain, and he was gone. The lifeless eyes held more terror in them than she had ever seen in a mortal.

Surprise kept her from noticing something even worse, but not for long. "Where?" she mumbled to herself as she closed her eyes. It didn't matter how hard she tried; she couldn't see it. This was beyond impossible.

Gabriella had been confused since she got here. There was more than a bit of anger as well, but mostly confusion. Not anymore. Now, all she felt was fear.

Pulling her wings back, she carefully laid Alger's body down and stood. The wolves and ravens had been gathering to see if she was able to save him, and she quickly grabbed the closest wolf by his leather chest piece and pulled him closer. She leaned in and stared carefully into the surprised wolf's eyes.

"No," she hissed to herself, pushing the wolf aside and grabbing a raven. The result was the same, and so she grabbed another.

"Angel, what's wrong?" The question came from somewhere to her left.

Gabriella leaped backward, drawing her swords. She crouched, flaring out her wings defensively, as she looked over the crowd.

"What are you creatures?" she shouted.

One of the wolves held his hands up in a passive manner and took a step forward.

"Get back!" she threatened. "Stay away from me! I demand to know where I've been taken! What is this place?" She cursed herself for not noticing the signs of the trap sooner.

"What's your problem this time?" Xuě shouted as she pushed her way through the crowd. Others had been trying to hold her back, and no one would tell her what was going on.

"Tell me what's wrong with your souls!" She pointed a sword at the raven as shock and fear caused her to demand something no mortal could answer anyway.

"What does that even-" Xuě's voice cut off as she recognized the body lying close by. "*No!*" Ignoring the angel's nonsense, she ran to her father's body and started wailing into his chest.

"I did this," she cried. "What was I thinking trying to bring you back?" Her crazed eyes glared daggers at Gabriella. "The demons have *never* attacked us here, and now my father's dead because of *you!*" She barely managed to finish shouting before breaking down again.

Gabriella realized all she was doing was scaring them for no gain, so she forced herself to calm down and relax her posture. Whatever was going on, these mortals weren't aware of it. Or if they were, they wouldn't understand it anyway. If this was a trap, they were probably prisoners as well.

"Whatever is happening here," she raised her voice for the crowd. "I will do everything I can to help, but I must go somewhere for answers.

However, I will not leave you unprotected." She closed her eyes briefly, and two familiar figures appeared next to her.

"Oh, Yǎniū, there you are," Qiàn remarked.

"What do you mean by that?" Her friend's comment hinted at yet another problem.

"Nothing, really," K'tar grunted. "We were talking to you, and you kind of vanished. Then, when we called out to you, you didn't answer. That's never happened before," he shrugged.

Gabriella's eyes narrowed since that should never happen. Celestials could not be everywhere as the All-Father could, but they were still able to occupy multiple places. The vastness of creation made it necessary to do so.

Ever since her friends had crossed over, a part of her was always with them. The only exception was the times they requested privacy. Plus, she hadn't heard them call out to her. They were her only two friends; she couldn't *not* hear them. Unless…

Unless *all* of her was here, but that couldn't be true. Could it? It was far too dangerous for a celestial to bring their entire essence to this side of creation. Even if that had happened somehow, it meant she should be far more powerful than usual. Not weaker.

It also meant that when she told Alger he had saved her life, it might have been far more literal than she realized.

There were whispered conversations throughout the crowd, but she ignored them. The sudden appearance of the two beings didn't shock those gathered—not after what had already happened today—but their identities did. Eighty years wasn't nearly long enough for Qiàn and K'tar to not be immediately recognized, so a certain amount of surprised conversation and pointing was expected.

Even Xuě was staring in awe, her grief temporarily forgotten.

"Something's wrong here," she told her friends.

"Is that Henwick?" K'tar asked, staring past the crowd. "Welcome home," she smirked.

"Why is it so dark?" Qiàn was blinking and trying to force her eyes to adjust. "The world isn't broken again, is it?"

"Yes, and that is all I know so far, but it's very bad." The couple exchanged worried glances before nodding to her.

"I need you to keep them safe and learn what you can until I get back." She put a hand on each of her friends' shoulders. "The demons here are true demons," she said thoughtfully.

"Good," K'tar grinned toothily.

"Protect and defend only." She was speaking to them both, but only looking at the wolf.

"We understand," Qiàn patted the hand on her shoulder.

Gabriella smiled and brought her wings forward. Very gently, she touched a wing tip to each of their foreheads. Nothing had changed about the situation, but somehow, having her friends with her made her feel as if she could handle it.

"You're leaving?" Xuě asked angrily. "How can you be serious? After what you've done," she spat the words.

"You don't understand," Gabriella said, feeling terrible for what this raven had suffered, but growing tired of her attitude.

"Don't misunderstand me, *Yǎniū*," she used the angel's name as a curse again. "I'm happy to see your backside. You've brought nothing but ruin to us, and all you've done since I brought you back is kill my father." Xuě's grief and rage were blinding her to the fact that the angel had saved both her and her wolf.

"The best thing you can do for us is leave. I'm just disgusted that you actually can. I would think you would feel at least some obligation to help us."

"I *am* trying to help you," Gabriella tried to keep the anger out of her voice.

"Really?" Xuě glanced noticeably at her father's body. "In that case, perhaps you should stop," she hissed.

"Child, I have had enough of you." Gabriella stepped closer to the young raven. "I am aware of the loss you have suffered, that all of you have suffered. Do you believe you are the only one? That no one else in creation has ever suffered? That *I* have never suffered?" She knew she was losing control but couldn't stop.

"Would you like to know the *only* explanation for what is happening here? The only possible thing that *might* account for what I have seen?" Her voice was getting louder, and some in the crowd were already starting to clutch their ears.

"The very walls of creation are crumbling!" She shouted, and even Xuě took a step back as her wings flared reflexively. "Can you wrap your pathetic mortal brain around that? None of your physical lives mean *anything* on balance against what might be at stake here!"

"Yǎniū!" Qiàn cried out from behind her.

Gabriella forced herself to calm down. She had always been plagued with such terrible emotions. Angels weren't supposed to feel the things that she always seemed to feel the most strongly. She had gotten better at controlling herself, but it wasn't easy to always account for being so broken.

Looking around, she could see the painful consequence of beginning to lose control of her voice. All she was doing was continuing to frighten them. It wasn't their fault for not understanding. Even Xuě could be forgiven, given the terrible perspective through which she had been forced to view life.

Great, so I can add shame to my wonderful feelings right now.

"Xuě, think what you will of me, but I'm going to save all of you whether you want me to or not."

"Just go," Xuě sounded more tired than angry. "Abandoning those around you is the one thing you're good at."

Gabriella took a slow and deep breath before bringing her left wing in front of her body. She took a small handful of feathers and winced slightly as she yanked them free.

"These feathers," she placed them in the raven's hand, "are the purest part of me. There is nothing in creation that can prevent me from returning to collect them. Does this satisfy you?"

"I suppose it will have to," she reluctantly shoved the feathers in her pocket.

Gabriella spared a final glance and nod to her friends and vanished.

Xuě continued muttering under her breath for a few moments before stepping up to the pair the angel had summoned. As angry as she was at what Gabriella had caused in this world, at least one good thing had happened. Her grief was still being tempered by shock and wasn't enough to prevent the awe at meeting her heroes.

"Great-grandmother, great-grandfather," she began to bow, "it is an honor-"

Qiàn's powerful slap sent Xuě to the ground. "You are no descendant of mine. From this moment forward, you will address me as 'Your Majesty.'" "But-"

"And you will only speak when spoken to," Qiàn cut her off. "Am I understood in this?"

"But-"

"I asked if you understood." Qiàn raised her hand again.

"Yes, Your Majesty," Xuě ground out, clutching the side of her face.

"Husband, see to the state of their defenses and logistics. Please report to me when you have finished."

"Yes, dear." K'tar kissed the top of his wife's head before strolling toward the city gates.

"The rest of you," she addressed the crowd. "Am I correct in assuming you know who I am?"

The few faces not still frozen in shock and wonder nodded quickly. "Good. I need to know everything that has happened in this world since

the date of my death. Every fact, rumor, or story. No piece of information is too small. You," she looked down at Xuě, who was finally picking herself back up.

"I require a comfortable office and fresh tea, *huā chá* if it's available. See that all who wish to speak are formed into a line."

"Yes, Your Majesty, but there will be many who wish to speak." Xuě kept her eyes lowered. "What you ask will take considerable time."

"Then stop wasting it." Qiàn thought for a moment in case she was forgetting anything. "Oh, and have couriers sent immediately with appropriate dispatches."

"Excuse me?"

"Please tell me your foul mouth isn't matched by a lack of

education," Qiàn rolled her eyes. "A courier is someone who carries messages from place to place."

"I know what a courier is. We just don't use them anymore."

"We don't have time for this nonsense. The capital needs to be informed of my return. Oh, and Greensboro. The Eastern Kingdom's capital is too far away, so they'll have to relay the message themselves for now."

"You misunderstand," Xuě said, her eyes far less respectful than her voice. "We don't use couriers because there's nowhere to send them. This world is dead, and we're all that's left."

Chapter 3

Kukkug's Lair

Kukkug stared at the ceiling of the cavern, resisting the urge to carve out his eyes from the boredom. As tempting as it was, he would never forget how painful it had been when he actually did it.

It had been necessary to rip information out of the minds of several mortals. How else would he properly understand how things worked here?

Learning extra things like how food tasted had been delightful, but he had accidentally learned several other things he wished he hadn't, like how to experience proper pain.

His eyes had restored themselves almost instantly, but his sudden scream had leveled the abandoned city he was playing in.

Everything had been so wonderful and exciting when he first got here, but that was so long ago. At least, he thought it was a long time ago. Was this truly how mortals experienced time? How did they not all go insane?

Thanks to the knowledge he had absorbed, he understood how to do just about everything. After the first couple of times he did anything here, however, he would just get bored again. Even eating food wasn't much fun anymore. At least, not enough fun to counter the tedium of preparing it.

He tried to teach his demons to cook for him, but couldn't get them to understand the concept. It also seemed he didn't possess the knowledge of where to find the necessary ingredients if they weren't already inside whatever building he was exploring. He gave up on the whole idea some time ago.

Exploring had been quite fun for a while, given how different everything appeared from his new perspective. It was amazing how little of this world had been occupied by the mortals. Perhaps a consequence of their population being devastated by Thraxsis's influence and their original Great War?

He had no idea.

It was a significant problem for his plans though. Almost nothing could stop what he was doing, and it had been just as easy as he predicted. The problem was that the world's population was the most crucial variable.

If he were dealing with billions, everything would have been over almost immediately. Even millions would be okay. But what did he have? A few hundred. Although he was willing to admit that it was mostly his fault.

He had never visited this part of creation before. How was he supposed to know the mortals would all simply die? By the time he realized what was happening and applied the necessary control, it was too late. If not for the presence of the wolves and ravens, he would have failed by the second day.

Those creatures possessed enough protection to survive, but he had also been unprepared for how impossible it had been to control his demons. Even when faced with certain destruction by his own hand, they couldn't help themselves from slaughtering every wolf or raven they found.

He had gotten admittedly desperate.

Kukkug had been forced to destroy every demon that had crossed over. That part had been easy, but preventing others from crossing over to take their place had been decidedly more difficult. Keeping the doorway both open to his realm and closed to his demons had taxed even his abilities. At least it had been interesting.

Once the survivors had naturally gathered, he had placed a barrier around their city. Certain that the barrier would keep his demons away, he allowed them to return. Their presence in the world helped speed the process; otherwise, he wouldn't be bothering with them at all.

What would the survivors think if they knew they were only still alive because he was actively protecting them himself? It was an amusing thought.

In the end, it didn't change the result, only how long it would take. He also couldn't deny the vast increase in power from stealing every soul on this world since the moment he arrived. Granted, even that number would have been higher overall if more had remained alive to have additional children.

His plan wasn't supposed to take long enough to require thinking in generational terms.

On balance, the numbers might not seem impressive. What worth did even a hundred thousand souls have when compared to the near infinite number that were constantly flowing through creation? The difference came from these being souls he wasn't supposed to have.

Everything he was stealing was working to tip the balance in his favor, and the wolves and ravens had been beyond his expectations. It shouldn't be possible for him to take those souls, and only his physical presence here allowed it. They were blended with an energy that should not be able to exist in his realm.

Something about the light of his former home being blended into the soul itself was acting as an interesting loophole. The effects had been…fascinating. He could stop everything he was doing right now, and the victory he had already won might be enough.

As he looked to the doorway back home, Kukkug was tempted to do just that.

If he was being candid with himself, he really did want to go back home. At least briefly. This place was beginning to feel better, especially so close to the doorway, but it wasn't the same yet.

Unfortunately, he was forcing this world itself to do something it did not want to do. Leaving, even briefly, would undo his progress.

The stolen souls would still be his, but the world would revert to its version of normal relatively quickly. He had come too far to give the other side time to counter what was about to happen.

Despite his current theory about the Old Man's impotence, Kukkug had to allow for the possibility of being wrong. There was no doubt the Old Man was a sneaky one when he wanted to be, but did he possess the power to properly interfere or not?

Even if he didn't, he could certainly tell others what to do.

The drawback of executing such an obvious and open strategy was that the counter to Kukkug's plan was equally obvious. Any counter would still fail, provided the Old Man couldn't personally involve himself. An answer he simply wouldn't have until it was too late for adjustment. Well, he had known from the beginning that this idea carried risk.

"I'm so bored!" He yelled at the cavern ceiling as he allowed his thoughts to continue brewing. "Are you bored?" He looked over and grimaced at the decayed head to his right.

He stretched out a wing and touched the tip to her forehead, and Shūfāng's head was instantly restored to its former perfection. He kept forgetting to do that.

"Sorry about that, dear," he apologized. "Better?"

The life had long since faded from the eyes, as Shūfāng was currently in the Dark Realm, being used with the others. Still, the head itself held a particular sentimental value for him. At least it wasn't a dripping mess anymore.

"Oh? What's this?" He trailed off with eyes slightly unfocused. "Well, it certainly took her long enough."

He had expected her arrival much sooner than this, but it didn't really matter. She was the only possible counter to what he was doing, and there was considerable uncertainty about how the next phase would play out. There was almost nothing she could do to stop him, even if she understood exactly what was happening.

It was too late for that.

The entire reason the rules said they couldn't come here was that this side of creation couldn't handle them. There was no struggle. Whichever of them came first simply won. That had technically been her, but she hadn't been trying to take anything, so she only added to the prize.

Kukkug had effectively won the instant he appeared here. Everything that has happened since represents the process of achieving his victory. The Old Man's direct interference was the only thing that *might* change things, but his time here was a fair amount of proof that wouldn't happen.

The uncertainty came in how exactly to handle her. Obviously, they would have to fight, but what would that entail? Something like that had never happened here. They were not indestructible beings, but on this level of creation they may as well be.

Kukkug could annihilate her anytime he wanted, but the energy required to do so would rip a hole in reality the size of this star system. Possibly even the galaxy. Creation would survive, but he would lose everything he was doing here. Plus, the Old Man would just recycle her energy into another.

Factoring in the cost of actually destroying her, and that was definitely the one thing he couldn't do. Unfortunately, given that idiot's ridiculous notion of self-sacrifice, she might force the issue because it was the only strategy that could at least delay him.

Assuming she could stomach the trillions of unknown lives it might instantly cost.

"Now what are you idiots doing?" He grumbled as he saw a mass of demons heading to attack Henwick.

That shouldn't be happening. What about the barrier?

"Oh, I hadn't considered that," he mumbled, trying to decide how to fix the problem.

Kukkug could still easily tell the difference between this world and home, but the demons didn't seem to be able to anymore. His barrier and constant scolding eventually allowed them to accept the wolves and ravens as cohabitants. Most of the time.

Nothing could make them see an angel that way. They were moving to attack her because their base instincts were forcing them to protect their home from the invader. This was problematic.

Well, not really, he supposed.

He removed the barrier immediately. His demons stood no chance against her. They were so outmatched that he doubted even the survivors were in any danger. The battle might also give him additional insight into how his struggle with her may go.

Meanwhile, he would need to empty this world of demons. There was no way for him to control them now, and he'd have to just deal with the consequences.

"Great, as if this wasn't taking long enough." He looked over at the head, noticing its lack of response.

He reached over to force the eyes and mouth open a bit. It wasn't much, but maybe now he could pretend she was answering him.

He had studied Gabriella's final battle with Thraxsis very carefully. It wasn't a perfect parallel, but it was the best example he had. For all of Thraxsis's foolish goals, that demon had grown in power far beyond what Kukkug had expected. Thraxsis had also learned and demonstrated a fantastic amount of control by the end.

By contrast, she had gotten lucky. The only reason she hadn't ripped a hole in this reality was that she didn't realize what was happening at the time. It appeared she had used exactly enough power to destroy him, rather than attacking with everything she had available.

Given her state of mind at the time, she likely hadn't known the rest of her power had even been available.

It had been fascinating to study, but essentially useless since the same strategy wouldn't work between the two of them. He wondered if he could send her back without completely destroying her. How exactly did these physical bodies work, and how necessary were they?

He continued watching her fight the demons while also examining the fingers of his left hand. His eyes widened as she was seriously injured. So, it would seem she didn't fully understand what was happening here. Her injuries were messy, too, but he knew she'd be fine.

On a whim, he ripped off a finger from his left hand and watched the blood start spraying. Ignoring the pain, he looked inside the injury to see the white of the bone. Oddly, this had not happened when he cut out his eyes earlier on.

He let the injury heal itself and reabsorbed the severed finger. A consequence of his wanting a body that understood this world, perhaps? Strangely, that change had taken longer. Having made the discovery in his own body and watching her lie near dying in the battle, he had an idea. What if he killed her body? She would be fine, but unable to interact here.

No, that wouldn't work. Even real, these bodies just weren't that important. A fact underlined by her instant recovery from the fatal wounds.

What about taking her wings? He already knew that would work, but was it possible to do it here? It was worth a try, and he could always fight her to a standstill forever. Time was on his side after all.

No, a prolonged physical fight might not work. Without being able to use his additional power, he had to admit he was not a match for her. No being was. Not in that type of fighting.

In fact, his eyes narrowed; this just became a significant problem. If her wings could be taken, so could his. Ejecting him from this world would be a partial victory for her. Worse, he had already moved openly and had to assume she wouldn't repeat her earlier mistakes.

Well, this just got more complicated.

He stretched and looked back to the doorway, his thoughts turning longingly back home. After a moment, he started smiling.

Before long, his smile turned into loud laughter. That would never work. Would it?

She's not that stupid.

Gabriella had always been a broken pile of emotions. She constantly made stupid choices and did plenty of silly things. However, he knew she wasn't actually stupid. She would never fall for such an obvious trap.

Although…

Her emotions had always been her weakness. In many ways, she was no different from him. She was simply an example of what happens when a being lives its life in denial, whereas he preferred acceptance. He could use that.

"Dear," he looked to Shūfāng. "I have an insane plan, and I need your help. Let me give you a history lesson of my relationship with my sister," he grinned in memory.

"Then, you can help me figure out the perfect string of conversation to drive her emotionally insane. I want her so blinded by emotions that she follows me," he said, his eyes flicking to the doorway, "no matter where I go.

"Once upon a time…"

*****

Henwick (Outskirts)

"This is not as much fun as I remember," K'tar complained as he followed Larg through the trees.

"This isn't real hunting, sir; it's not supposed to be fun." Larg tried to avoid direct eye contact with the legendary wolf walking next to him.

It had been two days since the battle outside Henwick, and the survivors were still uncertain what to do. The loss of Alger had been devastating, and his burial had a finality to it. It was as if there was no longer any point in even pretending they should all continue living.

Perhaps the angel would return and tell them what to do, but there was much heated discussion on that point. Queen Qiàn had not given them any instructions either. She had spent an entire day listening to people speak, and then simply asked not to be disturbed.

In the end, the necessities of survival prevailed, leading to their current activity. Whatever the future held, they needed food, and so a large group was gathering and directing game animals to those waiting to collect them. Thanks to the wolves' rapid healing, Larg had nearly recovered, and so he joined in, and K'tar had decided to come with him.

"Wasn't this done in your time, sir?"

"I suppose, but mostly by farmers or other men. I confess I don't really know what to do," K'tar admit.

"Just what we're doing now," Larg chuckled. "We follow the path we were given, make noise, and rustle the underbrush we pass," he shrugged. "That's about it. Others will collect the herd as it runs to them. Sorry, sir, but it's more important that we get the numbers we need, rather than have fun."

"I suppose," K'tar grunted. "But when we're done with this foolishness, I plan to go hunting on my own. It's been a while," he sniffed the air appreciatively.

"We normally don't go out at night anymore, nor do we go very far, but no one is going to stop you. Um, can I go with you? That is, if you do go hunting later, sir?" Larg looked over and tried not to sound too hopeful.

"Do whatever you wish, boy, and stop calling me sir. My name is K'tar." "I, I can't do that."

"I understand," K'tar chuckled, "but for a very long time in my life, I could not use my name. I like hearing others say it. It is respectful and enjoyable to me for you to do so."

"Um, very well, sir, I mean, K'tar," Larg forced himself to obey. "This is so strange," K'tar mumbled as he beat the underbrush around him with a large branch. "Sorry, I'm just used to being quiet. It's also still a bit odd to be in a forest this close to Henwick."

"So does that mean it's true?" "Is what true?"

"This forest," Larg waved his nearly healed arm. "Is it truly the Forest of the Angel?"

"Oh, people still call it that?" K'tar laughed. "Do you know of the final battle between our people and the Soul Eater?"

"Everyone knows that story," Larg nodded.

He spent several minutes detailing what the stories told of the terrible battle to K'tar. The information was remarkably detailed and far more accurate than K'tar would have expected. He didn't, however, appreciate the look of excitement in Larg's eyes and face as he told the tale.

"Well, that's more or less what happened," K'tar agreed. "Not sure I care for how excited you're getting. Thousands of dead on both sides," he started shaking his head. "Even corrupted men are still men," his eyes glazed over.

"In Raven's Realm, all races were valued and treated equally, and we did our best to spread that notion of equality to the Eastern Kingdom at the time. Never were we more equal than on that day, boy. That day, when the dead were so thick and mangled so as to not be able to tell the difference."

"I never thought of the story like that," Larg nodded. "You have to appreciate the brilliance of the Queen's strategy, though, to be-"

K'tar spun and shoved the younger wolf against a tree before Larg could react. His eyes had a sudden yellow fury that silenced anything else that was about to be said.

"*Strategy!* She chose suicide! And it's not just a story, you fool." K'tar leaned his face dangerously close to Larg's, but his eyes didn't see the wolf. "You want to know what I saw when it was over?

"Over six *hundred* dead ravens as a result of her *strategy*. Their bodies were so mangled, burned, and ripped apart that they were no longer recognizable as people. That sight haunted me until the day I died. It was sick and disgusting, and we still called it victory," he finished growling.

"K'tar," Larg risked putting a hand on the older wolf's wrist. "It *was* a victory, though, wasn't it? You defeated the Soul Eater."

"Yăniū defeated the Soul Eater," he disagreed softly. "I'm not convinced the rest of us accomplished anything worth the death of so many. Maybe I'm wrong," he released his hold on Larg and patted the wolf's shoulder. "Truth be told, I'm aware that we finally turned things around, but not sure I'll ever accept the cost."

"You learned the truth and saved the world," he insist. "Isn't that worth any cost?"

"Did we?" K'tar looked around at the perpetual darkness of his former home.

"Whatever happened later doesn't change what you all did then. It doesn't make sense to belittle what you accomplished simply because the future didn't work out the way you hoped."

"You sound a bit like them," K'tar chuckled.

"Like who?"

"Never mind, and sorry for losing my temper just now," he sighed. "Whatever the cause or the result of what we did, there was no glory in it. Guess it's still a bit of a sensitive topic for me."

"I'm sorry, but I disagree." Larg held up a hand quickly when it looked as if K'tar would grow angry again. "If it sounded in any way that I was being disrespectful earlier, then I apologize, but look around you.

"K'tar, we have nothing left. The stories of what happened before all this keep us looking forward. Whether people believe them or not doesn't change how important they are to us. Maybe it's true we glorify them too much, but it's our only source of hope. Proof that maybe we'll find another victory," he shrugged.

"Fair enough," K'tar relented, and the two began following their path again. "Anyway, it took a fair amount of time to take care of the dead following the battle. Once that was over, there were arguments over what to do about the land.

"Many said the land was cursed, given the amount of death and the Soul Eater's presence. Others argued that the land was blessed because the angel was victorious and present. The ravens," he rolled his eyes, "pointed out *logically* that the amount of remains and blood soaking into the ground could have made the soil more fertile, and the area should be cultivated."

Larg looked over quickly, expecting a grim joke of some kind, but K'tar just shook his head.

"You might guess their opinion wasn't very popular at the time," he chuckled in memory. "The discussion went on for some time, and there were plenty of other things to deal with. Eventually, when Yǎniū started visiting us, we asked her opinion. We figured that under the circumstances, it might be easier for her to just tell us the truth about blessings, curses, and the like.

"She told us not to worry about it. Sometime later, she was seen walking through the area at night. It's said she knelt down and spread her wings across the ground. A couple of days after that, the forest was here. It never seems to expand, and none of the trees can be felled. I guess the name was a pretty obvious choice."

"That's amazing," Larg brushed a hand gently against one of the trees. "Wait," he stopped suddenly. "This is normally where we hunt. It's not safe to go far from the city, and you can see the abundance of game."

"What's your point?"

"Well, if it's not just a story, should we be hunting in this forest?"

"Do your people not need food to survive?"

"Well, of course, but-"

"Then that's a stupid question, isn't it?" K'tar cut off his concern with a wink. "I'm more interested in hearing your intentions toward my great- granddaughter." He cast a side-long glance at the suddenly nervous wolf.

"You mean Xuě?"

"I only have the one," K'tar suddenly paused. "Right?"

"Um, yes. As to your question, though, I'm not sure how to answer it." "It was a simple question, boy. Are you her wolf, or aren't you?" "Honestly, I think I'm just her tool," Larg mumbled before looking embarrassed that he had said the words aloud.

"May as well spit out the rest." He encouraged, as he sniffed the air. It was really frustrating not to be allowed to chase anything, but spooking the animals in the wrong direction wouldn't help.

He listened as Larg slowly opened up about his and Xuě's history, although there wasn't as much information about Alger as he hoped. K'tar made a mental note to ask around about the former leader later. Anyone who could accomplish as much as he had was worth knowing better. Not to mention the wolf had been married to his granddaughter.

Most of Larg's story was naturally focused on Xuě, and the more he spoke, the less pleasant the information became. K'tar had heard enough comments from others that he was forced to allow for the possibility that the young wolf wasn't exaggerating. It didn't, however, make it any easier to hear.

"You are not describing a charming individual," was all he would offer when Larg finished.

"I can't lie," Larg shrugged.

"Yet you still seek to protect her?"

"No choice really, if I'm being honest about it." "Oh?"

"If I don't, no one else will." Larg paused for a moment, unsure if he should continue. "The people respect that she's the Raven Queen, but in truth, it's almost an empty title now. We hold on to it for the same reason we hold on to the stories, but the people followed Alger. Not her.

"Except for me, no one so much as talks to her unless they have to," he admitted sadly. "It's different now that Alger's gone, but any additional attention to her seems to just be sympathetic. In truth, the people are grateful for you and Queen Qiàn's presence because it means they *don't* have to turn to her for leadership."

"So, you protect her out of pity?" K'tar asked, careful to keep his voice low and neutral.

"No, it's not like that," Larg shook his head and seemed to stare at nothing.

K'tar could see the apparent confusion in the boy's thoughts and forced himself to remain patient.

"I really do care about her. She's the smartest and most beautiful raven I know, and I truly believe she cares about me. As hurtful and dismissive as she can be with everyone, even Alger at times, I feel like she's always at least tried to be different with me." Larg paused and narrowed his eyes.

"But?" K'tar encouraged as the pause continued to stretch.

"I don't think she knows how to be any other way, and lately her actions have grown more confusing. I see and hear her try to apologize more often, especially to the elders who tried raising and teaching her."

"That sounds like a positive change."

"Except she's done nothing to act any different," he argued. "Simply acknowledging your error doesn't mean much when you insist on repeating it. In fact, it just underlines how arrogant and self-centered she is." He reached out and grabbed K'tar's elbow.

"Please, you have to tell me how to help her. You and Queen Qiàn were the first, so you must know something. There has to be *something* I can do or say to help fix whatever's wrong with her."

"Sorry, boy," K'tar hated to deny the pleading look in Larg's eyes. "You're talking about entirely different things. When I was your age, I barely knew the difference between my own feet, much less had any dealings with ravens.

"Protecting them is a wonderful, yet horrible thing, no matter how you look at it. I spent a lot of years doing my part to keep Qiàn on the right path and to prepare her for the terrible life she would be forced to live.

Qiàn, you see, was destined to live a life of two extremes.

"The side everyone else saw was the amazing Queen. She forced everyone to be what they needed to be to save the world we were in. Every time we learned something impossible or terrible, she made everyone accept it and fight back anyway. Qiàn was a legend long before she died." He could see Larg nodding along with his description.

"That fits with everything the stories say about her."

"Do the stories tell of her other extreme? How her mind broke repeatedly under the pressure? How she was literally killing herself to force herself to be what the world needed? Do the stories tell of the number of times she fell asleep screaming about how much she hated the world and wanted no more part in it?" It was hard to keep his voice low, as K'tar's mind replayed several unpleasant memories.

"Um, no, there's nothing like that."

"As her wolf, do you know how I protected her?" He bared his teeth. "I would hold her and comfort her and then push her right back into the world she hated. Because we needed her.

"And she paid the price for it. Qiàn was only twenty-seven when we reached the turning point, but it was already too late. Our bodies weren't properly balanced, and she had pushed herself too hard too often. It was less than ten years later before it became apparent she wouldn't have much time, even for a raven.

"I'm sure if you ask her, my wife will say nothing except how glorious her final twenty years on this world were. I'll even admit they were the best years of my life as well, but she deserved more time."

"I'm sorry to hear about it like that, and I can see how different things were. There still has to be something I can learn from it though. I'm not willing to give up on her."

"Xuě is an example of what happens when a raven grows up without the guidance of another raven," K'tar tried to explain. "Even after raising Měilíng, it's hard to explain, but there's not much a wolf can do. Keep them on the proper path, give them their lumps when their arrogance gets out of control," he chuckled, "things like that.

"As for things like their eyes, and especially their minds, we just don't have the framework to reference. From what you've said, it sounds as if Xuě has already figured out the problem and just assumes it can no longer be fixed."

"Exactly," Larg agreed. "That's my point. We have to help her."

"You don't understand. We can't. In Xuě's mind, she is correct and will always be correct, regardless of factors like attitude or even reality.

Anything you say to her to help or correct her is likely to be ignored and might even drive her away from you.

"Or, she already sees herself as irredeemably broken, which will cause the same result if you try to interfere with her mind. There's only one thing you can do, and you won't like it."

"I know maybe you think I'm too young to say this, but I swear I'll do anything for her," Larg pleaded.

"Then just wait and be ready." "I don't understand."

"Reality has a way of breaking people who refuse to accept it. Wait for it to break her, and then be ready to catch her when she falls. It's an unpleasant thing to witness, but everything should connect quickly afterward."

"You really believe that's the only way?" Larg asked softly. "And that it'll happen to her?"

"I hope it does," K'tar grunted thoughtfully. "If it doesn't, then it becomes a question of what she'll lose first. Her sanity, or her life."

*****

Qiàn's Office, Henwick

"Don't you think that's a bit greedy considering we don't need to eat?" "What?" K'tar looked up from the very healthy portion of meat he had just been served. "It's not as if they have a lack of anything." He eyed his wife for a moment. "If you want some, just say so," he grunted.

Qiàn responded by smirking and holding her plate out. "Thought so," he mumbled, ripping his meal in half.

"Not quite what I meant," Qiàn commented, as a slab of meat was slapped onto her plate. "Whatever," she thought, not expecting anything different, and went to work slicing off small pieces to mix in her rice bowl.

There were plenty of available buildings in Henwick, and she had chosen a former school for her use. The classroom they were in was large enough to double as an office and private dining room for them. Which was fortunate since, for obvious reasons, no one had expected them to want dining facilities of any kind. A few pieces of quickly moved furniture had solved that problem.

"Why are you sitting like that?" K'tar didn't think it was comfortable for her to lean forward so much while trying to cut food. "If you're looking for me to say anything beyond that being a nice dress, you're wasting your time."

"Oh, really?" Qiàn twisted and started stretching seductively in the far too low-cut black dress. "And after all the alterations I had made after I found it?"

"Raven, teasing doesn't work when the other person enjoys

it," he winked.

"Excuse me?" She looked confused.

"Are you serious? The only reason your teasing and jokes ever made me feel uncomfortable was because I wasn't allowed to do anything about it.

That's long in the past," he paused to take another bite.

"You're my wife, and we know no one's going to bother us. So, truth be told, I'd just as soon have you lose the dress altogether," he grunted, laughing.

Qiàn gasped slightly and started to blush.

"Why are you acting like this is new information to you?" K'tar typically enjoyed his wife's antics, but she seemed oddly surprised by what should have been obvious information.

"I'm, I'm not sure. You're right, of course, but," she mumbled as her eyes started twitching. "Wolf, do your memories feel strange, like out of order, or missing, or anything like that?"

"A bit, but remember what we were told. Our personal reality is altered now based on our perceptions. We can't actually alter the reality of this world, but," he tapped the side of his head. "Being here again probably makes our old lives seem more real to us than our current ones."

"There's no logic to that," she tried to disagree. "Real is real, and how do you understand it?"

"I don't. I just accept it. Only you could have everything you've always wanted and still be mad because you can't figure it out," he laughed.

Qiàn threw a cloth at him. "That large boy sounds nice," she decided to change the subject.

"He is," K'tar nodded. "Boy's not certain of his age, but twenty-five is everyone's best guess. It's hard to imagine, given how mature he is compared to me at that age. We started seeing it with the new generation, but we didn't last long enough to really see them grow up."

"No, we didn't," Qiàn said sadly.

"It sounds as if Alger might have been grooming him to take over, but he's years away from being ready for that. They don't really have anyone in charge at the moment. A couple of people, both wolves and ravens, helped Alger, but no one here has any official titles."

K'tar's conversations with the survivors had shown a lack of hierarchy.

They seemed to operate closer to a large extended family, rather than the small town level of organization he would have expected the ravens to insist on. Anyone old enough to remember the "time before" was considered an elder, and that was about the extent of authoritative positions.

"Well, except Xuě," Qiàn pointed out sternly.

"Fair enough, but she's the non-entity you expected."

"I appreciate you avoiding her," Qiàn said as she put her utensils down. "I know how hard it must be."

"Do you?" He forced his voice to stay low. "I deserve to know her." "You will, I promise, but you have to let me finish with her first." "So, you figured out her problem? Can you help her?" He let himself sound hopeful.

"Her problem is the most obvious thing here," she waved. "Helping her would be easy if we had years, as it is," her voice trailed off. "You continuing to avoid her helps what I'm doing. Just promise me you won't interfere with my methods, no matter what I do or say."

"The look in your eye makes me think I'm going to regret this, but I promise."

Qiàn nodded sharply in thanks. "Back to the people here, I'll admit, the look on their faces when they came in with the food was pretty funny," she chuckled.

"Yeah, it's almost like they've never seen people who have

been dead for eighty years eat," he agreed.

"We probably made it even more confusing for them by waiting two days before bothering to ask for food," she shrugged between bites. "So, you really didn't see any supply concerns?"

"No, beyond the lack of horses, but that's not unsurprising. By my count, there are only three hundred and twenty-two survivors," K'tar hesitated at the sad number. "Not a lot of mouths to feed, and the enemy doesn't care about taking their supplies. I admit I'm a bit confused at the effect this darkness is having."

"How so?" Qiàn had her own opinions, but her focus had been on other matters.

"Well, the forest Yǎniū made seems unaffected by the lack of light. I guess we shouldn't be surprised by that, and they get plenty of fruit and medicinals from it. They struggle when it comes to growing certain grains and vegetables, but they don't seem to be struggling enough." K'tar thought about some of the extensive gardens he had seen.

"A lot of plant life around here shows signs of suffering, but it's still growing. I would have expected it all to simply die. Also, their skin tones look normal to me. I would have thought over twenty years of darkness would cause them to be a bit paler, especially those who were born since.

"All the ravens I've seen here have the same perfect olive skin you do.

The wolves' skin tones don't have the variety I remember, but that could be because there are so few of them left. It's just not what I expected to see under these conditions." Having concluded his brief report, K'tar went back to his food.

"Hmm, I was a bit surprised myself to see how well stocked they were with things like rice. It doesn't taste any different than I remember either," Qiàn stirred her bowl as she spoke.

"Hah, the rice is the only thing I do understand," K'tar's smile beamed. "If anyone can figure out how to grow rice where it shouldn't exist, it's a raven."

"Are you complimenting us or insulting us?" she glared at him. "Yes," he grunted. "Pity they don't bother with noodles anymore. At least my teeth can handle noodles." In truth, K'tar enjoyed rice on occasion, but given a wolf's pointed teeth, it was a bit of an annoyance to eat.

"Clearly there's plenty of game, but what about fish?" Qiàn had been unable to find any available.

"From what I'm told, lack of fish isn't a problem. That's something else I don't understand. The issue is that they don't like going too far from the city. Supposedly, Henwick is safe for whatever reason, but the demons take anyone who strays too far."

"You think you can convince them to go fishing tomorrow, provided you go with them?"

"Some sort of test?"

"Not really," she admitted. "I just want fish, and we both know the demons aren't a problem."

"Ah, so you figured that out as well?"

"Of course I did," she rolled her eyes. Whatever was going on here, if the demons wanted to kill these people, they would have done it twenty years ago.

"What about the rest? You know what's going on?"

"Sure, it's pretty obvious. Took less than an hour to figure it out actually." She looked up and seemed surprised he even asked her.

"Qiàn, it's been two days. Why haven't you told me anything yet?" "Honestly," she looked frustrated. "Because I don't understand the *how* or the *why* yet. As for the *what*, there are people here who saw it happen. There's no reason why any of them shouldn't already know what's going on, although I admit they don't have the perspective we do. That could be preventing them from accepting it.

"I was waiting to see if I could make the connections, but I think some of it is beyond our understanding. This is what I've figured out so far." Qiàn spent a few minutes filling in K'tar on the timeline she had put together.

"He's here? As in physically here?" K'tar's appetite suddenly vanished. "Yes, and this darkness isn't real darkness. That's why the effects don't seem to match what you would expect. Although," Qiàn wrinkled her nose in thought. "I admit I am not an expert in such matters, so it's possible it just hasn't been long enough.

"I don't know how long it would take for plants to actually die, or for people's skin tone to change," she shrugged. "In any event, this darkness isn't as simple as the sun simply not shining anymore."

"Qiàn, if *he's* here, there's nothing we can do. I don't even understand what he is, and don't pretend that you do." Until this moment, K'tar had thought there might be a way to help this world.

"Calm down," she reached across the table to take his hand. "Our job is to gather information and to be ready. The information is what it is. We'll wait for Yǎniū to come back, and then we can figure it out."

"That could be a while." "What do you mean?"

"You know how different time works there. Also, have you been trying to call out to her?" K'tar didn't need to wait for her answer, as Qiàn's eyes gave it immediately.

"When it happened before, I didn't think much of it. Then, she brought us here, and it's happening again. Raven, something's in the way," he struggled to find the words to match what his brain was screaming. "Something that shouldn't be there."

"She'll never abandon us, you know that."

"Unless it's something she can't control," he pointed out. "Even if she can come back, it could be tomorrow, or it could be ten years from now."

"My Wolf," she smiled to put him at ease. "That just means we should get comfortable. There is no logic in creating problems we cannot solve. We need only keep them safe and seek what comfort we can from each other in the meantime. As we always have."

"Yes, dear."

Chapter 4

Gabriella strode through the Great Hall, scoffing at its emptiness.

Of course, it would be empty. It was foolish of her to think for even an instant that any of her empty siblings would be taking notice of this problem, much less be willing to help. Still, there was an odd feeling to this emptiness, and so she stopped briefly to close her eyes.

That can't be right.

The physical appearance of the hall's emptiness did not really mean much, at least not in this realm. What Gabriella was sensing now, however, meant a great deal. More accurately, what she *wasn't* sensing.

"Ah, welcome home, dear."

Gabriella's sudden thoughts were interrupted at the sound of the All- Father's gentle voice. She quickly shook her head and finished approaching the throne, her eyes darting briefly to the still-empty silver throne at his right. Every time she felt drawn to sit on the throne, something seemed to distract her away from doing so.

There was a part of her that insisted she finally do so, but there were more important things to handle first. She stood confidently before her father, before bowing deeply.

"Something is wrong, Father."

"I still think your armor looks beautiful, but I wonder if you have yet to truly appreciate your choice in color." He ignored her comment.

"What? My choice?" She glanced down at her blood-red armor.

"The Angel of Voice, who has since acknowledged herself to be my Right Hand. At least in words," he added softly. "In practice, it would seem you prefer to be the Angel of Death," he arched a brow at her.

"I do not seek death, Father," she responded defensively. "I seek only to defend the balance, and I seem to be the only one even trying." She tried to keep her sudden anger in check. "It's not my fault no one else cares."

"It is not? Under other circumstances, your choice of words would be rather amusing. Tell me, dear, how are your methods progressing?"

"I don't have time for this," she sneered slightly. "Father, something is wrong with creation."

"Obviously. You claim to be the only one trying, yet you are the last one to notice." He cocked his head and smiled.

"I," she paused. She hadn't expected such a direct answer. "What are you talking about?"

"I am surprised you even bothered to return here at all, given what is happening on that world. Do you truly not understand?" He sighed at the question.

"No, I don't." Gabriella was growing more concerned. She heard what could only be exhaustion in her father's voice. That had never happened before, and she hadn't believed such a thing was even possible.

"Father, I returned here to find the answers. I, I don't understand why you're talking to me like this."

"If you believe something is wrong with creation, perhaps you should observe the state of the Dark Realm for a moment," he suggested.

"You know that's the one place angels cannot see." Gabriella was growing more confused, but she couldn't deny the serious undertone in her father's voice.

"Perhaps you should try?" "I can't," she insisted.

"Gabriella," the All-Father spoke loudly. "If there was ever a time for you to stop questioning me and simply do as I suggest, now is that time."

"Very well," she swallowed slowly at her father's tone.

Gabriella closed her eyes and attempted to follow his instructions. It wasn't long before she collapsed and began clutching at her chest, her wings automatically wrapping around her body for protection as she fell to the ground. After several heaving breaths, she forced her eyes back open.

"That was," she gasped. "That was," she could only stare in wide-eyed horror at the ground, as she braced herself with her hands.

"But you *did* see it?" he asked softly.

"I, yes," horror at what she had seen was slowly replaced by realization of the impossible thing that had just happened. "I did."

"Hmm, I am curious what has happened on that world since you left.

Perhaps you should check?"

Gabriella eyed her father warily as she climbed back to her feet. He could see anything he wanted for himself, but she decided it was better to play along until she understood what was happening. She closed her eyes to check on her friends, and after a moment, her face began to tense with effort.

"I can't see," she mumbled. "Why can't I see?"

"An interesting question." The All-Father chose to interpret her mumbled question as one directed at him. "I wonder what it really is that prevents angels from seeing certain places." He trailed off and simply leaned back.

She was about to say that obviously angels couldn't see into the Dark Realm because of the realm's opposing nature, but she held her tongue. What she had already experienced disproved that. She forced herself to consider the question logically, and it wasn't long before she inhaled sharply.

"He's there," she hissed.

The All-Father simply nodded slowly.

"That bastard's on *my* world!" She screamed, her wings shaking in rage. "Your world?" He questioned softly.

"You need to fix this!" She shouted at her father. Gabriella had had enough.

For so long, she had been the only one fighting. None of the other celestials ever helped her, and now this? She was tired of being questioned and scolded for no reason. *This* time, her father was going to help her, whether he wanted to or not.

"What would you have me do?"

"Cast him out!" she shouted. "What other choice is there?"

"Why?"

"Because he doesn't belong there!" Her deep blue eyes were filled with rage as she tried staring her father down. "The rules are clear about this, we don't belong-" her voice cut off as a connection snapped into place in her mind.

"Oh, no," she whispered softly as the rage vanished. Horror and shock took their place as she fell back to her knees. "I did this," she finally acknowledged, and her hands went up to cover her face. "This is all my fault, isn't it?" She started to cry, making her question barely audible.

"Mostly, although no being truly operates in a vacuum." He looked down sadly as Gabriella's wings wrapped around her body. "Fear of intervention or punishment was the only thing staying his hand. You proved these things would not come." There was no longer any point in coloring the truth.

He considered how to proceed, as the bundle of feathers continued to shake. This was the final focal point, leaving no choice but to force her to understand everything. The risk to her was no longer relevant, despite how much it hurt to see his daughter this way.

The probability of the balance being restored was minute, but it did exist. The likelihood of her destruction before the end of this focal point, however, was very high. Much of it would depend on his next few direct actions.

That was unfortunate.

The All-Father could not foresee the direct consequences of his own actions. In the infinite futures, he appeared to himself as a non-entity, yet he did make his own choices. So, he would have to guess. Without knowing what was truly wrong with her, the odds of guessing correctly were suboptimal.

"Please," she lifted her head slowly. "Please, do it anyway." He cocked his head at the tear-stained face looking up at him.

"I'm sorry for everything I've done. I'm sorry for not understanding," she pleaded. "Punish me if you have to, but don't let this happen because of me. Please don't let this happen," she cried.

She lowered her head, completely prostrating herself. Even her wings stretched out to cover the All-Father's feet. All while continuing her pleas.

"Daughter, it pains me to see you like this," he said truthfully, "but I will not do what you are asking."

"Why not?" She screamed and forced her physical body to stop crying as she rose from the floor. "Why can't you do something? Just this one time, actually do something useful!" Gabriella was losing control of her emotions and no longer cared how she was speaking to him.

"I did not say I could not do anything. I said I *would* not."

"What?" Her eyes widened further as her face tensed. "What could I have possibly done to make you hate me this much?"

"Hate you?" he smiled. "Daughter, you are my favorite. I have told you this many times."

"Then prove it!" She jabbed a finger at him in challenge even as her wings flared out.

He was about to answer when a thought occurred to him. It didn't seem plausible, but could it be true?

"Is it possible you have forgotten what I am?" he asked slowly. "I don't have time for your riddles, Father!"

"Tell me what I am. Now." He could not force her, but it was unlikely she would be able to deny his command.

"You are the master of this realm," she waved an arm around her, "and you command the angels. You're *supposed* to be the one countering the Dark Realm's forces," she sneered.

"You believe this to be true?"

"Because it is true!" she shouted. "You made it abundantly clear during The Fall. Not that you've done anything useful since. Why are you wasting time with this nonsense?" Her wings were trembling, and she was no longer sure which emotion was overwhelming her the most.

The All-Father's eyes narrowed. "You mentioned The Fall. The only thing I am certain about in your mind is that you no longer remember it. Your suffering vanished in an instant. The only explanation for this is that you chose to remove those memories."

"My suffering?" Gabriella was losing track of the conversation. "No one could forget what happened."

"So, tell me."

She forced her anger down. It was rare for her father to be so direct in his conversations. Even if she didn't understand what he was trying to say, at least he was talking to her. What choice did she have but to play along with what he wanted?

"The Dark One rose up against us. He sought to destroy the angels and take the power of creation for himself." Her breath caught slightly.

It had been the first time she had felt fear. The first time she had considered that celestials may not be indestructible. Despite the eternity that had passed, it was so clear in her memory. When she saw those dark blades coming for her...

"But you stepped down and shielded us," she smiled, forcing herself to focus on how it ended. "The angels cried out for you to destroy him for his ambition, but instead, you cast him to the Dark Realm. It was how you taught us mercy."

The All-Father was nodding slowly. It was all so obvious now. "What's wrong?" She could see a strange look in his eyes.

"I never considered the possibility that you would give yourself false memories."

"What do-"

He waved her silent. "It does clarify how I should proceed." He made his decision. "What is the purpose of creation?"

"Choice, at least that's what you keep telling me." "Why?"

"Because that's what you told me. I have no idea why," she rolled her eyes.

"All is foreseen, but nothing is foretold."

"You say that a lot, too, and I don't know what it means either." She didn't understand what he meant by claiming her memories were false.

"Do you understand what energy is, in its most basic form?" he asked carefully.

"It's just energy," she responded. "Energy awaiting its use in creation."

"It is boring," he stated loudly and clearly. "Can you comprehend what it is like for an entity of unimaginable power to occupy a never-ending empty void? A void filled with energy. Energy with such potential, but energy that did nothing but simply exist?"

She did not understand the purpose of the conversation, but she quickly recognized what was happening and refused to speak. The All-Father was talking about the moment of creation and doing so in a fashion he had never done before. She did not see how useful the information would be, but as an angel, she was deeply curious about what came before.

"So, I created two pure and perfect realms of opposing viewpoints. So diametrically opposite were these realms that if they should ever touch," he mimicked an explosion with his hands. "And so, the rest of creation was placed in between to hold them apart."

Gabriella nodded slowly, wanting to hear more.

"Finally, infinite beings were either created or allowed to

evolve to inhabit all the realms and universes, and the constant flow of life energy was established. With two opposing viewpoints to choose from, it was logical to assume approximately half would go in each direction. In this fashion, I believed the balance would be maintained eternally.

"I anticipated creation not working correctly. You see, dear, knowledge does not come from nothing. Not even for me. Concepts such as ambition and complacency, for example, affect the logical and perfect balance, yet they were unknown to me until I witnessed them happening.

"There were…other concerns as well, but safeguards were put in place." He paused, noticing Gabriella's captivated expression.

Never before had he spoken so long and maintained her full attention, without her interrupting him. This was verification that being direct with her had been necessary all along. It had failed with his son, and he feared trying again. If only he had been aware of her false memories.

"You are aware I can see the infinite futures made possible by the infinite choices of the infinite beings that make up creation?"

"Yes, Father," she nodded, still not understanding why he had chosen to tell her so much.

"Nothing is foretold, however, so I do not know which of these futures will come to pass until it arrives."

"But," her brow wrinkled in thought. "I don't understand. You know everything."

"You are not listening," he sighed. "Daughter, I realize I gave you Voice, but why do you insist on using it as your only method of communication? The words you use are so inefficient compared to how beings like us should be communicating.

"If you continue to force me to use them, then you must listen to the ones I choose. I know all the choices that can be made, but I do not know which ones *will* be made until they are. That is the entire point; for me to not know what will happen.

"Without choice, creation serves me no purpose. If the balance fails, the futures will begin to converge and become foretold. A foretold future serves me no purpose, and I will begin again." There was an ominous undertone to his final statement.

"What exactly do you mean by that?"

"Exactly what you think. All will cease, and I will begin again. I will use my acquired knowledge to avoid past mistakes."

"You, what?" Gabriella began stuttering as she tried to contemplate what her father had said. "But that's not necessary. Just fix it." There was something about this she didn't quite understand, or perhaps was simply unwilling to accept.

"Why would I? Isn't the puppet's future foretold by the puppet master?" She could feel her entire body starting to shake with fear and anger.

It couldn't possibly be true, but the answer finally became clear to her. "We're your…entertainment." Even as she said it, she couldn't believe it.

"Of course, you are." The All-Father sounded confused in response to her powerful emotions. "What other purpose could creation serve me?"

"I, that's, I," Gabriella was losing control of her voice, and her wings began shaking violently. She tried taking a step, but it became difficult to move.

"Calm down," he ordered. "You are the one forcing me to use these words, and it is your interpretation of the concepts that you are assigning to them. I am a being beyond even your comprehension. To say creation entertains me is an expression that goes far beyond your concept of love."

Gabriella forced herself to breathe deeply and slowly, and her body began moving normally again. That had been odd. The feeling of being briefly frozen. Hadn't she felt that before?

"I don't believe you," she finally said. "If what you're saying is true, then why are you talking to me at all? Why haven't you already begun again if the balance has truly failed?”

“It has yet to fail,” he corrected. “It most certainly will, but it would be a violation of my own laws to act before it is foretold. Also,” he paused, “I do not want to. My preference is for this version of creation to continue,” he admitted.

“Even though you claim it will not?”

“Correction, I *believe* it will not. I have grown quite good at guessing which future will come to pass; however, creation occasionally proves me wrong. Those are my favorite moments, in fact,” he smiled.

It was so hard to control her anger, but she had to try. She wasn’t entirely certain, but she sensed there was far more He was willing to say. He was waiting for something.

Gabriella forced herself to remember as many conversations with her father as she could. Emotional outbursts rarely seemed to work with him. She believed he recognized her various emotions; he was just not swayed by them. She would have to force herself to handle this logically.

Not exactly her strongest attribute.

“If I am to accept your words as truth,” she began carefully. “You are willing to let whatever happens happen, regardless of your personal desire.”

“I was very clear about that. If this version of creation cannot continue without my direct action, it serves me no purpose. My personal desire does not change reality.”

“It is hard for me to accept you will not even assist us,” she argued. “Perhaps because I never said those exact words.”

“I see,” Gabriella felt a flash of hope. She thought carefully about each word he had chosen to use since her return.

“You implied you have yourself made errors. Something about my memories, and perhaps other things as well.”

“Correct,” he agreed. “I am unable to foresee the consequences of my own choices, or to foresee the choices I make in each of the infinite futures. I must guess like any other. I am not always correct. I believe creation is better off with me making as few choices as possible."

"Another guess?" "Correct."

"I believe it is reasonable to request that you provide a level of assistance of equal value to the errors you have made." Gabriella made the demand clearly.

"It is impossible to assign value to something so subjective. Are you also implying I have never done anything correct to already balance my errors? You also fail to understand my abilities," he pointed out.

"You made an error in my creation. Certainly, you can at least fix me?" "As worded, your statement is inaccurate."

Gabriella's eyes narrowed, but he held up a hand before she could speak again.

"You are approaching information you are not prepared for. All is waiting for you, Dear One, as it always has been. However, if you insist on doing things out of order, I do not believe you will ever fully understand," he sighed.

"The futures in which the balance is restored have only two common threads. The first of which is that you know the truth, yet in none of these futures do I see how you finally learn it. My inability to see the cause is proof that your true memories were returned to you by my own hand."

"Of The Fall, you mean?"

"That, and some of the time before as well. Tell me, do your memories include a being named Kukkug?"

"No," she thought for a moment. "I've met so many beings, it is hard to be certain, but nothing important comes to mind. If this is so important and you are willing to do it, why have you waited this long?" Her memories were so vivid, it was more than a little disconcerting to think some may not be real.

"You do not understand, since you do not remember." He paused before deciding there was no point in hiding the rest. "Your suffering was so great, I almost destroyed you out of mercy. You would ask me to force this upon you again? My own daughter?

"The probability of this ending in your destruction is high, but the likelihood of you remembering and understanding on your own was nearly absolute. Given such knowledge, my choice was a simple one. I cared not for how much more time it would take, only that I could spare you.

"Unfortunately, it would seem the timeline creation as a whole has decided upon is one in which you gave yourself false memories. I also made a grave miscalculation when I began my methods regarding you," he smiled sadly. "I blamed myself when in reality, I should have blamed you."

Gabriella swallowed slowly at the statement, but she kept her eyes and wings steady.

"You see, I was faced with a problem almost certain to correct itself.

So, I examined the few futures where your understanding did not develop on its own to find the cause. I never did." He motioned for her to respond.

"So, you assumed the cause was you, and that's why you've never been direct with me about anything. You've spent all this time thinking you would do or say something wrong, so you essentially choose not to do or say anything at all." She was beginning to understand why it suddenly felt as if she was talking to a different person, or whatever he was.

"I feel that was phrased a bit too harshly," he winced, "but largely correct."

"What must I do?" "Make your choice."

"Doesn't sound as if I have one," she smirked.

"There is always a choice," he said, no longer smiling. "This choice will likely lead to your destruction."

"Is there a single future in which the balance is restored without me possessing this knowledge?"

"There is not."

"What must I do?" She repeated her earlier question.

"Gabriella," he sighed, "even a mortal would have figured that out by now."

She winced at the light rebuke, but her eyes found themselves wandering once again to the silver throne. So, it really had been that obvious after all. She stepped closer to the seat that had been calling to her all this time and turned around.

Carefully, she placed her hands on the arms and gently sat down.

Leaning against the throne's back, it felt no different than she imagined any metal throne would feel. It wasn't even very comfortable.

She turned her head and was about to ask a question when her deep blue eyes widened further at the intensity in the All-Father's gaze.

"Dear One, I am so sorry," he placed a hand on her head, "for what you are about to see."

Gabriella's body briefly stiffened before going completely limp.

Chapter 5

Celestial Plane, Before The Fall

"How many eyes do mortals need?" Kukkug grimaced at the strange creatures they were watching.

"As many as they need, which on that world is apparently four." Immaru laughed at her brother's question.

"They look ridiculous." He scowled and began searching for more pleasant worlds to watch. It was the only thing worth doing here, even if most of the mortal life he found amounted to little more than a waste of energy.

"You shouldn't say things like that, Kuk," she scolded.

The two of them were nearly inseparable, but she really didn't like a lot of the things he said. Although his having the ability to *say* them was all that really mattered to her. He wasn't like her other siblings.

"That's not my name," he rolled his dark eyes at her. "Shall I start calling you Ru?"

"I think Kuk sounds cuter, and no, please don't." She wrinkled her nose at the ridiculous sound of the shortened version of her name.

"I agree, it doesn't sound very good," he chuckled. "I'll never understand why you insist on talking. You know this isn't how we were meant to communicate." As he spoke, Kukkug continued waving through various worlds.

"I am Voice, and voice is what I shall always use," she said sternly. "I think you are interpreting what the Old Man gave you a bit too literally."

"Don't call Father that."

"Why not?" He shrugged his shoulders. "If he was the first being here, then he's the oldest, so it makes sense. I've learned other words to use to describe him, but I assure you, you will like those words less." He turned to glare at her.

Immaru met her brother's angry gaze for a moment before moving to sit next to him. She wrapped her right wing around his wings and back and forced his physical form closer to hers. Once she could feel him relax slightly, she let go.

"You had another argument with him, didn't you?" she asked softly, feeling him tense again.

"Not really. Just him ignoring everything I have to say and then filling my head with more lies."

"Father doesn't lie."

"That's all he does. Would you like to hear what he says to me?"

She shook her head slowly. "When he speaks to us, it is not appropriate to share his words."

"If you say so, but I know I don't belong here. I want to leave so badly, but he won't let me."

"We have to finish learning and understanding before we can be allowed to leave." She forced him to look her in the eye. "Brother, if you didn't belong here, then you wouldn't be here. It is that simple."

"Is it though?" He looked tired and unconvinced.

"I don't want the others to hear you speak this way," she whispered carefully.

"The others?" he asked in surprise. "You think I care what those fools think? I'm not even convinced they *can* think," he chuckled humorlessly.

"That's a horrible thing to say," she hissed.

"You only say that because they listen to you. They treat me as if I don't even exist," he mumbled.

"Look," she put an arm around his shoulders. "The barriers prevent us from leaving anyway, so it doesn't really matter if you want to go. You're stuck here with me whether you like it or not," she smiled and winked.

He leaned his head on his sister's shoulder and smiled. "I guess I'm okay with that."

*****

Kukkug couldn't take his eyes off the dozens of windows he had opened. He had been watching for some time, and these dozens were only the latest of thousands of others. It was fascinating.

The details were different.

Some groups were using handheld instruments. Some remained at great distances from one another. Some traveled over the ground and through the air in metal machines. Others had left the boundaries of the worlds they called home in even vaster machines.

The base principle, however, remained the same.

Groups of mortals seeking to end the existence of other groups of mortals. But why bother? Their existence was so fleeting, so what was the point? Still, it was the most exciting thing he had discovered so far.

"You shouldn't be watching things like that."

"Oh," Kukkug looked over his shoulder, "hey, sis." He quickly adjusted his posture so Immaru could sit next to him.

She looked across the various windows containing only destruction and death with anger in her eyes.

"I don't like this."

"It would seem to be their one unifying characteristic," he pointed out. "We don't have much choice but to try and understand it."

"It's wrong," she scolded.

"Sorry," he shook his head, "but you should know you can't make unilateral statements like that." He waved the windows closed and selected several more depicting different variations of the same thing.

"Please stop." She reached over and placed a hand on his

shoulder. "Aren't we constantly being told we need to understand?" He snapped his head to the side. "That means everything, Immaru. We can't simply ignore the things we don't wish to see.

"The sooner I understand whatever it is I'm supposed to understand, the sooner I can leave this place," he mumbled.

"This again?" she scowled at him.

"Yes, this again." He waved the windows closed and turned to face her. "I wish you could understand what it's like," he groaned.

"Then explain it to me," she encouraged gently.

"*I can't!*" He screamed in frustration. "Every bit of my essence is screaming that this place is wrong, or that I'm wrong, something's wrong!" He grabbed the sides of his head. "And instead of trying to help me, all he ever does is lie to me!

"I don't know how to use these words you make me use to explain how this feels." His wings started to tremble. "And it never stops!"

"Kukkug," she put an arm around him. "Would you like to know why I insist on talking this way with you?"

"Some nonsense about your interpretation of what the word voice means," he grumbled.

"I do it because you're the only other one who can," she smiled. "It doesn't matter that it's inefficient. It's different, and that makes it special. I also learned how to control my voice differently so that you would enjoy it more." Her blue eyes twinkled.

"You sound the same to me." He sounded confused, but she noticed his posture had started to relax.

"It's private now."

"I'm not sure I understand what you mean."

"When we speak like this, none can hear. Not even Father. You may say whatever you wish, and I'll never tell. You'll never be scolded or punished again, at least not for your words. Our conversations will be our little secret forever."

His eyes widened in surprise. "Really? How can you prevent Father from hearing?"

"He chose to give me voice before any other being in creation. A consequence of that choice is my ability to remain unheard if I so choose. I just didn't understand how until recently.

"I wanted to surprise you," she cocked her head. "I just want to help you feel better and be happy here with me."

He threw his arms around her, and they wrapped their wings around each other.

"I'm always happy being with you, sister," he wept softly into her shoulder, "but it's just *so hard*."

"I know," she patted his back. "Well," she quickly corrected, "I guess I don't, but when you do find the words, I'm always going to be here to listen."

He nodded into her shoulder before pulling back. "Would you like to see some beautiful things I found?"

"Yes, please," she nodded happily. "Wait, your definition of beautiful or mine?"

He simply laughed and opened several windows to vast glittering cities filled with amazing structures. Kukkug knew his sister preferred seeing the mortals themselves, rather than the overall worlds they occupied. Although he added a few openings to beautiful nebulae to add a bit of color to the collage he was creating.

"Wow." Her eyes were the size of saucers as she lost herself in the images. "It's still so amazing to see how different they all look."

"Personally, I'd still choose words like 'weird' and 'ridiculous' for most of them," he chuckled.

"They're beautiful," her eyes scolded him briefly. "All of them." "Interesting to hear you say that, considering your own choice in form."

"Well, I could only pick one, and naturally, I have my preferences," she shook out her long, pure blonde hair.

"And every one of the others just happened to pick almost the same form as you, a mere instant later." He let the statement hang with an arched brow.

"As did you," she pointed out.

"Obviously, I copied you intentionally, but that's not really a surprise. I'm saying the others did it by mere reflex. Powerful beings aside, those idiots can't think for themselves."

"Careful what you say about them, brother," she scolded angrily. "You said I could say anything I wanted to you."

Immaru started to groan. "I'm really going to regret this, aren't I?" She couldn't help but grin as Kukkug began laughing loudly. At least he seemed to be feeling better.

"It might be of interest for you to know that all the wonderful things you are seeing now were direct consequences of the things you saw before." He held his hands up quickly as she scowled at him.

"Hey, it's not my fault that violence amongst themselves seems necessary for their development. I was just trying to help you see it for yourself."

She continued scowling as she closed her eyes to look for herself. It didn't take long to find what she was looking for, and she quickly replaced the windows with an equal number of her own.

"These things came after as well," she said sternly.

The pair looked carefully over the barren and devastated landscapes. Entire worlds that had clearly wiped themselves out a very long time ago. More than one of the windows showed planets that had actually been cracked open.

"Everything in creation has two sides," he pointed out. "You are okay with this?"

"It doesn't matter. It's reality," he sighed. "You often talk as if I am the one who needs to fully understand everything that's happening, but you refuse to even accept that creation cannot continue without two sides.

"You don't have to agree with it, or like it, but you can't pretend the other side doesn't exist." He crossed his arms and smirked at his sister's angry expression.

"Why do you even care so much? Haven't you always said they were nothing but a waste of energy?" she countered.

"They are a waste," he shrugged, "but they are very amusing to watch.

Perhaps the only thing Father and I agree about."

"They aren't a waste," she insist. "We were created as we are, but they grow and develop from almost nothing." She began opening windows to show various stages of evolution from countless worlds.

"It takes a great deal of their time, but from a single cell to a truly sentient being? It's amazing." Her eyes widened again as she grew excited. "Then they get to come here and we can even meet them." She started clapping her hands together.

"I've met so many amazing beings who began life as mortal creatures.

The conversations I have with them are wonderful, and I don't understand why you don't join in meeting them yourself."

"They don't all come here," he pointed out. Immaru's expression immediately clouded over.

"See, you're trying to pretend the other place doesn't exist." Kukkug cocked his head and smirked.

"It shouldn't exist," she sneered.

"This is what is holding you back," he shook his head slowly. "There are two sides. Balance. The other place is just as important as this one. If you can't even accept that, you will never understand."

"I suppose we'll have to agree to disagree on that point, brother."

*****

Kukkug opened his eyes again in frustration. No matter how hard he tried, it wasn't working.

"What are you doing?" Immaru demanded as her form appeared

before her brother.

"You were able to sense that?" He had been certain he had found a way to hide his attempts. "I wonder what I did wrong?" he mumbled to himself.

"Sense it?" She looked confused. "You're scaring everyone, and most of the inhabitants here forgot what fear felt like. It's causing a lot of problems. Now answer my question."

"Fine," he surrendered. "I was trying to destroy myself, but I can't make it work. I either lack the ability, or the energy itself can't be destroyed." He cupped his chin.

"Anyway," he continued after a moment's thought, "I'm now trying to simply negate my consciousness."

Immaru simply stared, certain she had heard wrong. "What do you mean by that?" she asked carefully.

"Exactly what I said," his eyes narrowed in confusion. "Did I pick the wrong words?"

"You're, you're trying to kill yourself?" she whispered in horror.

"No, I don't think that word applies to us." He stopped to think again. "Erase. Yes, that's a better word," he nodded. "I'm trying to erase myself."

"It's the same thing!" She shouted at him.

Kukkug waved an arm dismissively as he closed his eyes to try again. "*Stop it!*" Immaru was forcing her essence to directly interfere with what he was doing. It was the only thing preventing it from working, but she was uncertain how much longer she could.

"I don't have much of a choice in the matter any longer, now do I?" he replied calmly. "This would be a lot easier if you'd just help me."

"Are you insane? I'm trying to stop you." She said the words before realizing he had tricked her into admitting it.

"As I was beginning to suspect," he grinned. "I'm going to release everything I have in opposing directions and then turn it inward."

"I don't know what that means." She was getting desperate.

He met her frightened gaze, and there was something in his eyes she had never seen before.

"I know. It's going to take everything you have to protect your precious realm. You won't have enough left to stop me."

"Just please tell me why," she begged as he began to close his eyes again.

"You know why." His body seemed to tense. "I can't stay here, nor can I

leave. The choice is obvious."

"Is this place really that bad?" she questioned sadly.

"It's a prison, and *I can't take it anymore!*" He arched back, wings fully extended, and screamed upward.

Immaru lashed out quickly to collect the uncontrolled energy and return it to where it belonged. Thankfully, it was only the equivalent of a minor outburst.

"But why?" she pleaded. "I can't help you if you don't tell me what's wrong."

"I told you, *I can't!*" He grabbed the sides of his head. "You make me use these words, but none of them work. *I can't find any that work!*" He started screaming again.

"Then tell me the other way."

Kukkug suddenly stopped screaming. "I can't do that." "You can."

"I won't do that," he corrected his wording.

"Why not?" She kept her voice as soft as she could.

"What I am doing, I am choosing of my own free will. I have no wish to cause you any suffering."

"Do you understand any of the words you are choosing?" she gaped at him. "You wish to spare me suffering, yet you threaten to go away? You're going to leave me alone forever, and you don't think I'll suffer from that?"

"Alone? You're never alone here." He didn't understand her line of reasoning.

"You're the only other one here like me," she insist.

"Are you crazy?" His surprise was temporarily distracting him. "We're nothing alike. We seldom agree on anything."

"So what? We're the only two who are different. Doesn't that make us the same? Kukkug, you're my brother," she started to cry.

"I didn't know we could do that," he mentioned at the appearance of her tears.

"Cry? Of course we can cry. I've just never had a reason to," she yelled through the sobs. "If you're going to do this to me, then I demand to see the truth. *So do it!*"

He hesitated briefly before finally nodding and bringing his right wing forward. Very gently, he touched the tip to Immaru's forehead.

Immediately, waves of agony and torment washed through her entire being. She didn't understand what they were, only that it was terrible. She was being torn apart from all directions, even as an impossible force was crushing her together. Behind it all was the feeling that her mind itself was screaming in pain.

Everything vanished an instant later, as Kukkug withdrew his wing. His sister's horrified gaze and clearly weakened state brought tears to his own eyes for the first time.

"It never stops," he offered quietly. "I don't understand," she gasped.

"Neither do I, but now you know why I have to do this." "*You can't!*" she cried.

"I'm sorry, but your desire for me to remain is selfish." He watched her recoil from the harsh truth. "You have seen I am enduring something that cannot be endured. If no one will help me, I at least deserve some peace." He began closing his eyes for the final time.

Immaru leaped at him, wrapped her arms and wings around him, and began to sing. After a time, she could feel him start to relax.

"Do you feel better now?" she sobbed into his shoulder. "I, I do," he admitted honestly. "What did you do?"

"I learned how to sing. I'll sing to you forever if you want me to.

Kukkug, I'll never stop protecting you." She let him go and met his surprised gaze squarely. "When the time comes, I'll go with you."

"What do you mean?"

"We can't leave yet, but when we can, I'll go with you."

"You would leave this place for me?" He couldn't stop his own tears.

"You're my brother," she smiled. "We can go as far away from here as you want."

He looked down, overpowered by the emotions she was displaying.

"I'm going to save you," she put a hand on his shoulder, "trust me. But you must swear to me you will never do this. You can never make yourself go away. Okay?"

"I, I swear," he moved closer and embraced her. "Can you please sing a little bit more now?"

Immaru smiled sweetly and began to sing.

*****

"I thought you agreed to trust me?"

The pair were standing together in the Great Hall, and she didn't like the look of finality in her brother's eyes. It had been getting more and more challenging to help him, and his final statement had held a note of certainty.

"I know, but I'm saying I no longer need to. I believe this is what I was always meant to do."

"We've had this conversation before, Kuk," she shook her head. "We can't cross the barriers anyway, so why even talk like this?"

"My name is Kukkug," he sneered, "and there is no barrier where I'm going. It's a little frustrating to not have seen the answer sooner, considering how obvious it is."

Immaru eyed him warily, having no idea what he was talking about. The barriers prevented them from going anywhere. Well, anywhere except…

Kukkug grinned, sensing she had finally figured it out.

"You, you're insane," she gasped. "You're choosing the wrong words again." It was the only explanation she could think of.

"I am not."

"Kukkug, there's a reason that type of protective barrier doesn't exist. You would cease to exist the instant you crossed over," she insist.

"I am not so sure about that. Even so, what does it matter?" he shrugged. "Either way, you'll all be rid of me, and I'll finally be at peace."

"How many times do I have to tell you that I don't *want* to be rid of you?" She moved to close the distance between them.

"I know," Kukkug's features softened. "Leaving you is the one thing I am truly sorry about," he said genuinely.

She threw her arms around him, but before she could begin to sing, he shoved her away.

"Not this time, but," he reached his hand out. "You did promise to come with me."

"You know that's not what I meant. We can't go there!" She yelled at him.

"I already told you I think you're wrong." "I *won't* go there," she corrected.

"I gathered as much," he nodded. "Well, wish me luck." He smiled, waved, and turned to leave.

"Take this seriously, Kukkug!" She shouted at his back. "I promised I would save you, and that's what I'm going to do!"

"*Why!*" He spun around and shouted back angrily. "Immaru," his voice softened, "you know I love you in my own way. You're the only one who ever tried to help me. The only one who never gave up on me.

"Unfortunately, you never stopped even once to consider that I didn't need saving. That I'm not the one who's wrong."

"You don't understand what you're saying," she held her hands up calmly. "Let's just talk about this for a bit."

"No. You fail to accept even the most basic concepts of reality. What you call understanding, I call ignorance," he began to sneer.

"Don't speak to me like I'm a child," she warned.

"Then stop acting like one! An arrogant little child who seeks to help everyone because she thinks she knows better than anyone," he growled. "Goodbye." He turned and began walking out of the hall.

"There's one thing I understand," she hissed, before closing her eyes. Kukkug found himself surrounded as the entire host of angels appeared, filling the Great Hall.

"What is this? Get out of my way," he shouted at the smiling faces before him.

"Remember, brother? They don't listen to you," she grinned.

"Immaru, this isn't what I want," he warned. "Tell your pets to leave." "You're giving me no choice!" came her exasperated response. "Father says we aren't ready to leave, so even if you have found a way, I can't let you."

"Listen to me," he turned slowly to face her through the growing crowd. "Whatever happens later is for later. In this moment, I seek only to leave.

There's nothing you can do to stop me."

"It is forbidden," she said sternly. "Don't worry. I promise you're only going to be gently suppressed to keep you safe. I'll make Father help you properly," she assured him.

"Please," he begged. "You don't understand. This does not have to happen."

"Stop speaking down to me," she said, her eyes hardening. "What are those?" She looked in confusion at the two strange dark objects Kukkug was suddenly holding.

He moved swiftly, as the closest smiling angel reached out for him. The angel's wings were severed even as Kukkug's other blade took the creature's head. The body simply vanished in a flash since there were no physical remains to be left behind.

The bodies were simple toys used to carry the wings that stored the angels' consciousness. It was the way Immaru had decided to be, and all others had followed her example. By severing the wings and destroying the body, Kukkug was able to send a temporary shock through the angel's true essence.

In this moment, the angel's true essence was unable to react and became vulnerable to his nonphysical attack. As he quickly lashed out with his true power, he easily rendered the angel into nothing but base energy awaiting its reuse in creation. It confirmed what his earlier experiments had eventually suggested.

Angels were remarkably easy to kill.

Immaru froze in shock as the body vanished. An instant later, a terrible scream entered her mind before quickly being cut off. She had no idea what was happening, and the host began to move as one. The angels had the capacity to defend themselves but had never had a reason to do so before, and she was too confused to command them.

It was a massacre.

As more screams entered and left her mind, the horrible truth began to suggest itself to her. It wasn't long before the hall was empty again, and she knew Kukkug was behind her. Immaru still couldn't move, but she felt the blades resting on her neck and wings.

"Do you understand now, you ignorant fool! *This didn't have to happen!*" He sheathed his blades after a moment, unwilling to kill his sister. He moved to stand in front of her and saw that not even Immaru's eyes were moving.

"These forms were your choice. How do you not understand that allowing yourself to become too emotionally overwhelmed causes you to lose physical control?" He shook his head slowly.

"Eventually, even you are going to figure this out." He leaned closer to the unmoving eyes. "Once you realize what you've done, maybe, just maybe, you'll finally realize that while I might not belong here, you don't *deserve* to be here." He tapped her forehead once before walking away.

"Tell the Old Man he's going to pay for his lies." He glanced over his shoulder one final time. "I'll keep the door open for when you finally decide to make good on your promise."

With no more obstacles in his path, Kukkug finally left.

Immaru remained frozen for a time, trying to comprehend the truth.

Angels were indestructible and eternal beings, but the never-ending echoing screams in her mind tried to convince her otherwise. However, it wasn't just a fact. The eternal nature of their essence was *an immutable law*.

The physical disappearances didn't really mean much. Not here. So, she tried stretching out as far through the realm as she could. No matter how hard she tried, however, she couldn't sense anything but the realm's regular inhabitants.

Even as the echoes wouldn't leave her alone, a memory came to her unbidden. A memory of when she had stopped Kukkug from erasing himself. He had said something about focusing on his consciousness and not his energy. Her horror began building further as the pieces fell together.

He had warned her. He tried to tell her what was going to happen, but she had been deaf to what he was truly saying. Everything she needed to know had been in her mind all along, yet she never bothered trying to truly understand.

They may as well have all died by her own hand.

She finally collapsed, not knowing how much time had passed. All Immaru knew was that she could no longer hear the horrific echoes in her mind. Those screams were easily drowned out by her own.

Chapter 6

Great Hall, Celestial Plane

The All-Father could feel the barriers weakening. It wouldn't be long before they began to tear open. This is what he had feared would happen.

He had caught Gabriella as she fell off the throne, and she had been screaming into his shoulder since. No matter what he did or said, nothing calmed her down. He was in direct contact, and not just physically, and it wasn't enough. That shouldn't even be possible given what he was.

It didn't matter that she didn't understand her genuine connection to this realm. That connection was very real, and if she was lost, then so too would be the realm. Of course, it was equally possible she would destroy the realm first by accident, but he supposed that wouldn't matter since the end result would be the same.

Many of the futures ended at this point, but not enough to suggest there wasn't a simple solution. So why was nothing working?

In theory, he could destroy and replace her easily. That would solve everything, but he didn't think he could ever do that. His own unwillingness would suggest that wasn't the *simple* answer.

He did his best to see his daughter through her own eyes.

Ever since the beginning, Gabriella had always mimicked the mortals. It had been amusing and relatively harmless, but he wondered if that was where the answer might lie. It seemed likely, considering her mimicry had only grown worse since spending time among them.

So, what was the mortal answer to the situation?

He closed his eyes and allowed trillions of images from millions of worlds to flash through his mind. Despite the significant differences between the various beings, the answer was remarkably similar. So, there really was a simple solution. Under other circumstances, this would be exceptionally fascinating.

The All-Father leaned back and slapped her.

Gabriella's screams cut off immediately, and after a moment's pause, she covered her eyes and began sobbing softly.

He closed his eyes briefly to verify no permanent damage had been done. Most of the inhabitants had not even noticed the disturbance. Some had grown a bit distressed, but they would recover easily enough.

"I loved him!" She cried through her hands.

"Of course you did, dear." He pat her head gently. "He is your brother."

"So, this really is all my fault?"

"Really, dear, your arrogance is astounding." He smiled as she looked up at him in confusion. "You believe it is through your choices alone that creation is driven? I do not even believe that about myself," he chuckled.

"Kukkug was always destined to return home." He held up a hand before she could interrupt him. "There is more that neither of you knows, but that information will not serve you in the coming conflict.

"His ambition and failure to listen to me caused him to leave without proper understanding. However, the moment he retook his proper place, his true powers and control began returning to him. Kukkug is misusing the Dark Realm in terms of maintaining the balance, and there is no counter to stop him."

Gabriella's eyes went again to the silver throne.

"It is too late for that. By the time you are his equal, it will be too late. It also would not serve to fix the differences between the two realms."

"The realms are supposed to be different," she argued.

"That is not what I meant." He paused, trying to decide how

much information he should provide. "You always complain that this realm is losing. How can this be the case when there is such a greater amount of energy here?"

"Because no one here does anything," she sneered.

"Kukkug has turned the Dark Realm into something akin to a machine." He decided to ignore her comment. "Perfect hierarchy and precise regimentation, with every bit of energy serving to fuel his exact desires. Clearly, his desire is not in alignment with maintaining the balance.

"Tell me, has complacency alone ever once been equal to ambition, much less defeated it?"

She shook her head angrily, forcing herself to stay silent.

"So, if it has never worked on a single world in the entire history of creation, then why would you expect it to work here?"

"All you're doing is repeating what I've been trying to say for a long time, Father! How can you scold me by agreeing with me? And where are the others?" She finally stood and waved her arms to indicate more than simply the empty hall.

"Their base instincts have forced them to act. They are protecting the balance as best they can, although they can do little more than delay the inevitable."

"So," her sneer was back, and she forced herself not to growl. "It only took the end of creation for those drekking useless pieces of energy to actually *do* something. How wonderful for them." The sarcasm dripped from every word.

"I caution you. Given the reality of the situation, the words you are beginning to choose are inappropriate." His voice rose slightly, but she didn't even flinch.

"Inappropriate?" Her wings began shaking. "If any of them *ever* listened to me, or *ever* helped me, we wouldn't be in this situation. You're lecturing the only being here who ever does anything about this realm's complacency. It doesn't make any sense." She threw her arms up in frustration. Before she could start yelling again, a frightening thought occurred to her.

"Unless," she hesitated. "They aren't real, are they? That's what really happened back then, isn't it?" Her voice was starting to break as she began to see the true horror of her actions.

"I am not certain I understand your question."

"It all makes sense now," she whispered. "Because of me, the real angels were murdered, and the ones now are empty fakes. Nothing but energy and basic instincts." She collapsed again.

"Gabriella!" He shouted at his daughter before she could start screaming. "Calm. Down."

She just looked up, eyes filled with sadness and horror.

"You have all the information you need to find the answers you seek, but you are already allowing your emotions to twist it into untruths. You need to calm down and think it through."

There was more he wanted to say, but there was no point. It seemed impossible that she hadn't found the missing piece, considering she had just seen proof of what she was. At least the beginning of what she was anyway.

It had been a significant amount of information, yet he had no idea what the actual impact on her mind and emotions was. Perhaps she needed more time for it to settle. If that was true, additional information could make it worse.

"Fine," she sniffled. "If you won't tell me, then at least fix me. You owe me that much," she demanded.

"I cannot."

"You have to!" She rose back up and jabbed an accusing finger at him. "I didn't create myself. The flaws in my being did not come from my own hand."

"Those statements are technically accurate, but your request remains one I cannot grant. You have what you need."

She forced herself to try to think calmly. Her emotions were spiraling out of control, but she had already seen how much better her father responded to logic.

"If this is all true, what's the point? It doesn't matter what his goal is if it results in the destruction of all creation. Unless he truly desires self-destruction enough to take everything else with him."

"He does not. Kukkug has been quite happy since returning home."

"Then why can't we just talk to him?" She couldn't believe what she was saying, but the sudden idea had a certain logic to it. "Winning is pointless if the reward is destruction, so if we explain that, as you did for me, surely we could come to an agreement?"

He was impressed. It wouldn't work, but he hadn't expected her to calm down quickly enough to suggest something so reasonable.

"A wise idea, but search your new memories for what the result will be."

She closed her eyes for a moment and nodded. "Kukkug always called you a liar."

"Correct. In this case, I have already tried, but he merely laughs and ignores me," he shrugged. "Kukkug believes I cannot begin anew. Further, he believes once the balance completely fails in his favor, he will be able to take the power to create and potentially even destroy me."

"That's not possible," she gasped. "Are you certain?"

"Aren't you?

"Not really." He grinned at her expression. "I am certain of my ability to begin anew. As for my destruction? I do not foresee it, but does any being? I find it a fascinating consideration at least. In any event, does the reality matter in this instance?"

"No," she was forced to admit. "If it's what he believes, he'll never stop. So, I guess force truly is the only option," she nodded sharply.

"If you believe it is."

"You really aren't going to tell me what to do, are you?"

"I have made that clear. I can be more specific as to why if you like, but I assure you, the knowledge will make you feel worse."

"I'll be the judge of that, so if you don't mind," she waved for him to continue.

"Technically speaking, Kukkug has not yet won, but he has come far enough to prevent you from winning. That is reality. However, there are still futures in which the balance is restored, as I said before. It is against my personal laws to tell you how this is achieved, but in truth, I simply do not know.

"Beyond the two common threads I mentioned, I cannot identify any key choices or points that have obviously successful outcomes. It all appears as random chance." He smiled sadly as her eyes widened.

"Which means it comes down to the only places you can't see, and you already told me I can't win." She reflexively touched her temple as she was speaking.

"I sense something else is bothering you?"

"Many things," she chuckled sarcastically. "But the biggest one is that I still don't understand how everything could ever be foretold, no matter what happens."

"Meaning?"

"Accepting everything you have said about the infinite futures, until something happens, there will always be at least one future in which it doesn't. So, the future will never be completely foretold, thus you would never need to begin anew."

He smiled broadly. "I am very proud of you for working that out, and you are technically correct. Allow me to choose words you will understand more easily." He paused in thought, wanting to make sure he was understood correctly.

"If the infinite futures are all bad or all good, then I no longer care. Even if technically, they represent different bad or good things. So, if the balance fails beyond restoration in either direction, I will begin anew."

"Very well," she nodded. "It would seem my path is rather simple," her eyes hardened. "I know where Kukkug is, and it doesn't matter how powerful he's become. If I pour my armies onto that world, there won't be much he can do," she started to grin.

"Correct, and you would save one world at the expense of all others. Despite that world's current importance, it does not sound balanced to me," he pointed out. "I already told you where the others are. That includes your armies, and every wolf and raven soul inhabiting this realm."

Her mouth dropped open, and she quickly closed her eyes. It was hard to keep her breathing under control as she saw what was truly happening.

"Gabriella, Kukkug has not initiated his latest scheme. He has initiated what he intends as the final war for creation. You may make whatever adjustments or choices you wish, but each will have its own consequences."

"I-" her eyes were still bouncing back and forth under closed lids. It wasn't touching other mortal worlds in the same way, but it was happening everywhere and on every plane of existence.

"I know how to fight," her eyes flew back open, "but I don't know how to fight a *war*!"

"If only you knew others who did," he mumbled back.

"You keep saying I can't win, but that there are still futures in which I'm successful."

"Correct."

"Those words mean the same thing." "In this context, they do not."

The more she thought about it, the more Gabriella had to face the truth. If everything truly was at stake, there was only one thing she could do. She quickly knelt down, drawing her flaming sword and holding it out.

"Choose another."

"Who?" He made a show of looking around the empty hall.

"It doesn't matter," she kept her head bowed. "You have scolded my arrogance, but it would seem in these final moments of creation, I am to choose for all.”

“Perhaps, although Kukkug could make the same claim.”

“The last time I chose for all, it ended in the destruction of the angels.” A few tears fell to the floor.

“Correct.”

“If I am destined to fail, then you must choose another,” she insist. “Gabriella,” he sighed heavily. “You have a choice, as you always have.

You may continue to fight knowing you cannot win, or you may lay down your sword knowing no others remain to pick it up.”

She remained in place for a time. It seemed her only choice was in which way to fail. If that was true, she supposed she might as well do the one thing she knew how to do. She rose, replacing the sword in her right wing.

“I suppose I’ll never see you again.” She let the statement hang.

“As you yourself said, anything is possible until the moment something happens.” He tried to sound hopeful as his daughter finally made her choice.

“But you do not believe I will return?” “I do not,” he was forced to admit.

“Well then,” she bowed deeply. “Goodbye, Father.” Gabriella began leaving the hall, but she suddenly stopped and looked back over her shoulder. “What’s the second thread?”

“Hmm?”

“You said there were two common threads. You explained one,” she tapped her head. “What is the other?”

“Ah,” he grinned. “Your desire to shield and save others is necessary for what you truly are. I sense that seeing your true memories will serve to strengthen this desire. However, there is no successful future in which you act alone.”

She nodded her thanks for the additional information before continuing to walk away.

"A word of advice," he called after her. "Consider it a reward for what you have accomplished thus far."

She stopped but didn't turn around.

"I urge you to contemplate the difference between your battle with Thraxsis and the battle you recently fought. You may find the results quite interesting. Finally, please remember to stay calm."

Her body stiffened, and she inhaled sharply at his final words. If he would just fix what was wrong with her, then staying calm wouldn't be a problem. Not wanting to belabor a failed point, however, she decided it was best to simply leave.

As he watched his daughter vanish for the last time, the All-Father felt his cheeks become wet with more than a bit of surprise. Apparently, there were still things he didn't know he could do.

Chapter 7

"You really think it'll work?" He looked over, not yet convinced their idea was viable.

Shūfāng's empty eyes stared back, giving no answer.

Kukkug took a moment to gently adjust the head's facial features and manipulate her mouth so her tongue would be slightly visible. He had learned that not only could he prevent decay and rigor mortis, but he could force different muscles to tense or relax as he pleased. As long as he maintained contact.

"No, lying to her isn't a problem," he rubbed his chin. "I'm just not sure she'll believe it."

Shūfāng's jaw was opened and closed a couple of times.

"You're right, of course, dear," he admitted. "It's going to all come down to the delivery. So, I suppose all that's left is deciding the rest of the battle. The two she left behind are a bit curious as well."

It had been obvious when Gabriella had left the world almost immediately after arriving. It wasn't really unexpected. She was probably off on a useless attempt to wring answers out of the Old Man. Given what she was, it was perfectly logical that she would leave soldiers in her place.

"What's that, dear? Oh, well, yes, it is strange it's only two, but you don't understand what's happening everywhere else." He grinned at his silent companion. "Trust me, the rest of her armies are quite occupied at the moment.

"I wonder who they are? If I could only bring two, I'd definitely choose my favorites, and they do represent an additional variable." Kukkug's eyes went back to the doorway as he examined his thoughts.

When he had been watching this world, his focus had only been on her.

At the time, he couldn't have cared less for those around her. He allowed the careful reexamination of his memories to continue, as the rest of his plan fell into place.

"There's really only one thing they can do, and that assumes they figure out exactly what I'm doing. It makes sense to counter that, since anything else they tried would fail anyway. What do you think?"

The unblinking eyes stared back.

"That's a good point, and it'll make things pretty simple. They're going to attack, assuming I still care about trying to kill as few as possible. Any one of those three could theoretically cause a problem. That," he pointed to the doorway, "can't defend itself, and there's only one of me.

"Unfortunately for them, my new plan means this world no longer matters and forces me to leave anyway. So, all I really must do is flood the area with demons," he shrugged. "If they're outnumbered dozens, or even hundreds, to one, there isn't much they can do.

"It should be enough to even keep her soldiers busy. I mean, pure souls aren't that much more powerful, even wolf and raven souls. There should be plenty of time to play with my sister uninterrupted." He began nodding to himself, even as his eyes suddenly unfocused.

There was no way to be certain, but it would seem he knew who those two were after all. The more he examined them, the more they didn't appear on the same level as mortal souls. That didn't make much sense, but the difference in their power felt familiar.

Had his sister done something to them?

In her battle with Thraxsis, a single wolf and raven managed to fight effectively and shared a similar feeling. Kukkug carefully rewound the two mortals' timelines. Usually, that wouldn't have been possible here, but this being the world of their birth was a nice loophole.

Both their lives flashed through his mind. There were a few enjoyable moments, but it was mostly rather dull. Some of it was familiar since he had already watched rather closely once Thraxsis had awakened. It became fascinating when the mortals he was watching first came into contact with the Soul Eater.

He froze the timeline when Thraxsis finished killing them all and moved off. Well, that didn't make any sense. These events happened before the others, so how could they be dead? He restarted the playback, and it wasn't long before Kukkug was laughing loudly.

Really, sister, you're making things too easy for me.

"It would seem they aren't soldiers at all, but my sister's pets.

Well," he focused back on Shūfāng, "good news for you, I suppose. You'll get to meet your grandparents. Isn't that exciting?" The mouth was forced open and closed twice.

"Well, if you insist. I'll make sure to prepare something special just for them," he grinned. "I really am too good to you, dear," he looked at her, awaiting a proper response.

The features were manipulated to give him a stern glare. "Fine, you're right," he rolled his eyes. "I need to take this seriously and address the biggest problem. The most likely outcome is my crazy sister slicing this body to pieces," he groaned.

There was no choice but to start training and learning how much power he could use here. Kukkug had been watching mortals fight since the dawn of their time, not to mention the direct experience he had stolen from some of those here.

It couldn't be *that* difficult to learn. Could it?

He stood up and stretched before collecting his companion and heading out. Deciding that having partners might help, he closed his eyes, allowing a few dozen demons to cross over and join him. It's not as if he had anything better to do.

"Well, dear," he looked at the head cradled gently in his right arm, the long dark hair spilling nearly to the ground. "This should be fun. Don't worry, I'll find a nice place for you to watch."

*****

Henwick

"Here you are," Larg announced as he entered the room. "Raven, I've been looking for you all day. What are you doing in this part of the city?" After questioning several others, he had heard Xuě had been wandering the abandoned areas of Henwick for days.

"The Queen wants a complete report of the contents and integrity of every building we aren't using," she answered while marking down notes.

"Why? Anything useful has long since been moved out." Larg was confused at the clearly illogical task.

"Because it's going to take me a long time, which prevents me from causing problems anywhere else." She shrugged, picking up her lantern and moving to the next room.

"Oh," he hurried to follow her. "Raven, that's actually what I came to talk to you about."

"Please stop calling me that." She put the lantern down and began examining the new room.

Larg had frozen in his tracks. Her statement was not a very good sign, and he wasn't sure whether to address it. In the end, he decided to stick with his original purpose.

"I think she's gone too far with how she's treating you. It's not right, and I think you should say something to her privately about it."

"You just don't understand," she said, starting to take notes while still not looking at him.

"I understand that it's wrong, and it hurts me to see you treated and spoken to that way."

"The solution to that is fairly obvious, Larg," she shrugged. "Stay away from me," she said very clearly. "You really don't get it, do you?" She added after it became clear he wasn't going to answer.

He just glared at her in a mixture of sadness and confusion.

"Fine," she put her pad down, and found somewhere to sit, facing him finally. "Other than my father, you're the only one who's ever been nice to me," she smiled slightly. "So, you deserve the courtesy of having me spell out reality."

Larg nodded slowly, found his own chair, and remained a respectable distance from her.

"You know now the true reason for me summoning that fool back to this world was no more than that she deserves to die along with us," she reminded him.

"Need I remind you that *fool* is not only an angel, but has already saved this world once?" he kept his voice neutral.

"Larg, that's complete horse dung," she shook her head. "She held a sword in the final battle, who cares?" Xuě's eyes grew angry. "If not for Qiàn and K'tar, that winged idiot would be nothing but an undiscovered pile of bones in the middle of some random forest.

"Nothing she has accomplished could have been done without the two of them. Worse, anytime they aren't watching over her, she's a miserable failure." Xuě looked as if she would start spitting on the ground.

"Xuě, that is a gross over-simplification of the truth, and ignores a lot of things," he warned.

"I don't care," she hissed. "My point is that those two are the heroes, *not* her. I never imagined my actions would result in them being here as well, and it changes everything." She started smiling, and it appeared genuine.

"How so?"

"Don't you see? I don't know if there's a chance for all of us, but if there is, those three working together can find it. Every single one of us needs to be ready to give everything we can, to *be* everything we can, if there is to be any hope."

"Xuě," he finally started to smile. "If you don't mind me saying so, you are starting to sound like a real queen." His smile faded as her expression suddenly changed.

"Only because you haven't fully applied what I've said," she said sadly. "Due to the worthless person I have allowed myself to become, I simply have nothing to give, save my absence."

Larg was shocked by how easily she said the words.

"Do you honestly think someone as great as Queen Qiàn wouldn't see through someone as pathetic as I am in an instant?" She cocked her head at the rhetorical question. "She chose her words very carefully after the battle. It wasn't a public scolding. It was a public *denouncement*.

"She knew me for less than a minute and stripped my title. Which also happens to make it much easier to keep me out of sight, so I can't screw up anything else," she finished quietly.

"That's what I'm trying to talk about," he shook his head. "She went too far."

"Aren't you listening to me? Going too far is one of the main things Queen Qiàn is known for, along with always being right. This is no different. All I have to offer others is to make them *less* than themselves through my very presence.

"I may be arrogant, but I've always been honest with myself," she tapped her temple. "Everyone else knows it as well, and deep down, so do you."

"Look, I agree you haven't been the nicest person, but personally, I'm better for knowing you. Since you know I can't lie, doesn't that disprove what you said?" he smirked.

"Not really," she disagreed. "It just proves you're an immature fool." Her eyes stopped moving and hardened.

"That's not-"

"Stop talking," she cut him off. "Just look at yourself and think. Even at your young age, somehow, you're one of the best warriors we have. Clearly, my father was training you well. Who else could have protected me so well against so many demons?

"You aren't ready to command them all in battle, but you are surely prepared to be a leader. I also know you've come to see K'tar as the mentor my father was, and he seems to have taken a liking to you as well. Your time should be spent learning from him and helping as a liaison between him and the others.

"Everyone is preparing for what will probably be the final battle for this world, but they still lack the will to fight. Join them and spread the fire you somehow still possess to the rest of them. That's the future you can have, the fate you *deserve*.

"Larg, I don't know how you grew to be this strong, especially with me holding you back," she said with a sad smile. "Wasting that strength on me now, when it's our people who need it, is an act of criminal negligence. You need to stop."

"Time spent with you is not a waste," he said, trying to talk slowly and gently.

"*Yes, it is!*" She shot up out of the chair, clear anger in her eyes. "If you can't see it, then it's just another example of what my presence does to others. What do you even hope to get from me anyway?" She threw her arms up in frustration.

"Is it my body? Believe me when I say there are many others who are interested and far more deserving of you than I am. I'm barely worth the air I breathe, much less your affection," she screamed.

Larg stood and stepped toward her. "Raven, that isn't-"

She slapped him. "*I said, don't call me that!*"

Larg's eyes were wide with shock, and his jaw had gone slack. "What is it going to take to make you understand!" She slapped him again. "Does that clarify things for you? Stay away from me!" Her expression softened. "Take your rightful place. Help save the world and just let me fade away.”

“Very well.” Larg turned and began walking from the room, before stopping two paces from the door. “I don’t agree with you, but I will respect your decision, *Raven*.”

*****

Qiàn’s Office

Xuě handed the thick stack of papers to Qiàn after being escorted into her office, noticing a freshly broken window on the room’s right side. It wasn’t too surprising to see, given the state of some of these buildings, but the blankets underneath it seemed odd.

“Thank you for what I’m sure was a thorough report,” Qiàn offered, as she immediately tossed the papers into a refuse bin.

“Of course, Your Majesty,” Xuě bowed, trying to control her expression. She had known the task was pointless, but she had still worked hard to ensure its accuracy. Qiàn could have at least waited for her to leave.

She waited a moment for any further instructions. When none came, Xuě bowed again and began to leave.

“Wait,” Qiàn called out suddenly. “Why are you wearing that ring?” The question held a hint of anger.

Xuě turned and looked at her left hand. “Oh, my mother was not wearing it during the attack. Since it was so close to the day I was born, I think it just didn’t fit comfortably. Larg found it when we were searching for the cloth to summon the angel,” she shrugged.

“That wasn’t my question,” Qiàn glared at her. “That ring is meant to be worn by the queen.”

“Your Majesty,” she bowed again. “I assure you that is not why I am wearing it.”

“Take it off,” Qiàn demanded, pointing to a spot on her desk.

“Please,” Xuě froze, “it’s all I have of-” “*Now!*”

Xuě slowly stepped forward, removed the ring, and placed it gently on Qiàn's desk. Trying to keep the anger out of her eyes, she started to bow a final time.

"Tell me, if I were to ask your people about you, what would they say?" "Nothing good, I imagine," Xuě responded to the unexpected question. "How can you be that oblivious to the world around you?" she mumbled just loud enough for Xuě to hear. "Your popularity is higher than you can probably imagine. In fact, many are already comparing you to me." "That doesn't seem likely."

"I agree, it is a bit disgusting." Qiàn noticed Xuě's eyes twitch slightly at her choice of words. "Still, it is true, nonetheless.

"The young Queen who, after failing to garner support, embarked on her own perilous quest to save her people. Facing a world full of demons with none by her side, save her wolf, she traveled for days searching for an item no one believed was real.

"Then, after miraculously surviving to find the item in question, the young Queen found herself pursued by a demon horde. With her own two hands did she fight her way to the remnants of the old shrine. Finally, under the desperate cover of her Wolf Protector, the Queen summoned an angel. Yǎniū, the savior from the time before.

"Your story grows even more exciting, considering the great battle that took place upon your return. The horror of the young Queen witnessing the death of her heroic father, mixed with the excitement of our return," she waved towards herself. "The public display between us is easily explained by you being overcome by grief.

"Moreover, now that your people have seen your greatness, they are blaming themselves for their past opinions of you. You were never at fault. It was they who failed to recognize the truth, given this dark and twisted world. Even the way I am treating you is being misunderstood.

"What do they truly know or understand of how the Raven Queen is born? My inappropriate and derisive actions toward you must be some sort of secret training method, known only to our family. Worst of all, everything I do is being attributed to you, since your actions are what brought me here.

"This is the current story your people are writing of Xuě, the Raven Queen. It makes me sick," Qiàn finished with a disgusted sneer.

Xuě was frozen in shock, not believing half of what Qiàn had just said. She had sounded so serious, though, and how much interaction had she honestly had with her people since this had started?

"Your Majesty," she started finally. "Half of what you said is completely insane, and the other half bears little resemblance to the reality of what happened."

"That's how the best stories are written," Qiàn smirked. "It does, however, leave us with a bit of a problem." She reached down and pulled a dagger from her belt.

Xuě's eyes followed the dagger as Qiàn placed it on the desk. "For the first time in over twenty years, your people are at least trying to rise to the challenge this world represents. I can't ignore that, but I know the truth. More importantly, you know it as well."

"What truth would that be, Your Majesty?" Xuě said quietly, still looking at the dagger.

"The truth of how worthless you are. Every passing moment is another opportunity for you to prove it to them, and thus undo everything you accidentally accomplished. It is time to end your story favorably before you have a chance to ruin it with the truth of what you are."

Xuě looked away from the dagger and stared in horror at what she saw in Qiàn's eyes.

"The enemy who already destroyed the world feared the new Queen. Such was her greatness; they came for her in the night. In an attempt to finally destroy her people, the demons took away their Queen." She paused, as Xuě's breathing became slightly erratic.

"Imagine how your people will fight in your name," she continued softly. "The Dark One himself will be hard-pressed to contain their rage. You will go down in history as one of this world's greatest martyrs. It is far better than you deserve."

Xuě couldn't believe what Qiàn was saying, but the Queen's eyes weren't even moving. She was focused entirely on her, and the seriousness in her eyes was deadly. But this conversation couldn't be real, could it?

"You've wanted to do this for a long time. I already know that." She reached out and touched Xuě's hand gently. "It's a hard thing to justify, though, isn't it? Even with logic as twisted as yours. You seek permission. Well, I not only give you permission, but I insist it is your duty.

"Only I will know the truth, and I already told you the story I will tell. The only way to give your life any meaning is with your death." Qiàn withdrew her hand and leaned back in her chair.

Xuě looked back at the dagger and didn't know what to do. The truth was, Qiàn was correct. She had wanted a way out for so long. In the last year or so, Xuě had projected her feelings of hatred onto the angel. Ever since she had heard that final story and thought there was a chance to bring her back.

In reality, all the powerful feelings of hatred she had toward Yǎniū were false. Since she had always been too much of a coward to take her own life properly, it was simply easier to redirect the feelings onto another. Now, however, it sounded as if she could finally do it and even have something good happen from it.

Something bothered her about the whole conversation, though. It was rather hurtful to hear her own feelings about herself being thrown in her face by another, but it was more than that. Qiàn seemed to be trying too hard, and a small kernel of defiance awakened inside her.

"Sorry, Your Majesty, but I'm not ready for that yet," she forced a smirk.

"I don't care."

"Excuse me?" Xuě had not expected that response.

"A person who doesn't deserve life isn't really worthy of opinions now, are they? Especially not on balance with what your people need. Hurry up, and I would prefer you do it by the window." She nodded her head to the right.

Xuě looked and gasped as she realized what the blankets were for. It would seem Qiàn had been planning this all along, but something still didn't feel right.

"Your Majesty, I've been studying and idolizing you since I was old enough to read. I understand this is some sort of test, but you've gone too far."

"I'm offering you a way out. A way to be remembered in a positive light, and you believe it's just a test," Qiàn arched a brow.

"Obviously," Xuě shrugged. "I feel I know you pretty well. If you truly believed the only way I can serve my people is in death, you would've already killed me yourself." She allowed herself a smile as she beat Qiàn at her own game.

Qiàn slowly stood and leaned slightly over the desk. As her eyes came within inches of Xuě's, she allowed them to turn completely black. Xuě suddenly began to look less confident about what was happening.

"You think you know me? You arrogant little *bitch*." She watched Xuě flinch from the insult. "You know nothing of what I am now, or the chains that bind my actions.

"Whether I like it or not, we are of the same bloodline. Previously, striking you was the limit of what I am capable of. Believe me, if it were within my power, you'd already be dead!" She continued glaring with her blackened eyes, as Xuě fell back in horror.

She suddenly realized she had misread the situation. It had all been true. The one she idolized most wanted her dead, and she still didn't have the courage to do it herself. As she fixated on those black eyes, Xuě finally lost control of her tears.

"What, what are you?" Xuě gasped as she continued stepping back.

"What I always have been, and what I always will be," Qiàn

stated clearly. "The Raven Queen." She continued glaring as Xuě looked as if she were about to fall over.

"You already know what you have to offer. That blade will be waiting for you. Waste no more of my time until you are prepared to use it." Qiàn turned her head to the right and spat on the floor.

Xuě stumbled backward a few more steps before turning and fleeing through the door.

Qiàn listened carefully, hearing the footsteps fade into the distance, before finally collapsing back into her chair. Her eyes turned back to normal, as her head dropped into her hands, and she started to cry.

"Have you lost your drekking mind?" K'tar shouted as he appeared next to her desk.

"Do you think that was easy for me?" She looked up at him, tears running down her face. "I had no choice!"

"I can think of a dozen better ideas," he insisted angrily.

"And they all would have failed!" she screamed. "She's too far gone, and there's only one person here who can truly help her. The boy ignored your advice, making it nearly impossible for it to happen on its own.

"You don't understand how our minds work. I had to break her mind so badly that her instincts take her to the one place she needs to be. I had no choice," she repeated quietly, as she went back to crying.

K'tar moved to sit next to his wife and held her. Having watched the entire exchange, he was furious at how Xuě had been treated. However, it was true that he didn't fully understand the best way to help her. In the end, all he could do was what he had always done.

He let Qiàn cry into his chest as he stroked her hair and whispered to her. After a few minutes, she seemed to calm down enough to talk.

"What was that nonsense about bloodlines? And how did you do that with your eyes?" Despite what had been happening before his hidden eyes, K'tar had been torn between shock and amusement for that part.

"Oh, that," Qiàn grinned. "She really is quite clever," she nodded in approval. "I didn't expect such a coherent counter. The only reason I cursed at her was to buy a couple of seconds to think. The bloodlines thing was the best excuse I could come up with," she shrugged.

"The eye thing was for added shock value. Apparently, we do have a bit of control over our appearance, as long as there's some sort of basis in reality for us to focus on. My eyes did turn black on occasion while we were alive, so I can do it now whenever I want." She let them flash back and forth.

"It's no stranger than us walking through objects, or simply vanishing, whenever we want. In fact, Yǎniū's body is actually more real than ours are now. It's kind of funny when you think about it," she giggled.

"If you say so. Anyway, if nothing else, we need to keep Xuě out of harm's way," he finally said. "It could be that she is all we have left." "I don't want to talk about that," Qiàn warned.

"We can't ignore it, Raven. We know they aren't back home, and-"

"No!" She cut him off. "Wolf, please," she begged. "I know what you are trying to say, but I can't handle it right now. We have to wait for Yǎniū to come back. We'll make her tell us the truth. Until then, please don't make me talk about it."

"Very well."

*****

The door to Larg's bedchamber flew open so violently that it sent him halfway to the ceiling. He struggled to get himself properly upright after falling back down, but a sudden weight impacting his chest flattened him.

Luck, more than anything else, allowed him to recognize Xuě an instant before he ripped the attacker's head off.

It had been three days since their last meeting, and avoiding her had not been easy for him. Now, here she was seemingly screaming and wailing into his chest, clutching him as if her life depended on it. The only reason he knew he was awake was from the pain of her nails slicing his back open.

"Am I really that bad? Why does she want to kill me?" She screamed into his chest. "You have to protect me! I don't really want to die!" She continued to wail.

Larg wasn't awake enough to hear half of what she was screaming, and the half he heard didn't make any sense.

"You were right, she's gone too far! She's insane! Protect me!" She screamed.

Larg tried blinking the sleep from his eyes and rubbed his face with one hand. The other had reflexively started stroking her hair.

"Calm down, what's going on?" It was the best he could come up with, as his heart finally started slowing back down.

"Wolf, you have to protect me. She wants me to die! I swear I don't want to die!" Her words were muffled since she was still screaming against his chest.

He could feel how wet his skin was from her tears, and could finally clearly see the state she was in. Slowly, he adjusted his posture to sit correctly and hold her more comfortably.

"Raven, please," he said gently. "Stop crying. Of course I'll protect you. Just tell me what's wrong."

Chapter 8

Henwick

"I still can't believe it," K'tar admitted as he stretched out on the large bed.

"I told you to trust me," Qiàn winked, as she ran her fingers up and down her husband's chest.

The former classroom across the hall from her office had been converted into a bedchamber for them. In terms of space, it was easily twice the size of what they had enjoyed in the castle, even if the furnishings were a bit sparse. Although they didn't really need much aside from a large bed and the necessary implements to make fresh tea.

"She's like a completely different person. How is that possible after only two days?"

"It's hard to explain, but I've told you in the past what a wolf's presence does for us. Her case was far more extreme, so somehow the presence itself was enough. She needed to *accept* it. In any event, the effect is nearly immediate."

No one had seen Xuě the day after her final meeting with Qiàn. The following day, however, had seen Xuě moving amongst the survivors in a way she hadn't done since they arrived. She had been mingling, offering suggestions, asking questions, and doing it all with an attitude none had ever seen from her.

Never with her wolf more than two steps away.

"Her abilities are very impressive," Qiàn pointed out. "It's just that her mind was moving in the wrong direction. Larg changed that. It really is that simple for us. The hard part is admitting it in here," she tapped her chest.

"I never had to worry about that part, given that my childhood was more or less normal, for a princess anyway, and you were always there. Given the horrible life she's been forced to live, it was a bit more complicated in her case, but it all worked out." She pat his chest and bent up to kiss his cheek.

"Let's give her one more day to settle into her proper self, and then we can truly get to know her as a member of the family," Qiàn added happily.

"Sounds good to me," he nodded. "Hopefully she doesn't hold a grudge for-"

The sudden flash in the room cut off K'tar's comment. They both sat up quickly, trying to keep the bedcovers wrapped around their bodies, as Yăniū stretched out her neck and shoulders.

"A bit more subtle than your usual entrances," Qiàn commented.

"Huh? Oh, the lightning thing is more for fun than anything else," she grinned. "How long have I been gone?"

"Just a bit over three weeks," K'tar answered.

"Okay, so everything should still be about the same," she mumbled. "We have a lot to talk about before we meet with the others," she said sternly.

"Fine, but do you mind turning around?" Qiàn asked. "What?"

"This is our bedroom," she pointed out. "I am aware of that."

"We're not exactly clothed at the moment," K'tar offered as way of a better explanation.

"Who cares?"

"We do," they both echoed each other.

"You're being ridiculous," Gabriella scoffed, but she turned around.

Qiàn and K'tar quickly retrieved their discarded clothing and coughed slightly as they sat back down on the bed.

"Well, that was a lovely waste of time," Gabriella commented as she turned back around. "Can we get started now?" She grabbed a chair and moved to the best spot she could find to keep her wings out of the way.

"We would like for you to clarify something for us first," Qiàn started, as K'tar's hand found hers.

They had done their best to ignore reality, but now that Gabriella had returned, they couldn't ignore it any longer. It was likely the answer was relatively harmless, but neither would be satisfied until she confirmed it for them.

"Sure, what's wrong?" She noticed the odd look in their eyes.

"Where are our children?" Qiàn asked slowly and clearly.

They both inhaled sharply and exchanged a worried glance at the angel's instant, involuntary reaction to their question.

"That is a question that should be addressed at a later time," she replied softly.

"We are addressing it now," K'tar's voice was a low growl.

"They aren't back home, in fact, not many we left behind are, and obviously, there's almost no one left here now," Qiàn waved her arm gently. "The best theory I have is that somehow everyone is simply *stuck* somewhere, but I don't really understand such things."

K'tar noticed that as Qiàn was speaking, Gabriella had averted her eyes.

"How can such a thing be possible?" Qiàn forced herself to stay calm as she asked the question. The angel's reactions had begun to fill her with a dread she had never known.

"Nothing can be served by this conversation," Gabriella pleaded. "Please, you both have to trust me." She still couldn't look at them.

"Yǎniū," K'tar growled, squeezing his wife's hand. "We're doing nothing further until you answer our question."

Gabriella nodded slowly and forced her blue eyes to look directly into both of theirs. She had been expecting this question. Well, dreading it was probably more accurate.

"No one from here is stuck," she forced the words out. "Every mortal who has died on this world since he arrived is in the Dark Realm." She knew they would've already figured out on their own that the Dark One was here.

"You said wolves and ravens couldn't go there." Qiàn's statement was automatic.

"I know, but my brother's presence here changes some of the rules," she explained gently.

"Your, your brother?" Qiàn's voice was empty and confused.

Gabriella saw her friends sitting frozen on the bed, trying to comprehend what she had said, and wasn't sure what to do. She stood, allowing her wings to extend slightly, and began walking toward them, but froze when Qiàn stood up as well.

The raven walked up to her, her head only slightly higher than Gabriella's neck. Her eyes were frozen as she looked up into the angel's and gripped her breastplate with both hands.

"Get them back." The plea was spoken too weakly to be considered a demand.

"Qiàn, I-"

"They're innocent, they're all innocent." Qiàn's weak words ran over whatever Gabriella was trying to say. "How could you let this happen?"

"Qiàn, please-"

"I want them back." Her grip started to tighten on the angel. "I want my children back *right drekking now!*" Her frozen eyes turned crazed, as all remaining weakness left her voice.

Gabriella tried to raise her hands to gently touch Qiàn's arms. "It's not-"

"Creation is not a playground for your family's drekking problems!" she shouted in Gabriella's face. "Do something!"

She didn't want to have to use force to calm her down, but Gabriella didn't know what else to do. Suddenly, a large hand found Qiàn's shoulder, and the raven relaxed, albeit only slightly.

K'tar looked completely pale, and his eyes lacked any of the fire she was accustomed to seeing in them. Somehow, however, the wolf was able to maintain his composure.

"Raven, please, this isn't helping."

Qiàn's head snapped around to face her husband, but she didn't interrupt him.

"It's already happened. We have to help her win first, then we can worry about fixing things." He noticed something flash in Gabriella's eyes as he finished speaking. "What's wrong?"

"It's, it's not that simple." She didn't want to continue.

Lying or withholding the information would be better. They deserved to be spared. Unfortunately, she knew they would learn eventually, and if they ever discovered she lied to them about this, they'd never forgive her.

"A soul's alignment to its realm is permanent. The two of you are proof of that."

"We don't know what that means," K'tar said carefully, although the change in Qiàn's eyes said she suspected the answer.

"Everyone here is being corrupted," Gabriella spoke slowly, "but the two of you remain unaffected because you've already crossed over. The potential remains to change the alignment of any living being, but after death, it's too late."

"I do not accept that," K'tar growled, even as Qiàn's body started to shake.

"I'm sorry," Gabriella could feel the tears in her eyes. "Even if we win, I do not possess the ability to move souls between the opposing realms. I can't, I can't save them," she finally admitted clearly.

It was too much, even for K'tar.

As they both broke completely and fell, the only thing she could do was move to catch them in her wings.

*****

"That's odd," Larg stopped before opening the door to the former school.

"What?"

"I don't hear anything anymore."

"Are you sure you heard anything in the first place?" Xuě grinned as she reached up and pinched one of his pointed ears.

"Ow." He playfully knocked her hand away. "Yes, and that flash in the window was obvious."

They had been wandering around aimlessly, not quite ready to call an end to the day. It had been a busy day, and Xuě was exhausted, but it had been the first good day of her life. There was also something she felt she had to do.

She didn't remember much about the night she ended up in Larg's room. There was a lot of crying and random words with little coherence. The entire following day had been nothing but long conversations, many of which were effectively unimportant. The whole time, her emotions seemed to spiral in completely random directions.

Then, she woke up this morning feeling amazing. Her mind was moving as quickly as ever, but it was…quieter. Things were easier to understand. She recognized the number of dark things she still held inside, but there were good things as well.

She felt…balanced.

Having never experienced this herself, she found it to be one part of the old stories that was difficult to believe. Driving away any other raven who tried teaching her from their personal experience hadn't helped either. It was pointless to continue denying reality.

She suddenly found herself grabbing the hand of the person who saved her. Well, *one* of the people.

Larg and she had spoken much of Qiàn and K'tar. She had her own theories now about why Qiàn had been mistreating her, and Larg confirmed them by admitting his own conversations with

K'tar. As hurtful as it had been for her, it had likely been equally hurtful for Qiàn.

Now that it had worked, it was possible Qiàn feared the situation would reverse. What if she resented Qiàn for going as far as she had? Xuě desperately wanted to speak with her. To explain that she understood, and everything would be okay now.

Simply put, she just wanted to truly meet them, not as her heroes, but as her great-grandparents. It would be the perfect end to this lovely day.

"Well, it is late," he pointed out. "Perhaps they were, you know, busy," he winked.

Xuě blushed. "Aren't they dead?"

"To be honest, I don't think I know what that word means anymore. I mean, they eat a lot more than any of us do," he laughed.

"Well, whatever they were doing seems to be over, and we know they don't really need sleep." She reached for the door handle.

"Raven," he reached out and quickly grabbed her wrist. "Is that something you really want to walk in on?"

She drew her hand back quickly, as her eyes twitched. "That is an excellent point."

"Come on." He started pulling her away. "They might not need sleep, but we do, and don't forget what that flash probably meant. I have a feeling tomorrow is going to be a busy day."

"Agreed."

*****

Xuě and Larg stopped a respectable distance from where the angel seemed to be making pleasant small talk with a group of survivors. The last two days had been confusing for everyone.

They had anticipated some sort of meeting or discussion the day after she tried meeting Qiàn and K'tar, but nothing had happened.

In fact, no one had seen any of them since. None wanted to believe the worst, but on this twisted world, rumors couldn't be helped.

Xuĕ never would have imagined that *she* would be the one encouraging faith. Most of her people seemed as surprised to hear such things from her as she was for saying them. In truth, she had begun growing concerned herself, just not for those reasons.

A few hours ago, however, she heard talk that the angel was back and talking amongst the people. Rather than seek her out right away, Xuĕ ensured proper preparations were begun for what they were likely to need today. She also needed time, and Larg's help, to prepare herself.

She had much to make up for with this angel.

It was still strange to see how she somehow dissipated the darkness everywhere she went. There was no additional light emanating from her or anything like that; it was far simpler and somewhat stranger. The darkness simply wasn't around her.

There was an almost perfect bubble around her, showing what Xuĕ imagined their world was supposed to look like. Supposedly, some had questioned her about this. So far, the angel had simply smiled and said she would explain later.

Drawn as her eyes were to the phenomenon, it took her a moment to notice something even stranger. Where were her great-grandparents?

Gabriella walked up to them, wearing a pleasant smile. She nodded slightly and seemed to notice Xuĕ's confusion.

"They'll be along when they're ready," she said softly.

"Um, okay," Xuĕ nodded in return. Had there been an undertone of sadness in the angel's voice? "About before," she tried unsuccessfully to meet the angel's gaze.

Gabriella quickly raised a hand to stop her from continuing. "You may have expressed yourself inappropriately, but much of what you said was correct. We need say no more about it," she insisted.

"Very well," Xuě sighed, before bowing in thanks. "Still," she reached a hand into her pocket. "I do not believe it is appropriate for me to have these." She reached a hand out, holding the feathers she had been given.

"If that is your choice." She nodded again and attempted to retrieve her feathers. "Hmm," she mumbled as her fingers seemed to pass through them, before brushing Xuě's palm.

"What does that mean?" Xuě asked in confusion.

"I gave them to you freely. They cannot be retrieved until their purpose has been served," she shrugged.

"What purpose?"

"If you find out, let me know," Gabriella chuckled. "Ah," she looked over Xuě's shoulder. "It seems we are ready to begin."

Xuě turned, as she returned the feathers to her pocket, and saw Qiàn and K'tar approaching. She couldn't help but smile, although her voice caught before she could call out to them. The darkness prevented her from seeing them clearly, but something was wrong.

"Hello, everyone, we hope you all weren't waiting long," Qiàn called out to the group.

There were a few moments of pleasant and respectful greetings all around before Qiàn motioned Xuě to come closer.

"Yes, Your Majesty?" She bowed deeply.

"You left this in my office the other day, dear." She smiled and held out the ring Xuě had been wearing. "You really should be more careful with your mother's things."

"Yes, of course." She took the ring, and after an almost imperceptible nod from Qiàn, put it on. "Thank you," Xuě finished cautiously. From this close, she could see the problem.

It was their eyes. Despite their interactions and overall expressions, there was a sadness in them she hadn't seen before.

"We really should get started," Gabriella interrupted them.

"Yes, of course," Xuě spoke up before Qiàn had a chance. "The main administration building has been prepared for you. It has not been used in a long time, but the building's size should make you more comfortable if many are to attend," she indicated the angel's large wings.

"How thoughtful, thank you," she said with a smile.

"And by now, there should be plenty of fresh apples waiting for you," Xuě allowed herself a small smile. It was still surprising to her how easily smiling had become.

"Really?" Gabriella grinned. "The stories could not possibly have been that detailed."

"No, but the forest you created makes it obvious. Such a large variety of fruits can't be available in the same climate, yet half the forest is still made up of apple trees," she smirked.

"Even more of a reason to get started. If you don't mind leading the way?"

"K'tar can take you," Qiàn interrupted. "I would like a moment." She glanced pointedly at Xuě as she uttered the request.

"Yes, of course," Gabriella agreed, no longer smiling. Whatever the results, she had heard the details of Qiàn's methods and disapproved.

Although she recognized that right or wrong, it wasn't her place to interfere.

"Larg." She laughed as the young wolf snapped to attention at being addressed. "Would you mind gathering as many of your people as you can? There is something I wish to tell everyone before we begin."

"Yes, Miss Angel!" the wolf shouted before running off.

"I told you to call-" Gabriella gave up as he was clearly too far away. "Well," she looked to K'tar, and arched a brow.

K'tar nodded and, with a grunt, led her off, leaving Qiàn and Xuě alone.

The two ravens stood simply staring at one another. Xuě waited until it became clear Qiàn did not want to speak first. "Were you bluffing, or did you really know?"

"I didn't need to know," Qiàn answered. "The mind can be a terrible place, and I am adept at making others believe what I want them to believe to serve a necessary purpose."

"No matter the damage you do, or who you hurt?"

"That is correct," Qiàn admitted. "The purpose must be served. Answers must be found, and problems must be solved."

"Would it surprise you to know you were correct?" "Saddened, yes, surprised, no," she answered softly.

"I even tried to do it once," Xuě forced the admission.

"That is difficult for me to accept," Qiàn's eyes started twitching more at hearing how far she had gone.

"You believe I would lie about such a thing?" Xuě cocked her head.

"No, but you are very clever and clearly still alive," she inhaled slowly. "I do not believe you would have failed, or if you did, it is likely you would have continued trying," she pointed out logically.

"Larg stopped me."

"Truly?" There was a hint of disbelief in her question. "He has grown quite friendly with my husband, yet hasn't mentioned such a thing."

"I don't think he knows," she explained. "He was just at the right place at the right time. If I'm being honest, he does that a lot," she mumbled.

"They always are," Qiàn smiled, "even if they don't know why." "Shortly after my first attempt, my father told me the story of you hiding the cloth with the angel's blood on it. It gave my life new purpose."

"Punishing Yǎniū?" Qiàn kept her voice free of any judgment. "Yes, only then could I allow myself to die, so that's why I never tried again."

"I see, and now?"

"And now, thanks to you, I'm a different person," she smiled slightly, as she carefully inhaled. "I do have a single remaining concern."

Qiàn merely nodded for her to continue. It was difficult for her to handle this conversation on top of the horrible news Gabriella had given them.

"Am I a real person?" She raised her gaze to see the sudden confusion in her great-grandmother's eyes.

"I'm sorry, but I don't think I understand," she offered carefully. "My current happiness is less relevant to me than how quickly it

happened. How can this be real? How can a mind be trusted when it can be swayed so easily?" Xuě's voice began to break slightly.

"Oh, honey." Qiàn stepped forward quickly and embraced her.

Xuě's shoulders tensed, but it wasn't long before she responded in kind.

"Has the truth of what we are been lost again?" Qiàn asked gently. "No, but I don't understand it. I don't care how many others agree this is normal; it doesn't make it logical," she sniffled slightly. "I'm scared I'm not the one in control."

"It's okay, dear." She patted her back a few times before stepping away. "My current perspective allows for a more simplistic explanation." She waited a moment for Xuě to recover her composure.

"The energy required for a full celestial is divided in half and then attached to mortal souls. While the mortal body and consciousness imprint on the soul, this energy works in the opposite direction. It alters the mortal body and mind, transforming them into wolves and ravens.

We are given wondrous abilities, but they come at a cost."

"We only have half of what we need," Xuě filled in correctly, as Qiàn paused. "Yes, but that doesn't explain my concern."

"Because you are thinking in terms of being half as strong,

or something of that nature, but that is not accurate. This energy changes us in such a way that we cannot survive without the other half. Somehow, on this world, we adapted to being apart anyway, but your generation is appropriately balanced.

"Xuě, to put it simply, you have two choices. Be with a wolf, or die,"

Qiàn finished with a shrug.

Xuě's eyes started twitching as she considered the explanation. "Why such a clear separation based on gender?"

"Our kind was created to fulfill a particular purpose, but all beings must choose their path freely. A method was devised to ensure we chose properly, despite being born with this knowledge locked away." She cocked her head and waited for Xuě to comment.

"No sane being would choose extermination over procreation," she nodded slowly.

"Correct. As for you personally, your mental trauma is real, and somehow it was blocking the influence Larg's presence should have been having on your mind. Briefly breaking your cognitive functions allowed your mind to reset. Thankfully, your base instincts took you to the proper place for it to happen."

"What if I hadn't?"

"There's no need to worry about such things now, dear," Qiàn smiled sweetly.

"Tell me," Xuě demanded. "What would have happened if I had gone anywhere but to Larg that night?"

Qiàn's smile vanished as she sighed. "Either your mind would be beyond saving, or you'd be dead."

"You are saying we were created this way?" She gasped in horror. Qiàn nodded quietly.

"That's terrible!"

"Whether I agree or not isn't relevant," she shrugged again. "They do not see mortal death as we do. From their perspective, if we aren't going to do our jobs, we need to die as soon as possible to be retasked. We've also been on this world far longer than our kind should be anywhere, and we've interacted with another mortal race."

"Why does that matter?"

"We have developed and grown closer to normal mortal beings than we were ever intended to. It is more accurate to call us all normal women with the appearance and abilities of ravens than normal ravens. The same can be said of the wolves."

"This is a bad thing?" Xuě's eyes narrowed as she tried to keep up with the information.

"On the contrary," Qiàn crossed her arms. "I think it's wonderful, but it greatly complicates our existence. Any wolf and raven should be able to work together properly at any time. Unfortunately, it's not that simple for us.

"Tell me, do you see yourself having similar feelings for any wolf other than that boy?" She grinned as Xuě blushed slightly.

"Well, my feelings are a bit of a mess still," she laughed humorlessly, "but I know the answer's no."

"And because of that, no other wolf can ever help you," she shrugged. "Still, as I said, I am thankful for this difference. If being a proper raven means trading the love I feel for my husband? To not even understand the feeling? Drek that," she wrinkled her nose and shivered.

Xuě couldn't help but laugh.

"Whether it's good or bad, the existence of those feelings is enough proof that you are real. You still have a lot of work to do, but you're going to be okay." She took Xuě's hands into her own. "You believe that, don't you?"

"I do now." Xuě smiled again, but this time with a tear in her eye. "Good, because there's something else I need you to understand." Xuě's eyes quickly locked onto hers at the subtle, but noticeable, change in Qiàn's voice.

"I sought to help my great-granddaughter, and I couldn't be

happier with the results. As for your other persona," Qiàn allowed her voice to trail off.

Xuě tried to maintain eye contact but failed. As her gaze dropped to the ground, she couldn't do anything but nod meekly.

"I returned that ring to you because you have every right to it, but only as a memento of your mother. You aren't ready."

She knew she shouldn't be surprised. Nothing she had accomplished in the last few days could make up for nearly two decades of improper training and development. Honestly, it hadn't really meant anything to her anyway.

Except...

Except that for some reason, it suddenly meant *everything* to her. "My people need a queen," she said softly.

"They're my people now," Qiàn responded equally quietly. "Xuě," she placed a finger under Xuě's chin and gently raised her head. "Look at me. This is not a test. It is a simple reality." She tried offering a gentle smile.

"But I can still-"

"You can act as my liaison," Qiàn cut her off quickly. "Nothing more."

Xuě looked as if she was about to say something more, but chose to remain silent.

"When all of this is over, you can take your proper place and help your people rebuild." She reached out and embraced her again. "Until then, don't mistake arrogance and pride for positive intentions and skill," she whispered.

"Yes, Your Majesty," Xuě whispered back.

Chapter 9

"Ah, there you are." Gabriella smiled as Qiàn and Xuě finally joined the growing crowd outside the former city hall building. "Qiàn, there's something I still need to check. Want to join me?" she glanced upward as she asked the question.

"Of course," she grinned in excitement. "Husband?" "There's a reason wolves don't have wings," he growled.

"Suit yourself," she shrugged, moving to join the angel in the center of the crowd. As Qiàn walked, suddenly her eyes flashed gold, and fiery golden wings sprouted from her back.

There were gasps throughout the crowd, as most looked on in wonder. There were more than a few, however, who were old enough to look on with sadness. Not being able to transform wasn't as bad as remembering the feeling and no longer being able to.

No sooner had Qiàn joined the angel than they both launched straight upward. It wasn't long before they vanished from sight.

"Um, excuse me, but where are they going?"

K'tar and Larg both turned at the sound of Xuě's voice.

"Oh, hello, Xuě," K'tar grinned broadly. "I'm happy to hear you're doing better, and very sorry for remaining so distant. Hopefully, now we can change that?"

"Thank you," she returned his smile. "I'd like that." Her gaze returned to the sky as Larg stepped up next to her. "I think I remember Yǎniū doing something similar right after arriving. The flying part was fun, but not the first part."

"The whole thing was horrible, and I prefer you not bring it up." Larg looked slightly queasy as he remembered the terrifying flight. He'd easily choose fighting demons over repeating that experience.

K'tar laughed loudly, recognizing the look in Larg's eye,

before slapping the young wolf's back hard enough to cause him to stumble forward.

"But I don't understand," Xuě spoke up again.

"Yǎniū likely wants to test a theory or two, so she needs to see all this from the other side. Unprotected mortals can't survive the trip," he shrugged, as if expecting the explanation to make sense.

"I, what?" Xuě exchanged a confused glance with Larg, as K'tar went back to looking up.

"Well, that didn't take very long," he mumbled at the incoming streaks. "That's them?" Larg questioned.

"What else would it be?"

"They're on fire!" Xuě exclaimed.

"Calm down." K'tar rolled his eyes, waiting for the pair to touch down gently back in the center of the murmuring crowd.

"As beautiful as always," Qiàn remarked with a smile more genuine than most of hers had been lately.

"Some of us were doing more than simple sightseeing," Gabriella smirked.

"And?" K'tar prompted.

"There's nothing wrong with this star system's primary," the angel shook her head.

"So, you were right?" he groaned. "Unfortunately," Gabriella agreed.

"There's no other sentient life in this system either," Qiàn added. "Although we had already guessed as much."

"So, we shouldn't have to worry about the numbers suddenly changing?" K'tar wanted to be certain.

Xuě and Larg simply stared, not comprehending the conversation.

"No, the closest life I sensed is at least ten light-years away," Gabriella cupped her chin. "That's my best guess anyway. It's hard for me to judge distances, and I wasn't able to check to confirm."

"That doesn't sound good." There was a note of concern in K'tar's voice.

"It isn't, but it's also not unexpected," Gabriella sighed. "I'm being suppressed too much to simply go flitting about this galaxy on a whim," she shrugged. "On the other hand, he must be similarly restricted; otherwise, this would already be over."

"How?" Qiàn spoke up. "If all that matters is him getting here first, shouldn't he be able to do whatever he wants?"

"Yes, but what if his physical presence is required here for whatever he's doing? It's also possible he doesn't know how. Remember, he's never been to this side of creation before.

"Fact is, it's been over twenty years here. If he was going to relocate a billion or so other mortals here from another world, he would've done it already," Gabriella pointed out.

"Excuse me," Xuě waved for attention. "I don't understand some of the words you're using. What are you talking about?"

"Oh," Qiàn started to answer. "It's nothing for you to worry about. We are simply eliminating variables. Yǎniū, we really should get started with the rest."

"Agreed, but I want to make an announcement first," she said sadly. "You're going to tell them?" K'tar growled softly.

"I don't want to, but I believe they have the right to know the truth."

Qiàn and K'tar nodded their understanding and moved to enter the building. They saw no reason to be subjected to this information a second time.

Xuě and Larg quickly followed them but stopped as Qiàn turned to look back over her shoulder.

"You both need to stay and hear what she has to say," she whispered.

Xuě inhaled sharply as she once again saw something terrible in Qiàn's eye. K'tar hadn't turned around at all, but his head was clearly hanging lower than it had been. Larg reflexively took his raven's hand as they turned back to face the angel.

Once Gabriella was certain she had everyone's attention, she took a deep breath and began to explain what had been happening to all their fallen.

*****

Kukkug's Lair

Kukkug spun, slicing a demon in half while his wings shredded a second target. A pair of trees got caught in the crossfire as well, but he barely noticed them.

"Still too slow," he grumbled to himself, before leaping upward toward a trio of winged demons.

Using the demons for practice wasn't as helpful as he had been hoping. It hadn't occurred to him that they were incapable of attacking him. As much sense as it made now, it was still annoying. The best he could do was make them attempt to simply touch him.

At least it provided him with moving targets and allowed him to practice evasion as well. Unfortunately, it wasn't anywhere near the same astesting himself against a truly aggressive opponent. He also hadn't anticipated his body's seeming lack of coordination.

It didn't make any sense.

Back home, he could hold an entire universe in the palm of his hand. Here? He was lucky to fly in a straight line. Having already been in this body for so long, it had been rather shocking to discover he had somehow gotten worse.

The need to focus on too many things at once, without being bound by the fundamental laws of this reality, was causing the problem. His physical body was still bound by those same laws, which was making the situation worse. Simply wanting something wasn't enough; he had to know how to do it.

Simple movement had come to him automatically in the beginning, but focusing on moving *and* fighting had been too much. He might have wanted to charge and swing his sword to the right, but what actually happened was that he would leap up and fly to the left. Worse, he couldn't try too hard without risking this world's total destruction.

He had given up on trying to use two swords, like her, almost immediately. Using his wings as actual wings helped as well. He began noticing that putting in the proper physical effort made focusing easier.

At least he was getting better.

Kukkug twirled and danced through the air, as the trio of demons did their best to touch him. Forcing himself to focus on movement alone, he was easily able to avoid all three. Accounting for momentum had been strange, but it seemed he had finally mastered that.

Tucking his right wing while flaring the left allowed him to execute an unexpected turn. The demon streaking toward him fell to the ground shrieking, having been sliced in half. The brief attack, however, had a noticeable impact on his maneuvers.

Kukkug flew upward and flipped around. Even as he destroyed the demon on that side, he felt the third touch one of his legs. He still couldn't even properly handle this much.

It was beyond unacceptable.

Screaming in frustration, he clenched a fist, and every remaining demon was crushed into non-existence as he returned to the ground. A pity he couldn't use that ability on her.

"I know, I know," he mumbled to the sole spectator. "But I don't remember hearing you giving any useful tips either!"

The slanted eyes stared at him in lifeless rebuke.

"I'm sorry, dear," he apologized quickly. "It's not as if this is your fault." He cradled the head and started stroking her hair. "I shouldn't have yelled at you.

"May as well go back for now." He was anxious to get closer to the doorway. The direct energy flow should help him feel better.

"Guess it doesn't matter too much," he shrugged. "I'll just offset the difference with numbers. Even she can't fight me, plus a hundred demons or so." His eyes narrowed as he considered the comment.

"At least I don't *think* she can." He chuckled as they came back into view of the cavern. "What's this?" He closed his eyes briefly. "Finally," he mumbled as he rushed the rest of the way back to the doorway.

Kukkug made himself as comfortable as he could before gently setting his companion in his lap. He opened a window, checking to make sure she had a proper viewing angle.

"It seems she's finally ready to do something," he laughed. "I admit there's a part of me that doesn't want to know. Maybe this will be more fun if it's a surprise later. What do you think?"

He tilted the head back far enough for him to look into the eyes, and the mouth was forced to move a bit.

"Agreed," he sighed. "This is too important to leave anything to chance. Well," he readjusted the head to join the viewing, "let's watch their secret meeting."

*****

City Hall, Henwick

"I'm sorry, but I don't understand a lot of what you said," Xuě admitted.

Gabriella had finished explaining everything she had already told Qiàn and K'tar. Given that she was talking to mortals, she had left out some of the more complicated details and concepts, but it was still difficult for them to accept. It was the main reason she had insisted that no one attend this meeting except Xuě, Larg, and a select few elders.

Larg put a hand on Xuě's shoulder. "What do you mean this darknessisn't real?"

"Think about it," Gabriella started to answer. "Yes, this world is always dark, but has no one noticed the temperature still changes between day and night? Not to mention the animals still flourish and maintain typical day/night cycles?" She waved a hand at them before grabbing another apple.

"Yes, Miss Angel," Hóngwén answered from the back of the room. "A great deal was recorded about this phenomenon in the very beginning, but we never figured it out," she shrugged. "It makes no sense to us, but we believe our own eyes."

Xuě nodded to the elder for speaking up. Hóngwén had been an adult back when the ravens were still trying to understand what was happening. Before everyone had given up.

"It's more complicated than that," Gabriella answered. "How so?"

"You wouldn't understand it, and the information doesn't really change anything. Just trust me on this." She took another bite from her apple before continuing.

"No." Hóngwén's simple response drew all eyes to her. "If you had no intention of explaining, then you shouldn't have said anything at all about it. You may see us as ignorant children, but we are not, and I personally take offense to being spoken to that way."

"Well said, Hóngwén," Xuě spoke up.

The elder nodded curtly in her direction but offered no other sign of thanks for Xuě's support. The young raven stifled a sigh at the additional evidence of what she had been seeing lately.

Qiàn had technically been correct when she had described Xuě's overall rise in popularity amongst her people, but only if one looked at simple numbers. It had been sufficient for her plans in that conversation, but it wasn't the whole truth. The few survivors who had already been adults before this started had no use for her.

Any improvement she had made in the last few days didn't come close to erasing the previous two decades. In addition, while the younger survivors saw nothing but her recent great successes, the elders were old and wise enough to see them for what they were: accidents. The elder ravens especially practically hated her.

They knew her problems were almost all self-inflicted. The exact issues each of them had tried to help her foresee and avoid as she had been growing up. Just to be angrily cast aside. In some ways, seeing her suddenly improving so easily had lowered their opinion of her even more.

Oh, so *now* the "want to be queen" decides to listen? Congratulations on taking twenty years to solve problems most ravens solve for themselves within days. Definitely someone worthy of ruling over us…

Xuě wasn't sure how to mend those particular fences, but at least this time she knew she wouldn't give up. The sound of an apple being dropped back on the table drew her attention back to the angel.

"Very well," Gabriella bowed slightly, "I will do my best." She rubbed her chin for a moment before looking over her shoulder. "Qiàn, if you can think of better words to use, please do not hesitate to interrupt my explanation."

"Agreed."

"Okay, this," she stretched her arms out, "is the physical. All around us and stretching further than you can imagine. However, creation as a whole is far more than the physical." She paused a moment and looked around slowly.

"What is happening here has an effect on the physical realm, but it is not primarily happening in the physical realm. Simply put, you are all under constant attack, but you have no way of identifying or understanding it. You perceive this darkness because the part of you that transcends the physical is screaming in your minds, trying to warn you."

Xuě, along with two elders, raised their hands for attention.

"Please hold a moment," Gabriella gestured for them to be patient. "I believe if you allow me to try and explain exactly what is happening, rather than focusing on the darkness itself, it will all make more sense." She waited to receive nods from around the room.

"I am forced to use words that make sense regarding your perspective, but are, in reality, inaccurate. It likely doesn't matter given what's at stake, but it makes it difficult for me," she sighed.

"You think in terms of good and evil, and maybe that makes sense against a mortal opponent. I use many of these words as well, as I prefer this type of communication. The difference is that I am capable of understanding the true difference between the two perfect and opposing realms, and you are not."

"Excuse me, but good and evil *are* opposite," Xuě cut in. "It seems a logical perspective to take. Also, we all know that demons represent a very real and *very* physical threat."

"First, the demons are nearly completely irrelevant to what is truly happening, as is this entire physical world. Secondly, you are correct about good and evil, but the words have very subjective meanings. It simply isn't good enough.

"The base energy of each realm is so diametrically and objectively opposite, they would-"

"Yǎniū," Qiàn stepped forward and cut her off. "Just use words they know and be done with it. Otherwise, we'll be talking in circles all day, and they still won't understand."

"Alright." Gabriella inhaled slowly and deeply. "The balance of creation is mainly maintained because this side of creation is not perfect. Moreso, this side of creation was not designed to even handle perfection.

"Over the course of eternity, however, we've seen that mortals seem capable of even more than we ever imagined. Even perfection. It is incredibly rare, but possible, and it's happened enough times that I see the similarities to what is happening here."

"Explain to them what you mean by that," Qiàn suggested quietly. "Um," Gabriella was at a loss. Was she really going to be forced to explain it so poorly? Well, accurate or not, it was either that or say nothing.

"The life energy mortals possess, what many of you call a soul, can act as a conduit to the physical world around you. It gives you the ability to unknowingly affect the alignment of all base energy, even if that energy is in the form of inanimate objects. It's largely irrelevant, unless of course enough of you attain a pure enough level of perfection."

It was clear her audience was paying close attention. The squinting eyes and furrowed brows, however, made it equally clear she was losing them.

"This table," she patted the table next to her, "can be an evil table." She quickly held her hands up to stop the sudden murmuring. "I'm being serious, but maybe now you realize why words like good and evil don't work," she smirked.

"If more than half of the living mortals on a world attain a state of perfect purity, they can alter the alignment of the actual world itself.

There is potential for this to begin spreading even further. So, in the rare instances where this happens, we step in."

"And do what?" Xuě asked, as if she were afraid of the answer.

"We finish the job, but most importantly, we remove the world from this side of creation. From the perspective of the inhabitants, they are getting what they want. The only real difference is that the world is taken to a realm designed to handle it," she shrugged.

"That doesn't sound so bad," Hóngwén said slowly, and a bit uncertainly.

"It isn't. To be honest, it's quite exciting actually," she started to smile. "To see mortals able to attain something like that on their own," she said a bit wistfully. "Of course, if the world goes in the other direction, it can be a bit terrifying." Her eyes clouded a bit in memory.

"Anyway, what I have mentioned is a very rare, but natural occurrence.

Here, however, I believe it is being done by force."

Qiàn coughed slightly for attention. "You have always believed yourselves under attack. This is not an attack. This is an abduction. Your deaths are not what the Dark One seeks. He wants this world.

"In fact, most of the death here was likely an accident. He needs souls inside living bodies for this to work, and the more the better. We believe he was unaware of how to control his power or his demons here, until it was too late."

Gabriella smiled her thanks for Qiàn's concise summary.

"It probably doesn't matter, but do we know why he wants this world?" Xuě asked.

"Unfortunately, we do," Gabriella lowered her gaze. "Every time I touched this world, I increased its power exponentially. I ignored the rules because I wanted to see my friends. In so doing, I turned this world into a target he couldn't resist.

"There's a reason we aren't supposed to interact with mortals." She forced herself not to cry. "Whoever gets here first wins. From the moment he set foot on this world with the intention to stay, it was over. So, you see, Xuě, you were right after all." She looked up, smiling sadly.

"Everything happening here truly is my fault."

"So?" Larg growled. "Just fight back and tell us how to help you." "Beings like us can't really fight here," she admitted, and her wings seemed to droop slightly. "He was already present, and so he's been suppressing me since I arrived. If I resist, or if he tries harder, it's all over.

"Any true battle between us would destroy far more than just this one world. Neither he nor I wants that, even if it is for different reasons. We could fight physically, but I'm not sure if that would accomplish anything," she admitted.

"Surely you have some idea of what to do? Otherwise, why are we even having this conversation?" Xuě tried infusing her voice with confidence.

"Not really." She picked up another apple. "I just wanted to be honest with everyone, and I was hoping that by talking it through, maybe I would think of something." She couldn't help but be reminded of her Father telling her she couldn't win.

"Well," Xuě was forcing herself to think of something. "Can we stop him without fighting him?"

Qiàn slowly turned her head to face her, and Xuě swore she saw the faintest of grins before the Queen returned her face to a neutral expression. "What I mean is, you already told us what and why, but exactly *how* is this happening?"

Gabriella seemed to study her for a moment, but didn't respond.

"You said this was being done by force here, but it's something that has happened naturally more than once." Xuě decided to take encouragement from the angel not immediately silencing her. "In the past, how did you intervene to finish the job?"

"Hmm," Gabriella wrinkled her nose. "We just take the world. The other celestials and I, I mean. It's easy when it happens naturally, and it's in accordance with their base instincts, so it's one of the few things my siblings actually do."

"What about when the world goes in the other direction?" Qiàn questioned?

"I never really thought about it," she shrugged.

"Is that why the demons are here?" The suggestion came from K'tar. "I don't think so. They're more independent than celestials, but not even close to as powerful." She sat down and started eating another apple as she considered the possibilities.

"My brother is a lot stronger than I am now, so I wonder if he can do it by himself?" She mumbled the question to herself. "Still, it sounds too risky considering he's acting against this world's desires."

Everyone watched as the angel pondered what suddenly seemed to be a crucial question. Slowly, she stood and began pacing around the room. When she left without a word, even Qiàn and K'tar seemed to hesitate to follow her.

Finally, Xuě decided there was no point in waiting and signaled for everyone else to follow her out. They quickly caught up to the wandering angel but were careful to remain a respectable distance behind her. Xuě looked about to say something, but Larg put a hand on her shoulder and shook his head.

Gabriella stopped after crossing the main hall and seemed to stare blankly at the doorway. After a moment, she simply opened the door and waved everyone closer.

"Do you feel that?"

"The breeze you mean?" Larg asked, clearly confused.

"This is the world, and that's the Dark Realm." Gabriella first indicated the building before pointing outside.

"What?" The question was echoed by multiple voices.

The living mortals began stepping back, and even Qiàn and K'tar seemed confused.

"Huh?" Gabriella looked over her shoulder. "It was just a metaphor," she rolled her eyes. "Calm down.

"Is it really that easy?" The angel was mumbling to herself again. "Why not do it that way? I mean, why take any risk, or put forth any effort?" She started rubbing her chin. "I wonder why we never thought to try that?"

"Yǎniū?" K'tar questioned loudly. His ears had no trouble hearing the mumbled questions, and the other wolves weren't brave enough to speak up. "My brother opened a doorway directly to the Dark Realm somewhere on this world. The pure energy from that realm is simply flowing through naturally, much like the breeze you now feel. It's directly corrupting your souls—and, through them, the world around you.

"His presence is allowing it to happen, but he's not actually doing anything himself. That's the simple explanation anyway," she shrugged. "In other words, we don't really have to defeat him after all." She smiled broadly and nodded toward Xuě.

"We'll still have to fight him, but closing the doorway should solve the problem." Gabriella was staring at nothing, and everyone present could almost feel her mind processing variables and information quicker than any of them could hope to do.

"Alright," Qiàn nodded. "How exactly do we do that?"

"The more important question is *where*?" Gabriella frowned. "Normally, we would seek the darkest, or evilest, if you prefer, place on this world. The problem is this world isn't evil, or at least it wasn't when he got here. This world is larger than any of you really understand, and he could be anywhere."

"What about that cave you saved us from way back?" K'tar suggest. "You told us that was Thraxsis's home, and it felt pretty evil to us."

"Right," she started to nod slowly. "Right," Gabriella repeated more confidently. "By the time my brother got here, the influence would have had another what, seventy-five years or so to fade?"

Xuě nodded to confirm the angel's understanding of this world's timeline.

"Still, it was unbearable even after a thousand years, and it's likely the only choice." Her eyes started shining a bit brighter. "We might have a chance after all."

"I'd still like to hear how." Qiàn returned to her earlier question. "That's where the two of you come in. Since he doesn't know you're here, it gives us an advantage."

"That's an assumption, Yǎniū, not a fact," K'tar pointed out.

"It's a fact," she disagreed. "You guys don't understand. What he's doing is making everything in this world look the same. It affects our ability to truly see."

"Correction," Qiàn started to counter. "It's affecting *your* ability to see. There is no evidence that-”

“You have to trust me,” she cut her off. “He can likely see me just fine, but the two of you are just two more souls, and that assumes he can separate individuals. Even your alignment is hidden, given how close you are to me.”

“But what about when you-” “Qiàn, you need to trust me.”

Qiàn grudgingly nodded, but the disagreement remained clear in her eyes.

“We’re coming too,” Xuě spoke up confidently.

“No,” Gabriella disagreed. “The three of us can make the journey rapidly. Your people would need a week or more. We simply can’t afford to wait that long.”

“You have no choice,” the young raven insisted and glanced to her wolf. “You are attacking three targets,” Larg took over. “The Dark One, his doorway, *and* the demons, but you only represent two attackers because they must fight together,” he waved toward Qiàn and K’tar.

They were both forced to nod and concede the point.

“I believe I understand the type of strategy you are going to propose, Miss Angel. With only the three of you, it will fail. You will either be delayed too long or overwhelmed separately.”

Hóngwén and the other three elders present each voiced their support, and Gabriella moved to stand in front of Xuě and Larg.

“I already told you what is happening here, and what will happen should any of you fall. Even if we win, there won’t be anything I can do.” She tried to keep her voice calm, but tears were already forming in her eyes. “Please don’t make this choice.”

“If we don’t, you can’t win at all. So, logically, there really isn’t any choice,” Xuě pointed out.

Gabriella was about to argue further, before a memory of one of her Father’s warnings clarified in her mind.

“Very well, but keep the numbers low.” She agreed sadly. “He can outnumber us whenever he wants, so let’s take advantage of him not wanting to really kill anyone he doesn't have to. He'll likely engage you with as few demons as possible, hoping to simply scare you away.

"If you bring everyone, he may decide it doesn't matter anymore and defend with thousands," she sighed, resigning herself to the inevitable. "I suppose those two can even blend in better if a group of mortals comes with us and just splits off when we get close enough."

"Agreed, we'll prepare a force, and if you'll allow it, I plan to lead them." Xuě held her eyes steady and stared hard into the angel's sad blue pools.

"Absolutely not!" Qiàn shouted, stepping up behind Gabriella.

"If that is your choice," Gabriella answered, ignoring Qiàn's comment. "Yǎniū, she's not ready!" Qiàn hissed, trying to keep her voice down. "That's enough, Qiàn," was all Gabriella would offer.

"I forbid it!"

"*Qiàn!*" Gabriella's head snapped around. "This is not your choice to make."

K'tar grabbed his wife's hand and gently pulled her back, but everyone could hear the powerful wolf grinding his teeth. The raven looked away but offered no further argument.

Xuě tried to hide her disappointment.

"As for the plan of attack, it's relatively simple, really. Nothing's going to happen until we get very close, and when it does, we simply charge our respective targets. It's not a very clever strategy, but that's where you two change everything.

"If I head for the doorway first, he'll likely sense my intentions. So, I'll keep my brother busy, they'll handle the demons, and the two of you charge for the doorway. You won't run into anything you can't easily handle, and all Qiàn has to do is fire light directly into it. At that point, if we act quickly, we win."

"It can't be that easy," K'tar argued.

"It's because other than me, he doesn't know anyone's here that can threaten the doorway itself. So, he'll be focused entirely on me. Also, the timing has to be perfect. You can disrupt the doorway but not close it. This is where it gets tricky.

"Qiàn, after you attack the doorway, both of you need to run away immediately, and we will switch places. The two of you hold off my brother, while I close the doorway completely."

"*What?*"

Gabriella winced at the volume of their sudden shouts.

"That's insane!" K'tar yelled. "He'd destroy us instantly. How does that help you win?"

"Just listen," she gestured calmly. "Believe it or not, fighting him will be a lot easier than fighting Thraxsis was."

They both looked ready to start shouting again, but Gabriella's glare kept them silent.

"Thraxsis was less than an insect by comparison, but because of that, he was able to fully use his power, provided he was careful. My brother is as weak as I am here, even if for opposite reasons. To put it in terms you can understand, if either of us so much as sneezes the wrong way, this world would vanish from existence.

"Defeating him would be impossible for you two, but you should be able to *survive* against him without too much effort. Also, you only need to buy me a few seconds."

"If he's really that limited, it sounds like we'd be better off fighting him three on one," K'tar suggest.

"Except I'm not certain if either of us can be defeated on this side of creation. I know firsthand that celestials can be killed, but I don't know if we can be killed *here*," she admitted.

"I'm going to try to take his wings. In theory, that should at least send him home for a time, which is effectively a victory for us. However, since I can't guarantee whether or not that is possible, I don't want to waste our surprise on it."

"Can you do it?" Qiàn whispered the question.

"Of course she can," K'tar growled. "No one can beat Yǎniū in a physical fight." He gave a broad and toothy smile. "That's not what I meant."

"I can do it," Gabriella's eyes fell briefly. "He's not really my brother anymore," she inhaled slowly. "If the opportunity does exist to kill him, or even just send him home, I won't hesitate."

Everyone gave her a moment of silence to regain her bearings.

"Anyway, the instant you attack the doorway, it will cause a disruption that both of us will feel. It should surprise him, whereas I'll be expecting it. Even if he's able to follow me immediately, I'll still have a head start. He also would never expect two souls to dare to attack him directly.

"Hopefully, before I enter the cavern, you'll already be waiting outside to knock him off my tail. That should be all that's necessary. I truly only need a second or two to understand what I'm looking at, then I can close it."

"Excuse me," Xuě raised a hand slightly. "I know we agreed closing the doorway is the priority, but it sounds like we will still need a way to deal with your brother."

"Everything will sort itself out after the doorway is closed," Gabriella said carefully.

"Yǎniū," Qiàn's eyes started to twitch, "what are you planning?"

Gabriella groaned, not really surprised that the raven refused to let her off the hook so easily. If there was ever a time to lie, it would be now, but she just couldn't face these people with dishonesty.

"The doorway being suddenly closed not only stops what is happening here but should serve to interrupt my brother's concentration. Only for an instant perhaps, but in that instant, I will no longer be suppressed," she explained.

"I don't understand how that helps us." Qiàn seemed to consider the point for a moment. "The way you explained it, neither of you can act in that way here, so it doesn't really matter which of you is dominant."

"I have a great deal more experience existing on this side of creation.

That gives me the advantage of being able to act without unthinkable consequences." Gabriella was trying her best to keep her answers vague, even knowing Qiàn would likely not accept them.

Xuĕ glanced around and saw the same look of confusion on everyone else that she knew she was wearing, except for K'tar. K'tar's expression was very carefully neutral.

"Yăniū, speak plainly," Qiàn demanded.

"Very well," she sighed. "The instant I feel myself no longer suppressed, I intend to burn this world clean myself. It will happen in less time than you can blink."

Qiàn and K'tar went wide-eyed and inhaled sharply.

"The demons will be destroyed, and this darkness will instantly vanish.

It won't destroy my brother, but it will serve to send him back home. Since it's the one thing neither of us should ever do, he won't expect it and won't have a chance to respond."

Xuĕ was having difficulty comprehending what Gabriella was talking about, but it sounded like victory to her. Still, there had to be a reason why her great-grandparents looked so horrified.

"That sounds like a good plan then, right?" Xuĕ tried to gently interrupt the silence.

"Tell them the rest," Qiàn whispered loudly.

"It doesn't serve them any purpose to know," Gabriella whispered back, with a tone of warning in her voice.

"Do it, or I will."

"It won't change anything." Gabriella glared at the defiant raven, her eyes demanding that she remain silent.

"What she's suggesting," Qiàn's eyes glared back as she spoke, "will end all life on this world."

There was a series of gasps before total silence reigned over the six mortals listening.

"Your plan is to kill us?" Larg spoke up first, his yellow eyes wide with shock.

Gabriella flashed Qiàn a final angry glare before returning to her signature smile and turning to face the others. She spread her wings slightly and began holding out her arms in a calming manner.

"There's no need-"

"We've done nothing wrong," Hóngwén cut her off. "Just let me-"

"Are you punishing us for letting this happen?" One of the wolf elders, Arahk, called out the question.

Gabriella kept trying to calm everyone down, but the more the others spoke, the more panicky and confused they were getting. Her attempts at gently defusing the situation weren't even being heard. There was a reason she didn't want this information shared.

"Why is no one listening to me?" Her gaze lowered, and her wings drooped. "I explained all this already. Don't you understand what's at stake here?" Even as she half mumbled the words, she could feel her anger threatening to break free.

Her hands became fists at her side as she fought for control. This was the only way. Why couldn't they see that? She could feel her wings start to shake.

"This goes beyond death!" She shouted as her wings suddenly flared out.

Qiàn and K'tar were unaffected, but most of the others were sent to their knees, clutching their ears.

"I'm sorry, I'm so sorry for what's happening here." She retracted her wings and began pacing back and forth in front of the others. "But it's already happened. Your fates are sealed.

"No matter how long you live, or how worthy you are, every one of you is facing an eternity of suffering and torment. That assumes creation is even allowed to continue. This is the *only* way to prevent that from happening.

"Your mortal lives mean very little on balance, and quite frankly, your bodies are in the way. But you don't need to be afraid." She forced her voice to soften and her smile to return. "I speak not of your end, but merely your beginning."

She spread her wings and arms. "When it's over, I'll take you all into my wings and bring you back. And not just you, but countless others." Her voice grew more serious.

"I will turn this world into a bastion of light and fill it with your people in the forms they were meant to be. Indeed, I cannot enter the Dark Realm, but I'll rip it open with my own hands if I have to. I'll allow wolves and ravens to pour directly into it, in limitless numbers.

"We'll take the stolen souls back by force if we have to." She clenched a fist in front of her face. "We're going to save every single one of them." Gabriella was forced to stop talking to get better control of her breathing.

In allowing her anger to turn so quickly into excitement, she had been gulping more air than her body required for simple speech.

"Yǎniū," Qiàn spoke very softly and gently. "It's not going to work." "You always speak to us of balance being the ultimate goal." K'tar tried to support his wife's argument. "What you are suggesting is not balance, but only a reverse of the current situation."

"No, it isn't," Gabriella shook her head violently enough to dislodge half her blonde hair from its clasp. "I only seek to retrieve what was taken. It will serve to restore the balance, not break it."

"And you think your brother will simply allow any of this to happen?" Qiàn started raising her voice. "The Dark Realm is going to just allow itself to be invaded? Yǎniū, it'll never stop there." Qiàn rubbed her face and eyes, still not fully believing what she was hearing.

"Let him try and stop us," Gabriella sneered. "I am tired of this horse dung. If my brother wants a war, then I'll give him a *drekking war!*" she shouted.

"Your entire strategy is predicated on the element of surprise!"

Qiàn shouted back as she gestured angrily. "Something we have *no evidence* to assume! This isn't going-"

"*Know your place, soul!*"

Qiàn reeled back, as if physically struck, before K'tar caught her. "Qiàn, you may still have difficulty accepting this, but your title became meaningless the day you died. This is *my* fight! I want you both at my side, but if you aren't willing to obey my commands, I'll find a way to send you back home." She tried to maintain a neutral posture, but her anger was evident in how her wings were poised.

For a moment, it appeared Qiàn was going to argue further, but K'tar tightened his grip on her noticeably. She glanced up, and he shook his head despite the clear sign of anger in his eyes.

"We will obey, *Angel*," Qiàn forced herself to agree.

Gabriella's eye twitched as she heard her closest friend address her formally for the first time. There was nothing to be done about it; however, this was simply too important. She turned back to face Xuě and pretended not to notice the trails of blood coming from the ears of the six mortals present.

Just what I needed, another reason to be ashamed of myself. She quickly buried the thought.

"How long before your people can be ready?"

Xuě took a moment to finish composing herself. "The people and supplies can be ready within a day, but it'll take longer to gather enough horses." "Warhorses will be here and waiting for you," Gabriella responded with a nod before turning to leave.

"How?" Xuě called after her. "We aren't even sure where to find them anymore."

Gabriella stopped walking long enough to shoot Xuě an angry glare over her shoulder.

"Um, never mind." Most of Xuě's surprise had faded, but the look inthose blue eyes awoke a small kernel of fear.

"Have someone inform me when all is ready. I am not to be disturbed before then." Gabriella left the building without waiting for a response, leaving six frightened mortals and two angry souls in her wake.

Chapter 10

Kukkug's Lair

"A week? *A week!*" Kukkug shouted, causing cracks to start forming along the cavern's ceiling.

Realizing what he had done, he quickly leaned over to protect his companion. At the same time, he extended his wings to touch the tips to the cavern wall and ceiling to repair the damage to the stone. Once he was satisfied the potentially annoying cave-in had been averted, he straightened his posture.

"Sorry about that, dear," he whispered as he started gently brushing dust and bits of debris from the long hair. "It was just a bit frustrating to hear we have to wait so long when we're ready now." He looked back through the window.

She had already left whatever building they had been in. The mortals and her two pets were suddenly engaged in multiple confusing and excited conversations, but none of it mattered to him. He waved the window closed with an angry sigh.

"How long is a week anyway?"

The lifeless eyes gave no immediate response.

"They call every rotation a day, and every revolution a year," he mumbled to himself. "So, there are other increments in between, I guess? Hmm, I should have this knowledge," his eyes narrowed.

Kukkug searched his mind, examining the information he had stolen since he had been here. Fundamental concepts were the most difficult, but he eventually figured it out.

"How tedious," he groaned. "And what a stupid plan. I expected better of you, sister," he chuckled.

The eyes stared at him in judgment.

"You're right," he forced himself to admit. "Given what she

knows, it's not a bad plan at all." He stretched and scratched at a bit of dust in his hair. "It's a little disappointing that she assumes she knows everything, though. So many obvious errors," he shook his head slowly.

"I mean, how does she not know that I can see and hear everything on this world that I want to? That I can literally watch every step she takes?" The fingers of his left hand traced random patterns in the dirt as he considered the odd situation.

"Perhaps I've been making false assumptions as well," he admitted quietly. "It's been so long," his voice trailed off. "I assumed she had either been destroyed by the Old Man out of pity, or that she had more or less grown into what I am. What if the answer is somewhere in between?"

The dead mouth opened and closed a few times.

"I'm not sure, but she doesn't seem much different from the last time we were together." His eyes glazed over wistfully. "I admit I hadn't considered that, although it does mean it'll be easier to defeat her."

The mouth began to answer, even as the eyes seemed to soften, and Kukkug was forced to look away.

"I know what you're trying to do, but that was a long time ago. This is what I've been preparing for, and if I have to kill her, so be it."

The mouth stopped moving, but the eyes seemed to stare through him, demanding more.

"No, it was all lies, just like the Old Man, but with her it was much worse. It's like I already told you. She actually made me believe, and then she broke her promise," Kukkug's voice caught.

Suddenly, Kukkug's vision seemed to distort, and his face felt strange.

He reached up and touched his eyes, only to have his fingers come back wet. How very odd. Is this what crying felt like in a physical body? He wondered why he was doing it.

His goals had been so clear for so long. Even when he watched her suffering as a mortal fighting Thraxsis, it had been a source of much-needed amusement. Why was watching her now causing so many strange emotions to come to the surface?

"I just want to hear her sing again." Kukkug heard the words before he even realized his lips were moving. Before long, he was weeping softly.

"Well, that was odd," he mumbled, wiping his face clean. "I suppose we should decide the best way to use this extra time." He wasn't sure what had briefly come over him, so he decided it would be best to simply ignore it.

"I can't even prepare, at least not yet," he groaned. "If I start bringing demons through now, they'll just charge to attack her," he explained to his companion. "Without my help, I don't think any number of demons could stop her, so what's the point?"

The eyes asked him the obvious question.

"I can't risk going too far from the doorway. She definitely got that part right," he shrugged. "So, we have to wait for them to get close and then bring all the demons through at once. Fairly simple, but I'm getting tired of waiting."

The mouth began moving again.

"True, I did say I would prepare something special for your grandparents." Kukkug considered the possibility and decided that controlling a single demon should be easy enough.

He stood up, cradling his companion in his right arm, and faced the doorway. Carefully, he sent out a call for Greater Demons. Unfortunately, he couldn't be more specific about what he wanted from here. So, his only option was to wait and see what came through and send back any demon that wouldn't work.

It took a while, but eventually one of the largest demons he had ever seen lumbered through the doorway.

"Oh my, aren't you adorable?" he grinned at the demon who barely fit inside the cavern. "Come along," he said, waving and moving to leave.

The giant demon growled and hissed, but followed his master obediently.

Once they were outside the cavern and tunnel, Kukkug looked over the demon more carefully. It wasn't what he wanted, but that didn't matter. He could alter the demons however he wished, but there were limitations to doing so on this side of creation.

He could do anything he wanted, as far as altering these creatures, except for changing their overall mass. What he wanted was rather large, but this demon had more than enough mass to work with.

"You're going to do something vital for me. Does that make you happy?" Kukkug barely came up to the demon's waist.

The Greater Demon hissed and seemed to bow slightly.

"Good," he smiled. "Now, I have to change you first. It's going to hurt a great deal, but you're okay with that, aren't you, cutie?"

There was more hissing and bowing.

"Excellent." Kukkug stepped to the side and placed his companion on the ground. He carefully turned the head away and gently closed its eyes. "You shouldn't watch this, dear."

He turned back to the demon and flexed his fingers. "Let's get started."

*****

Henwick

Gabriella opened her eyes and saw K'tar standing patiently with his arms crossed behind his back.

"Did you forget how to knock?" "Would you have let me in?"

"I said I didn't want to be disturbed."

"Then you have answered your own question," he grunted. "What are you doing?"

When he first entered the room, Gabriella seemed to be meditating.

K'tar had been surprised that it seemed to have taken her so long to notice he was even here.

"Now that we know where he likely is, I was trying to focus on that area to see if I could see anything useful."

"Did it work?"

"No," Gabriella sighed. "What do you want?"

"How could you ever imply we wouldn't stand with you?"

Gabriella's eyes fell. "I didn't mean for it to come out that way." "We will always stand together, no matter what." K'tar inhaled deeply.

"But in this case, it simply means we are agreeing to fall with you." She winced noticeably before looking back up to meet his gaze. "You're wrong, Yǎniū," he said sternly. "And you know it."

"How can you say that when this is the only way?" "I didn't come here to argue with you."

"Oh, really?" She smirked and crossed her arms. "I admit that I expected one or both of you to try doing exactly that. May I ask why you aren't going to bother?"

"For the same reason I never wasted time arguing with Měilíng, especially when she got old enough to start manipulating her brother."

Gabriella's smirk vanished instantly. "You see me as a child?" She asked slowly.

"Your actions are rather similar in a way, truth be told," K'tar shrugged, ignoring the angry tone in her voice. "I don't mind providing helpful information and support to children, but arguing with them is beneath me and an enormous waste of time."

She stood quickly, slamming her palms flat on the table. "You can't even comprehend what I am!" She shouted, not noticing how easily K'tar had goaded her into the sudden outburst.

The wolf merely sighed and shook his head slowly. "I don't need to,

Yǎniū. I know *who* you are," he responded clearly.

"What's that supposed to mean?" she demanded loudly.

"On many occasions, you speak with such intellect and authority, and you seem to have no shortage of confidence. However, you spend equal time complaining and blaming others, and your arrogance is beyond anything I've ever seen. Considering who I have for a wife, that last point is especially impressive," he grinned slightly.

Gabriella forced her anger down as she glared at him. "Is that all?" she asked through grinding teeth.

"More or less." If K'tar was concerned in the least by the furious angel facing him, he didn't show it.

"Forgive me if I think I have a valid reason to do those things, and that this certainly isn't the time to bring them up," she hissed.

"I'm not the one spending a great deal of time complaining about always being alone, but as I said, I have no wish to argue."

"I *am* alone!" She shouted. "Don't you realize that's one of the main reasons we're in this mess?" Her wings flared partially in frustration.

"You would truly say such a thing to my face?"

Gabriella cocked her head in confusion until she recognized the faint look in the wolf's eyes. Anger and confusion were quickly replaced with shame and sadness.

"Oh, no, no," she stuttered briefly. "Please, K'tar, please tell me you never thought that's what I meant."

"That word has a clear definition, and it's what you said. We both have to suffer through hearing you say it a lot, and you're usually quite angry when you do so," he pointed out.

"No, never the two of you." She extended her right wing across the table to where K'tar was standing and let it press against his left side. After a moment, she withdrew her wing and fell back into her seat.

"I've existed for so long, but never in the way I've existed since meeting you both." She covered her face with her hands as she felt her eyes watering. "I never meant to make either of you feel that way.”

“We know it was never your intent, but the fact that you can say the words so easily means you aren’t thinking clearly,” he said gently.

“I spoke to her so horribly,” she mumbled through light sobs.

“I wouldn’t worry too much about that,” he waved a hand dismissively. “Really?” She looked up in surprise and disbelief.

“Yǎniū, she’s your friend,” he said, as if the point was obvious. “I also happen to know you’ve been the victim of at least one volatile exchange with her.”

Gabriella’s eye twitched at the unpleasant, yet distant memory. “So, if you ask me, you owed Qiàn that one,” he chuckled, before finally moving to sit across from her. K’tar reached out and gently took one of her hands.

“As for this strategy of yours, it *is* wrong. You’re making too many assumptions and ignoring too many facts. I trained you better than this, Yǎniū.” His eyes pleaded with her to see the errors.

“You taught me how to hold a sword,” she smirked. “This isn’t quite the same thing, K’tar.”

“I see.” He nodded sadly before withdrawing his hand. “If that’s truly all you learned from me, then I owe you an apology. You’re the only student I ever failed.”

“K’tar, wait!” She reached for his hand to stop him from leaving the table. “I spoke poorly,” she apologized. “It would seem even I don’t always know how to use my voice properly.” She bowed her head slightly.

“You taught me so much more than simply how to fight. Although, to be honest with you, I’m not sure you understand just how important the pure physical training has turned out to be. I certainly never would have guessed, even if I had known I would be returning to my old form.”

“What do you mean?”

"Controlling this body is not difficult, but it is *very* different than controlling the physical shell I used to have. It is hard to explain, but nothing works the same. If not for my time as a mortal, simply walking in this body would take an impractical amount of focus.

"My body changed as a consequence of saving you both the first time. My time as a real mortal in between meant I was already prepared when I returned to this existence. The only reason I can fight as powerfully as I can now, and as easily as I do, is because of your training.

"In fact, the more I think about it, the more I think this will be our biggest advantage in the coming battle."

"Meaning what? You said your brother was far stronger than you, even if he can't fully use that strength."

"He's been here over twenty years. He's likely found a way to make his body like mine. If for no other reason, as a way to properly understand and interact with this world. He would have no way of realizing the enormous disadvantage that would be until it was too late.

"I know firsthand what he can do," her eyes clouded over briefly. "But that doesn't mean he knows how to do any of it in a body like this." She stretched her arms out.

"Hmm," he considered the information. "I see what you're saying, but twenty years is a long time on a world like this. We can't underestimate his intelligence or ability to adapt," he cautioned.

"Of course not, but simply realizing the problem doesn't make it go away. He'd have to relearn everything, and he'd be stuck training himself. Meanwhile, I was taught personally, long ago, by the greatest trainer on any world."

K'tar couldn't help but avert his eyes in embarrassment as she squeezed his hand.

"It's not just that either. I remember everything else you taught me," her voice got lower. "That's why I'll never stop fighting. It's why we have to do it this way, despite how unwise the strategy sounds."

K'tar's eyes narrowed as he realized Gabriella was fully aware of how unlikely her plan was to succeed. She nodded slightly, as if to confirm his realization.

"There are other strategies, Yǎniū. We don't have to take things that far just to stop what's happening here."

"We do if we're going to fulfill my primary objective." "Isn't that simply to fix this world?"

"No, that's just a means to an end." She inhaled slowly. "I'm going to save everyone. I'm going to get them back."

K'tar's body tensed as Gabriella's eyes hardened.

"I was telling you both the truth before. There's nothing I can do personally, but a direct assault on the Dark Realm might work."

"Yǎniū," K'tar swallowed carefully. "I can't even comprehend what that type of battle would be, but there's no way simple souls would be able to do it. I don't care how many of us try, and even if it's all wolves and ravens. Without the support of full celestials, we stand no chance."

"You're thinking in terms of a full assault. A simple raid should be possible," she countered.

"You speak as if we would have a clue what to do once we got there," he shook his head at the ludicrous idea. "And what about the risk of things escalating out of hand? What happens if the All-Father steps in, as you said he might?"

"So what?" she whispered. "He already said I couldn't win, and maybe he's right about everything else as well."

"What are you really saying?"

"I'm saying that maybe it really is time to start over. If innocents can simply be taken with no consequences, if I can't even save the children of my friends, then maybe creation is already irreparably broken. If it's already too late anyway, why not attempt one final impossible victory?"

"You don't really believe that." He forced her to look him in the eye. "I can't even look at either of you without hating myself, and that's an emotion I already don't know how to handle. How can either of you even still call me your friend after what I've done?" She started to cry again. "I have to get them back!"

As Gabriella continued to cry, K'tar wasn't sure how to handle the situation. He knew she was struggling, but hadn't realized it was this bad. He also had to force himself to admit he had little experience providing this type of comfort to anyone outside of his family.

It wasn't long before he realized how foolish it was not to remember that Gabriella was part of that family.

He stood and moved to sit next to her. He noticed Gabriella instinctively start to wrap a wing around him, but raised a hand to gently push it away. Instead, he chose to put his arm around her and let her continue crying into his shoulder.

"Qiàn and I aren't perfect," he started. "There was a lot of anger, even hatred, and more than a little blame. Truth be told, some of that still remains." He could feel her body tense as he made the admission.

"It doesn't change how much we both love you. We will get through this together, and that means *with* you." He turned towards her and lifted her gaze to match his.

"Neither of us could *ever* hate you, not really. Yǎniū, the fact that you're willing to enact this impossible strategy solely to save everyone just makes us love you more. It doesn't, however, change the fact that the strategy is impossible." He smiled sadly.

"Anyway, if it makes you feel any better, we both decided you were wrong," he added matter-of-factly.

"About my strategy?" she smirked sadly. "You've made that abundantly clear by now."

"That's not what I was talking about."

She stared into his eyes, a bit confused, for a moment. When she realized what he meant, she started shaking her head slowly.

"I'm so sorry, K'tar," she forced herself to not start crying again, "but I'm not. I realize I've made plenty of mistakes, but this is different. Creation has many rules that can be violated if one is willing to accept the consequences, but it also has immutable laws.

"Some things are simply the way they are and cannot be changed. I would never lie to you about this, and you understand enough about what I am that you should know to take my word for it," she finished softly.

"I understand that's what you *believe*," he smiled. "We have simply decided to disagree."

"K'tar," she sighed, "I guess I can see why you might cling to this belief, but not Qiàn. She's too clever and logical to ignore the blatant evidence that I simply know better in this case."

"On the contrary, we are agreed in this. In fact, it was a rather obvious choice. My wife called it a simple binary equation. Either you are right, or you are not.

"If you are correct, then we no longer have any reason to keep fighting. If you are incorrect, then we have every reason to continue giving everything we have. See," he shrugged, "the choice is obvious."

Her eyes widened at the seriousness of his tone. "I don't know how to respond to that," she admitted. "I'm torn between feeling sorry for you both and being in complete awe of you."

"Would you settle for simply listening?" She nodded silently.

K'tar leaned down and kissed the top of her head before patting her back and standing back up. He began pacing the room as he considered the coming battle.

"If you close the doorway, but do nothing else, what will happen to this world?" he asked.

"It will revert to its original state." "Even if he's still here?"

"Yes, remember he isn't really doing anything himself.

Moreover, it will happen very quickly. The corruption the people here are under would fade just as quickly."

"Then why can't we just do that?" He scratched his ear. "It sounds like an easy way to accomplish what needs to be our primary objective."

"It's too risky." She forced herself not to simply dismiss his idea but to honestly think it through. "Remember that he *would* still be here, and whatever he does next could be even worse. There's no telling how angry he would get after losing all the progress he's made here.

"Since I'm here now, anything new that he does after the doorway is closed has to be done in conflict with me. It would be the type of conflict we both wish to avoid, but what if he doesn't care? He is much stronger than I am in that regard, and he knows it.

"He might decide to take the risk of Father interfering and simply destroy me. I would be able to hurt him, but not stop him," she admitted.

"What exactly would happen in that case, aside from your destruction, I mean?"

"That's not bad enough for you?" she laughed sarcastically. "As I said before," she got serious again, "it would create a hole in this reality. I'm honestly not sure what the true consequence of that would be, but it's likely Father would choose that moment to start over regardless."

"You said your brother doesn't believe that would happen, so assume for a moment it doesn't," K'tar rubbed at his chin. "What would happen to him in such a battle?"

"It's never happened before, so I'd have to guess." Gabriella drummed her fingers on the table as she tried to consider it. "I wouldn't go down quietly. It's likely it would take him considerable time to recover, and it's possible he would even be completely dormant until he did."

"Alright," he nodded. "So, answer this question. Even if we stop him here, is it enough by itself to turn the tide of the overall war?"

"No," she forced herself to admit. "Too much is happening everywhere else, and fixing this world doesn't by itself return the extra souls he's taken from here. Arguably, stopping him here does nothing but delay the inevitable."

"If that's true, then I find it highly unlikely he would bother taking the risk to confront you directly. Even if the doorway gets closed. He's invested too much, and quite frankly, he's too smart to do something that stupid. He would likely retreat immediately and work to consolidate the victory he's already won." K'tar couldn't imagine someone taking unnecessary risks when they were already winning.

"I agree that makes sense," she said reluctantly. "The problem is that the possibility exists that my fears will be justified. Even if it's only a small chance, it's still too much since I can't stop him." She pursed her lips as she considered a compromise.

"The only way I can guarantee this world's safety is by acting first, the instant the doorway is closed. Although once I've cleansed this world, we can stop, rather than launching the assault I suggested. It would also serve to be a stronger victory for our side than simply closing the doorway and hoping for the best."

"You are certain you can do what you suggest? Despite the difference in power?"

"Easily," she confirmed. "I have the advantage of experience here and better focus, and I wouldn't be confronting him directly. As long as I act immediately, it'll work, but that means I'll only have the one chance."

"I think it still warrants more discussion. We shouldn't give up trying to find a way to save their lives," he insisted.

"There's no point until we know more, and we won't know more until it starts," she gestured helplessly. "Honestly, one of the most important variables is how vulnerable we both are in physical combat, and neither of us will know until we fight. This discussion could all end up being a waste of time."

"How so?"

"I'm confronting him as a means of distraction, but if we're actually vulnerable, I'll be able to take his wings rather easily," she shrugged. "Then it would simply be over, at least here anyway. He'd be immediately sent back to the Dark Realm, and maybe even dormant for a short time if we're lucky."

"Well, I agree that would be nice, but assume he's prepared for it."

Gabriella started shaking her head. "He can't. It's not a question of power in this case, but ability."

"You can't afford to underestimate him. Assume he's prepared a counter for that possibility," he said a bit more sternly. "One way or another, it's a long, boring journey to the target, which means plenty of time for additional consideration. Just stay calm, and think it through," he kept his voice gentle.

"You know, I'm starting to get really tired of people telling me to do that," she mumbled. "I know you'll probably say it's just another example of me blaming others, but in this case, that really is the truth. It's not my fault I get overwhelmed so easily by these emotions."

"Everyone gets overwhelmed sometimes, Yǎniū. That's why you have-" "Just stop it," she cut him off. "It's different for me, and that's just the way it is. I don't think you'd be able to understand."

"You don't really think I'd let you leave it at that, do you?" "Fine," Gabriella exhaled slowly once it became clear K'tar wasn't going to drop the subject. "Mortals," she gestured at him, "can feel anything there is to feel, and how you respond to that predominantly affects how you end up aligning yourselves.

"You grow from almost nothing, developing and evolving over vast periods of time into beings able to understand and comprehend these different feelings. Of course, you can still be overwhelmed from time to time—any being can—but you *do* have the capability to handle it and make your choice. It doesn't guarantee your success, but at least you have the tools.

"Technically, wolves and ravens don't evolve in this fashion, but at least you are still born and grow. Also, your minds were patterned after our studies of countless other fully evolved mortal races. Unfortunately, celestials don't work that way." She gestured toward herself.

"We're created as we are, intended to be fully aligned in only one specific direction. Despite the eternity of my existence, I am as I was the day I came into being. My knowledge and understanding have increased, but I will never have the capacity to handle certain things because I wasn't created with that ability."

"Hmm," K'tar considered her words carefully. "Sounds like an excuse to me," he shrugged.

"Dammit, K'tar!" Gabriella was on her feet again. "Aren't you listening? Angels can't feel dark emotions! We can't be angry or hate, or anything like that." She desperately wanted him to understand.

"Since we can't feel these emotions, our minds aren't designed to handle them. Unfortunately for me, Father wasn't paying enough attention when he created me," she practically spat on the floor. "So, somehow I get those emotions, yet the typical lack of ability in handling them."

"I see you're still comparing yourself to the other celestials?"
"I, what?" She was certain she had misheard his question.

"Sorry, forget I said anything," he waved dismissively. "I should probably go and help them get organized."

Gabriella barely heard him, still struggling with what he had said before. Not just what he said, but the look in his eyes as he said it.

"You know something?" She called out softly as he was leaving. K'tar stopped but didn't turn around.

"Either you or Qiàn managed to figure out something about me, didn't you?" Her voice was pleading and hopeful.

"It doesn't matter, Yǎniū," he answered without turning. "We won't offer you the answers you seek."

"How can you say that to me and still call yourself my friends?" A note of anger was slowly entering her voice. "Especially if you're going to scold me about how I've been acting regarding this very issue."

K'tar let out a long sigh before finally turning. "Are you an individual?"

"Huh?" The odd question confused her enough to interrupt the sudden anger that had been building.

"From the first day we met you, we've naturally treated you as the separate individual you appear to be. That never changed, despite how much you have." He nodded to indicate her wings. "Having met other celestials, I confess that I am no longer certain if that distinction applies or not."

"I can see how it would be confusing," she admitted. "There are many levels of celestial beings, and the word angel isn't a perfect description. Among the great many words mortals use to describe us, it happens to be my favorite," she shrugged. "Maybe I do use it too loosely."

"That wasn't really my question."

"Okay, if I understand what you are asking, then yes. I am a very different kind of being, but my consciousness is every bit as individualized as yours. I just don't understand why you would ask that."

"Have you encountered a single piece of evidence throughout your existence that suggests the others fall into that category. Aside from Kukkug, of course."

"Of course they do," she groaned loudly at the clear waste of time. "I said *evidence*, Yǎniū. I did not ask you for your personal belief."

He moved quickly to sit back across from her.

Gabriella opened her mouth to respond, but K'tar interrupted her by quickly grabbing both her hands from across the table.

"One of the most amusing and irritating things about raising children is the questions they ask."

Her features tensed at the additional reference to children, but Gabriella didn't interrupt him.

"At first, you do the best you can," he shrugged, "even when they're clueless about the subject matter they're questioning. However, there comes a time when you have to slowly stop. When, instead of answering, you begin showing them how to learn and experience things on their own.

"Usually this is a simple thing, but sometimes it's not. You advise and insist, just to be scoffed at and ignored. You know the right answer, but have no choice but to watch them suffer when they get it wrong. It's a necessary part of our growth and development," he smiled sadly.

"I already said that celestials don't-"

"The principle is the same," he cut her off. "The inability to find the answer can mean an inability to apply the information. Also, there are some things that no one else should ever answer for you. Not if you consider yourself an individual.

"I don't care what type of being you are. No individual can fully see the world through another's eyes and perceptions. Our answers to these questions will never be *your* answers. The moment you insist on relying upon the answers of others is the moment you cease being an individual and instead become nothing more than a puppet."

"You sound like him sometimes," she chuckled. "Who?"

"Never mind," her eyes fell.

"Yǎniū," he placed a finger under her chin to lift her face back up. "We care about you too much to ever color your truth, but you need to keep in mind that the only things we know are things you have told us. That, and a limited outside perspective, but it was enough. You already have everything you need."

"Please," she whispered. "I already know I can't win, and any decision I make is going to be wrong." She could feel tears forming again. "I need you to tell me what to do. Please," she begged again.

K'tar drew his hand back and considered her request. "We call it self- reflection. It's the best advice I can give you."

"What does that mean?"

"You have nothing else to do until we get there," he pointed out again. "Spend the time simply thinking about and reflecting upon yourself and nothing more."

"Easy for you to say," she smirked. "You don't have infinity inside your head."

"None of that matters right now." He held up a hand to forestall her response. "Forget about the rest of creation, your armies, what your brother's doing, all of it. Just focus your thoughts on yourself. Your knowledge, memories, your feelings." He reached out and squeezed her hand again.

"Just stay calm and think it all through. You've already done some of it to figure out why you were so weak when you first arrived."

"Technically, I'm still just as weak, but it's a matter of focus considering the suppression I'm under here. I simply wasn't paying attention, assumed I would win anyway, and almost lost complete control because of it.

Against Thraxsis, the one thing I had in abundance was focus. Well, that and unsuppressed power," she smirked.

"You still figured it out though. Do the same thing again. Stop overcomplicating things and just think it all through."

"I'm sorry," she shook her head. "You're asking me to put myself above the probable end of creation."

"In my opinion, it's the most important thing you can do *for* creation," he insisted. "Trying to do the right thing doesn't help if you do things out of order."

Her eyes tightened at the familiar comment. "Just promise me you'll try."

"Alright," she finally agreed.

K'tar smiled softly, nodded, and began to leave.

"I know Grath lived in almost perpetual fear and awe of you, but is this how you kept Měilíng under control?" she called after him.

"Nope," he looked back and smiled. "I always gave up halfway through, gave her a fresh lump on the head, and sent her to her mother to deal with. You're easy compared to her." He began laughing to himself as he walked back through the wall.

Gabriella simply stared after him, unsure as to whether she'd just been insulted or not.

*****

"Arahk, we don't have time for this," Xuě tried to insist.

"On that we are agreed," the large wolf grunted.

"You were in the meeting, so you know what needs to be done. I suggest you see to it." Xuě did her best to sound as commanding and confident as possible.

"I don't know what game you're trying to play this time, Xuě, but I know where my loyalties and hopes lie. I will act when I receive orders from my Queen." He crossed his arms and stared down at the child who had ignored his training and advice more than once over the years.

"Has the wolves' superior night vision somehow failed you?" Arahk began to growl softly but didn't respond.

"According to tradition, this task should fall to my wolf," she waved to Larg, "not you. However, in the absence of my father, you are our strongest and most experienced warrior." She nodded slightly in respect.

"I would be a fool to not recognize you as the proper choice, but if you insist on refusing my command, I will."

Arahk was about to respond, but hesitated at the piercing gaze that seemed to be staring into his very being. There was something different about those eyes from what he had seen before. He glanced briefly at the young wolf standing behind her and slightly to the right.

He had seen that boy following her around since they were both pups, but something felt different there as well.

"Alright," he finally agreed. "How many?"

"I believe it would be fitting to base it on the personal guard the Queen used to have. Twenty-four of each, with you leading the wolves and Hóngwén leading the ravens. I know there will be plenty of volunteers, but do we have that many who are able?"

"We do; however, the ravens have been unable to train properly for a very long time," he pointed out. "When you also consider the darkness, perhaps it would be better to use only wolves."

"No." Xuě shook her head sternly. "This is our world. We will fight for it together."

"Very well," he bowed slightly. "I will inform you when all is prepared."

"See that you do." Xuě nodded her approval and left the room with Larg in her wake.

Chapter 11

Kukkug's Lair

"Why isn't this working?" Kukkug mumbled as he looked over his otherwise perfect creation.

The large demon offered no answer and simply stared down at its master, awaiting instructions.

"I already said I wanted you to speak, so speak!" he demanded.

The demon opened its maw and uttered a series of grunts and hisses. "I don't understand the problem, just talk, you idiot." He threw his arms up, and Kukkug's wings began to flare slightly in frustration. He rolled his eyes as the demon started to cower.

"Calm down, I've spent far too much time on you to just tear you apart," he reassured his creation. "Obviously, my simply willing something to work isn't enough here, so now what?"

Except for its inability to speak, Kukkug was quite proud of the perfect facsimile he had created. However, he refused to give up until every detail met his expectations. The problem was that on this world, his wanting something wasn't enough. He had to know what to *do*.

He began to absently scratch his neck, even as he was grumbling and moaning in frustration. His fingers drew back suddenly, as he felt something strange. Was that it? Placing his fingers back on his neck, he moaned loudly to confirm what he had felt.

Strange vibrations were coming from somewhere inside his neck. He was reminded once again that this was a *physical* realm.

"I hate this place!" He shouted to his left, leveling several trees. He took a few deep breaths and forced himself to calm down. Allowing himself to get too angry wouldn't serve his goals.

"Okay, so I need to understand how creatures here can talk in these physical bodies and then recreate that in you," he mumbled. How did he talk? Did he even know?

"I know you have to breathe. You're breathing right?" He watched the large demon as it bowed slightly. "Yeah, you're breathing. So, you need whatever this is," he gently squeezed the portion of his throat where he felt the vibrations coming from.

"I wonder why you don't have one," Kukkug mumbled as he contemplated the problem. He had taken the knowledge he needed when he first arrived, and his body had changed accordingly. Unfortunately, it seemed that knowledge did not include exactly how certain aspects of his body functioned.

It would seem his body had a piece inside that helped make sounds, and it was better than whatever the demon had. That must be why the demon couldn't make the proper sounds he wanted it to. What bothered Kukkug was why he didn't understand the details.

"Dear," he walked over to where he had left his companion. "How does this body talk, and why don't I understand? I took knowledge from several of you, and I should understand how everything works."

The eyes simply stared back at him.

"What do you mean the knowledge is specialized?" Kukkug scoffed at the ludicrous idea. "What do you fools do if your bodies break? You can't just fix them yourself? You have to go to one of these specialized people? That's ridiculous!" he yelled.

"This entire side of creation is nothing but a mistake," he groaned. "Fine," he forced himself to calm back down. "I can figure this out," he nodded as he stretched his wings out.

"I don't need to understand how it works. I just need to give you what I have and scale it to your size. Mine will restore itself, and everything should be fine." He smiled as he realized he had found the perfect solution.

"Okay," he looked around and walked to the hillside next to his cavern's opening. If he was going to rip out a portion of his throat, he needed to see what he was doing.

Kukkug reached out with his right wing and touched the tip to the hillside. A small amount of molecular rearrangement, and he turned the grass and rocks into a beautiful reflective surface.

"This isn't going to work." He realized he wouldn't be able to maintain eye contact with the mirror he'd created because he would have to look up while cutting.

Closing his physical eyes, he brought his right wing in front of his body and allowed himself to see through it. The third-person view was quite helpful, and he looked up and began making various noises. He gently moved his fingers along his neck and carefully localized what he was looking for.

Once satisfied, Kukkug lengthened his fingernails and began to cut.

*****

The first few days of their journey had been a near-impossible test of frustration for Gabriella. It was quickly apparent they had been too optimistic about the speeds they expected to maintain. The wolves' vision was cancelling out the darkness as a factor, but two decades of overgrowth and neglect had taken their toll on the roads.

She could have made the same journey hundreds of times by now on her own, and Gabriella had been tempted to do just that. If for no other reason than to see for herself what lay ahead, rather than everyone relying on her best guess. Eventually, her annoyance and frustration had faded, and the relaxing monotony of travel had taken its place.

There wasn't a shred of actual difficulty in the journey itself, beyond the slow speed. They had even abandoned most of their supplies after the first day. With no one left alive to encroach on the area, food and water could be found so easily and, in such abundance, it seemed foolish to bother carrying very much.

In fact, now that it had been nearly a week since leaving Henwick, she felt calmer than at any other time since arriving. It was the perfect time to follow through with K'tar's suggestion. Although self-reflection was proving more difficult than she thought it would be.

There were so many questions and uncertainties, many of which she had never considered before. Perhaps that was a good thing, and maybe even the entire point of doing this, but she wanted actual answers.

"Excuse me, Yǎniū, but do you have a moment?" Xuě stepped her horse up to the angel's right side as she spoke.

"Oh, hello, Xuě." Gabriella looked around briefly. "Larg isn't with you?"

"We are stopping for the evening soon," she shrugged. "It is Larg's turn to organize the hunting parties. He is very excited to show off for the elders and has already begun making arrangements. I was told I would be in the way," she chuckled.

"That doesn't sound very nice," Gabriella commented. It was very odd to see Xuě without her wolf directly behind her.

"On the contrary," Xuě argued. "Larg has spent nearly every waking moment of his life trying to protect me, even though I mostly didn't understand it. For him to set me aside temporarily means he's finally comfortable in my own healing process.

"It's also nice to see him finally being assertive," she nodded to herself. "He may be young, but he's outstanding. I want the others to see that, especially Arahk and K'tar." She looked over and noticed the angel's eyes had clouded over slightly.

"You do not approve of Qiàn's chosen methods regarding my condition?"

"No, Xuě, I do not," Gabriella admitted. "I am delighted that you are doing better, but what Qiàn did was wrong. The ends do not always justify the means, and forcing you to suffer that way was unacceptable." Gabriella looked over to the young raven and tried to smile.

"Despite my own agreement that it was the only way?"

"That merely indicates a lack of intellectual understanding of your condition. I wish I had been here," she trailed off.

"Fortunately for me, you were not," Xuě insisted harshly.

"What exactly is that supposed to mean?"

"Yǎniū, your entire existence is a contradiction, and that's based on your own words," Xuě offered matter-of-factly. "I was in a horrible place, and my great-grandmother fixed that. To think you could have done better is laughable. So, if you disagree with her methods, do us all a favor and keep that information to yourself."

"What do you know of my existence?" Gabriella was doing her best to keep her anger in check.

"This journey has given me the unexpected blessing of having plenty of time to spend with them." Xuě nodded to the transformed wolf and raven who were leading the loose formation. "The hours I get to spend with them simply talking every night are wonderful, and they speak about you a lot."

"Do they?"

"Yes, although I believe they alter the information slightly so that I have an easier time understanding it. It would seem you are stuck in a loop of foolishness, and so for that reason alone, your opinion carries very little weight with me."

"Should I even bother asking you to expand on that?"

"In short, your issue is that you believe celestials, or angels, are made a certain way to do and think certain things. You believe you are different in what you think and feel, and because you should be the same as them, it is cause for concern." She arched an eyebrow in question at the angel.

"That's an oversimplification, but not inaccurate," she admitted. "There are obviously errors in your base assumptions, and if you can't see that, then I can't rely very much on your opinions now, can I?"

"Well then, Xuě, if you're so smart, then tell me what errors I am making." Gabriella groaned and rolled her eyes at the raven.

"Isn't it obvious?" Xuě gave her an incredulous look. "You insist that the information itself is accurate, yet the two sides of the equation are not equal. Logically, you are in error regarding the equation itself," she shrugged at the obviousness of it all.

"You are either wrong about what the other celestials are, or you are wrong about what you are. It is also possible you are simply wrong about the information; however, it is more likely the error lies in your assumptions."

"Look at me, Xuě." Gabriella flexed her wings. "Do I not look like an angel?"

"I don't know what an angel is supposed to look like," Xuě shrugged again. "Do I look like a half celestial demon killer?" She smirked as she looked down at herself.

"How many times have you told us the physical realm means very little regarding what is truly happening? Yet, you use your physical appearance as the main justification for what you think you are. Another contradiction."

"Xuě," Gabriella sighed, "the animosity you have toward me isn't helping anyone."

"If that's how you feel, then I apologize," she nodded her head. "I only sought to answer your questions as directly and honestly as possible. As I said before, I deeply regret my actions and words to you when you first arrived.

"However, that regret doesn't mean I like you. I know the truth of the stories, and where my faith lies," she nodded again toward her great- grandparents.

"I'm sorry you feel that way." It was all Gabriella could think to say.

"I don't doubt your intentions, just your ability," Xuě clarified.

"If any chance for our salvation exists, it's with them, not you."

"If your only goal is to insult me, I have better things to do," Gabriella managed to grind out the words more or less evenly.

"Whatever my opinion of you is, the fact remains you have information I require. I will have this information."

Gabriella suddenly started laughing. "You're an arrogant little whelp, aren't you?" She looked up, still smiling. "If I told you how much you remind me of Qiàn when she was your age, you probably wouldn't believe me."

Xuě looked ahead, her eyes narrowing sadly. "I wish she felt that way."

"I don't understand."

"You heard her at the meeting," Xuě sighed. "We're getting along great as family members, but she doesn't think I'm ready for this, or anything really. She can separate her personal and professional feelings far better than I."

"Xuě, that's completely wrong."

The raven snapped her head around at the angel's words.

"They're problem with you is born from their inability to separate their personal feelings from anything. I told you what is happening here, and the fate of all your dead. Unfortunately, most of you didn't understand it because of your limited perspective. They do.

"Do you remember I called you Měilíng when I first arrived?"

"Yes, that was a bit strange."

"Time does not work for us in the same way it works here. The never- ending flow of life energy is one of the few things we have to mark time by. Měilíng never entered our realm. This by itself is no cause for concern. It simply meant her time had yet to come.

"When I arrived, I saw the resemblance and mistook you for her. It made sense at the time." She stretched and rotated her shoulders. "She wasn't back home, so obviously she was still alive here. It wasn't until I realized how much time had passed on this world that I began to see the problem.

"Once I brought those two here to help, how long do you think it took before they put the pieces together? To realize none of their loved ones were back home or here? They cornered me and forced me to tell them the truth." Gabriella paused as she forced herself to dredge up the memory.

"I had to tell them their own children and grandchildren were gone, suffering for all eternity, and that there was nothing I could do. It broke them both in a way I've never seen before." Her wings began to shake. "All I could do was hold them inside my wings."

"Is that why no one could find you or them for a full day?"

Gabriella nodded. "They're my only friends, and I couldn't help them. I tried to sing to ease their pain, but I couldn't. I felt their loss so personally that all I could do was cry with them. So, you see, Xuě," she reached out and touched the raven's shoulder.

"They don't want you here, because you are all they have left."

Xuě nodded but didn't know what to say.

"Such a sad conversation." Gabriella wiped her eyes clean. "How about I tell you a story about Qiàn that even she doesn't know?"

"Well, I will admit you have piqued my interest." Xuě started to grin.

"You are well-versed in the stories of the final battle against Thraxsis, but the night before that battle, I met them. My intention was to kill them both." She held up a hand to forestall Xuě's automatic response.

"I did not believe we could win and sought to set them free. However, in the heat of the moment, I instead broke the chains in K'tar's mind, allowing them to finally be together. It was this night that Měilíng and Grath…began."

Xuě blushed but spoke up quickly. "Is it true that my great uncle was named after a horse?"

"What?" The question had thrown off Gabriella's train of thought. "No, although Měilíng teased him constantly about that very thing," she chuckled. "K'tar's original warhorse was indeed named Grath, but K'tar selected the name because it belonged to his predecessor.

"K'tar idolized that man, and that's where the name Grath came from. Of course, Měilíng was a terrible child and tormented her brother constantly for being named after a horse. K'tar was harsh with her, but I always thought he should've been harsher." Her eyes became wistful.

"Get back to the part my great-grandparents don't know."

"Oh, well, they are the first people I ever met on anywhere near equal footing, but they aren't the first wolf and raven couple I have interacted with. There were a pair of heroes from your Great War who were the first."

"Very little of that information has survived," Xuě commented, "save that the entire war was a mistake. How could anyone from that time be considered a hero?"

"You aren't wrong," Gabriella agreed. "They happened upon each other by chance, and over time began to realize the world was wrong. They never discovered the full truth, but they agreed the world was living a lie." The angel grew silent for a moment.

"They made the foolish choice to try and do something about it."

"What happened to them?" Xuě was intrigued by the idea of learning information that no one else living possessed.

"They were two people possessing nothing but half-understood truths seeking to challenge a world at war," she answered quietly. "What do you think happened to them?"

"Oh," Xuě nodded sadly.

"They met their end as best as they could, but it was horrific enough that it threatened to influence the imprint on their souls. I watched it happen." Her eyes clouded over.

"I assume you did nothing to prevent it?" Xuě tried to keep her question neutral, although there was a hint of accusation in it. "You assume correctly," she admitted freely. "When I heard the screaming from their souls, I collected them," she shrugged. "I feared they were so damaged as to be destined for erasure, and I sought to prevent that from happening.

"I promised to heal them, and when they were ready, to return them to this side of creation. I was unsure I could fulfill my promise, but I believed they deserved another chance at the lives they desired. After that, my memories of the incident become…muddled."

Xuě didn't fully understand some of what the angel was talking about,

but it was easy to see Gabriella's sudden confusion.

"My Father did…something," she finally continued. "I believe my memory was altered as well, and not because of my choice. Since then, I remember the proper truth, but it is as if I am seeing both versions overlaid on top of each other." She shook her head and began to absently scratch at her hair.

"Despite my past accusations toward my Father, I am beginning to realize he has taken a more active role in this world than I believed."

"Considering how bad things seem to have been here, it is far easier to believe we have all been forgotten."

"I can understand why you would think that, but the fact remains that at least you are all still here," Gabriella pointed out.

"I'm not sure I understand what you mean by that."

"Thraxsis set you against each other in a way you were unable to resist. This alone guaranteed either your direct destruction or that you would simply die out. There was no other possibility. Yet on this world, female wolves and male ravens began to be born. This should not be possible.

"Also, the Race of Man did not evolve on this world as mortal life is supposed to. They were created in place, with complete knowledge of a history that never happened." She carefully met the raven's gaze. "Xuě, it just so happens that the Race of Man is the mortal race wolves and ravens were based on.

"My Father has this ability, but the entire point of this side of creation is to simply see what life can do on its own. However, it is the only explanation that explains this world's timeline."

"If I am to believe what you are saying, it sounds as if we were being given alternate choices for procreation," Xuě suggested.

"That is my belief as well," she agreed. "The Race of Man made the situation far worse, regarding the war, but without them, you all would have simply been gone. He wanted you all to have as much time as possible, in the hopes you'd find your own answers."

Xuě nodded again. "Get back to the two you were talking about and what it has to do with them." She waved at her great-grandparents.

"Oh, well, they were kept within my own celestial body until they were ready, but then I became mortal. My consciousness was on this world, and I no longer had control of the rest of me. They took advantage of the situation and escaped," she laughed.

"To where?"

"Inside her." Gabriella nodded toward Qiàn. "I don't understand."

"Two new lives began the evening before the final battle," she grinned. "The perfect place for two souls seeking new life to go hide."

"Such a thing is possible?" Xuě did not really understand and was forced to simply take the angel at her word.

"I would say no, except that it happened," she shrugged. "At the time, Qiàn and K'tar's souls were in reality pieces of my former body. Those two used that as a kind of bridge to escape the barrier unaided. Or maybe my Father did it. I have no idea.

"Anyway, they saved Qiàn's life during the battle. In more than one way."

"And she really doesn't know?"

Gabriella shook her head. "These were not two fresh souls

awaiting an imprint but fully formed individuals completely aware of the world around them. Qiàn's mind remained clear during the battle because she was protected by the power of three. It also allowed her to finally transform properly.

"Also, at the end of the battle, K'tar was dying, but Qiàn was already dead. The two of them held what was inside of her in place long enough for her original soul to return and restore her. Something else I did not believe to be possible." Gabriella began to smile.

"You creatures are constantly surprising us." "You mean wolves and ravens?"

"I mean mortals," she corrected gently.

"So, these two souls became my grandparents?"

"No," she shook her head. "They desperately wanted a chance to be together, but not as brother and sister. They had simply been pure souls for so long that they didn't fully understand the difference anymore. I placed them elsewhere once I discovered them."

"And now?"

"I'd like to think they found each other, raised a family, and had the wonderful, loving life together they deserved." Gabriella's features fell noticeably as she spoke.

"But?"

"But, I can tell you they are not back home. This can only mean they were still alive when my brother came here, yet they are not among the current survivors. So-"

"So, based on what you have told us, they're in the Dark Realm now,"

Xuě finished for her.

Gabriella nodded as tears began to form in her eyes. "You accused me before of only being good at abandoning those I care about, but you were wrong, Xuě. I don't abandon others, I simply fail them, and the more I care about or love someone, the worse I fail."

Xuě looked at the crying angel, unsure of what to say. The truth was, Xuě agreed with Gabriella's opinion about herself, but that didn't mean she didn't want to help her.

"Well, anyway," Gabriella wiped absently at her eyes. "At least you are smart enough to place your faith where it's deserved."

"Angel, I-"

"It's alright. The truth is, I agree with you on that point as well." She glanced over to the east and seemed to stare at nothing for several moments. "There is a place I wish to visit. Please tell them I will return before we resume tomorrow."

"If you wish," Xuě agreed.

Gabriella reached out to touch Xuě briefly with one of her wings before suddenly launching off into the darkness.

Chapter 12

Abandoned Mine, Eastern Mountains

"Thank you," Gabriella smiled as she reached for the cup of fresh tea. E'kul merely grunted before limping back to his bedridden wife.

Gabriella had been following a curious instinct when she came to inspect the couple's former home. Never did she expect to actually find them. Although from the look of their aged bodies, had she waited even a few more months, she wouldn't have.

"I admit that I didn't expect to see either of you ever again, at least not here," the angel shrugged.

"In turn," the raven started to speak. "I will admit this is the first time I regret losing my sight." She waved her hand to indicate the milky white pools she had for eyes.

"I can fix that if you like."

E'kul perked up noticeably at the angel's words, but Yǔqíng simply shook her head sadly.

"I have no wish to see what has happened to my world. Even if it is to see you again, Gabriella, it is too high a price to pay. Oh, but I can only imagine how glorious you must appear to the eyes of a mortal," Yǔqíng smiled a bit wistfully.

Gabriella quickly looked down and away.

"What is wrong?" Yǔqíng inquired.

"How do you know anything's wrong?" she answered a bit wistfully.

"You don't need eyes to see some things," Yǔqíng answered. "My husband's hand tensed, and I can only guess it is due to whatever he sees in your actions. Your breathing is also a bit erratic," she shrugged.

"Why must all the ravens on this world be so clever and

arrogant?" she chuckled softly. "It's just that I don't feel particularly glorious at the moment," she admitted.

"Why not?" E'kul asked.

"That's not important right now," she sighed. "I'd rather talk about the two of you. Mostly, why do you live here, and how are you both still alive?"

"We haven't quite hit our one hundredth birthday yet, and what's wrong with this place?" the wolf growled.

"I admit you must have wonderful memories of it, and you certainly have made many improvements." She looked around the large cavern, noticeably impressed.

Holes had been dug through the rock above to allow for natural light, and there were covers ready to be swung in place in the event of inclement weather. The covers were attached to pipes to let the water flow outside. She even saw a way of heating the covers and pipes, so that snow and ice would melt quickly and safely run outside.

The cavern was also well furnished with anything a couple could realistically need. Everything from kitchen furnishings, clothing and wardrobes, tables and chairs, and finally the large bed, on which the silver- haired raven was relaxing.

Gabriella scrutinized the couple. The first wolf and raven she had personally met, all those centuries ago. She did not know them as she knew Qiàn and K'tar, but they truly had been her first. Compared to members of the Race of Man, they looked good for their age. Their frailty was apparent; however, Gabriella knew they didn't have much time left.

"I can't imagine raising children in a place like this, though," she shuddered slightly at the thought, but stopped as a clearly dark mood settled over the others. "What's wrong?" she asked gently.

"We couldn't," Yŭqíng started to cry. "I mean, I couldn't, not after what they did to me."

E'kul reached over with his other hand to start stroking her hair. "I know that technically I was already dead, but I still felt it. I *felt* it!" She leaned forward as the hand joined with her husband's found its way to her stomach. "The way they cut open my belly to get to the *abominations* inside. To make sure they were dead too. *I felt it!*" She screamed through the sobs.

"Makes sense," Gabriella mumbled. "You hadn't completely passed over, and so-"

"I don't think she was asking for an explanation!" E'kul snapped as he embraced his crying wife.

"Right, sorry," Gabriella apologized, and sipped her tea awkwardly for a few moments.

"Well, anyway," the wolf's voice was back to normal. "We just couldn't put ourselves through it again," he shrugged, but Gabriella could see his eyes held much more.

"I think it's time the two of you tell me why you live here," she flexed her wings slightly.

Yǔqíng nodded. "Do you mind, dear? I'm a bit tired." She was wiping tears from her cheeks.

"Certainly," he grunted. "We were nineteen when we found each other, and it was unbelievable. To suddenly know all the strange thoughts and dreams were real."

Gabrielle leaned forward and smiled as E'kul's hands were becoming more animate.

"I could see the look in her eyes as well. From that first instant, we both knew who we were and that there would never be anyone else. That we would never need anyone else." He paused a moment, taking a deep breath, "and then we ran away."

Gabriella shook her head. "I don't understand. What were you running from?"

"Everything," he said softly.

"We didn't even tell our parents." Yǔqíng took over the storytelling to give the old wolf a break. "We bought all the supplies we could afford and came straight here. "Well," she paused, "We did deviate to see Queen Qiàn in person along the way." She smiled in memory.

"She was so regal and beautiful. The perfect image of a warrior queen.

Such a pity she died barely a year later."

"When we arrived here, we weren't surprised to see the cavern infested with trolls," E'kul chimed in. "They like the more extensive tunnel networks of former mines more than natural caves, but they were easy enough to handle."

"How do you keep them out though? Not to mention how well supplied you clearly are, I mean, given your current condition," she finished as gently as she could. To be honest, she doubted the couple could handle even a single troll, much less live surrounded by them.

"Kill enough of them, and the rest wise up soon enough," E'kul chuckled. "They're also terrified by our other forms, and so they leave us be."

"You can both still transform?" Gabriella almost choked on her tea.

"Of course we can," Yǔqíng interjected, slightly confused by the question.

"Anyway, regarding the supplies, the trolls gather most of them for us.

I'm sure you saw at least a few useful items at the entrance to the mine," E'kul let the statement hang into a question.

"I did," she agreed, "but how did you get trolls to work for you?"

"Well, they don't really work for us," he corrected. "They may be stupid compared to us, but they're a lot smarter than people think. After enough trial and error, they learned the things we need. They don't want us to kill them all, so they provide us with these things."

"Even in your current state?"

"They see our lack of appearances as a sign we are satisfied," the raven grinned. "As my husband said, they are still pretty stupid."

"Okay, I guess I'm with you so far, but I still don't understand the running away part."

Yǔqíng looked toward her husband and nodded.

"We know the real reason you were surprised to find us alive," E'kul grunted. Whatever happened to this world, the two of us should have died in the fighting. Where else would two brave warriors of our caliber be?

Certainly not hiding for nearly eighty years in an abandoned mine." "I wasn't going to say anything about it," Gabriella responded neutrally.

"But it's what you were thinking," E'kul challenged. "Admittedly, yes," she couldn't lie to them.

"We failed you, Angel," Yǔqíng started to cry.

"I'm sorry, but I don't understand. Please stop crying." She started to get up but stopped at E'kul's raised hand.

"You made a promise to us, and upheld your end, but we wasted it," he said, looking down. "We've wasted this new life you granted us," he admitted shamefully as Yǔqíng merely nodded.

"Perhaps you should both simply start from the beginning," Gabriella suggested.

"Very well," E'kul agreed. "Our lives together have been a blend of love and terror. The moment we realized the truth of who we were, we were terrified of losing it again. That's why we ran away."

"But what is it you're afraid of?" she prodded.

"Death, everything, you name it," he lowered his eyes again. "We ran away to hide from the world, so that we could maximize how long this life would last. Maybe it doesn't make sense, considering we have proof of what comes next, but it's the truth. We left our courage and bravery in our previous lives."

"You both demonstrated tremendous courage when you saved Qiàn after sneaking inside her body. That wasn't very long ago, cosmically speaking anyway," she countered.

"That was different, considering what we were. Now that we're corporeal again, it's different. I guess we just weren't ready to come back." He started weeping softly as Yŭqíng began patting his hand.

"Is that the reason you came, Angel? To judge us?" Yŭqíng asked quietly.

"I sense there's plenty of judgment in this room already, without me adding to it." She watched as they both dipped their heads in agreement and shame. "But, more important to me at the moment is that I couldn't sense you. I still can't, by the way." She started extending her wings forward. "May I?"

The couple nodded, and Gabriella touched a wing tip to each forehead while closing her eyes.

"Ah, there you are," she mumbled, and started to grin, but the grin quickly turned to confusion. "That's odd."

"What's wrong?" Yŭqíng spoke up first.

"Nothing, and that's the problem. I sense no corruption."

"Well," E'kul started to answer, "whatever is happening on this world never found us here."

"You don't understand," she withdrew her wings, "it doesn't work like that. This is not a physical fight, and it's covering your entire world." She narrowed her eyes and wrinkled her nose, "Just let me think a moment."

The couple sat silently for a moment, not knowing what else to do. "I think this is my Father's work," Gabriella spoke softly.

"What do you mean?" Yŭqíng asked.

"To be honest, when I made my promise to you back then, I didn't know how to fulfill it. It was hard enough to extract you from the normal flow and prevent your erasure. The destiny of all wolves and ravens, too broken to continue," she admitted sadly.

"I didn't know what to do next, and then my Father was there, and then *something* happened, and then it was over. I was told to care for you until you were ready and then send you back here. My memories are not very reliable in many areas.

"Some things I forgot by choice, while other things my Father wiped out. Now, I have all my true memories back, but it's like seeing two lives next to each other." She shook her head, as if to clear it. "However, his intervention is the only thing that explains why you haven't been corrupted."

"The All-Father is protecting us?" It was difficult for either of them to accept.

"Not directly, no, but if I am right, you *did* come into direct contact with him. He is a being beyond our comprehension and has the power to match. His touch is blocking the corruption and keeping my brother and me from sensing you."

"Your brother?" E'kul inquired.

"Okay, it's about time I explain what's happening on this world." She spent the next hour giving the best explanation she could, including her plans for one final desperate battle.

"That is quite a story," Yŭqíng offered.

"It's not a story."

The raven nodded to concede the point.

"Well, your counter sounds a bit hopeless," E'kul said plainly, "but if anyone can pull it off, you and your friends can."

"Maybe, but we could use help."

"What are you…you can't really be serious?" His eyes went wide, even as his jaw went slack.

Gabriella simply stared back at them, flexing her wings a bit,

"She's blind, and I can barely walk." He was gesturing furiously, which brought on a coughing fit.

Yŭqíng handed him a bottle from the other side of the bed, and E'kul paused to clear his throat.

"You would, of course, not be as you are now," Gabriella said as gently as she could.

"No," was all E'kul would say.

"Dear," Yŭqíng tried to interject quickly.

"I said no," he repeated sternly.

"How much time do either of you think you have left?"

"It doesn't matter," E'kul was starting to sound angry. "We want every last moment of it. That's how terrified we are to die. It may sound shameful or cowardly, but it is the truth. Please stop making me repeat it."

Gabriella was about to answer when Yǔqíng raised a hand.

"May I speak on this?" she asked, waiting until she heard verbal consent from the others. "I know what you fear, husband, because I fear it as well. It is why we made such cowardly decisions throughout our lives."

"Raven, I-"

"I believe you said I could speak," she cut him off. "It was worse for me than it was for you, dear, because I had to endure something you never did."

"I know, Raven," he spoke gently, as he moved a hand to her stomach.

She shook her head. "That's not what I meant. I meant that I had to watch, and not just at the end, but every time before. Every time you fought to protect me, I could do nothing but watch.

"I knew how that day was going to end the moment that bag was suddenly pulled over my head." She paused a moment as fresh tears began to form. "Once I was tied to that stake, and the bag was removed, things just got worse.

"I saw you hiding in the crowd and knew what you were planning. I knew you saw my signals to run away, just as I knew you would ignore them. You fought so bravely in that hopeless battle, while all I could do was watch and burn." She began crying softly.

"It didn't do either of us much good in the end," he whispered, trying to comfort his wife.

"At least you got to fight." She looked up at him with eyes that could no longer see. "It sounds as if the world we knew is truly gone completely. If there is to be one final hopeless battle to bring it back, then this time I want to fight." She turned to face the angel.

"I want to fight."

"Are you sure about this?" E'kul prodded.

"Yes, and there's more to it than that." She turned back to her husband and squeezed his hand. "We are both ashamed of the choices we have made.

However, we both know we would make the same ones again, despite our regret. As cowardly as those choices were, they are the *only* reason we are still alive now to make *this* choice.

"My Wolf, don't you see? If we make the right choice now, it vindicates us. Our past cowardice is forgiven." Her unseeing eyes were full of hope.

Gabriella was careful not to say anything. Things were progressing the way she needed them to, and she didn't want to risk screwing it up. She did feel a bit guilty about how she had manipulated the situation by making them repeat things out loud that she already knew. Still, with creation itself at stake, she could no longer let rules stand in her way.

"Alright, Raven," E'kul finally spoke up. "If this is the direction you choose to fly, I'll choose to follow as I always have."

Yŭqíng smiled and leaned over to kiss her husband. Once they separated,

E'kul looked to the angel.

"What must we do?" he asked.

Gabriella stood and began to spread her wings. "I believe you already know the answer to that."

E'kul swallowed loudly as the wings reached around them both. "Is it going to hurt?"

"You don't need to worry about that." She gently finished closing her wings. "Just go to sleep," she whispered sweetly. "When you wake, come find us. Choose your moment."

Gabriella began to sing softly. A song that could never be heard or understood by mortals, until the time of their passing. Her song accelerated what was already happening inside their bodies.

After they had fallen deeply into their final rest, she laid them on the bed, making them as comfortable as possible. They would wake up when they were needed most, and not before. As she left the cavern, she spared a final glance at the elderly couple.

Gabriella had been walking a very fine line for a long time, and she couldn't help but wonder if maybe this time she had gone too far.

*****

Outside Kukkug's Lair

"Perfect," Kukkug exclaimed after hearing his creation's voice. It was nice to know all the time spent on this project would pay off.

"See, dear," he turned the head back around, "I told you I could do it.

Well," he addressed the demon, "it'll be two more days before they're in range, maybe three." He rubbed his chin for a moment.

"There's no point in bringing any of the others across this early. Can you resist the urge to attack them until the appropriate time?"

The demon bobbed its large head up and down twice.

"Alright, good, but I still want you inside the cavern with us, so I can watch you. It's not that I don't trust you, but I don't trust you," he chuckled, picking up the head and moving to return to the doorway.

After another pair of head bobs, the demon followed, despite its curved horns scraping across the ceiling. Scrapes that appeared very similar to the old markings already present.

Kukkug settled in and set his companion on his lap as he watched the attack force continue to advance. His sister had rejoined them, which was good.

Gabriella had ventured off toward the eastern mountain range, but he didn't have a clue what her reasoning was. Perhaps she was trying to enlist the trolls' aid? Those creatures were certainly

193

powerful enough to be useful, but too stupid to be adequately controlled. The fact that she had come back empty-handed was proof enough of that.

His sister must be getting desperate.

*****

Attack Force, Two Days from Target

"Welcome back," Xuě said respectfully, pulling her horse up next to Gabriella's. "Where did you go?"

"Just a little sightseeing. Did they ask about my absence?" She nodded toward her friends.

"No, they just said you normally do your own thing, and to not worry about it."

Gabriella could hear Larg laughing from his position behind and to the right of Xuě.

"You truly don't have much faith in me, do you Xuě?" she asked.

"I believe that much has already been made abundantly clear, but if you perhaps meant whether or not I have changed my opinion since our last conversation, no, I have not."

They both heard Larg loudly suck in air and gasp as the raven arguably insulted the pure celestial being to her face.

"And here I thought we were on such good terms now," Gabriella smirked as she gave the overly sarcastic response.

"As I have said before, I regret some of my actions and words toward you," Xuě said softly. "However, that is not the same as believing you will be successful," she shrugged.

Gabriella's shoulders tensed at the words, and Xuě immediately regretted speaking them.

"If it makes you feel any better, Yǎniū, I was being honest before when I said your intentions are good. I truly believe you are doing the best you can," she offered sincerely, "just that it won't

194

be enough." She looked toward her great-grandparents.

"If salvation exists for us, it is with them. Anyone who knows the stories knows this to be true. Tell me the truth, Yǎniū," she sighed, "where would you be without them?"

"A pile of undiscovered bones in a dark forest somewhere," she grinned humorlessly as she threw the words back in the raven's face.

"How did you know-"

"I know everything, Xuě." She faced the raven and dropped the complete control she had over her physical form ever so slightly.

The angel's pure blue eyes changed. Suddenly, there were images of other worlds, stars, and even whole galaxies, as all of creation seemed to flash by. She stopped as she saw the wolf and raven's expressions begin changing from wonder to fear.

"Xuě, listen to me," she said softly. "I appreciate your honesty, and I also agree with most of what you have said. I have learned so much from my friends and by watching others. Maybe there's only one chance in infinity for us to be successful," she paused.

"Even if that's the case," she finally continued. "I believe that we can find it together. I also harbor no ill will toward you for anything you have done or said to me. In my own way, I find your words as valuable as theirs."

"That's kind of you to say."

"Now that that's out of the way, I assume you have more questions for me?" she arched a brow at the raven.

"How did you know?"

"The only time you go out of your way to talk to me is when you have questions," she chuckled to herself.

Larg's guttural laughs could be heard as well.

"I suppose that is correct, even if you refuse to answer most of them,"

Xuě accused.

"I can't give you knowledge mortals are not supposed to possess," Gabriella said, rolling her eyes.

"Your very presence here does that," Xuě countered.

"That's a fair point, I'll admit," she sighed. "I suppose the rules aren't essential anymore, at least until we fix things." She wrinkled her nose as she considered the situation for a few moments. "Okay, if it directly assists us, I will answer any question you have," the angel decided.

"That's excellent, considering our main question is why we can't transform anymore. Solving that problem will make us far more effective in the coming battle."

"I agree, and I'm surprised it took you this long to ask me."

"Honestly, Miss Angel," Larg spoke up finally, "we've been talking a lot with Qiàn and K'tar, and the elders who came with us. We still can't figure it out, and in some way, I think we may actually fear the answer. However, it is a question we must face."

"And K'tar and Qiàn couldn't help?"

"No, all they did was embarrass us," Larg growled.

"It was a logical question, Larg, and it made perfect sense coming from their perspective," Xuě cut in.

"Okay, now I'm curious, what did they say?"

Larg refused to answer, but Xuě saw no harm in it.

"Qiàn asked us if we had shared a bed properly yet. If the answer was no, she ordered us to do so immediately."

Gabriella's laugh was so sudden and loud that it attracted the attention of several other riders.

"I know Qiàn is very direct, but she didn't have to say it like that, especially in front of Hóngwén and Arahk," Larg complained.

"And what, may I ask, was your answer?" Gabriella asked mischievously.

"None of your concern," Xuě snapped, although she blushed deeply. "Besides, that is obviously not the problem, considering our people as a whole are not celibate."

"Good observation, and I am happy you have become comfortable enough to take the final step while there's still time to enjoy it," Gabriella grinned.

"I didn't answer that question," Xuě insist.

"No, but your face did."

"Well, since my privacy has been violated, may I ask if you've ever…you know?" Xuě asked sheepishly.

"Of course I have," she winked.

"Wait, really?" Xuě and Larg echoed each other.

"Oh, don't look so surprised," she rolled her eyes. "You already know I was mortal for over two years, and most people found my body to be perfect. I was also convinced I would die along with everyone else," she explained.

"Under those circumstances, why wouldn't I take advantage of everything mortal life has to offer?" She allowed the rhetorical question to hang for a moment before continuing. "However, I am unable to form the type of bond K'tar and Qiàn have for one another, or the bond the two of you have.

"I feel love for all mortal life equally, and while I do have friends who are closer to me than others, I will never experience the type of love one has toward a mate. K'tar and Qiàn have told me this prevents me from truly experiencing the physical side of things. I suppose they are correct, but as I said, I have no frame of reference."

"I see," Xuě was nodding slowly.

"Whatever the two of you wish to believe, my advice to you is to simply face facts. There is a very good chance all of us will be dead, or worse, within two or three days. Enjoy the time you have left as much as you can."

"Can we please get back to why they would say that at all?" Larg cut in.

"Remember the stories, Wolf," Xuě began before the angel could. "The false law kept our people apart. Being together physically was impossible, so doing it successfully later *proved* the law false. That's what broke the wolves' chains."

Gabriella was nodding along with Xuě's succinct explanation.

"But, Yǎniū, as we all know, it's not the same problem now. We all know what we are supposed to be, so why can't we do it?"

"The best I can do is guess, and I don't think you'll like it."

"We need the information, Yǎniū, please," Xuě prodded harder.

"Your people don't want to, and that includes the two of you," she said simply.

"That can't be right," Larg grunted. "It's all we want right now." "I'm sorry, but it's true." She held up her hand to stop the coming interruption.

"Xuě, you're in a unique position. Your mind was broken for so long, and suddenly, you feel better. It's giving you a much more positive outlook on things, and I believe Larg is sharing that with you. But it doesn't change what you feel deep down about this world.

"I know that Qiàn explained to you how both wolves and ravens on this world developed differently and for a longer period of time than is normal. May I assume you have shared this information with Larg?"

She nodded.

"Well, because of this, a stronger emotional bond between a wolf and a raven is necessary. It's also easier to mentally block yourselves. Xuě, your people don't want to be demon killers. They just want to *be*, and most of them simply want to die," she finished sadly.

"Sorry, Yǎniū, but I have to disagree with that," Xuě shook her head.

"I believe I was an exception."

"You misunderstand." Gabriella tried to correct the conversation. "There is a difference between wanting to die and being willing to do it yourself, as you were. Your people wake up angry with this dead world, and when they lie down to sleep, they are not happy about the day they lived. No, they are furious about repeating this empty existence for even another day.

"They find happiness in small doses when they can, and they are too proud to take their own lives, but that's it. Why do you think every single one of your people volunteered for this mission?"

"Because it's the last chance we have of saving our world," Xuě answered confidently. "What other reason could there be?"

"Well, you're half right, but it isn't to save the world. This *will* be the final battle for this world, and perhaps more. I have told you all what is at stake, but you don't really comprehend it. To them," she waved an arm to encompass the entire formation, "it is just their last and best chance to die bravely." There were tears in her eyes.

"You all hate this reality, but you've all accepted it. Accepted that you've already lost. Xuě, have I described demon killers to you?" Xuě looked thoughtful, as Larg looked away completely.

"Yǎniū, you speak of fear and acceptance, and maybe you are correct.

There are, however, other emotions to consider."

"Yes, there are," Gabriella met the young raven's steady and piercing gaze.

"The emotions you have mentioned are not the emotions that drive me."

"What drives you, Xuě?" Gabriella's eyes were hard. "Tell me why you are here in this moment, seeking to defend a dead world?"

"You keep saying this is the final battle. Are you certain?" "I am."

"Then, logically, this is my last chance. Not to prove myself. No, it is too late for that. This is the last chance for me to take vengeance for my parents." Her gaze seemed to cloud over slightly, growing dangerous. "No matter what, Yǎniū, I *will* have my vengeance."

Larg growled his agreement.

"I urge caution to you both. Fear and the desire for vengeance are natural, but if you let them control you, these feelings are the most common things that lead mortals to darkness."

"Good," Xuě uttered the single word with such conviction it took the angel a moment to respond.

"Excuse me?" It was the only thing she could think of saying.

"Look around you, Yǎniū." Xuě paused a moment as she waved an arm around the area. "It's about time we had some darkness on *our* side. "Come on, Wolf, it's time to make our rounds."

Gabriella wanted to call after Xuě. To tell her the path she was walking was too dangerous. However, something held her tongue. Instead of shouting a warning, she found herself carefully contemplating what Xuě had said.

Chapter 13

Kukkug's Lair

"It's finally time!" Kukkug practically squealed as he hugged his companion. "You," he pointed to his creation, "find somewhere high up. Remember, I want everything the same, including the opening crash.

The massive demon dipped its head low before lumbering out.

"Now, for the others," he mumbled, waving his hand at the doorway.

The cavern quickly became too crowded, so he moved outside. It didn't matter since his command had already been given. The demons began forming groups automatically, and he walked among them even as the numbers in each group continued to grow. In general, they acted according to his will, but he needed to issue specific commands to keep them focused.

"Okay, big boys," he stepped in front of a group of Greater Demons. "Your job is the most important." He waited for the answering hisses. "Keep my sister's pets busy.

"They'll likely destroy you all, but you don't care about that, do you?"

The group of fifteen Greater Demons hissed acknowledgement of their task.

"Good. Just help my surprise slow them down, while I play with my sister. As for the rest of you," he faced the growing masses, "kill them all. When every member of their force is dead, you may head for their city and finish the rest." He ran his gaze slowly from left to right.

"I'm serious, the attack force must die first. You," he motioned for a winged Greater Demon to come forward.

The indicated demon obeyed and knelt down.

"Take charge of your winged brethren and help keep my sister busy." The demon hissed in confusion.

"Of course you can't win," Kukkug rolled his eyes, "but better you than me. You only need to keep her fighting while I talk to her. When she breaks, you'll know when it happens-leave her alone and join the others," he explained.

"You don't need to fight; focus on controlling the others. I plan to use hundreds. In addition, every demon who comes across will have the ability to sacrifice their long-range attacks in favor of growing wings. You may decide this evolution is useful."

The demon hissed again, and Kukkug placed a hand on its head. Suddenly, the creature grew larger and more intelligent.

"There," he said, satisfied with his work. "They will listen to you as if it were me, and more are still coming through. Don't fail me," he grinned.

The demon commander bobbed its head once and then began hissing instructions to most of the other groups.

"Well, now that that's taken care of, let's get you settled," he whispered to his companion.

As Kukkug reentered the cave, the flow of demons automatically parted around him. Once he returned to the cavern housing the doorway, he looked carefully for the best spot. Using a wingtip, he carved out a small alcove at eye level. When finished, he gently set the head down.

"Okay, dear," he spoke to the still perfectly preserved severed head. "You just wait here and keep your eyes peeled. Let me know if and when they make it this far." He bent down and kissed the forehead gently.

"I'm counting on you," he hollered back over his shoulder as he moved to get in the proper position for the coming battle.

✳✳✳✳✳

"Raven, I'm not afraid to admit that I'm getting very nervous about this."

"You and me both," Qiàn answered the voice in her mind. "We're close enough that we could get attacked at any moment, so be ready." "I'm always ready."

"I know." Qiàn was riding comfortably on the large wolf's back, not even bothering to crouch yet. Her wings were half spread, and her eyes glowed gold with anticipation. The staff clasped to her back was glowing gold as well, clearly no simple wooden weapon.

"So, I'm guessing Yǎniū hasn't briefed you on any alternate strategies that may actually work?" Qiàn asked hopefully.

"You know she hasn't," K'tar's mental voice answered. "I'm starting to think we may have made a mistake in not telling her what we know."

"Correction, what we *believe*," Qiàn gave her head a quick shake, "and we didn't." Qiàn's voice held nothing but confidence. "Yǎniū has to be who she was meant to be, not what we tell her to be. You know that already." She leaned forward to scratch the wolf's neck.

"Despite what's at stake?"

"The level of risk, or consequence if you will, does not change the base equation," Qiàn insist. "She'll think of something. She always does. We just need to be ready to back her up."

"And soon by the feel of it," K'tar agreed. "You feel it as well, I assume?"

"Can't miss it. I hope the others can handle it." Qiàn felt as if the darkness around her was trying to crush her. Even without a real body, she felt physically ill.

"As long as they don't get too close to the cave, they should be okay. Besides," K'tar's sentence was cut off by Gabriella, suddenly launching into the air ahead of them.

It was hard to tell, but K'tar believed he saw another winged being hovering in the sky. That had to be him, and Gabriella's launch was the signal to begin the battle. Wolves and ravens charged in every direction, beginning their bloody diversion, while K'tar sprinted directly for the cave. He could feel Qiàn rising to a crouch, while she unhooked the staff from her back.

"How long?" K'tar shouted inside Qiàn's mind. He knew speed and surprise were their primary assets.

"Can you maintain this pace?" she asked, watching the trees flash by. "Yes."

"About five minutes, but that's only if we don't stop to fight. Do your best, but I'm no longer certain that's possible." Qiàn's raven sight pierced the darkness, revealing that one of their primary assumptions was being proven false.

There were far more demons than predicted. This was no simple scare tactic, but a final extermination. To make it worse, if they stopped to lend assistance, the primary goal of the battle would be unfulfilled.

Gabriella had been wrong, and the only chance for victory would be to write off the entire attack force. Sacrificial lambs, led by their own great- granddaughter. Even if they did win, it would be another fifty wolves and ravens stuck in the Dark Realm to suffer for the rest of eternity.

These thoughts, and more, plagued both their minds as K'tar forced himself to move faster. Speed was the only thing that would save anyone, and the only thing he cared about. He ignored the demons and even the thick trees all around them, preferring a straight line.

Qiàn wielded her staff like the expert she was, sending bursts of light in all directions and crushing the life from any unfortunate demons who got too close.

The demons tried to band together to block their forward

progress. It didn't work.

K'tar simply howled at their foolishness, dissipating five of them with his jaws and powerful forelegs. The rest were left so far behind, so quickly, there was no point in even attacking them. It seemed as if nothing could stand in their way.

At least, until a large crash nearby rocked the ground beneath them.

They didn't notice it at first, but the smaller demons began fleeing the area. The path to the cave was clear.

"RRRRRAAAAAVVVVVEEEEENNNNNSSSSS!"

K'tar skidded to a halt so suddenly that Qiàn was nearly thrown free. The horrific battle cry froze their blood—or at least would have, had they had any. They separated, leaping in opposite directions, barely avoiding the green fire that came for them.

It was impossible, they knew that. He was gone, long since destroyed; they knew that, too. Their extra senses screamed at them, telling them this was nothing more than an above-average Greater Demon.

It didn't matter.

Qiàn and K'tar were second to none. Only a full celestial could match their raw power, but they weren't perfect. They were dealing with too much. Their world ruined again, their descendants stolen, and now this? To face the same creature that had effectively killed them twice before? A beast they had seen destroyed long ago?

It was too much.

Neither of them understood the concept of falling back or retreating. Regarding others—units they commanded, for example, certainly, but not for themselves. It was the only thing keeping them fighting, but their movements were too slow and uncoordinated. There was too much shock and fear.

Qiàn was swatted aside as if she were nothing but an annoying bird, while K'tar was kicked away with similar ease. Neither of them sustained any serious injury. Yet another piece of evidence that this creature was not an actual threat.

It still wasn't enough to counter what their eyes and ears were telling them.

K'tar lost his concentration and reverted to his normal form, holding a sword and a large tower shield. Qiàn was able to keep her wings, but her eyes cleared as she moved behind her husband, staff at the ready.

"What do we do?" K'tar growled loudly, without looking back.

"I, I don't, I don't know," Qiàn screamed, her voice cracking a bit.

They both took an involuntary step back as the demon closed the distance. The vicious claws on each hand warned all others to stay away. Its bulbous red eyes gleamed in the darkness, and its giant triangular maw seemed to grin in anticipation.

Suddenly, golden arrows seemed to pepper the demon's face from above.

Another raven came streaking downward, tossing aside her bow in favor of daggers. She slammed into the beast's face, burying daggers in its eyes.

At the same time, a wolf burst from the trees, tossing the remnants of a demon aside. The wolf charged the massive demon's legs, loudly growling the whole time.

Between the two fresh attackers, the demon was knocked over. They were both able to avoid the creature's claws, which were moving far more quickly than anything that size should be able to. Qiàn and K'tar were frozen in shock. At least until the demon began opening its enormous maw.

"No!" Qiàn shouted and lunged forward, only to be stopped by K'tar.

"Xuě, get back!"

The other raven ignored the warning and instead shoved a hand into the demon's mouth. She jammed a blade up into the upper half of its jaws and was rewarded with a roar of pain. All the while, the wolf was doing his best to rip one of its legs off.

"It's a Soul Eater, Xuě, you have to run!" Qiàn cried out.

Xuě simply waited for the demon's mouth to be completely open before shoving both her wings completely forward. Screaming in defiance, she forced her wings down the demon's throat and fired light directly into its body. The beast tried closing its mouth, but Xuě's wings and body kept it forced open.

Qiàn and K'tar continued shouting warnings, despite Xuě and Larg ignoring them. Finally, the demon blew apart.

"That was for my mother." Xuě spat on the ground where the demon had been. "Are you two okay?" She looked back at Qiàn and K'tar.

Larg was howling loudly in victory, and K'tar changed forms to join him. Despite his successful participation in the battle, Larg lowered his head briefly to the larger wolf.

"We're fine, dear." Qiàn stepped forward to embrace her. "That was amazing, but how?" She asked the obvious question.

"You know that thing wasn't the same, right?"

"Yes, I see that now, forgive our momentary weakness. However, that wasn't my intended question."

As if on cue, howls came from all directions, and two dozen ravens burst through the treetops. Their brilliant golden wings dissipated the darkness all around them. It was magnificent enough to distract them from how badly outnumbered they all were.

"We have decided to no longer accept this reality," Xuě answered. "It's time to create our own," she declared, as Larg ran up to her.

Qiàn hugged her again. "I'm so proud of you."

"You never told me how much it hurt," Xuě whispered back.

"Well, you were effectively ripped apart, just not physically. Don't worry, dear, it only feels that way the first time," Qiàn laughed. "Now, I want you to take your ravens and-"

"Don't the two of you have a mission to complete?" Xuě cut Qiàn off with her question, as she hopped on Larg's back.

"Of course, but-"

"Then I suggest you get to it." She nodded smartly, dismissing Qiàn and K'tar.

Qiàn smiled, "As you wish, Your Majesty." She bowed her head slightly before jumping onto K'tar's back. "Xuě!" she cried out before the pair disappeared into the trees.

Xuě turned her head just in time to see the golden staff twirling toward her. More out of reflex than anything else, her right hand shot out to catch it. No sooner had her fingers wrapped around the weapon than a burning sensation began to course through her hand and arm.

"That staff is not meant for mortal hands," Qiàn called out, "but it's a weapon befitting a queen. I trust you are capable enough to survive until I return to collect it?" Qiàn asked as she drew a pair of long daggers for herself.

Xuě simply held the staff high above her head, as Larg howled. Then, they both darted toward the sounds of battle.

"Try not to think about it, Raven," K'tar offered, once Xuě and Larg were out of sight.

"How can I not?" she sighed. "You sense the numbers as well as I do." She was doing her best not to cry. "Even transformed, the attack force doesn't stand a chance without us."

"I know, but the doorway must be closed first. You know that."

"It's hard to care about creation when it no longer contains those precious to you."

"If it makes you feel any better, there's a large group of the bigger ones between us and the target," he pointed out.

"It does, actually," Qiàn grinned, and crouched lower. "Let's go."

*****

Gabriella did her best to get within range of her brother, but it wasn't working.

Wave after wave of winged demons were blanketing the sky.

They weren't difficult to handle, but they were in the way. It took time she didn't have to deal with them. All the while, her brother hovered just out of reach.

"Stop this foolishness and face me yourself!" Gabriella screamed, knowing he would hear her.

"No," came the simple reply. Despite the distance, it sounded as if he were standing right next to her.

"*Coward!*" she accused.

"Simply intellect and prudence, dear sister," he laughed. "I'm about to win. Why would I risk that on a fight I am sure to lose?" he scoffed. "Sorry, but it's not my fault you're still the arrogant and ignorant child you always were. One of us had to grow up."

Gabriella forced herself to fight harder and faster than she ever had.

She was twirling so quickly that small, brief tornadoes were forming and affecting the combatants on the ground. The ravens, which she was both amazed and thankful to see, were getting the worst of it. With little to no experience in the air, they couldn't handle the additional disruptions in the air currents.

It still wasn't enough. She wasn't sure if taking her brother's wings would work, but she couldn't get close enough to even try.

"I'm going to stop you!" she cried, as she sliced another demon in half.

"No, you aren't." He rolled his eyes, not caring that she was too far away to see it. "Time is on my side, after all, and as you can see, you can't so much as touch me."

As frustrated as she was, Gabriella tried to remember that this whole fight was just a distraction. Her main job was to keep him busy while her friends disrupted the doorway. Kukkug challenging her this way was proof in her mind that he didn't understand her true strategy.

"Even after all this time, you still speak to me as a child," she sneered.

"Even after all this time, you insist on acting like one," he said matter-of-factly. "Despite what I did, you're nearly clueless about the world around you. You seek to repair a balance you do not understand, and, as such, cannot stop me.

"Your suffering was so great that even I could feel it," he grinned, "and I relished it. When it vanished, I thought you either destroyed or that you at least learned the truth, as I have."

"I may have been living in ignorance for a time, but that time has passed." With a powerful movement of her wings, the demons around her were blown away. She made a beeline for her brother, but dozens more demons moved to intercept her.

"I'll never forget again," she growled.

"Forget?" Kukkug looked confused. "You forgot?" After a moment, he started laughing so hard that tears filled his eyes. "I know you don't understand what happened, but I never imagined you would be so heartless as to forget." He continued to laugh at her.

"What is there to understand?" she hollered back. "The mortals would call you a murderer, but I know you're far worse than that. You have to be stopped!"

"Murderer? What are you talking about?" Kukkug paused in thought for a few moments before suddenly laughing again. "That's what you think happened?" He was holding his sides. "This is too much. This body can't handle what you're doing to it." The words came out in a garbled mess as Kukkug was nearly doubled over.

She had no idea what game he was playing, but she was growing furious. It was bad enough that she had to remember the truth once already; to have it implied she was still wrong was beyond irritating. She reminded herself again that this was just a distraction. The more time he wasted talking, the better.

"Fine, brother, why don't you enlighten me, while I continue destroying your creations?" She yelled the question as she split another demon in half.

"If you wish, but it's rather simple," he shrugged. "I've never killed anyone, at least not on purpose, ergo, not a murderer. I let these adorable little cuties do all that for me. In fact, my own creations," he waved to indicate the demons, "are the only things I've ever intentionally destroyed.

Well, except those two lovely ravens I met when I first arrived here.

Although technically, they attacked me first when all I wanted was a conversation. I believe mortals would call that self-defense."

The ludicrous statements shocked her. So much so that a demon got close enough to rake its claws across her back. The instant pain dragged her out of her stupor.

"I watched you kill the other celestials, the angels. You did it right in front of me, you lunatic!"

Kukkug shook his head. "We're eternal beings, you little idiot," he snapped back. "You can't kill an eternal being, so instead, I just took them with me."

"What are you talking about?" She finally got close enough to strike, but he merely laughed and levitated out of reach.

"Dear sister, tell me, where do demons come from?"

"You twist souls into dark and monstrous creatures to mirror yourself!" she screamed, feeling her anger beginning to rise again.

"An over-dramatization, certainly, but not totally inaccurate," he admitted. "So, tell me where *Greater* Demons come from?"

Gabriella hesitated at the question. She had no idea, but she didn't care either. There was no reason for her to even consider the question.

"You use more souls to accomplish the same thing," she finally answered.

"More so-" he cut himself off. "You really believe that idiocy, don't you?" He started shaking his head and chuckling. "I suppose it's better than facing the truth."

"What are you talking about?" she scoffed. She could still hear the voices and screams of her murdered siblings and wouldn't allow herself to ever forget them again.

"A perfect being, forged out of pure happiness and joy," Kukkug began to explain. "What would happen to such a being if it were suddenly exposed to never-ending suffering and torment? How long would it last? What would it turn into?" His grin became a sneer.

"No." It was all Gabriella could muster. She could already tell what her brother was trying to say, and there was simply no possibility of it being true. Was there?

"It is true, sister." Kukkug clearly knew what she was thinking. "When they are ready, I mold them. I shape them into what I need; however, a core of the original always remains."

"Shut up!" She was already moving more slowly. Her body was trembling with so much anger and hatred that she didn't even notice the demons had stopped attacking her.

"Deep within the recesses of the mind of every Greater Demon is one of your former siblings begging, no…demanding, that you save them. When you destroy the demon, their consciousness is simply recycled into a new demonic form."

"Liar!"

"You are the last of them, and not only have you failed to answer their call, but you chose to *forget them!*" He started laughing again, loudly enough that those on the ground heard nothing but thunder.

"I don't understand this game, brother, but it ends now," she said as she tossed her swords away. Instead, she drew the flaming sword from her right wing.

"Oooo, pretty," he commented dismissively. "Before you settle on what is truth, and what isn't, I urge you to simply listen. You claim you can hear them again, so what exactly are you hearing?" He crossed his arms and simply waited.

The voices in her mind were getting louder. It was expected, given the conversation they were having, but something was wrong.

There was no pattern. A memory should be repeated over and over. These voices were constantly changing. Icy claws worked their way through her very essence, as she realized the final truth.

Gabriella wasn't remembering the past. She was hearing the present! "Ah," Kukkug saw the realization in her eyes. "You figured it out, didn't you? I didn't murder our siblings. Oh, no, no," he grinned. "I took their wings *and brought them with me to hell!*"

She couldn't move or speak.

"Again with this?" Kukkug moved to within inches of her. "You really are still just a child, aren't you?" he sighed. "Easier to take your wings and be done with it, I suppose." He moved behind her, raising his sword.

Gabriella braced herself for an attack that never came. Unable to even turn her head, she had no idea what her brother was doing.

For his part, Kukkug was trying to strike, but something was preventing it. So, the Old Man had made it impossible to do such a thing here after all. That was alright.

She couldn't see the failure, and his primary strategy was already bearing fruit. As simple-minded as his sister was, it wasn't difficult to have her believe anything he wanted.

"This was supposed to be fun," he made sure to mutter loud enough for her to hear, "but you're ruining it for me." He moved back in front and stared directly into Gabriella's motionless eyes. "So, this is what I'm going to do.

"I'm going to go down there," he pointed with his sword, "and rip your pets apart." He could feel his sister's emotions spike even further out of control. "That's right, I know everything that happens on this world, he leaned forward, "including your little strategy," he whispered. "I won the instant I set foot on this world, you ignorant child.

"I'm not taking those two souls either." His grin grew broader. "Instead, they will be ripped into non-existence. Then, I'll assist with the extermination of this world. Finally, when you're truly the last one left standing, I'll come back for you.

"You failed again," he whispered the final comment as he plummeted back down, sword at the ready.

The frozen angel was left behind, no longer even worth the attention of the remaining demons.

*****

"I think that thunder was Yǎniū and her brother," Qiàn guessed. "Agreed, and that last group slowed us down too much," K'tar growled.

"Speaking of which," he trailed off as a final pair of Greater Demons charged them. He increased speed, ignoring the closer demon.

As they passed the first demon, Qiàn leaped upward. Using her wings, she twirled through maneuvers far too complicated for the demon to track. Once close enough, her daggers and wings cut it to pieces.

K'tar met his target head-on, ignoring the claws raking his sides. Where Qiàn relied on speed as her primary defense, he just trusted in his ability to take the hits. The demon wasn't able to do anything as he held it down with his forelegs and used his jaws to rip it apart.

"K'tar, move!" Qiàn screamed.

He leaped away quickly, not even stopping to question his wife. It was that pure trust in Qiàn's judgement that saved him from the Dark One's blade. Clearly, something had gone wrong with the plan, but there wasn't anything they could do about it now.

The two of them had discussed how to properly face the Dark One and realized it would mostly come down to Qiàn. There was no doubt that his dark blade and wings would easily slice K'tar apart. They would need to dodge, which meant they required Qiàn's speed and precision. K'tar would try an occasional strike to help distract him, but Qiàn would be facing him head-on.

She blurred into position, as K'tar leaped in the opposite direction, and managed to deflect his blade. Shockingly, he looked little different from the average man. Sure, he had black armor, wings, and a black sword, but he didn't *look* very imposing.

It was the *feel* of facing him that told you this was no ordinary man.

The internal fear. The terrifying feel of shadows closing in from all around you. It was too much for a non-celestial. Even Qiàn could barely handle it.

There was no way for Qiàn to win, but she wasn't trying to. The only viable strategy was to hold him off until Gabriella showed up. By focusing on pure defense, Qiàn could at least survive, for a time anyway.

The Dark One was faster in his overall movements, but Qiàn was quicker close in. Anytime K'tar tried to strike, he was tossed aside by one of the Dark One's wings, as if by reflex. So, he forced himself to stop for a moment and study the fight, and in doing so, noticed the main advantage Qiàn had.

The Dark One's body was real, but Qiàn's wasn't. He might be able to ignore certain laws, but his body had to move within its own limitations. Qiàn's body didn't.

Ravens had a way of moving, even when simply walking, that was beyond graceful. It was the way they moved, accentuated by their exotic features, that made them so *popular* with males. Even K'tar was comfortable admitting how seductive Qiàn was, whether she was trying to be or not.

There was nothing seductive about her movements now.

Qiàn's movements were limited only by her imagination, and she had mastered three-dimensional movement even while alive. In death? Watching her now was almost nauseating. Parts of her body flowed like water, while parts remained as rigid as stone. Anytime the Dark One's sword or wings struck, that part of Qiàn's body simply wasn't there.

The battle wasn't the quick, simple victory the Dark One had been expecting, and it was clear he was growing angrier as it drew on.

Unfortunately, it was equally clear that he was rapidly growing stronger and faster. It would seem the more he fought, the more he learned how to use his celestial abilities in this realm.

That was a problem. One mistake from Qiàn, and it would be over for them both.

As he prepared to charge in to assist his wife, instinct alone caused him to look to the left. He was shocked to see another Raven Rider approaching at full blinding speed. Transformed or not, the others had been told to stay away from this fight. Proximity alone would slowly kill the mortals. Of course, in his current form, he couldn't talk to anyone but his wife.

All K'tar could do was charge in support of the fresh attackers.

Fortunately for them, the Dark One's frustration was blinding him to all others besides Qiàn.

Qiàn leaped straight backward to dodge his wing attack. At the same time, the second raven leaped up, flipped over, and rammed her stave into the base of his skull. There was an explosion of golden fire, and the force of the attack knocked him slightly off balance. Both wolves took the opportunity to slam into his body and take him to the ground.

Not wanting to take unnecessary risks, all four combatants immediately backed off to a safe distance.

The Dark One was already counterattacking with his wings. Had they been any slower, at least two of them would have likely been destroyed. As it was, the second wolf had a nasty gash along his left flank.

A gash that showed golden light instead of blood and began closing almost immediately. K'tar's eyes widened as he realized the new pair were not simple mortals.

How was that possible? The question would have to wait.

The four took turns distracting the Dark One. He didn't have any long- range abilities, which was their saving grace. Of course, the ravens' golden fire didn't seem very useful either, so they were forced to move in close.

Anytime the Dark One focused too much on a single individual, the wolf or raven would simply run away, while the other three flanked him.

Even with all four of them, however, there was no way to actually defeat him. It was still a matter of simply buying time. Where was Gabriella?

The Dark One was clearly getting even more frustrated and surprised everyone by ceasing his attacks.

"*GET BACK!*" Qiàn screamed the warning with barely a moment to spare.

The Dark One began to twirl, allowing his wings to slice and scissor in all directions. The wings kept growing larger and moved haphazardly. They did their best to evade, but Qiàn lost about half her right wing in the process.

"Raven, look up!" K'tar needed her to see what his eyes already detected.

"*SCATTER!*" She cried the order, even as she picked herself back up off the ground. She grabbed and mounted K'tar as he ran past and forced her wing to restore itself.

A simple red streak was coming towards them so quickly that it was outpacing the thunderous boom that was only now being heard behind it. The Dark One seemed confused that everyone had backed away, until he turned and looked up himself. No one was close enough to see the satisfied smile on his lips.

Gabriella collided with Kukkug with a force that left a sizeable crater and should have liquified both their bodies. The shockwave alone tossed the wolves and ravens further back, as if they were made of straw. Of course, the two celestials used the power of their wings to instantly restore their bodies, even as they were being destroyed.

As they bounced out of the crater, they were literally at each other's throats. While the celestials battled, the ravens shook off their shock and quickly remounted their wolves.

There was little time to understand what was happening. Qiàn and K'tar still had a mission to complete, and there were hordes of demons everywhere. They tried ignoring them and simply charging through, but that strategy left them too vulnerable to the demons' long-range abilities.

They easily slaughtered any demons they encountered, but it was taking too long. So far, the new pair was doing their best to help, but their presence alone was confusing.

"I don't understand," Qiàn called out, as her newly formed wing took the head off another demon. "Yǎniū told us reinforcements could no longer cross the barrier, and why are there only two of you?"

"That's not where we came from, and who's Yǎniū?" Yǔqíng answered, spraying golden fire from her stave.

The two wolves were sprinting around in circles. They were killing anything they could find, but remained within support range of the two ravens who were flipping and twirling right above ground level.

Despite the battle they were actively fighting, and despite how desperately they needed to reach the doorway, K'tar kept looking back toward Gabriella's fight.

Neither celestial seemed to be using swords anymore. It was all fists and wings. Every blow seemed to send fresh shockwaves through the area, felling trees and tossing combatants on both sides around. The fight itself seemed too personal, and he didn't like what he was seeing.

K'tar would be lying if he claimed to fully understand his new existence or what was at stake. He didn't need to. His new home represented all that was good and joyous in all of creation. He truly believed that and gladly fought for it.

Gabriella was a pure representation of that home, even if she didn't fully understand herself.

He had always known there were secret depths and strengths to her that she had yet to discover. Logically, her brother and his home represented the opposite. The enemy. However, in this moment, save the color of their wings and armor, he couldn't tell the difference.

He was watching two monsters trying to rip each other apart.

*****

Gabriella was holding her brother's breastplate at the neck as she repeatedly drove her fist into his face. At the same time, their wings seemed to be engaged in a separate battle of their own. All the while, Kukkug simply smiled, restoring his body as quickly as it was injured.

"Why are you mad at me?" Kukkug tried to sound confused. "I've been nothing but honest with you from the beginning." The fist slamming into his face didn't affect his speech. "It was through *your* actions that the others were taken and are suffering. Surely you remember that?"

"*SHUT UP!*" Gabriella paused and screamed.

Kukkug took the opening to twirl and used his wings to slice open her chest.

She restored her body and moved almost too quickly to be seen. One moment her hands were empty, and the next moment she had buried a sword in Kukkug's chest. She grinned at the sudden look of shock on his face and sneered as he spun around and retreated.

*****

It didn't seem right to K'tar.

Yes, Gabriella was the better fighter, but her brother had been getting better and faster since the battle had begun. Yet, he had left himself wide open for that last strike. K'tar's hunter's eye and instinct told him something was wrong. When the Dark One began retreating toward the cave, warning bells went off in K'tar's mind.

"Wolf, what's wrong?" Qiàn could feel him trying to move even faster. "And do you recognize those two?"

"I'm Yǔqíng, and this is E'kul," Yǔqíng spoke up as she heard Qiàn's question.

"Well, thanks for the assist." Qiàn nodded politely at the raven, as E'kul ran alongside K'tar. "At least it looks like she's winning," Qiàn shouted, although both wolves shook their heads as they continued moving at full speed.

"Raven, something's wrong with Yǎniū, and I think this is a trap," K'tar warned.

"Qiàn," Yǔqíng yelled, "my wolf says something's wrong. The angel is being drawn into a trap."

"My wolf agrees, and how did you know my name?"

Yǔqíng grinned. "You aren't the kind of person someone forgets," she laughed.

"Uh huh." Qiàn was confused, having never met the couple before. "Anyway, K'tar, what do we do?"

"Get to the doorway as quickly as possible and then execute whatever brilliant plan you come up with."

"I was afraid you were going to say that."

*****

Xuě flew past the demons as if they weren't even there. A mere touch from her staff and they simply exploded. The power of the object Qiàn had loaned her more than made up for the pain of wielding it. Unfortunately, the other ravens weren't so lucky.

The transformed ravens could see more clearly, but that also meant they could clearly see how hopeless it was. There were clouds of demons filling the sky, and their wolves couldn't support them from the ground. Xuě spotted Hóngwén and moved to link up with her.

"Hóngwén!" she had to shout to get her attention. "Report!"

Hóngwén fired three arrows at once, destroying one of the two demons bearing down on her. She dipped down and spun to the right, putting two arrows into the remaining demon, successfully dissipating it.

"Your Majesty," she responded without slowing her rate of fire. "It's going badly."

Xuě moved closer and fired streams of golden light at any target she could see.

"We are outnumbered more than we thought possible. To make it worse, most of them have never flown before. I'm trying to organize the others into-

"*Your Majesty!*" Hóngwén cut herself off before she screamed and surged forward, shoving Xuě out of the way. The range was too close for arrows, and this demon was enormous. She brought her wings forward quickly to slice it apart, but the demon simply caught them both.

With a pull and twist, both wings were ripped free. Xuě tried to catch her, but as the body spun and fell, she got a clear view of her eyes.

Hóngwén was already dead.

Xuě was frozen in shock. There were no other visible injuries. The simple loss of her wings had killed her, and as the enormous demon looked down, Xuě knew she was next.

Chapter 14

Kukkug could almost *feel* Gabriella hot on his tail, and it was fortunate. He had been running out of lies that would make any sense to her. In fact, he was surprised at how easily the lies he had told worked, but supposed it was just a sign she was further gone than he had expected.

He was disappointed at his failure to destroy even one of her pets, but there hadn't been time. He was just so limited here; whereas, the wolves and ravens could do whatever they wanted. And where had those other two come from?

The more he fought, the stronger he was becoming, but his sister had recovered too quickly. Although the word "recover" wasn't the best term to use to describe the fountain of rage pursuing him. As the cave came into view, his grin grew broader.

He would have everything he ever wanted very soon.

*****

"*Drek!*" K'tar punched the cavern wall, burying his arm up to the elbow in the stone.

They had made it to the doorway just in time to see Gabriella pass through it. Given the cramped space, all four had reverted to their original forms after seeing the angel vanish.

"Well, let's go," K'tar grunted.

"Wait!" both ravens called out before K'tar and E'kul could pass through.

"For what? Qiàn, there isn't much time." "I agree," E'kul added.

"Do you realize where that doorway leads?" Yŭqíng tried to point out.

"Of course we do, but what difference does it make? We need to help her!" K'tar shouted.

"Wolf, please." Qiàn reached out quickly to take his hand. "Everything we know about this existence says she's already gone. That it happened the instant she crossed over. It's already too late," she said sadly.

"You actually believe that?" he growled.

"It doesn't matter what we believe," Yǔqíng spoke up. "Logic dictates-" "Your logic is worth a pile of horse dung right now!" K'tar argued, pointing a finger at both ravens.

E'kul stepped up next to him in a clear show of support. "You expect us to simply sit here and wait for creation to end? How about the fact that it hasn't ended yet? As long as we exist, there's a chance," he argued.

"Raven," K'tar said softly, "We will act as one, as we always have, but we must both be certain of the choice. It's a simple binary equation. Do you believe we have a chance, or don't you?"

Qiàn forced herself to calm down and think. "You're right."

Yǔqíng's eyes widened, but Qiàn motioned for her to not interrupt.

"Yǎniū, the angel you call Gabriella, gave us a significant amount of information. Basically, if we fail, everything will be replaced, or something like that. So, yes, our continued existence is proof there's still a chance."

"She did say something like that to us," Yǔqíng finally agreed. "So, it makes sense that we should go with you."

"No," K'tar shook his head. "Where we're going, numbers won't matter, but here they do."

"He's right, Raven," E'kul admit. "They're getting overwhelmed out there. We might be able to turn the tide."

"Alright," she nodded reluctantly.

"Are you sure we have never met?" Qiàn asked the sudden question as the pair were turning to leave.

"Well, technically, we saw you in a parade long ago, but we

know you better from the inside."

"What's that supposed to mean?" Qiàn's brow wrinkled in confusion. "When this is all over, ask Gabriella about us," Yǔqíng grinned. "Um, okay." Her eyes widened, and she gasped at what she saw behind Yǔqíng. "When you're finished here, please take care of her for us." Yǔqíng looked back and saw the head. "Of course."

"And whatever you do, please don't let Xuě see it." Qiàn took a moment to explain who Xuě was.

"Understood, but why does it matter?" E'kul questioned.

"Wolf," Yǔqíng cut off whatever Qiàn was about to say. "Look at the resemblance and consider how much time has passed. That's their granddaughter, which makes her…" she trailed off.

"Understood." He needed no further details. "You have our word Xuě will never see or know of this."

"Alright," Qiàn nodded her thanks. "We've wasted enough time. Good luck, you two."

"And you," Yǔqíng responded.

The two ravens embraced quickly, as the wolves grunted and clasped each other's forearms.

"Well," Qiàn bent her right arm, sticking out the elbow, as the others left the cavern.

K'tar linked his left arm through the offered opening. "Ready?"

"As ready as I'll ever be," she flashed him a brilliant smile. "So, be a good husband, and take me to hell."

*****

Gabriella had just enough time to realize she had been tricked before she burst into flames.

How much of what she had been told was a lie? All of it? There was no way to be certain, but Kukkug's laughter, heard above her screams, verified the trap.

Once again, she had let her emotions dictate her actions. Once again, she hadn't stopped to actually *think*, and once again, she had rendered anything already accomplished into nothing. She had followed Kukkug to the one place she could never go and handed him final victory.

Her wings were gone almost immediately; all that was left was for the rest of her body to follow. The best-case scenario was that the All-Father would start again as he had promised.

Why? The single question entered her mind so softly she almost didn't notice it.

Why were her wings already gone, yet her purely physical body remained?

How was she still capable of thought if her wings, her true essence, were gone? Why was she even burning at all? Shouldn't she have simply ceased to exist in an instant?

Why? The question repeated itself.

She heard it above her brother's laughter. She heard it even above her own screams, as her flesh melted away. Slowly, very slowly, she started to understand. Suddenly, it wasn't just her flesh that was melting away, but her misconceptions.

Gabriella was correct in her base thoughts.

The pure and perfect celestials-the angels-from her home could not exist here. Pure happiness and joy had no place in the Dark Realm. Those celestials would be negated instantly; however, Gabriella's thoughts were finally catching up to the present. She finally understood the question she should truly be asking.

What does any of that have to do with me?

*****

Qiàn and K'tar appeared and immediately felt ill. Other than that, there wasn't much to indicate they were in the Dark Realm. They were surrounded by a mix of rocky terrain, with several chasms, but it didn't seem as foreign as they had expected. Visually, it was actually brighter than the world they left behind, which seemed odd.

Of course, the massive hordes of demons were an additional clue as to where they were. Well, that, and the burning angel in front of them.

They looked back over their shoulders and saw that the doorway was gone. Not knowing what else to do, they rushed to their friend's aid.

Unfortunately, the light and heat from the flames were so intense that they couldn't get close enough to do anything.

The wolf and raven looked at each other, helpless, and suddenly the flames began to die down. Then, they vanished altogether.

Gabriella's wings were restored in a flash, and they seemed even larger and more brilliant than before. The angel was on a knee, head bowed, gripping a sword in either hand. Her left hand was on the ground, bracing herself, while her right arm was extended, as if for balance.

The Dark One was no longer laughing, and Gabriella's heaving breaths could be clearly heard by all.

"What game is this?" he demanded angrily. "Angels can't exist here any more than I can go back home!"

"You're right, brother," she mumbled. "You've been right about so many things, but you made one mistake." Her head snapped up, and Gabriella's eyes were pools of blue fire. "I'm no angel!" she declared with pride, before catapulting herself at Kukkug.

Qiàn and K'tar changed forms immediately. The Dark One was too much for them, but limitless demons were moving in to aid their master.

It was a single celestial and two souls against the entire Dark Realm.

*****

Xuě attacked first, jamming the end of her staff into the massive demon's chest. Unlike before, this demon wasn't destroyed so easily. No matter how much light she poured into it, the demon was able to keep restoring its body.

She had an idea and just kept flying upward.

The staff was long enough for her to be out of the creature's attack range. Also, keeping the pressure dead center on its body prevented it from escaping. Unfortunately, Xuě didn't know what to do next. The demon wasn't even struggling anymore.

It was just smiling and waiting.

Obviously, this demon was different. It knew that after a certain height Xuě would have to stop. K'tar had said something about that to her once, even though she didn't understand why. She had to admit, it was getting harder to breathe and noticeably colder.

She needed an idea, quick.

She dodged a strike from the demon's left claws and pulled her staff to the right, all while maintaining full upward momentum. The demon was thrown slightly off balance to her right, but was already beginning to correct itself with its own wings. She pulled her staff back suddenly and twirled to the left.

The creature tried catching her wings, but Xuě was too quick. She flipped up and then let her body drop as her wings sliced downward. Its arms were sliced off first, then came the head, and finally, its torso was bisected.

"That was for my father." She spat downward at the already dissipating pieces. Satisfied, she took a moment to focus on her labored breathing and enjoy the view.

In her current form, the darkness was not a factor, and she had never seen such beauty: the various shades of green, the mountains, the huge patches of blue. Even landmasses that had never been touched. Not even in the old stories.

Her world was *huge*!

The cold and thin air was becoming more than a simple nuisance, and so she quickly flew back down to rejoin the battle. It wasn't going well. The problems were evident to her, but she didn't know how to fix them. That responsibility had been Hóngwén's.

She paid no attention to the pain in her arms as she fired streams of light everywhere. It was effective, but lacked control, and then suddenly, a raven she had never seen before was corkscrewing through a mass of demons.

How did she move like that?

"Are you Xuě?" the raven hollered.

"Yes, who are you?"

"Not important. Your people are fighting the wrong way. The demons are focusing on you in the sky, so the wolves can't support you."

"I figured that out, but what choice do we have?"

"Stop using your wings to fly. Your people don't know how. Get back into the trees where you belong. Use your wings as weapons and shields."

"Wait, isn't that dangerous?" She couldn't get the image of Hóngwén's dead eyes out of her mind.

The other raven closed the distance quickly. "It's what you were created for!" She grabbed Xuě's light armor with her left hand, pulling her closer even as she pointed down to the right. "So shut up, get down there, organize your people, and *drekking fight*!"

"Wh, what about you?"

"I'm not bound by this world's laws." She proved her point by executing a series of impossible maneuvers that ended with another trio of demons destroyed. "Now go!"

Xuě nodded and dove for the treetops.

*****

"Wolf, how are things down there?" Yǔqíng's voice resonated within E'kul's mind.

"Confused is the best way to describe it," he answered. "I think all the demons took to the sky, so the wolves have nothing to fight. They aren't taking it well," he chuckled. "Also, I don't think they know how to talk to their ravens in this form."

"I surmised as much, but you'd better figure something out fast. The ravens will be in the trees soon, along with all the demons."

"Which direction are they coming from?" "Every direction."

"Wonderful," E'kul grumbled as he howled loudly.

Most of the wolves had been following him already. Likely, it was mere instinct. Recognition that he was something different, or the superior warrior, or something else of that nature, and his howl seemed to attract the few not already in the group. He returned to his normal form and quickly shouted a few basic commands and an overview of the situation.

It wasn't difficult. "The ravens are bringing the demons to us. Work in groups to support both the ravens and each other. Kill them all." What else needed to be said?

E'kul transformed back and issued a final commanding howl. "So, Raven, are you going to join us? I'm not ashamed to admit I'm feeling a bit lonely," E'kul said as he could hear the first ravens crashing through the trees.

As promised, the ravens were pursued by groups of demons.

Even as the ravens began flipping and twirling among the branches, wolves were leaping and pulling demons to the ground to be ripped apart. Despite how many demons were falling for the trap, they seemed to refuse to change tactics. It was odd, but the wolves and ravens had no idea that the massive demon Xuě had killed was effectively the horde's brain.

The demons still vastly outnumbered them, and they could still fight, but they could no longer fight *smart*.

"Sorry, husband, but I need space to work with," Yǔqíng

responded. "These demons aren't as difficult to fight as I thought, and they weren't prepared to deal with pure souls. Better for me to stay up here and break up the groups."

He spared a glance upward and could see his wife in the distance. Her movements were so fast, she seemed to be burning golden lines across the sky.

"Alright, but drop back down if it gets to be too much," E'kul insisted.

"Agreed, and you stay careful as well. If the demons decide to sacrifice their wings, they'll regain their long-range abilities."

"How do you know that?" "I have no idea."

He looked around and didn't see any demons like that yet, but he suspected it was only a matter of time. Just as he knew the demons weren't the only ones being killed. There weren't many, but the bodies of both wolves and ravens littered the area.

Despite their change in tactics, E'kul expected it to get worse before it got any better.

*****

The two celestials were striking each other with such force that shockwaves rippled around them, preventing their allies from closing the distance.

Unfortunately for Gabriella, many of the demons didn't need to get close. She winced in pain as volley after volley of dark spines stitched their way across her body and wings. Kukkug seemed immune to them, and so the demons were simply blanketing the area.

"I'm not sure how you still exist, sister, but it doesn't really matter," Kukkug said confidently. "This is my realm. The one place in which I can never be defeated."

"There's a first time for everything, Kuk," Gabriella smirked, defending with one sword as she continued striking with the other.

Unfortunately, despite her confidence, it wasn't long before she noticed changes coming over the battle.

Any time she tried to block or deflect a strike, his sword went through her blades to hit her. To make it worse, her own swords were beginning to pass through him, seemingly doing no harm. She was forced to dodge while attacking nothing but air.

It was becoming increasingly apparent that her greater skill may not be enough.

His nose wrinkled a bit in annoyance at her choice of names. "Are you noticing it yet? The reason why you can't win?" he began to gloat. "My body is no longer a true physical creation like yours. There's nothing you can do to stop me here."

She forced herself to ignore what he was saying and focus, knowing it wasn't that simple. It might be true that her brother commanded this realm, but this realm also represented a place where she didn't have to hold back. Her physical body might have its disadvantages, but this fight wasn't really physical.

Every time her swords or wings passed through him, it was an opportunity to lash out at what he truly was.

She was also aware that her friends were tearing through the realm, destroying demons by the dozen. They weren't giving up, despite the uselessness of their actions. The energy of destroyed demons returned to the Dark Realm to be reformed. Since that's where they were fighting, the enemy was effectively infinite.

If a single wolf and raven could fight a hopeless battle against impossible odds, then she was confident she could find a way to stop her brother.

As the fight drew on, Gabriella noticed herself getting stronger, and despite her pain and bloodied wings, she began moving even faster. She moved in to attack from the side while sweeping her wings in another direction, just to have a fresh wave of spines stitch their way across her back.

All it did was make her angry.

More and more, she was having difficulty focusing through the rage that was threatening to boil out of her. Through it all, a part of her mind began to wander, contemplating her newfound strength and sudden spike in emotions. She considered the few things she had learned recently, and the answer was suddenly crystal clear.

The reason why she had always been able to feel the things she hated feeling. The reason she could exist here and fight so well. How did she not see this truth sooner?

Being broken had been necessary. She was being prepared.

No perfect celestial from her side could ever truly counter this threat. Those she considered siblings had no place here. This was a place of torment and rage, and who felt any of that more than her?

Her past mistakes had been trying to hide those feelings, or to complain and blame others. That's why they always took her off guard and overwhelmed her. She finally saw them for what they were.

Simply tools to be used, and she used them now for all that she was worth. This had always been her true purpose.

Kukkug's blade continued finding ways to slice into her body time and time again, even as her wings were peppered with more spines. She had never before felt so much prolonged pain, but none of it mattered. Nothing mattered to her anymore, as she raged against the brother she used to love.

"Maybe I can't stop you, but I can fight you," she sneered. "As long as you're fighting me, you won't be able to do anything else."

"That's your brilliant plan?" he sounded unimpressed. "To simply fight me until the end of time?"

"I tried giving you everything I had, and you *still* turned your back on us," she screamed at him.

"You never understood or cared about what I needed," he yelled back. "It doesn't matter anymore, brother." She dodged his blade before sweeping her wings forward. Abandoning all further attempts at defense, her swords followed as she struck downward towards his head. Focusing everything she had, Gabriella knew it was an attack that would hurt him.

"I am the Right Hand of the All-Father, and I will *not* let you continue."

His sword came up in time to block her strike, but the force of it forced him to a knee.

"If I have to fight you forever, *then so be it!*" she shouted over the locked blades. Gabriella's eyes appeared as if they would set Kukkug on fire at any moment.

"Oh, so you sit to the Old Man's right, do you?" he scoffed and grinned. "Who do you think sits to his left?" he whispered.

"Wh, what?" Gabriella lost her focus as she heard the impossible.

Kukkug used his wings to knock hers out of the way before slicing her chest partly open. It wasn't until he buried his blade into her stomach that he realized she was no longer fighting back.

"You didn't know that?" he asked in apparent disbelief.

Gabriella responded by clutching her wounds and coughing up blood.

"Oh, come on, you can survive that." He waved dismissively at her, even as she crumbled to the ground. He threw his own blade down, so that it sank halfway to the hilt into the rocky surface.

"What did you mean?" she gasped as her wounds slowly healed.

Kukkug crossed his arms, looking frustrated. "You really are still the ignorant child I left behind," he shook his head. "It's about balance, you idiot. I personally disagree, but at least I understand it."

Gabriella lunged at him, swords at the ready, but Kukkug simply side- stepped the attack.

"Just stop," he rolled his eyes. "I tried to tell you this type of combat won't help you here. I was only allowing it because I thought it would be fun, but you disappointed me in that regard as well." He pinched the bridge of his nose in a very mortal manner.

Suddenly, Kukkug was struck by multiple streams of golden fire.

The demons had stopped fighting the instant their master had, and K'tar and Qiàn were taking full advantage of it. She was crouched on her wolf's back, as he charged full speed to Gabriella's aid. As powerful as Qiàn was, the streams of fire were coming directly from her wings.

Kukkug turned, seeming to not notice the attack, and nodded dismissively in their general direction.

The wolf and raven were blown backward, screaming and howling until they disappeared in the distance.

"Idiots," he mumbled. "All three of you," he said a bit louder, facing his sister once again. "How many times must I remind you of where you are?" He continued grumbling to himself as he walked up to Gabriella.

Her hands tightened on the hilts of her swords, but she refrained from attacking. If there was a way out of this, she knew she had to stay calm and think things through. Unfortunately, no longer being able to sense her friends' presence was making it complicated.

"I'm guessing you don't even know why I'm doing this?" he asked conversationally.

"Because whatever you used to be, you've become an insane monster." She managed her response through grinding teeth.

Kukkug started to clap slowly. "Marvelously done," he said sarcastically, while rolling his eyes again.

"Fine, I'll play along." She started pulling spines from her wings and body. "Why?"

"Because you broke your promise to me. Because you never came," he finally admitted.

"You *are* insane, aren't you?" She couldn't believe her ears. "You really thought I'd follow you after what you did?"

"Oh, come on," he gasped. "Those creatures are our version of cattle, barely. You must know at least that much by now. Still," he paused, "I knew you'd be angry with me. I just figured you'd get over it. It was supposed to be the two of us against everything.

Shaping things the way we want," he shrugged.

She narrowed her eyes, doing her best to judge her brother's words. No matter how closely she looked at him, she didn't detect any dishonesty. In fact, if there was a single word to describe how he looked in that moment, it would be "exhausted."

"Kukkug," she said, sitting down and patting the space next to her.

After a brief hesitation, he sat as well. "Your words and actions are contradicting themselves."

"Nice try," he chuckled.

"Just think," she started. "You're mad that I didn't follow you here to be with you, but you just finished executing a plan that led me here for the purpose of my destruction. Moreover, you seemed surprised that I wasn't instantly negated." She paused, waiting for him to speak.

"Okay, I admit that doesn't make sense," he nodded slowly. "Did you set this trap just so I would be here with you?"

"I guess I don't know for sure, but it doesn't matter anymore."

"What do you mean by that?"

"Exactly what I said, sister. Now that you're here, I win, and there's nothing you can do about it."

"Tough words, Kukkug, considering I'm still here and ready to fight you." Gabriella was still mostly covered in blood, but her injuries had healed entirely.

"You still don't get it," he sighed. "This is my realm. You can't really challenge me here. I was only fighting you to waste time and have some fun, but your ignorance of reality is robbing me of even that."

"If all you're going to do is insult me, I'd rather go back to fighting."

"Sorry, sis, but I'm not in the mood." He held up a hand, and Gabriella was frozen. "I could destroy you in an instant."

"Do it then," she tried calling his bluff.

"You need to learn how to think of more than just the present moment." He forced himself not to simply sigh again. "After I destroy you, then what?" he shrugged.

"I can't destroy your energy. That's why I was hoping you would simply be negated out of existence. The total loss of what you are would tip the balance more than far enough, even if I didn't actually gain anything." He stood, crossed his arms, and began to pace back and forth. "Unfortunately, that didn't happen," he groaned.

"If it's possible for you to exist here, then it's also possible your energy will go back where it came from after I kill you. The Old Man could just recycle your energy and power into another, and I'll be back to where I started. Also, what if your replacement doesn't suffer from your glaring weaknesses and stupidity?"

Gabriella flinched at the insult.

"No," he shook his head. "I gave up a tremendously powerful world for this opportunity. So, you're safe until I figure out how to keep your power here after you die. Once that happens, it's all over, and I win.

"If I can't figure it out, well, I'll have to keep you prisoner here to at least take you out of play. I'll still win that way, but it'll take longer." He grimaced at the thought of having to wait and waved his hand.

"There's a third option, Kukkug." Noticing her freedom of movement had returned, she stood back up but made no move to touch her weapons.

"Do tell," he smirked. "You can simply stop."

"Why would I do that? I'm winning."

"Because you can have what you want without having to wreck creation. I realize there's a lot I don't understand, but I really am trying. I'm here now. I don't belong here, but obviously, I can exist here. Don't you see?"

"All I see is you stalling for time."

"Just listen," she insisted. "I can visit you. We can even visit creation together. That's what I was really promising back then. As long as we go together, the balance should be maintained. You don't have to be alone anymore," she risked a smile. "You could even come home to visit me," she began to sound excited. "It makes sense since I can survive here."

"That's the best you can do?" A warning tone was creeping back into Kukkug's voice.

"Huh?"

"All the extra time you've been given, and the best idea you have is a reverse of my own trap."

"What are you-"

"The Old Man wouldn't hesitate to destroy me if I set foot back there." "No, brother, Father wouldn't-"

"You're out of time," Kukkug said softly, before lashing out with his wings.

She barely managed to dodge the surprise attack. "I'll sing for you!" she screamed before he could strike again.

Kukkug froze.

"Brother, please." She straightened back up and held up her hands. "Please," she said again. "Just let me sing for you."

"How dare you?" he hissed. "How dare you!" Kukkug's entire body started to twitch in rage. "I wish only to end you. I would never resort to such torture," he growled.

"It's not torture, brother," she smiled sweetly. "Just a promise." "Need I remind you *again* of where you are, fool?"

"You may command this realm, but I will always be Voice." She moved slowly, as if approaching a wounded animal. "Just let me sing for you."

Kukkug's eyes seemed to change slightly. "I might not understand this trick, but it won't change your fate."

"Perhaps not, but it may change yours," she said softly.

"You would never offer your song to a being who has done what I have done." Despite his argument, Kukkug's overall posture was less aggressive.

"I made a promise to sing to you forever if that's what you needed. Do you remember?"

Kukkug nodded as his wings began to droop. "That promise stands."

"But why?" He sounded honestly confused.

"Because you're my brother, Kuk," she started to cry. "I've been trying so hard to hate you for everything you've done and everything that's happening now, but I can't," she admitted. "I still love you, and I just want my brother back."

Kukkug's jaw went slack at Gabriella's actions, and he had no idea how to respond.

"You belong here; I understand that now. I am so sorry for holding you back and making you suffer for so long, but that's over," her smile broadened. "Why can't we just be together now? Just let me sing to you."

Kukkug's eyes were actually wet as he watched his sister cry for him.

There was a slight nod as his wings drooped the rest of the way to the ground.

Gabriella nodded back and began to approach him. Her wings flared out behind her, and even through the bloodstains shone more brilliantly than ever as she prepared her true voice.

Kukkug dropped his head, embarrassed at his own display of emotions. At least, until Gabriella was close enough. Then, the wings that had been harmlessly lying half on the ground swept forward and up.

Before she could react, the wings wrapped around her body underneath the base of her own. The wings pulled her close enough to almost be able to bite her brother's nose, and then they began to constrict. There was a series of cracks and pops within her body, and then he simply held her in place.

"You made that too easy," he laughed and leaned closer to her ear. "Do you understand what is happening?" he whispered. "The final consequence of you choosing a body like that."

"What have you done to me?" she gurgled through the blood starting to pour out of her mouth.

"I'm simply killing you, nice and slowly," he answered gently. "Your wings are trying to restore you, of course, and I'm absorbing that power through you."

Blood was coming from her eyes and ears as well. Gabriella realized he was right. Her body was being used as a conduit.

"I'm sorry, sister," his eyes held a hint of genuine sadness, "but this is the best way. I'm trying to make it as painless as possible for you."

"Please, don't do this," she choked. "Father will destroy everything if you do this."

"You still believe his lies?" He shook his head. "This is the only way. Once I take the power to create for myself, I'll make a new family. A family who won't abandon me!"

"I understand you don't believe as I do, brother, but this action you are taking is permanent." She had to keep trying to reach him. "If there's even the slightest doubt in your mind, you need to stop." It was getting harder to talk. "Let's fix creation together."

"Don't make this harder than it has to be." He tried to smile softly. "No matter what you say or do, Gabriella, you can't win."

Kukkug's final words echoed what her Father had said, and she suddenly had the answer. She quickly wrapped her own wings around them both, making sure they completely covered his.

"Nice try, but it won't work for you," Kukkug sounded exasperated.

Gabriella simply smiled and jumped to the left. The chasm she was aiming for was more than close enough.

*****

Larg did his best to maintain a circle of privacy around Xuě as

239

others took stock of the situation.

"May we?" Yǔqíng asked politely, before approaching too closely. "Of course," came Xuě's weak response.

"We have completed our search," Yǔqíng began, as E'kul grasped Larg's forearm. "There are no demons here, and no sign of the doorway they were using."

"Okay, thank you," Xuě said tiredly. "What's in the bag?" She indicated the sack E'kul was trying unsuccessfully to hide.

"Just a few supplies we require," Yǔqíng told the best lie she could think of and met Xuě's gaze harshly.

"Fine," Xuě nodded. "We'd all be dead if not for the two of you, so I guess you're entitled to a few secrets."

Yǔqíng nodded her thanks.

Xuě turned to observe the other survivors gathering the bodies and pieces of bodies.

Yǔqíng saw the look in her eyes and got E'kul's attention. She made a subtle gesture, and E'kul led Larg a bit further away. She then gently took the glowing staff from Xuě's white knuckled grip and leaned it against a tree.

"There's no glory in this," Xuě mumbled, staring at nothing.

"There never is, not really," Yǔqíng commented. "Just necessity and death."

"I failed." "You won."

"Queen Qiàn would've done better."

"I disagree," Yǔqíng shrugged. "Technically, both times Qiàn faced a true demon in life, she died and required the intervention of a full celestial. You, on the other hand, merely had the assistance of two extra souls." She tried to offer an encouraging smile.

"Thirty-seven dead out of fifty," she gasped weakly. "Well, fifty-two if we count the two of you."

"The only thing worse than a battle won is a battle lost," Yǔqíng muttered.

"What does that mean?"

"I think you already know."

"There aren't even enough of us left to carry our dead." Xuě was fighting back the tears, and her body was still shaking all over.

"It's more appropriate for us to release them here anyway," Yǔqíng shrugged.

"I want Larg." Xuě hated how petulant she sounded; however, Yǔqíng merely smiled.

"A few moments alone with your own kind can be useful. He will be back soon enough." She pulled Xuě into a gentle embrace. "It's okay to cry, dear," she whispered into Xuě's ear.

"The Raven Queen can never show weakness," she whispered back, sniffling.

"I predate the queens, and I say you are wrong."

Xuě's breath caught. "The angel briefly referenced another wolf and raven whom she had met-"

"Yes," Yǔqíng cut off the obvious question and bowed slightly.

"But is this even really a victory, or did we do nothing but deliver thirty-seven more souls to the Dark Realm?"

"I can't answer that, but we must believe they will be successful."

"I just wish I knew what to do next." Xuě finally gave up and allowed her tears to flow freely.

"There's nothing we can do, honey," Yǔqíng embraced her again. "We can only release our dead, return home, and wait."

"Well," Xuě wiped her eyes and suddenly started to look happier. "At least I still have these." She shoved a hand inside her pocket, and all color drained from her face.

"Dear, what's wrong?" Yǔqíng didn't understand the sudden look of fear and distress.

Xuě withdrew the hand that should have been clutching Gabriella's feathers to show it held nothing but dust.

*****

As the pair fell into nothingness, the final connections formed in Gabriella's mind. She couldn't win because no one was supposed to. All she had to do was successfully restore the balance.

That was it.

The first half of the answer came when Kukkug had mentioned their Father replacing her should she be destroyed. Well, the same thing could be said about Kukkug. She had no idea what was at the bottom of this chasm, but somehow she *knew* it would be enough to destroy them both.

Then, the All-Father could replace them both and use his newly acquired knowledge and experience to avoid past mistakes. More importantly, for the briefest of cosmic moments, the Dark Realm would have no master. No being with the power to maintain hold of the stolen souls and energy. The balance would be restored.

The only part of creation that needed to begin anew was the broken part. The two of them.

Gabriella could feel him struggling, but it didn't matter. Keeping her wings closed was easier than opening his. It wouldn't be much longer.

A part of her was frightened. What did death mean for a being like her?

But as the moments passed, she felt at peace. To finally understand. To finally know and fulfill her purpose. The anger, sadness, and confusion were all gone. She closed her eyes and sighed gently.

She was ready.

It was the sudden laughter that forced her eyes open again. The look on Kukkug's face was different.

He had been trying to destroy her from the instant this conflict began. However, he had also been talking to her normally. Except for the lies he had told to get her here, she had the impression that he could even be reasoned with. He even sounded regretful to an extent.

Not anymore.

The sound of his laughter and facial expression were both manic. The look in his eyes was insane. Whoever this was, she had never seen this person before. Her brother was truly gone.

"For the last time, fool, this is *my* realm. The very air obeys my command," he hissed.

No sooner had Kukkug spoken than invisible hands seemed to grip the tips of her wings. She fought against it the best she could, but it made no difference. Her wings were pulled open, and Kukkug was able to unfurl his own and halt their descent.

The hands didn't stop there.

Gabriella screamed as both her wings were bent, twisted, and broken backward. Suddenly, her brother had her by the throat, and his right arm was fully extended. Her screams were cut off as the grip tightened. She could do nothing but claw uselessly at the fingers and wrist.

"This chasm is another way to keep your energy here. Well, most of it anyway," he shrugged. "I merely wanted to spare you that particular horror." He glanced downward briefly. "But, if you insist." He let the words hang as she continued her useless struggles.

"Believe it or not, I really am going to miss you." His eyes softened a bit. "Your pure arrogance is something to behold, and far beyond even my own. I plan on destroying your home, but never in my wildest fantasies do I see myself actually going there.

"Yet here you are. You seek to challenge me in a place where I have not only a limitless army, but near infinite power. What do you have here?" He paused to twist his hand, and the sound of Gabriella's neck being snapped echoed in the seemingly empty chasm.

Gabriella's flailing stopped, and her arms dangled limply.

"Just a useless body and two broken wings," he laughed. "Goodbye, sister." Kukkug let go.

She was being pulled downward with the grace of a broken

ragdoll, and her brother was dwindling in the distance. However, she felt a spark of hope as she was reminded of the two other things she had here.

K'tar shrank his size down to that of a normal wolf before landing on Kukkug's back and starting to rip at one of his wings. Qiàn simply dove straight down, using the power of her own wings to catch up to the falling angel. Unfortunately, the raven's wings weren't strong enough to support them both.

"You have to fix my wings!" Gabriella shouted. "How?"

"The hard way!"

Qiàn did her best to straighten the angel's right wing. She ignored the pained noises from Gabriella that followed every "snap." Once finished, the single mighty wing was enough to halt their descent. Qiàn then quickly helped straighten her entire body, making it easier for Gabriella to restore her spine.

The angel's left wing was bent and twisted far worse than the right one had been. It was actually pressing down on her left shoulder, preventing her from using that arm properly. No matter how hard Qiàn tried, the wing refused to budge.

"Yǎniū, I can't fix the left one!" she yelled.

Gabriella pulled out a sword with her right hand and nodded to the wall. With Qiàn's help, she got close enough to bury the blade into the stone. She then braced herself, facing the wall.

"You need to reach inside my right wing," she told the raven, who was hovering behind her.

"What?"

"Just do it!"

Qiàn reached her hand forward and gasped as it seemed to disappear inside the blood-soaked wing.

"I give you my sword, of my own free will," Gabriella mumbled. "What did-" Qiàn stopped talking as she felt the pommel of a sword appear in her hand. She tightened her grip and drew Gabriella's flaming sword.

"Qiàn, I need you to cut it off," she said sternly. "What are you talking about?"

"What do you think?" she muttered, bracing herself more carefully.

Qiàn's eyes went to the twisted remnants of her left wing. "No," was all she said.

"Do it now, hurry," Gabriella insist. "I can't!" Qiàn started to cry.

"It's in the way! Do it!" the angel shouted.

"Yǎniū, you said your wings were-"

"*SOUL, I COMMAND YOU!*" No soul could disobey the command of a celestial.

Qiàn's mind rebelled as she watched her body act on its own. Trying to make it as quick and painless as possible, she carefully lined the swing up with the wing's base. It didn't work. The powerful blade did almost nothing.

It was as if it refused to harm its own master.

She was forced to use the blade as a hatchet with one arm, while twisting and pulling with her free hand, as one would with a particularly stubborn sapling. All the while, she tried to ignore her friend's writhing body.

In those moments, Qiàn would have traded half her soul to silence the agonizing screams of the angel.

Finally, the wing came free with a hollow snap that Qiàn would remember for the rest of eternity. She dropped the severed appendage and watched it turn to dust almost immediately. Before she had a chance to speak, or even look up, Gabriella reached out with her freed left arm.

Quickly grabbing Qiàn's free hand, she lowered the raven as far as she could without releasing the grip she had on the sword in the stone.

"Qiàn, do you see it?" Gabriella called out to the dazed raven.

Qiàn looked up, still traumatized by what she had done. She immediately saw what Gabriella meant, and it paralyzed her. Far above them both, the Dark One was still struggling with K'tar.

The wolf's perfect position prevented Kukkug from dislodging him and interrupted his focus, but it wouldn't last.

She could see the Dark One already beating the wolf against the chasm walls.

The only thing saving K'tar was that by directly attacking the Dark One's wings, he was interrupting his ability to command the realm as a whole.

The point Gabriella was referencing was Kukkug's right wing. With the wolf working on the left, the base of the right wing was open to attack. At least if one had the precision of a raven. Of course, there was precision, and there was impossibility.

The target was so small and so far away. It was moving in too many dimensions, and it was so dark. Even in her current form, her eyes were having difficulty piercing the darkness of the chasm.

"Qiàn," Gabriella started more softly, "do you see it?" The question was asked gently, as if Gabriella sensed her friend's mental turmoil.

Qiàn looked from the target back to Gabriella and gasped audibly.

Visually, the angel had been through a meat grinder and lost.

Her remaining wing had very little white left in it. Her red armor had been useless against the Dark One's blade and was no longer the proper shade. Even her face was streaked with drying blood. The same blood that was matting down her brilliant blonde hair. The same blood that had sprayed on Qiàn's face and chest as she mutilated her friend.

It was her eyes, though, that stood out the most.

When they had first met, those deep blue pools had been filled with so much terror. Terror of everything around her. No longer. There was such power behind those eyes now. That was when Qiàn's gaze hovered above the angel's left shoulder.

That's what she meant. The thought echoed in Qiàn's mind.

There was no question, given Gabriella's current posture. It was then that Qiàn recognized Gabriella's fundamental truth.

Even if the angel didn't realize it herself yet. This angel who did so many wonderful things, but who made so many mistakes along the way. This ridiculous angel, who still didn't seem to understand that actions had consequences.

Qiàn finally knew why.

It was because Gabriella simply didn't care. She would always do what she felt was right. If the consequences were dire, well, she would face them head-on. She was the type of being who dared others to be better by her very presence. The kind of person who would *order and endure* her own mutilation, just to give someone else a single chance to win the day.

Qiàn knew that if she should fail, Gabriella would spend the remaining moments of her existence clawing at the fabric of this realm until there was nothing left of her. In that moment, the only thing Qiàn feared more than failure was admitting weakness to those eyes.

She made proper eye contact with Gabriella and nodded once.

Gabriella hurled Qiàn upward with all her remaining might. After adding the power of her own wings, the raven was moving quick as lightning. She wasted no time or effort on battle cries. No, Qiàn simply let her eyes dance.

The target was approaching quickly. She had to measure distances, angles, and speeds, all by pure sight. She adjusted her grip on the fiery sword and continually fine-tuned her angle of attack. Her target's movements only *looked* unpredictable. All she needed was to see a fraction of a second into the future.

Surely the Raven Queen could do such a thing.

When she flew past the Dark One, she felt no resistance. So much so that she thought she had missed. Qiàn extended her arms, allowing her body to flip around. What she saw brought a feral grin to her lips, as one of the Dark One's wings fell deeper into the chasm.

She wasn't done yet.

Qiàn sheathed the sword and dove back down.

K'tar finally succeeded in ripping off the other wing.

As the pair began to fall, the wolf kicked off Kukkug's back and changed back, allowing Qiàn to grab his hands. Of course, the added weight threw her off balance.

"The wall!" she screamed, as she started swinging him back and forth. "Ready!" K'tar answered.

On the next swing, Qiàn let go.

K'tar drew two swords as he slammed into the wall. He bounced and slid a bit below the angel before getting his blades into the stone.

Qiàn breathed a sigh of relief from where she was still hovering, far above the two of them. Suddenly, she felt something land on her back and saw a dark blade bisect her breasts. It reminded her too late of a variable she had failed to consider.

The sword was through her chest, but the pain was coming from everywhere. It grew even worse as the Dark One began to claw her back open. Qiàn had been injured in this form many times, but this was different.

Despite the demonic feeling, the feeling of pure darkness all around her, this was no demon on her back.

Qiàn could tell the difference as her very soul was being ripped apart by the most powerful angel in all creation.

As she fell further, she realized it didn't matter. They had clipped the Dark One's wings. His consciousness was trapped inside the body, with no ability to communicate or command the realm around him. Which meant there was no way for him to save himself. If final victory came at the cost of but a single soul, then it was a price worth paying.

Even if that soul was hers.

Golden light was erupting from her form as her vision began to fade. As she got closer, Qiàn could better see Gabriella's posture. The raven was suddenly reminded that "most powerful" angel didn't necessarily mean "best."

With the last of her effort, Qiàn slammed herself into the wall to the right of Gabriella.

The angel had her right wing poised above her, waiting to strike. In the exact moment, she reached out to grab Qiàn and brought her wing down as if it were a scythe. The Dark One was sliced in half and scraped from Qiàn's body. She closed her eyes and restored Qiàn's damaged soul as all three listened to Kukkug's echoing cries.

"So, is that it?" K'tar asked, looking up at the other two.

"I think so," Qiàn answered. She had managed to get daggers into the wall and was supporting herself, although her breathing was still a bit erratic. The injuries may have been restored, but their memory would take longer to fade.

"So, we won?" he grunted.

"Yes," Gabriella sighed, drawing the other two's attention to her broken and bloody form, "we won." She closed her eyes and let go of her sword.

The action took Qiàn by surprise, but K'tar caught one of her arms before she could fall any further.

"Yǎniū, are you okay?" he asked.

"She let go on purpose," Qiàn pointed out.

"That's ridiculous." He looked down, but Gabriella refused to meet his gaze.

"You need to let me go," she said softly.

"One of these days you are going to start making sense," he growled.

"Just restore yourself and get us out of here!" Qiàn shouted. "I can't anymore!" she yelled back.

"You fixed me," she countered.

"That's different. I'm a celestial, you're just a soul," Gabriella responded, as if it explained everything.

"So, why'd you jump if there's no way out?" Qiàn yelled the question. "It's not that simple," she corrected. "I fell in to bring my brother with me."

"What?" The wolf and raven echoed each other.

"Yǎniū, why do most of your plans revolve around killing yourself?"

K'tar demanded.

"I must agree, dear," Qiàn chimed in. "You seem to take the notion of self-sacrifice way too far. Perhaps you should talk to someone when we get back?"

"It's not like that," Gabriella argued. "I was nobly sacrificing myself to destroy the Dark One and restore the balance of creation."

"That's a terrible plan!" K'tar yelled at her.

"It was a pure and perfect moment. I finally understood my purpose and felt true peace, and you're both ruining it for me!" she shouted.

There was an odd silence before all three friends began laughing at their ludicrous situation.

"Look," Gabriella said gently. "I was wrong before. A soul whose alignment was forced can be reclaimed. By destroying him, all the stolen souls and energy will go where they truly belong."

"What about us?" Qiàn asked. "What do you mean?"

"We weren't stolen."

"Yeah," K'tar growled. "We were dumb enough to follow you by choice.

Will your plan work for us?"

"I, uh," Gabriella hesitated. "I'm not sure," she admitted. "Why am I not surprised?"

"Wolf, calm down," Qiàn cautioned.

"No!" he yelled back. "From now on, I make the battle plans, but first, get us the drek out of here!"

"Stop yelling at me!" Gabriella shot back, although she was grinning. "Qiàn, do you mind?" She lifted her left arm.

Qiàn took the hint and lowered herself to Gabriella's level. She returned the flaming sword before positioning herself to take the place of the angel's missing wing. Between the two of them, they formed a single large winged creature, and they scooped up K'tar before beginning their ascent.

"When we tell this story later, can we leave this part out?" K'tar grumbled as the two women cradled him like an overly large infant.

"Sorry, dear, but this is the only part I plan to remember," Qiàn winked, as the wolf groaned. "Yǎniū," she looked to the angel, "if we're just souls, why is he so heavy?"

"It's the weight of your emotional burdens," she shrugged. "You're making that up," the raven accused.

"Yep," she confirmed. "You both wanted to remain as you were, so you weigh as much as you did."

"Wolf, pretend you're a feather," Qiàn suggested.

"It doesn't work like that," Gabriella laughed. "Look, guys," she got serious. "I really don't know how to leave this place."

K'tar squirmed a bit in their grip and looked down. His entire body froze.

"What?" Qiàn looked down. "There's nothing down there." "I can see in the dark, even here," he pointed out. "What do you see?" Gabriella asked.

"I don't know how to answer that question, but you both need to flap faster."

"I know that's what this looks like, but it's not what we're doing," Gabriella pointed out.

"Well, whatever you're doing, do it faster, better, or more of it," he insist.

Qiàn and Gabriella exchanged a worried glance. They could count the number of times K'tar had displayed genuine fear in the past on one hand, and without using any fingers.

"K'tar, the only thing waiting for us up there is a never-ending army of demons."

"I'll take it!" he screamed.

Gabriella had no idea what to do until she remembered something vital. "My feathers!"

"Your what?" Qiàn called out. "Do you both trust me?"

"No."

"K'tar!" Qiàn scolded. "Yes, Yǎniū, we trust you."

"Then get rid of your wings. They're in my way."

Qiàn reverted to normal, and the trio began to immediately fall.

However, Gabriella was now able to wrap her single wing around them all. As they fell, wrapped in the angel's wing, she simply closed her eyes.

Chapter 15

"Raven, you really need to eat something," Larg said softly, placing a few plates of fresh food on the table.

The survivors of the assault had maintained their forms for the journey home, allowing them to make the trip in barely three days. The darkness covering their world had seemed to begin dissipating after the first day and was gone entirely by the time they met the cheering crowd outside the city.

Saddened as the people were by their heavy losses, it was hard to ignore the obvious signs of their success.

It would seem the world was fixed, and no one was in the mood to remain inside the dilapidated city. Supplies and furniture had been quickly moved outside and set up between the city gates and the forest, and the people had been celebrating ever since.

There was only one problem.

"I'm not hungry," Xuě mumbled. Her head lay in her arms on the table as she looked at the leather pouch containing the angel's dust. She had barely moved or said anything to anyone since their return.

"Yes, you are," he disagreed. "The fish is fresh and supposedly one of Qiàn's favorite dishes." He pointed to the plate of sliced open and lightly seasoned fish before selecting one for himself. Larg sniffed at it and took a large bite, consuming about a third of the fish at once.

"Personally," he said around the large mouthful. "I prefer animals with larger bones." He started working his tongue around in an attempt to separate the numerous small bones poking the insides of his mouth.

"I don't think you're supposed to eat it like that," she laughed slightly. Her head was still lowered, but at least she was grinning. "It does smell good."

He shrugged and simply swallowed, bones and all, before pushing the plate closer to Xuě. She straightened up and started slowly separating the fish meat from the bones, but her grin was already gone. Larg watched for a time as she ate, noticing how automatic her movements seemed.

"How can the people be happy and celebrate when their Queen does nothing but mope around?" he asked quietly.

"Doesn't seem to be stopping them." She looked around the field where everything had been set up.

Groups were taking turns handling cooking and cleaning, while everyone else enjoyed themselves.

Children were chasing each other around haphazardly, barely staying ahead of intentionally slow-moving parents. Games had been set up, and several friendly competitions had been underway for days. Many people were simply lying in the grass and staring at the sky.

"It shouldn't be that surprising," he shrugged.

"When are they going to stop?" Her question sounded dangerously close to a petulant complaint. Finished eating, her head was back down, and she was staring at the pouch again.

"You can't be serious. Not after everything we've been through here." He moved to sit next to her. "Raven, we won."

"Did we?"

Larg noticed her eyes dart to the glowing staff propped against the table. Her concern was obvious, but he had been hoping she would reach the same logical conclusions everyone else already had. He put an arm around her and forced her to lean against his shoulder.

"We have no evidence to conclude this is over," she mumbled.

"I disagree," he whispered back. "Just look around you." He waved around and up at the sky. "The elders say this is what the world used to look like. I admit the first day was pretty uncomfortable, given how sensitive all our eyes have become to light. Never thought I'd actually be happy for it to get dark again." He laughed in memory of the first true day/night cycle of his life.

"The battle for this world was not the only battle being fought."

He sighed and tightened his hold on her. "The truth is, Raven, we may never know what really happened. However, everyone is in agreement that they must have won as well."

"Based on nothing more than hopes and dreams."

"No, based on the fact that we are all still here," he disagreed gently. "The elders believe the answer is simple. They don't belong here. Something was wrong, and it allowed their presence to fix the problem. Yŭqíng and E'kul's sudden disappearance the other day supports that hypothesis."

"I've heard their theory, and I reject it."

"Based on what? It's not like you to reject the facts so easily."
"Because if it's true, it means I'll never be able to say goodbye." She started to cry softly. "They have to come back to retrieve their items. They said so," she whispered harshly, pulling on Larg's sleeve.

A sudden bright flash drew everyone's attention before Larg could respond. Recognition was immediate, and people began rushing towards the trio, but something was wrong.

Qiàn had her back turned toward the approaching crowd and spread her wings as far as she could. She wasn't really large enough to hold everyone back, but the gesture had its intended effect, and the crowd held its distance.

Xuě quickly grabbed the pouch and staff and began to hurry closer until Larg grabbed her arm. Her excitement turned to confusion, then to concern, when she saw his expression and his left ear twitch.

"You can hear what they're saying, can't you?" Larg turned his head and didn't respond.

"Larg, what are they saying? Tell me," she demanded. "It's the angel," he finally answered quietly.

"What's going on?" She kept pulling on his arm until he finally turned his head back to face her fully. For the first time in her life, she saw tears in his eyes.

"She's dying."

✳✳✳✳✳

"Yǎniū, you did it," K'tar exclaimed after gently laying the battered and bloody angel down on a nearby table and propping her head up.

The angel nodded but said nothing else.

"Okay, I think everyone took the hint and will stay back," Qiàn called out as she appeared on Gabriella's other side. "Hurry and restore yourself before they see you like this." She grabbed Gabriella's right hand and squeezed hopefully.

"I'm sorry, Qiàn, but I can't." "You said-"

"Qiàn," Gabriella cut her off. "You need to listen to me." She pulled her right hand free and brushed it against Qiàn's cheek, leaving a fresh streak of red. "I have nothing left."

"Yǎniū," K'tar spoke softly. "You got us this far. You can get us home.

We've always believed in you, and we're not letting you die now."

"It's not your choice, my friends." She stopped to cough up more blood and tried to control her erratic breathing. "You can return home whenever you wish, but please stay with me for a few moments more." She started to cry softly. "The problem with being Voice is that there isn't anyone to sing for me, and I don't want to die alone."

"Truth be told, Yǎniū, you looked a lot worse when you finally defeated Thraxsis, and that turned out okay," K'tar offered hopefully. "Don't be so fast to accept the inevitable."

"This isn't the same." She tried to prop herself up on her elbows but failed. "Do the two of you fully understand where we just were? What we just did?" She rested her head back and exhaled slowly.

Gabriella's blonde hair was discolored entirely and matted down with blood, and most of her face was still streaked with it. There was nothing wrong with her eyes; however, those deep blue pools stared into the eyes of both her friends.

"We did the impossible and got away with it. Everything and everyone is where they belong. Qiàn, K'tar, I can see them waiting for you," she winced in pain, "but it isn't over yet.

"The cycle won't be complete until I'm gone and replaced. My Father will use his new knowledge and experience to prevent past errors from happening again. The same cycle doesn't need to be repeated, but the current one must still end."

"For someone speaking of nothing but dying, you are certainly taking your time," Qiàn pointed out.

"Raven!" K'tar scolded her harshly.

"You're always so insensitive when you don't get what you want, Qiàn." Gabriella tried to laugh but ended up coughing again.

"I'm merely pointing out the likelihood that something else is going on."

"You're right, of course. I never could completely fool you, could I?"

Her right wing was limp against the side of the table and spread across the ground, and her eyes lost focus briefly. "I'm using what capabilities I have left to hang on a bit longer.

"It will not change my end, but I just want to rest a little before I go. Just a few moments of peace before I die. I feel I've earned at least that much. *Or is even that too much to ask?*" She seemed to shout her final question to no one in particular.

"I would like to speak to Xuě, please."

Qiàn nodded and left her side briefly and quickly returned with the younger raven in tow.

"Yes, Yǎniū?" Xuě tried to control her expression upon seeing Gabriella's condition, but her eyes betrayed her. When Gabriella slowly turned her head to face her, she could feel fresh tears starting.

"I want to thank you before I go," she said softly.

"I was horrible to you!" She cried out as the tears came.

"You were honest with me. More importantly, it was your pigheadedness that led me to give you my feathers. It's the only reason we made it back at all," she smiled. "I think we can agree their purpose has been served." She reached out her hand expectantly.

"Um, they aren't feathers anymore," Xuě explained as she placed the small pouch in the angel's hand.

Gabriella nodded. "They came from the wing I lost, but it doesn't matter. Even the dust represents a pure part of me." There was a small flash, and the now-empty pouch fell to the ground.

"Some of the dust blew away," Xuě admitted.

"That's okay. It likely explains how this world recovered so quickly on its own. I want you to know I'm proud of you, and of all your people. Tell them their loved ones are back where they belong."

"Really?" Xuě's sad eyes lit up.

"Yes, and they're proud of you too. They're waiting for you, but only when it's your time. Not before." Gabriella's eyes grew serious. "You understand what I am telling you?"

"Yes, Yǎniū, I swear," Xuě put her hand over her heart. "But this," she waved at the angel's broken body, "can't be real, right? You're just going to change again, like in the stories, right?"

Gabriella smiled sadly and nodded to Larg, who gently led the crying raven away. She raised both her hands slightly, and K'tar and Qiàn each took one.

"I love you both and have a final favor to ask of you." She paused, waiting for them each to nod. "When you meet my replacement, be nice to her. Help her and watch over her." Gabriella's eyes completely lost focus.

"We're doing the best we can. It's not our fault," she whispered as her eyes stopped moving.

*****

The moment it became clear that Gabriella had accepted her own death, Qiàn had largely stopped listening to her.

Despite what Gabriella had said to her before leaving for the assault, Qiàn still considered herself to be the Raven Queen, and she wasn't prepared to lose anyone today. So, instead of paying attention to the conversation, she was doing what ravens did best. Qiàn was watching. Everything.

It allowed her to see something everyone else had missed, and she was convinced it was the answer.

When Gabriella reclaimed the dust Xuě had returned to her, a tiny patch of feathers on her ruined right wing had been restored. It wasn't much compared to the overall wing, but it happened instantly.

So, she was being literal. The thought came to Qiàn's mind when she considered Gabriella's earlier words about having nothing left.

This simplified the problem but did not necessarily solve it.

Technically, Gabriella wasn't dying. She just needed more of whatever it was celestials used for power. So, what was that, and where could Qiàn get more of it?

She let her brain quickly process every interaction they had ever had, not only with Gabriella but with any celestial. No matter how small or insignificant, she considered every detail. Qiàn knew that time was not on her side, but that was okay. She was still a raven, and the answer lay in the beginning.

In fact, it was before they had even been properly introduced.

*****

As a wolf, K'tar had a different view of death than his wife.

259

Gabriella was his closest friend, and he wasn't happy to see her die.

This didn't change the fact that they had just won perhaps the greatest victory in the history of creation. The triumph hadn't technically been hers alone, but she had played the most integral part in it.

If her death was required, he would not dishonor her by arguing the point. Instead, he would hold her hand until the end and ensure her name was never forgotten. When they returned home, all would know of her accomplishments and sacrifice.

Her once blue eyes were now unmoving gray orbs, and she gave the appearance of already being dead. Given what she was, however, it was difficult to be sure. Still, the eyes were a bit unnerving to look at, so he reached out to close them.

Qiàn's hand lashed out and grabbed his wrist before he could do anything, and gently guided his hand to her forearm. He looked up in confusion. Confusion that only grew worse at his raven's strange grin as she leaned down to Gabriella's ear.

"Honey, before you go, I want to thank you one last time for what you did for us in the very beginning. It was such a lovely gesture, wasn't it, Wolf?" Qiàn's eyes glanced towards him, and K'tar started to catch on.

"Yes, Yǎniū, remarkably selfless, truth be told." He started grinning.

"The truth is, sweety, we don't need it anymore. In fact," she raised her head to look at the hovering crowd. "If this world is free of demons, then what need is there for demon killers?"

The closer wolves could hear everything and were passing the information along to their ravens. Xuě and several others figured out Qiàn's plan, and word spread quickly.

The wolves and ravens rushed forward and placed their hands all over the angel's body. When there was no more space, hands were placed on others who were in direct contact with her. It wasn't long before all the remaining survivors were connected to the angel in an unbroken group.

After a moment, the entire group began to glow, but none as brightly as Qiàn and K'tar. The glow intensified as everyone present chose freely to return the celestial energy they had been gifted with at birth. When the light finally faded, the group released their hold and retreated to a respectful distance.

The angel had been restored. Mostly.

As Gabriella sat up, looking confused, Qiàn tried unsuccessfully not to glance over her left shoulder.

"If it was going to grow back, it would have grown back," Gabriella mumbled.

Qiàn put her arms around her, as the angel began to cry softly, and Gabriella wrapped her remaining wing around the raven.

"What's wrong, honey? Don't you feel better?" Qiàn whispered.

"Why don't you ever listen to me?" she demanded, her voice soft through her tears. "I was done. You should have let me go."

"You've saved us more than once; we were only returning the favor," she whispered back.

"I never asked to be saved," Gabriella scolded. "I didn't want to be saved. I'm sick of being the way I am, and now I'm just as broken on the outside as I am here," she tapped her chest and head.

"Really, dear, you need to stop saying that." Qiàn's tone grew serious. "Don't take that tone with me, Qiàn," she glared at the raven. "You've overstepped yourself. My purpose has been fulfilled, and I can't face the others like this. I can't win, remember?"

"You didn't win, we did," she smiled. "It can't be that simple."

"It is, and so is everything else. You insist on overcomplicating everything, and it keeps you from seeing the simple and obvious answers staring you in the face."

"Like what?" she smirked.

"Like the fact that you haven't even begun to fulfill your purpose, much less completed it." Qiàn quickly put a finger on Gabriella's lips to keep her from interrupting. "What we just did was treat a symptom. The disease is still there.

"Yǎniū, everyone is waiting for you. Speaking as one queen to another, some of us are losing our patience." Qiàn grinned as Gabriella's eyes widened.

"Why didn't he ever tell me?" she gasped.

"He did, many times in fact, but you never listened. Now, hurry up and say goodbye to everyone so we can go home. I want to see my children."

Gabriella nodded and wiped her eyes before standing up and spreading her remaining wing. She motioned the crowd to come closer.

"Thank you all for what you have done, but please do not forget the consequences of your choice." She paused a moment. "You're all normal men and women now, so you former wolves better start cooking your food better and eating more than just meat. As for you ravens, it'll take time for you to get used to seeing the world through normal eyes." She paused for the inevitable groans and slight laughter.

"Your physical attributes may fade throughout the generations, or maybe not. You'll all just have to start making lots of babies and see for yourself," she chuckled.

The crowd grew uncomfortable, and more than a few blushed.

"What? It's a great big world out there, so you need to start filling it up."

"What if the demons return?" The question was shouted from someone in the crowd.

"They won't." Gabriella's expression grew stern. "The fighting never ends, but it will be kept outside of this realm. I will appoint watchers to ensure this will never happen again on *any* mortal world.

"I have also learned my lesson, and I'm sorry, but I can never return." There were tears in her eyes. "But you can still talk to me. Maybe I can visit you in your dreams."

Gabriella began to move amongst the crowd. She wasn't

imparting any special blessings or anything like that. She was just giving each individual the personal thanks they deserved. When finished, she stood before everyone with Qiàn and K'tar at her sides and waved goodbye.

Xuě and Larg rushed up to them before they could leave.

"When you return, can you tell my father that I'm sorry?" Xuě called out.

"He knows, dear, but we will deliver your message." Qiàn smiled and nodded to her.

"Thank you, and here," she reached out with the glowing staff Qiàn had loaned her.

"You can keep it, Xuě. It's a weapon befitting a queen."

"Qiàn!" Gabriella scolded. She reached out with her wing and touched the staff, absorbing the glow until it was simple wood. "Now she can keep it. No more interference."

Qiàn simply shrugged meekly and winked at the younger raven.

With a final wave, Gabriella grabbed the others and launched into the sky to the cheers and waves of the crowd. It wasn't long before K'tar started to fidget.

"Where are we going?" he asked, annoyed.

"I agree," Qiàn added. "Why didn't we simply disappear?"

"I told them we could never return, so I didn't want to simply disappear right in front of them," she shrugged. "Watching us dwindle in the distance will give them a better sense of closure. We'll vanish once we get inside that cloud up there."

"Wow, you're being serious, aren't you?" Qiàn eyed the angel in disbelief.

"If you insist on being a drama queen, fine, just don't drop me." K'tar issued the demand as he watched the ground continue growing smaller.

Chapter 16

Great Hall, Celestial Plane

How long had it been since she had been here? Another eternity it felt like. Did she even belong here anymore?

After so much pain, hardship, and confusion, Gabriella was questioning certain things more than she ever had. Although there were some things she was now certain of.

She inhaled deeply and fully stretched out her remaining wing. The celestial host facing her seemed to give no notice to her missing wing. In fact, they gave no notice at all.

"You," Gabriella pointed, "come here."

The celestial moved forward without hesitation.

She gazed carefully into its eyes. When finished, she carefully touched her wing to the wings of the celestial and closed her eyes to see. She nodded slightly after a moment. How very interesting.

"Get out," she commanded. "All of you."

The celestial host bowed as one and vanished.

I suppose that confirms it, Gabriella thought to herself as she approached the golden throne.

The All-Father did not wait and instead rushed to meet her. He threw his arms around her in an embrace that nearly knocked Gabriella to the floor.

"I did not think I would ever see you again," he whispered as he tapped Gabriella on the back.

She could feel her heart leap as her left wing grew back and restored itself, but she was careful to hide the excitement from her expression.

"I'm not thanking you, Father," she ground out through clenched teeth. "You don't have to, Immaru," he answered. "You never have to." He finally released her, and there were clearly tears in his eyes.

Gabriella had never seen that before. "I don't understand." She turned around and indicated the empty hall. "They obeyed my command so easily."

"Of course they did."

"Then why have I spent most of eternity practically begging on my knees for assistance, simply to be ignored?"

"Is it not obvious to you yet?"

"No, Father," she scowled at him. "If it were obvious, I wouldn't be asking."

"The celestials are not conscious beings in the way you and I are, but they are still beings of great power. What would happen if they obeyed your every passing whim and desire?" He paused to invite a response.

"I guess that sounds bad," she admitted.

"You foresaw this potential problem and designed them to obey your commands only. Since you lost and replaced your memories, you stopped commanding them."

She began nodding. "Because I thought it was your job."

"Correct, and I do not possess that ability even if I wanted to," he shrugged. "Your celestials ignore everything I have to say."

"But," her brow furrowed in confusion, "you're the All-Father." "Correct, yet I had nothing to do with the design of this realm. When you were designing the realm and the celestials, you decided that I could not be trusted to meddle with it." He laughed as Gabriella's eyes grew ever wider.

"You've always been arrogant, Immaru, but you did a wonderful job nonetheless."

"I remember that name from my lost memories," she pointed out.

"Yes, Dear One, the name of my daughter." He waited, hoping she would finally interpret things correctly.

"All the times you've said that," her voice trailed off as her eyes narrowed. "You were speaking literally?"

"Yes," he nodded. "In hindsight, your selection of a new name should have told me where the problem was. Had you simply erased the time from your memories, you would have still known your name. Somewhere in your false memories, you must have selected a new one," he shrugged.

"It is all so obvious now, and I am a little disappointed in the fact that I did not see it. Simply another gross error on my part, I suppose," he smirked.

"May I keep my new name, Father?"

"You may do as you wish, but to me you will always be my beautiful Immaru," he answered, smiling. "I merely hope that you are at least beginning to see your error in these words you have chosen to use to describe yourself."

"I don't know what you mean," she mumbled, trying to evade the point. "You think I do not hear your mind screaming? That I am unaware of you referencing yourself as 'broken' or 'imperfect?' To say nothing of our last meeting, where you threw this information into my face?"

"Facts are facts, Father," she said sadly.

"Yes, they are, Immaru, and the fact is imperfection is a necessity for life. You are not broken. You are simply alive. I am no different." He smiled at her shocked expression.

"But, you are the All-Father."

"Why do you feel the need to constantly remind me of who I am?" he laughed.

"You are perfect," Gabriella insisted.

The All-Father began shaking his head. "Have we not identified multiple errors on my part? How is this perfection?"

"I, I'm confused." Gabriella was reflexively flexing her wings as she tried to understand what her Father was telling her.

"Please call forth one of your celestials."

Gabriella nodded and closed her eyes. A moment later, another celestial was standing next to them, with its wings comfortably retracted.

"Dear One, this is a perfect being." He pointed to the celestial. "It is perfectly aligned with this realm, with no capability to understand anything outside its alignment." He held up a finger.

"This means it can only act within its base instincts or obey your direct commands. What does this being lack?"

She thought for a moment. "Choice."

"Exactly, Immaru," He nodded happily. "Without choice, there can be no true life, but to have proper choice, a being cannot be perfect. One must have access to both alignments. One must be able to choose incorrectly. This is what makes my creation special."

He turned and walked back to his golden throne, leaving Gabriella to contemplate what he had said.

"Wait," she called after him, and hurried to follow. "You referenced a few things I still don't remember. What exactly happened at the beginning of creation?"

He indicated the silver throne next to him and waited for Gabriella to seat herself. Given how far she had come, it seemed sensible to tell her the rest. It was necessary, in fact, considering he would be leaving soon.

"Do you wish for it to remain here?" He pointed to the celestial that was still simply standing in front of the thrones.

"Oh," Gabriella turned her head. "Go play outside or something." She could hear the All-Father chuckling at her choice in commands, but the celestial bowed and vanished.

"Immaru, if I value all things equally, then how is it possible for me to tell the difference between the alignments? Especially when you consider how subjective words like 'right' and 'wrong' or 'good' and 'evil' are?"

"I imagine you can still tell the difference," she shrugged.

"You've been watching for all eternity."

"I am speaking of the beginning, Immaru. Long before I gained conceptual understanding," he pointed out. "How could I possibly form the two perfect realms on my own? A single mistake would have ended creation before it began." He allowed a moment for the stakes to sink in.

"So, instead, I created two children to help me." "Kukkug and I," she cut in.

"Yes," he nodded. "You were each primarily aligned in one direction, but given the ability to feel and understand the other side. It was your minds that guided my power to create your respective realms. So, you see, Immaru, this entire realm is akin to your body."

Gabriella's features froze as she listened.

"When completed with your realms, you both assisted me in finishing the other side of creation and its bindings. The three of us worked quite well together," he smiled in memory.

"So, what happened?" Gabriella was almost afraid to ask.

"The two of you were inseparable," he sighed. "Flitting back and forth between all the realms and safely managing the balance. There was little for me to do but simply observe my creation as I had wanted to from the beginning."

"How could we cross the barriers so easily?"

"You are still thinking in terms of a normal celestial. You two are the ones who established the barriers. Of course, you could pass through them." He arched an eyebrow at his daughter.

"Right, sorry, please continue."

"As for what happened, well," he paused briefly. "You spoke with Kukkug during the recent battle. His ambition prevented him from accepting proper understanding, but what was his true downfall?"

"Loneliness," she answered quietly. "He felt betrayed by me."

"Yes, and it was your downfall as well." The All-Father lowered his head. "You were always enough for your brother, but despite how much you loved him, he was never enough for you. There is a reason why demons seem so much more independent than your celestials.

"Kukkug did that on purpose so his realm would require less direct oversight. As a safeguard, he created them far less powerful. You, however, created your celestials in your own image and made them immensely powerful, but added the safeguard of them being unable to act on their own."

"Father, not that this isn't interesting, but please tell me what I did." Gabriella could tell her Father was stalling for time. As if he didn't really want her to know.

"Even back then, you were fascinated with mortals and their lives, and you came up with an additional plan for your celestials. You meant for them to be a surrogate family, not fully understanding that this could never be. Eventually, you began to wonder what would happen if you simply joined the celestials.

"Perhaps you could have the family you dreamed of, yet maintain proper command of the realm. In fact, you even added this throne as a safeguard should you lose some of your abilities." He stroked the back of the silver throne.

"What you did not know was that you would immediately lose all knowledge of the time before," he sighed. "From your perspective, the moment you opened your eyes as a simple celestial was the first moment of your existence."

Gabriella started to open her mouth, but stopped at a slight movement from the All-Father's hand.

"As problematic as this was, by itself, it was a problem that would have been solved on its own. You can go anywhere, but this realm will always be a part of you and where you truly belong. It wasn't long before you even began commanding the others, even if you did not understand why they were listening.

"The true problem was Kukkug." He inhaled slowly. "When you vanished behind the barrier, he panicked. After seeing what you had done, he immediately made the same choice to be with you again."

"And in so doing, lost his memories as well," she said softly. "Correct," he nodded. "Unlike you, Kukkug was never intended to be in this realm for more than short periods of time. The very fabric of this realm tore at his essence in a way that you cannot understand. To make it worse, his lack of memories meant he did not know why he was suffering.

"Eventually, his instincts led him back home, but his ambition clouded his understanding. The Kukkug who returned home was not the Kukkug I created," he finished sadly.

"Father," she reached out to touch his arm. "If I am to accept this as truth, then it means all that has happened really is my fault. I'm not sure how I feel about that."

He began shaking his head. "Not your fault, but mine, Dear One. You may be the personification of arrogance, but you are no fool. The three of us talked almost constantly in the beginning. You asked me what would happen if you followed your plan.

"I never answered." He lowered his head again. "You grew tired of waiting and made your choice. The truth is, I simply did not hear you at the time. When I finally did it, it was too late.

"Seeing what had happened, I rushed to assist in correcting the mistake and made my second error. I chose to speak with Kukkug first. It seemed the logical choice," he grimaced. "It was he who was suffering, not you, and so I told him exactly what had happened and what choices to make to undo it."

"He didn't believe you," Gabriella said unnecessarily.

"No." There were tears in the All-Father's eyes again. "It is what created the rift between us, and nothing I could say would repair it." He paused a moment. "I understand now that if I had spoken to you, you would have listened.

"Immaru, I am begging you to understand." His eyes were

pleading. "At the time, I had lost both my sons. You were all I had left, and I could not risk any interference that might drive you away as well. It merely proves that in the end, I am a coward." He turned away, refusing to meet her gaze anymore.

"If I had chosen to speak with you first instead of Kukkug, you would have listened, and we could have saved him together. Please do not remember him for what he became, but instead for what he was. None of it was his fault."

"Father," Gabriella started when it was clear the All-Father had finished. "You said you lost *both* your sons." She let the statement hang.

"I see you have grown better at listening." He gave her a weak smile. "Yes, and what did you mean by not hearing me until it was too late?

You hear everything in all of creation."

"The act of creating is quite simple, Dear One, but controlling that which is created is often not. I foresaw the possibility of the creation of a great many things which could not be allowed to exist." He stroked his beard absently. "Elements of randomness and chaos that could grow to destroy everything."

Gabriella cocked her head to the side. "Even I know that creation requires a degree of random chaos to function properly."

"You are correct, but I am referring to chaos given form and function. Chaos with the ability to form its own realm equivalent to this one. Can you even fathom this?" There was a frightening note of concern in his voice.

"If this were to happen, choice would no longer matter. If chaos were that heavily interwoven into creation, all realms would fall." He began to sound angry. "I will not allow this. My creation will not fall to chaos!" He started to shout, and the entire realm began to shake.

"Father, calm down," she ordered. "If this really is my realm,

I can't have you here wrecking up the place."

He began to laugh suddenly. "How very amusing. Thank you, Dear One." He seemed to take a deep breath. "In any event, regarding chaos, I faced the same problem in the beginning as with the other realms."

"You couldn't tell the difference."

"Exactly." He nodded to her. "More than that, even if I could see the chaos, as you said before, some of it is needed. Too many potential complications, any one of which could end creation. So, as I did with the perfect realms, I found another way.

"I created a second son," he finally admitted. "He was a being of great power named Michael. Such was his power that you and Kukkug together would have been no match for him. His purpose was to protect us and all of creation from the chaos, which he had the ability to see."

She reached over to take his hand. "I'm afraid to ask."

"He was lost. I never foresaw the possibility of one of my children being destroyed by any hand but my own. For a time, I was unable to either hear or create."

Gabriella reached out with her nonphysical being and tried to truly embrace her Father, but he resisted. She refused to relent until she felt his answering embrace. The All-Father's physical form seemed only mildly sad, but she could now feel the true depths of his sorrow.

"You were grieving," she offered. "And I don't think you ever stopped." "So, you see, Immaru, there is your proof. You now know who to truly blame."

Neither said anything anymore, as Gabriella continued holding the Father she finally knew properly. Her mind went through her more recent memories, and she was ashamed by the hatred she had insisted on feeling towards him. Of course, he would never hold her accountable for it, but how much extra pain had he felt because of her?

"I'm sorry about Kukkug, Father. I tried so hard to find another way, but he just wouldn't listen."

"I know you did your best. One of you was destined to fall. I will admit, I am glad it was you who survived, but it does not change the fact that I lost another son." He released his nonphysical hold on his daughter. "It did, however, teach me something new."

"What do you mean?"

"I did not watch your conflict with Kukkug," he stated. "Knowing my children would be fighting to the death was bad enough. I could not bring myself to see it. However, I felt Kukkug's destruction the instant it happened, despite my best efforts to remain unaware.

"It was as if I lost a piece of myself. In a way, it is the closest I believe I can come to physical pain." He fixed her with a steady gaze. "I can tell you, Immaru, that I have never felt this before."

Gabriella's eyes narrowed. "You think Michael's alive, don't you?"

"Yes, this new experience of loss proves it to my satisfaction."

"Well then," Gabriella hopped off her throne and spread her wings.

"Come on and let's go get him!"

"It is not that simple." He waved for her to sit back down. "I do not know where he is."

"That's impossible," she insist.

"I would agree, if it were not clearly true." He sighed again. "I did not foresee the possibility of his loss, nor the possibility that he could be kept beyond my sight. Immaru, it is time for us to face certain facts."

"I don't like how you sound right now, Father."

"If I ever truly had the ability to foresee the infinite futures, it is gone. Also, my creation has grown beyond my ability to control."

"Well," she shrugged, "you didn't really want to control it anyway." "Correct, but I do wish to protect it."

Gabriella tried her best to follow the information he was giving her.

There was something he still wasn't saying.

"It's the chaos, isn't it? Too much of it came through back in the beginning," she shouted suddenly. "That's who has Michael!"

"That is one possibility, yes."

"It's the only possibility that makes sense." She left her throne again and began to pace back and forth. "He was created to fight the chaos, but despite his power, he lost. Since we're convinced he's still alive, then logically he's a prisoner somewhere."

"Where?" The All-Father couldn't help but grin at how excited his daughter was getting.

"Okay, I admit I have no idea."

"Well, I plan on going to look for him. I do not believe you need me to continue sitting on this throne for no purpose?"

"Can I help you?" Gabriella asked excitedly.

"Not yet, Dear One. You must first wait for your remaining abilities to return to you. When that happens, you will begin to see the disruptions throughout creation. In the meantime, you may remain in that form if you wish."

"Okay, but when you say you are going," she let the statement hang. "I will always hear you, Immaru. I have made errors, but I do not repeat them."

She smiled. "May I ask you a personal question before you go?" "Of course."

"There have been multiple occasions I have been convinced of my own death, simply to recover. Now, after learning what I truly am, was I ever in danger?"

"When you were in Kukkug's realm, you were vulnerable, but other than that, it is only you who has been your worst enemy."

"What do you mean?"

"Dear One, have you been listening? You are a limitless being. This realm, where all souls throughout creation who are deemed worthy go, was not simply designed by you. It is you. Your essence, your power, stabilizes one of the infinite sides of creation.

"However, your actual consciousness is not limitless. It is a very dangerous combination for one with lost memories. Almost anything you believe is true becomes true, not because it is really true, but because your power makes it so. It is how you so easily replaced your memories.

"If you do not wish to survive, your own power will kill you. However, if you truly never give up, no one can ever stop you. Thraxsis was less than an insect compared to you once I gave you renewed access to this realm. You were willing to sacrifice yourself, but you did not really want to die, and so you easily returned to celestial form.

"Your experience immediately following Kukkug's destruction was very different. You were convinced your time had come, and what's more, you no longer wished to survive. You felt yourself out of energy, but it was only because your own mind was preventing it. You could have restored yourself in an instant.

"To put it bluntly, Immaru, you were so convinced your death was necessary, your essence was killing you. You were committing suicide by accident. The wolves and ravens on that world, which provided you with energy, saved you. The energy itself was unnecessary, but the act of self- sacrifice served to interrupt your thoughts, and your friend's words helped you make the final connection you had been missing."

"So, they sacrificed what they were for no reason?"

The All-Father grinned. "Do not concern yourself with that. Those beings got what they truly desired as well."

"I don't understand."

"They didn't want to be demon killers. All those survivors ever wanted was simply to be normal."

"It sounds like I still have a lot of work to do."

"Yes, Dear One, you do. I suppose I shall be on my way and let you get to it."

"Promise me that whatever you find, you will do nothing without checking back with me first," Gabriella insisted.

"You barely have access to your full memories, and already you seek to command your Father?" He started to laugh. "Such unbelievable arrogance."

"I can't help it," she shrugged. "Father, I'm sorry," she forced herself to meet his gaze, "for everything I thought and said. I understand now and just want to thank you for everything."

He cupped the side of her face. "You never have to thank me, Immaru. You are my daughter, and I will always love you." He kissed her forehead.

"I love you too. Now go find my brother," she commanded with a grin. The All-Father merely smiled and vanished.

Faced with the empty hall, Gabriella knew what she had to do. She stood up, drawing her flaming sword, and faced the empty golden throne. After a brief hesitation, she twirled the blade a few times before quickly slicing the throne to pieces, which promptly dissolved.

There was much to be done.

*****

Gabriella faced the eyes of the celestial host and wondered whether her idea would really work.

She had moved her silver throne to the head of the table and began to truly study them all. Each one had a name, although she had never cared much for acknowledging them in that way. But what if she did?

Combining multiple celestials into a single being would create a being of far greater power. If she then acknowledged that being by its original name, she could gift it with independent life. There were dangerous potential consequences, but she needed help, and this was the only way to get it.

Kukkug had the right idea by creating his demons with independent thought.

"Do any of you remember anything ever being on this table?" she asked. The sightless eyes merely stared back at her, awaiting instruction. "What's the point in having a table if we're never going to use it?"

She closed her eyes briefly, and suddenly an infinite pile of objects appeared on the table. She selected an apple and tried to make up her mind as she chewed.

As she stood up to think better, the entire host mimicked her movements.

"Sit back down," she commanded in annoyance.

The host obeyed immediately and began simply poking at items they didn't recognize.

"Lucifer," she called out.

The celestial immediately stood at the sound of his true name. As he did so, several of the surrounding celestials seemed to suddenly merge with him.

"The Dark Realm needs a new master," she began, commanding the newly empowered celestial. "Someone has to do it, and I have faith in you."

Lucifer bowed, as his features and wings turned dark. "Do a good job and I'll replace you in a few eons."

He nodded as he spread his wings, preparing to depart.

"Oh, and Lucifer," she quickly started to add. "Do me a favor and simply punish souls for their misdeeds rather than running amok. All of creation will thank you," she smirked.

Lucifer winked, with a strange twinkle in his eye, and vanished.

That was odd, Gabriella thought to herself. *Did he have that strange look before or after I gave him his new job*? She supposed it didn't really matter.

"Gabriel." She waited for him to stand and finish absorbing the celestials close to him. "I'm not going to have time to sing anymore.

I need you to be the new Voice and my messenger. Can you do it?"

Gabriel bowed, far more gracefully than Lucifer had. "Well, don't let me keep you."

Gabriel spread his wings and vanished.

"Raphael, no, wait," Gabriella cut herself off. "We need to start writing these things down," she mumbled. Sitting back down, Gabriella selected a quill and several sheets of paper from the pile. It wasn't long before a new problem arose.

"I never learned how to write in this body," she groaned. She looked back up. "Do any of you know how to write?" she asked the confused celestials. "Of course you don't." She pinched the bridge of her nose. "I doubt any of you even understand the question.

"It's okay," she went back to mumbling. "I can figure this out." She forced herself to think it through calmly before suddenly snapping her fingers. All they needed was a good teacher, and what better teacher was there than a raven?

She had barely closed her eyes before Qiàn and K'tar appeared behind her.

"Yǎniū," K'tar greeted her, "it's about time. You've been pretty quiet since we got back."

"I've been a little busy," she smirked. "I didn't want to risk dividing my consciousness until I finish figuring things out."

Qiàn was simply looking around. "Yǎniū, you told us souls were not allowed to come in here."

"A lot of things are changing," she gave as her only explanation. "How's the new job?" Both Qiàn and K'tar seemed to be oblivious to the number of celestials so close to them. Or they simply didn't care. "About that, Qiàn, I could use your help."

"Always, but I don't know what help I could possibly offer here."

"I want to start keeping records, but none of us know how to write. Can you teach us?" she asked hopefully.

"You were mortal for over two years, Yǎniū," K'tar stated in confusion.

"Remember, Wolf, her Father limited her capabilities, so she was never able to perform the task," Qiàn reminded her husband. "I'd be happy to,

Yǎniū. Angels make the most wonderful students." She immediately moved to the table and began interacting with the celestials.

Gabriella took a step back to watch, and her confusion grew. It wasn't just Qiàn's confidence, but the way the celestials seemed to be freely interacting with her. This was learning a new task, not something in direct accordance with their base instincts. They should have been ignoring her.

"K'tar," she started as Qiàn seemed to be taking total command of the group, "you know how much I love you both, right?"

"Of course, Yǎniū, and truth be told, we're quite fond of you as well," he grinned.

"So please don't be offended by this, but Qiàn understands she's not a queen anymore, right? This is my realm," she turned to face K'tar fully. "She's not in charge anymore."

"Hah," he started to laugh. "If you want to tell the Raven Queen she isn't in charge, be my guest. I'm the one who has to live with her."

Gabriella faced the group of celestials again. "Maybe later." Something else K'tar said was nagging at her mind. "What did you mean by living with her?"

"What did you think I meant?" He arched an eyebrow at her. "Speaking of that, I'm supposed to invite you to dinner. Everyone's going to be there, and we'd be honored if you would join us."

"You lost me."

"Honestly, I still can't figure out if we all live in the same castle or if we all have different castles that somehow occupy the same space. It drives Qiàn nuts," he laughed again. "You know how ravens are. That crazy woman will never stop trying to find a logical explanation for this place."

"K'tar," Gabriella was losing her patience. "In the name of my Father, what are you talking about?"

"I'm confused," he cocked his head. "Where do you think we go when we aren't with you, or when we request privacy?"

"I guess I never thought about it," she shrugged.

"Wow, Yăniū, do angels have a word for narcissism?" He shook his head as Gabriella grimaced. "Somewhere over there, I think," he pointed out a window that had appeared. "You can't see it from here," he shrugged.

"What are you talking about?" she asked, looking out the same window. "What are *you* talking about?"

"There's nothing out there except the light of the realm," she insisted.

"Your eyes must not have restored themselves properly."

Gabriella glared at the wolf in annoyance, but on a whim, she touched his shoulder. Looking back out the window, she immediately gasped and took a step back. Terrain, structures, and contraptions of all kinds seemed superimposed onto one another and stretched further than even her eyes could see.

She had always known that all things were possible here, but she had only applied that knowledge to what she and the other celestials did. For the first time, she saw her realm through the eyes of a soul. She realized that while she had insisted on doing nothing but fighting, it was the other celestials who had been managing the realm she had been ignoring.

"How do you understand any of this?" She gasped the question, still recovering from her awe.

"I don't," he shrugged, "but another angel showed us how to live here properly. An angel who wasn't you, I might add." He glared at her.

"You two are never going to let me forget that, are you?" She rolled her eyes.

"Never," he shook his head. "You claim we're your only friends, and you promised to be there. We heard your song, but when you weren't there, we were terrified. Thankfully, someone else was."

Gabriella turned back from the window to face him. "So, about this other angel?"

"Yǎniū, honey?" Qiàn called out before K'tar could answer. "Yes?"

"Where's Lucifer?"

Gabriella's eyes widened, and her wings twitched. "How do you know Lucifer?"

"Oh, such a lovely young angel," Qiàn responded as she left the group.

Gabriella was too distracted by Qiàn's method of referencing a celestial who was older than time to interrupt her.

"He showed us all manner of things here and refused to leave us until we were comfortable and the terror of crossing over had vanished." She smiled in memory and then held up a finger. "However, you know how I feel about debts, so I started teaching him things as well.

"Angels are perfect beings, after all. Once they possess the proper conceptual understanding, they can do just about anything. Teaching the others will go more quickly if he helps, but I don't see him."

Realization began to dawn in Gabriella's mind. "What exactly did you teach him?" she asked through grinding teeth.

"Reading and writing for one." Qiàn started tapping her chin. "We discussed other emotions and feelings and how to properly interpret them." She paused as Gabriella's eyes seemed to catch on fire. "Why are you looking at me like that?"

"You gave a celestial outside knowledge and understanding that exceeds its base instincts!"

"So? Isn't that what you just asked me to do?" She waved back at the table, where the others were writing.

"Under my supervision, and this is just a task. It has nothing to do with how they feel or could feel in the future." She started rubbing her eyes in frustration.

"I still don't see the problem," she shrugged.

"You gave Lucifer the ability to self-evolve!" she shouted. "So, he was already independent when I empowered him further. I have no idea what the consequences of that are."

"What do you mean? Where is he now?"

"I sent him to the Dark Realm to take over," she answered.

"Oh," Qiàn scratched her cheek a few times. "That's bad. You shouldn't have done that."

"Dammit, Qiàn!" Gabriella's wings flared out, although Qiàn seemed to not care. "This is *not* your kingdom. You have got to stop screwing around with things you don't understand!"

"Well, maybe I wouldn't if there was something preventing me from doing so!" Qiàn shouted back. "I refuse to believe this is the first time this has happened in the entire history of creation."

"Souls who come here are simply grateful to spend eternity in the happiness they deserve. They don't mess with my drekking angels!" She jabbed a finger in Qiàn's face.

"You didn't even know they were yours until I told you." Qiàn jabbed her own finger right back at Gabriella. "You were too busy consigning yourself to death on that world. Again!"

Gabriella sputtered for a moment, having no idea how to talk to the raven.

"Maybe if you'd spend a little more time checking in with us, we'd know about your plans and could help you instead of getting in your way." Qiàn crossed her arms a bit petulantly.

"Wait, is that what this is? You think I'm ignoring you, so you're acting out to get my attention?"

"Maybe." Qiàn glanced off to the side.

"I'm with you all the time." Gabriella was careful to control her voice. She really didn't have time for this.

"Not in the beginning, and not since we got back, and you've never simply experienced the realm with us. I'm willing to bet you've never really experienced it at all, despite having created it."

Given her recent revelation with K'tar, Gabriella couldn't dispute Qiàn's accusation.

"I understand you must be busy, and I know I can't comprehend everything that is going on, but I don't really care either," Qiàn said honestly. "I always get what I want eventually, and I want my friend back.

"If I have to mess with an angel or two, or the very fabric of reality, I'm okay with that. I'd like to think that we had at least a small hand in getting you back where you belong." She dropped her head. "I just don't want to be forgotten."

"I don't know if you're insane or just incredibly arrogant." Gabriella reached out with her wings to embrace the raven. "I suppose I could always use another advisor."

"Really?"

"Of course, Qiàn." She held on another moment before letting go. "Thanks for the support, K'tar," she yelled sarcastically over her shoulder.

"I wasn't getting anywhere near that argument," he laughed. "Although if you ladies are done fighting, what is the plan regarding Lucifer?"

"Honestly, it's for the best," Gabriella said after a moment's consideration. "His job is more difficult and important than the other jobs I'm assigning, so it might help that he's a more powerful angel."

"Aren't you worried that he might challenge you like before?" Qiàn asked.

"No," Gabriella shook her head. "My brother was equal to me. Lucifer is one of my creations. He can't even leave his realm without my permission. I have a more important question for you two."

"What is it?" K'tar asked before Qiàn had a chance. "What's for dinner?"

Epilogue

Gabriella stared, fascinated, down the length of the too-large table.

There were an incredible number of people here, yet somehow everyone was close enough together to have private conversations with whoever they chose. She saw it wasn't just wolves and ravens present either, as Qiàn was conversing with her father.

Given who she was, Qiàn had offered her a place at the head of the table. Gabriella hadn't been comfortable accepting, however, and had instead opted to remain at the opposite end. The chair next to her had been removed so that she could sit in the center, making it easier to fit her wings.

A few people had spoken with her throughout the meal, though they seemed more interested in talking to each other. She listened in on most of the conversations, and the general theme was comparing stories from each individual's life. It was good that so few were bothering to speak with her. It gave her a better opportunity to appreciate the experience.

How had she created this realm and had no idea how souls used it? *"Having fun, Dear One?"*

The voice in her head surprised her at first, but it could only belong to one being.

"I told you I would always be there for you, Immaru," the All-Father added, sensing her surprise.

"Hello, Father, and yes, this is more enjoyable than I thought it would be. I just do not understand how I didn't know about this. Especially if I created it all." Gabriella continued eating, even as she had her mental conversation.

"Because after you replaced your memories, you were too busy fighting and complaining to truly see," he chuckled in her mind.

"I guess I'll take your word for it," she sighed to herself.

"Unfortunately, I believe I may have already made mistakes."

"Of course you have. It is not easy contemplating infinite variables, is it?"

"No, it isn't."

"Raphael would have been the better choice, although I will admit that Lucifer was the most entertaining one, so thank you for that." He began laughing again.

"So glad I could accommodate you." She groaned inside her head as the laughter continued. *"What do you think of what I've begun doing with some of the celestials?"*

"I think it is a bold choice with both potential positives and potential negatives, as any choice would have."

"Kukkug did it with his demons, and I can see how useful it must have been for him. I need help, Father," she admitted.

"His safeguard was his demons' lack of power. Your celestials are incredibly powerful, and the new ones you have created are far more so. By giving them true life, you have given them true choice. This means they have the ability to choose against you," he warned.

"I think it will be okay. My Archangels—that's what I'm calling them — seem to enjoy the responsibilities they've been given, and they execute their tasks however they see fit. Besides, it's not like any of them could ever hope to challenge me." She gave a mental shrug.

"It is your realm, Immaru. Handle it however you wish." As was normal, the All-Father managed to respond to her without clearly agreeing or disagreeing.

"Well, anyway, any luck with Michael?"

"Not as of yet. I am beginning to think he will not be found here." *"I don't understand what you mean by 'here.'"*

"It does not matter at your stage of development," he responded, clearly closing the matter.

"Very well," she gave in. *"Father, I was thinking. Now that you can differentiate better, can't you destroy the chaos yourself? Once you find it, I mean."*

"In theory, although I am unable to focus my ability the way you can.

If the chaos has grown too large, there is a high probability that I will destroy far more by accident."

"Oh, that sounds bad."

"It is why I made children. Your minds are my focus." "So, you can use me to do it?"

"Unfortunately, no, Immaru, as you were not created for this purpose.

Using you would result in your destruction for no gain."

"So why not create another child with the same purpose as Michael?" "I will not replace my son when I know he is alive!" His voice began growing angry.

"Not replace, Father, just to assist," she made her mental voice sound as soothing as she could.

"After the pain I have suffered, I will create no more children." "Even if creation is in the balance?"

"I will create no more children," he repeated with a sense of finality.

Gabriella accepted that that particular matter was closed. Not knowing what else to say, she chose silence. Looking around the dining room, it was clear Qiàn was trying to make eye contact with her. Gabriella took a moment to tip her drink in Qiàn's direction.

"Have you figured out what they are, Immaru?" The voice was back, sounding much more relaxed.

"The demon killers?" She was confused by the simplistic question. *"Father, that's probably the only thing I've known for sure throughout this whole ordeal."*

"Then perhaps it will come as no surprise to you that you were wrong about them as well." He was laughing in her head again.

"Of course I am." She had to stifle a sigh of annoyance. *"Well, go on and tell me what they are."*

"Firstly, Immaru, they were not created by your hands, or those of the other celestials, but by mine. I have no true control in your realm, but I can introduce something new. Provided that something is in accordance with the realm's purpose."

"Okay," she couldn't help but narrow her eyes slightly. *"That's not how I remember it, but I'll take you at your word. It still doesn't change the fact that they're demon killers,"* she insist.

"No," he stated. *"You use them as demon killers because it is in accordance with your and the other celestials' base instincts. It is, however, not their true purpose."*

"Okay, Father, you have my attention. What is their true purpose?" *"Despite the successful turn things have taken, I foresee the cycle repeating. Time has a way of erasing memories. Mistakes of the past will be repeated. Knowing this, I introduced a safeguard."*

"I can only assume you are referring to me." Gabriella assumed that if she wasn't the topic of his concern, he wouldn't be having this conversation. *"Trust me, I learned my lesson."*

"As I said, time will negate that. Eventually, you will grow lonely again, and knowledge of the consequences will fade."

"If that's true, then how is the introduction of the wolves and ravens supposed to stop it?" As she asked the question, she noticed both Qiàn and K'tar watching her with smiles.

"Immaru, as you created the celestials to be stewards of the realm and watch over creation, I created the wolves and ravens to watch over you."

www.ingramcontent.com/pod-product-compliance
Lightning Source LLC
Chambersburg PA
CBHW020125310726
48970CB00006B/1734